THE FAR CRY

Persephone Book N° 33
Published by Persephone Books Ltd 2002

Reprinted 2003, 2007 and 2010

First published 1949 by MacGibbon & Kee

Endpapers taken from a late 1930s English
printed linen in a private collection.

Typeset in ITC Baskerville by Keystroke,
Tettenhall, Wolverhampton

Printed and bound in Germany by
GGP Media GmbH, Poessneck

on Munken Premium (FSC approved)

ISBN 978-1-903155-23-3

Persephone Books Ltd
59 Lamb's Conduit Street
London WC1N 3NB
020 7242 9292

www. persephonebooks.co.uk

THE FAR CRY

by

EMMA SMITH

with a new preface by

THE AUTHOR

and afterword by

SUSAN HILL

PERSEPHONE BOOKS
LONDON

To Ralph Keene

PREFACE

The Second World War was in its final stages when I gave up working a pair of narrow-boats on the Grand Union Canal in order to join Greenpark Productions, a small documentary film company belonging to Ralph Keene. My determination for as long as I could remember had been to write, and I therefore contrived to get accepted on to the Greenpark staff as trainee scriptwriter. My other equally devouring ambition was to travel abroad. The war was nearly over at last. I was twenty-one, had never been in a foreign country and, as the product of minimal schooling, knew practically nothing about anything. This ignorance of mine appalled me. I wanted to learn everything about *everything*; or as much of it at least as was possible, and the quicker the better. All I had ever seen of the world had been from the deck of a diesel-engined canal-boat chugging up and down an English waterway between London, Birmingham and Coventry in wartime. It seemed to me a painfully constricted view. This being the case, it was indeed an amazing stroke of good fortune – I thought so then and I still think it today – to have had the chance of attaching myself in the spring of 1945 to a documentary film unit which eighteen months later was commissioned by the Tea Board to make two educational films on a tea-garden in far-away Assam.

One dark and drizzly day in September, 1946, five of us went aboard the *Andes* and sailed out of Southampton, to the band's playfully seductive rendering of 'Indian Summer'. It was the first voyage the *Andes* had embarked upon after being re-converted from a troop-carrier to a pleasure-cruiser, and she was ablaze from bows to stern with spanking new white paint, the mere sight of which was a treat for eyes accustomed to the gloom of black-outs and the pervasive dirt and dinginess of Britain at war.

Our team consisted of director Ralph (a.k.a Bunny) Keene; cameraman George Still, and his aide-de-camp Teddy Faber; Laurie Lee, who in those days was chiefly renowned as a poet; and myself. Laurie was to be our scriptwriter. This coveted position I was as yet by no means qualified to fill, yearn for it as I might. Instead I was labelled assistant-director, which title, flattering but specious, meant in reality that I was the unit's humble bottle-washer and dogsbody. My jobs were to have included the supervision of loading and unloading equipment, acting as continuity-girl, typing out and posting off the daily progress reports, and making sure my masters were kept amply supplied with cigarettes and toothpaste. These official duties would begin as soon as we reached Bombay, but meanwhile three weeks of sybaritic bliss at sea stretched ahead of me, an interval celebrated by feasting on purest white bread instead of the greyish utility loaf of wartime, and drinking a previously unobtainable nectar of freshly-squeezed orange-juice. Every spare moment – that is

to say, all the time not used up in eating, bathing, dancing or playing deck-quoits – I devoted to keeping a detailed account in my diary of this magical Cinderella-like transformation.

However, no sooner had we docked than it became abundantly clear the first of the responsibilities which ought to have been mine was wholly beyond my powers to fulfil. We learnt immediately on arriving that owing to the rumoured imminent withdrawal of the British Raj from its Indian Empire the sub-continent was in a highly volatile condition, and it was considered neither safe nor suitable for a very green young woman to be at large, unaccompanied, in Bombay's excitedly seething dockland. As a result of this state of affairs the task of baggage-minding, clearing the Customs and so forth, fell at once on to the competent but understand-ably resentful shoulders of George and Teddy, who exacted revenge for the rest of the trip by exploiting me as their personal messenger-girl. More than compensation, though, for any wounded pride was the extra free time I could spend in communicating with my diary.

Looking back from the vantage-point of old age at the young person I was in 1946 I realise now that the ignorance I so deplored was really a blessing in disguise. I went down the gangplank at Bombay, and India burst upon me with the force of an explosion. I was totally unprepared for it. Engulfed by a teeming multitude of exotic strangers – foreigners – by raucous noises, brilliant colours, pungent smells, the huge surprise of it almost overwhelmed me. Had I been more sophisticated and less astonished the impact would have been slighter and the loss to my diary doubtless greater. But from

then on each moment was vibrant with the thrill of a discovery that had to be recorded, and because such youthful impressions have no store of similar memories to refer to or compare them with, they can be as vivid as the rising of the sun at the dawn of a cloudless newly-created summer's day, glittering, unique. To capture the wonder of that experience, to pin it down, so that not a single iota of it could escape me and be forgotten, became my priority, and I scribbled, scribbled accordingly. I might be hopeless at my job and mocked unmercifully by George and Teddy, but I knew I was quite able to keep a diary, and keep it I would.

We crossed the huge expanse of land that lies between Bombay and Calcutta, from the western to the eastern seaboard, by train, travelling for several nights and days crammed, all five of us, into a small stinkingly hot four-berth compartment. It was I who slept on the floor. And since I added no comment, not even an exclamation mark, to this plain statement of fact, I must assume the arrangement met with, not only the others' approval, but mine also.

From Calcutta we journeyed on further north to our ultimate destination, an assembly of tea-gardens centred on the village of Nazira, with a faint view of the distantly enticing Naga Hills. We were lodged in a large bare white-washed bungalow-type building which had – I think we were told – been originally intended to serve as a hospital. It had no doors and the birds flew in and out of round openings like unglazed portholes at cornice level. Pleasantly airy to start with, we found these quarters increasingly chilly as the season progressed. But here, happily enough, we made camp of a

sort and remained, with the exception of our scriptwriter, Laurie, until the shooting of both films was completed.

Our first film was intended for a teaching aid, to illustrate all the various stages of tea production from growth on the bush to its being packed in chests and shipped off to markets overseas. The second film was for entertainment, a lyrical re-play of the courtship and wedding ceremony taking place between two tea-garden workers, Ramdas and Mangri, a charmingly responsive Assamese boy and girl who were actually already married. Laurie left the unit early, having seen as much and made as many notes on location as he needed to, but the rest of us stayed on in Nazira over Christmas and January before flying home and arriving at Heathrow in a snowstorm towards the end of a phenomenally cold English winter.

My Indian diary, while extolling the beauty of fireflies and the pleasure of the burra-sahib's swimming-pool, expresses a shockingly intolerant attitude towards the club culture of the tea-planters who were so kind to us. They, more charitably, deemed us a bunch of amusing if uncivilised oddballs, and were liberal with their hospitality. For myself, because I persisted in waving sociably to the villagers and their children as we tore past them daily in our Land-Rover, covering the patient uncomplaining dhoti-clad figures in dust, I earned the description of 'jungly', a term that gave me considerable satisfaction.

Retrospectively – for it did not occur to me then – it seems very strange indeed that although the Second World War had so recently terminated and its hellish campaign against the

Japanese been fought in the jungle of a Burma practically on the doorstep of where we were blithely shooting peace-time films, no mention was ever made in my hearing of that horrific – heroic – struggle, of who was involved, to what extent, or who spared. It might never have happened. Perhaps the nightmare – the danger, the fear, the horror – was too close for comfort. Perhaps a sufficient number of years had to elapse before the nightmare was made safe enough to approach and investigate as history. Or perhaps it was only to us that no one could speak of a suffering particular to those who had been there; and we had not.

Part way through the summer of 1947 I decided, on a reckless impulse, to cut adrift from Greenpark Productions and strike out on my own, sink or swim. I went to France where I promptly fell in love with everything French, and above all with Paris, dream city of aspiring writers. But I had, alas, a woefully small amount of money saved up on which to keep myself afloat in the city of dreams, and by winter there was nothing left. The short stories I had had published were very short and very few. Altogether the situation was worrying.

Rescue came in the shape of two letters, one from the literary agents, Curtis Brown, and the other from James MacGibbon, then of Putnam's publishing house, in each case suggesting the time could be ripe for a full-length book about life on a canal in wartime, a subject I had so far only briefly dealt with in the short short stories. Much encouraged, I hurried back to England and down to my mother's cottage in Devon, where, supplied by her with free food and shelter,

I managed to produce in three months the manuscript of *Maidens' Trip*. And my sponsors were justified in their prediction: the time *was* ripe, and the book was a best-seller.

Financially solvent, I once more took up residence, alone with my typewriter, in a tiny room in the Hôtel de Tournon, Paris. The next book I wrote was going to be a *real* novel, but it still had to have a background that was authentic. Luckily, the material to provide its authentic background lay ready and waiting for immediate use, requiring only to be extricated from the hectically scribbled, hardly decipherable pages of my Indian diary. The interwoven story-line I would invent, of course, together with the people needed to carry the story along. In my mind the characters of *The Far Cry* were entirely fictitious, and I believe most of them – certainly the leading actors – do owe as much to imagination as is usual with creatures of fiction. That Teresa, the child at the centre of the tale, had a good deal of me in her personality I was not then able to perceive and would have hotly denied. But indeed, how could it have been otherwise?

The Far Cry was published by MacGibbon & Kee, and, since I was now fairly and squarely launched on my chosen career, it ought to have been followed up smartly by a third best-seller. Instead I got married. And for seven years, apart from the occasional newspaper article or magazine story calculated to pay our telephone bill, my typewriter mouldered quietly away on a shelf.

Then the unexpected happened. I found myself a widow, with a family of two small children to raise. We moved, the three of us, to Radnorshire, Wales, where slowly, slowly, at a

snail's pace – because there was so little time or energy to spare for it – I began to write again, books for children and one novel for adults (so far unpublished).

Now my typewriter, that old friend, is back on the shelf. I shall not disturb it again. But to have had *The Far Cry* rescued from oblivion and once more back in circulation after being for so long out of print, is a great pleasure for me, as I hope it may also be a pleasure for a whole new generation of readers.

Emma Smith
Putney, 2001

CONTENTS

THE FAR CRY

PART ONE
DEPARTURE

I

The birds came and picked holes in the sleeping ears of Teresa Digby. Their sharp cries insisted on her waking, but she, confusing these sounds with the early sounds of a summer morning, made no haste to be done with her drowsiness. As though it was summer the chintz fluttered and through the chintz the sunlight was mellowed into pools of golden water. Awake, she lay in bed, dreaming of sleep. And in she drifted on the slow tide of returning senses, between the shrill twittering of sparrows and starlings, to beach herself on the smooth hard sands of her thoughts; to be scraped in particular by one pebble, one thought, one word – breakfast.

Late! She was late! She was late for breakfast! She heard the birds then as a host of angry screamers, and springing out of bed scuffled for clothes, shuffled into shoes, and caught back her long hair with a red elastic band. Her fingers, she noticed, were trembling from hurry, and she frowned at them, even put them in her mouth and bit them to stop their shaking. Still they shook. She threw open the window and leant out to press them firmly against the slate sill – slate that was cold in spite of the sunlight, for it was not summer after all but the last week of September – saying to herself in that arrogant tone so easy to assume when the conversation is internal:

'Well, I don't care; I don't care.'

Her flesh shook, her heart pounded for no reason, no good reason, she told herself, for no fear. And she flushed with impatience at the idiocy of trembling out of fear of nothing. She touched the small ivy-leaves, whose fluttering could be excused on account of the faint wind that was stirring over the whole garden, and taking courage like a resolution slammed the window shut. Then she ran hurriedly down the stairs and strolled into the dining-room.

Aunt May was already at breakfast. She said nothing to Teresa and Teresa said nothing to her, having chosen to play the part of sulky disgrace rather than any of the other parts she might have chosen from a repertoire acquired during nearly fourteen years of being late for breakfast while staying with Aunt May. Her aunt, for her part, preferred this attitude to pertness or pretended dreaminess, though she disliked all of Teresa's attitudes, and Teresa too, together with most other little girls. So, thinking intensely about their ideas of one another, they ate and drank their way through breakfast. At the end of it Teresa directed a striking look across the table and said: 'Why isn't he here? I thought he was coming last night.'

'Your father,' said the old lady, wiping her lips on her napkin in order to spread out those softly uttered words as long as possible, 'spoke to me on the telephone. He missed a train. He'll be here sometime this morning instead. Could you not smooth your hair before coming down to breakfast?'

'What do you mean, *smooth* it?'

This was really very rude, and Teresa, who often frightened herself, added quickly: 'I did. I combed it.' And as this was plainly a lie, the fright increased. Teresa's face appeared to go even thinner and Aunt May's face to grow fatter, in the same way as the qualities of light and shade alter immediately before a thunderstorm. However, no storm broke for at that moment Teresa's father arrived. Hearing his voice first at the front door, they sat perfectly still, waiting. Then they heard his suitcase being flung down on the polished floor of the hall. Then the door behind Aunt May was hurled open and Teresa saw him come in.

The natural likeness between his face and hers was accentuated by her own at once and involuntarily imitating the same expression as his wore. Only her air was even graver, her features more immobile. Also, her skin was marked by a certain bluish transparency that gave the impression of being as much a spiritual as a physical attribute – a transparency, in any case, long ago lost by Mr Digby, even supposing he had ever possessed it. The moment he appeared her eyes fastened themselves upon him in fascinated apprehension, rather as small and helpless creatures caught on an open moorland cower away from the menace of talons and beak overhead, without the strength to flee. Her eyes, however, were unusually large, and, for all their shrinking, with something forcedly bold about them. He tossed his mackintosh far away from him into a chair and his hat somewhere else. He did not kiss his daughter, but not because he had forgotten. There were times now and again when he did forget and kissed her, and times when he remembered other things, not exactly Teresa, and then he kissed her.

'Teresa,' he said loudly, 'I want to talk to your aunt – now. At once. It's most important – urgent business – understand? Go into the garden or something, but don't go far away. I want to talk to you too in a minute.'

Teresa went into the garden and wandered up and down the grassy plots hugging her arms about her, shivering partly

because of the early hour and the month of the year, but more because her father had taken away her shield of defence – that is to say, her attitude. This he did every time they met, and, what made it worse, without knowing that he did so. Now why was it, she wondered, that with her Aunt May she had always a perfect armoury at her disposal, a glinting array, every weapon of which she was skilled in handling, while with *him* she was left without even a shell into which she might creep. One glance from him, the merest suggestion of a glance, and she was as helpless as a wretched specimen impaled on the point of a collector's pin. Her Aunt May, she explained to herself, as carefully as though it was for the first time, understood hypocrisy. She knew every shade of mood in Teresa's large assortment. Teresa could change a mood to puzzle her, maintain one to exasperate her, and be labelled accordingly throughout every minute of the day by her plump and hostile aunt.

But with Randall Digby, her father, it was different. Attitudes he did not observe, and so they ceased to exist. Hypocrisy, about which he constantly talked and from which, one understood, he ceaselessly suffered, he did not recognise when it came into the same room or sat down beside him. Since, he knew, the world abounded with and was made ugly by it, he was forced to discover it hidden in every guileless action and in the most unlikely people. Double-dealing flashed round him like swords. He searched for and longed to discover innocence, and suffered terribly. And was gullible, no one more so, a perfect fool of a man, thought Teresa, kicking a rose tree as she passed, and shuddering with the anticipation of what he was going to say to her. Yes, a fool, she knew, she

6

knew. For she had watched him fixedly since her first year with an eye that saw more than movements. Then why was she stiff and shrieking – shrieking, not aloud, but in a voice that only she could hear, a voice buried deep in the darkness of her innermost being? 'Help, help!' it cried, but as no one could hear, it was not of much use – why was she nerve-white like a twig of willow with the bark peeled away the moment his step sounded outside a door or his voice called? Why was she even now walking up and down, feverishly arguing with herself in Aunt May's garden – and she allowed her attention to swerve aside for an instant in order to think how much she detested Aunt May's constricted garden, with its pretence at amplitude, its little stretches of gravel, its rose-bushes so studiously pruned and propped: she wished the voluptuous topple-heavy blooms were out, just ripe to be snipped that afternoon by Aunt May's scissors, so that her kick – and she lashed out with her foot again and again – might scatter the petals, ruin the roses, depriving Aunt May of her gorgeous flowers and part of her pride. Teresa, it must be made clear, was not really as full of hate as her angers seemed to indicate: her passions would have melted into tears but that she was in love with no one at all, and the tower of tears inside her was a frozen tower.

In the meantime May Digby was saying to her brother in the dining-room: 'Now, Randall, tell me what all this nonsense is about. But first of all, sit down. No, wait – we'll go into the drawing-room. Eileen wants to clear away.'

'Never mind about clearing away,' said her brother impatiently, 'I'd rather stay here. What does it matter?'

He threw himself heavily down in a chair, for to stay on in the dining-room when Eileen should have been clearing away the dirty crockery and sweeping up the toast crumbs was to break a minor rule, and, his news being dramatic, the more rules that were broken round the breaking of it, the greater was its drama. Miss Digby resigned herself and folded her hands. The previous day he had sent her a wire, arbitrary, violent, as the telegrams of his life had always been:

'Fetch Teresa from school immediately. Arriving this evening. Randall.'

Miss Digby had accordingly driven the six miles over to Teresa's school in a hired car, interviewed Teresa's headmistress, mentioned family affairs in a voice of dignified mystery, and driven Teresa the six miles back with her nightdress and toothbrush stuffed into a satchel. She had done this in disapproval for histrionics disgusted her, but the pride of being her brother's confidante was ever stronger than her disgusts. Then he had missed the last local train, had wired her again, had telephoned her, and here he finally was, keyed-up, cyclonic, darting significant glances all round him and behaving, thought Miss Digby, more like an irresponsible boy in his teens than a man of over sixty.

'Well, Randall?'

He shrugged his shoulders, and said in an ordinary voice: 'Lilian – she's coming back. Arriving in England next week. Can you believe it?' Lilian was his second wife who, for ten years, had pleased everyone by living in America.

This bombshell – for it was indeed a bombshell – strained Miss Digby's studied placidity very much. Being the world's confidante often was a strain on a character naturally unsympathetic and inelastic, and poor Miss Digby had to suffer from time to time for the satisfaction it gave her. She did not love her fellow-men. She loved herself much better, and thought herself superior to almost everyone except Royalty. But somebody, when she was still only a girl, had said:

'May is such a good listener.'

This casual sentence had marked and moulded her for the rest of her life. She had grown impressive and serene upon it. The discreet corners of her mouth controlled the heavy sensuality of her cheeks. Now she was old, but her brother, and others, still came to her, still had to pour out their troubles to her, still needed her careful advice and useful silences, and the flattery in this way given and in this way received was consequential and as necessary as breath. Notwithstanding she and Randall bore a deep contempt for one another. Notwithstanding it often was a strain, but then so are all rôles, even the least energetic. For now, at this moment, she would have liked to have broken out with some wild exclamation at the mention of that odious ghost, Lilian, to have thrown her hands in the air or banged on the table, she and her brother being more alike than either of them cared to think. But instead she had to pinch her lips up, and squeeze her hands together, and say with soft, but only slight amazement: 'My dear Randall! What an extraordinary thing! When did you hear?'

'Why, yesterday of course. I wired you the moment I'd read her preposterous letter. You shall read it yourself later on.' He was marching up and down again, ruffling up his hair and

9

skidding absurdly on the polished floor and mats every time he turned sharp round. 'She's preposterous,' he shouted, 'just the same as ever after ten years. No – worse, worse. You shall read her letter.'

'But why? Why is she coming? After such a long time – ten years – it seems such an odd thing to do. What about her husband?'

'Lilian has divorced her husband,' replied Mr Digby, stopping jerkily in front of his sister and making a large sarcastic gesture; 'that is to say, of course, he has divorced her. One understands very well what the situation really is. Lilian never was in the wrong. Lies – my dear May, her letter is full of 'em. You shall read it later on – twelve sheets of paper written on both sides. What a dangerous woman she is! I always said so, of course, only now it's worse, she's over forty – forty-two – more dangerous, a ravening animal rushing round the world – rushing after me. Well, I tell you flatly, May, I'm going to rush away from her.'

'Randall, do sit *down*! Jumping about like that at half-past nine in the morning! And of course you're being absurd. Of course Lilian isn't chasing after you. Look at yourself in the mirror if you don't believe me. You never would take trouble with your appearance, though you could have been quite handsome still – you had quite an air in your young days – if you'd only cared for yourself in the proper way. But really, now, it's ridiculous. You're deluding yourself. You're an old man, Randall, you might as well admit it, and a shabby old man too, you silly fellow, and with no money to speak of. Lilian must have six times as much money as you, or more. Just ask

yourself a plain sensible question: why – for what reason – should she chase you?'

Mr Digby had listened to her angrily and as she finished speaking he flung himself down again in a chair and drummed on the floor with his foot. 'My dear May, you astonish me. Use your head, think – think a moment. Money – of course she has money; more than she knows what to do with I dare say. As for my being old, I know how old I am; I know what I look like too' – he grimaced a little as he said this, from the pain her remarks had given him – 'No, no, my dear May, she wants something else, something I've got and she hasn't: Teresa.' At the mere thought he sprang up again with his eyes blazing. 'Imagine it, the impudence! The child she didn't give a snap of the fingers for – hey? And now, *now*, at this stage, she wants to be a mother. America gave her dollars but it couldn't give her flesh-and-blood, like I did. Well, she's not going to get it now, not from me, oh no! Oh, most certainly, certainly not!'

Miss Digby, who since Teresa was four years old had helped to bring her up, said: 'I understand your feelings absolutely, Randall. I feel the same myself. But the whole thing can be settled legally, in a civilized manner. There's no need for you to go into hiding with Teresa, which seems to be what you're intending doing. Melodrama is so unbecoming at your age, Randall, and so bad for Teresa. Goodness knows, she's melo-dramatic enough as it is. No, really, Randall,' she added in a burst of vigorous petulance, 'I can't have you behaving like this – snatching Teresa away from school, sending telegrams, turn-ing up at odd hours, raising the roof with your rumpus

– my roof. It's too disquieting for Teresa and too ridiculous for all of us.'

'Teresa isn't your child,' he answered rudely. 'She's my daughter. I'll put her to school and take her away as often and just as I please.'

'Indeed you won't. Or if you do I wash my hands of Teresa and you and all your affairs. I know you're upset, Randall, but that's no excuse for ingratitude. When Teresa was a baby and you at your wits' end you were pleased enough for me to take charge of her. I think you forget that, Randall. I think you forget that I've done my best for her ever since – and for you too – and that it hasn't always been convenient for me to do so. I don't say I've been like a mother to her – a child has only one mother, say what anyone will. But I've given her affection and lodging, and seen her grow up, and corrected her manners. You do wrong now to throw it in my face, for I have an interest in her as natural as yours.'

She spoke indignantly and ended up puffing and flushed, for her feelings had been really hurt by her brother's words.

Mr Digby, made to feel ashamed, scowled and clicked his tongue. 'Of course I'm grateful, you know I am. Surely I don't have to say so? As for your advice – well, come on, what is it? Your advice,' he added in a stilted voice, 'has always been valuable to me, as you ought to know, my dear May.' Her advice was of no value to him and he never acted upon it. She was valuable in a different way, by being someone into whose lap he could pour himself: thoughts, words, suspicions, deeds, intentions – every so often out they had to come, higgledy-

piggledy, and someone had to receive them. Miss Digby was a suitable receiver.

'Then if you want my advice I'll give it to you, and after that I'll say no more. Lilian has forfeited all right to Teresa. Nothing is clearer than that. You must see your solicitors at once, today. Put the matter entirely in their hands and then forget all about it. They can deal with Lilian much better than you were ever able to.'

Mr Digby was silent. He tapped his teeth. Apparently he was thinking over what she had said. His sister watched him with confidence, her head a little on one side. His eyes were gleaming with secret amusement, but he kept his lids lowered and she could see only the hand tapping at his teeth and the seamed profile. When he wrenched himself round towards her she was shaken with surprise as though by a hiccup. Sweeping with one spidery arm a wide contemptuous circle, he cried:

'Solicitors! What can solicitors do about Lilian? I lived with that woman, I know her, like nobody else does. I've got the sense to be afraid of her. Solicitors indeed! I know a better trick than that.' His large and brilliant eyes, inherited by Teresa, shone and sparkled until they were beautiful. They held Miss Digby's attention. She waited. He leaned towards her, smiling. 'Ruth,' he said, almost in a whisper, 'Ruth, my dear May, not solicitors. Teresa and I are going to visit Ruth.' With his burning excitement he kept them both silent for a few moments. Miss Digby closed her eyes.

'Impossible,' she murmured, 'Randall, you must be mad.'

'Mad enough,' he cried, bursting up from his chair again, 'mad enough to save my own skin. Mad enough to beat *her*. Let her come to England. No one shall stop her. And when she arrives, what will she find? Nothing. There'll be no arguments, no words, no explanations, nothing. No one. The birds will have flown. To India, May, to India.'

He ran to a window and threw it open. 'Teresa,' he shouted into the garden, 'Teresa, Teresa,' drowning her answering cry, 'come here. I want you.' Turning back into the room he said more calmly: 'It's all settled, May. I've booked the passages.' He had made his sister tremble and for the moment she could think of nothing to say.

Teresa came into the dining-room and stood by the door. 'What is it?' she asked, nervously stammering. Miss Digby found her tongue, and turning her stout body towards the little girl, answered in a voice of bitter fury:

'Your father has lost his head, I think. He's taking you away – to India – next week.' Then she got up and swept past her niece out of the room like a gust of the Lord God's wrath.

'Well?' said Mr Digby to his daughter.

'Well what?' she said, staring at him.

'What do you think of it?' He looked back at her benevolently.

'Are we really going to India?'

'Yes, of course. Didn't you hear what your Aunt May said?'

'Shan't I go back to school?'

'No.'

'Well, I'm glad of that.'

Mr Digby, who had made himself an old man before it was necessary by just such excessive bursts of emotion, dropped down exhaustedly into his chair and gazed moodily at his sister's grate, unattractively filled during the summer months with crinkled paper and soot. He tapped his teeth. There was a short silence. Teresa bit her underlip and fidgeted.

'We're going to see your elder sister, Ruth,' said Mr Digby at length. 'Do you remember Ruth?'

'Yes, a bit. Not very well.'

Ruth was Teresa's half-sister, the child of Mr Digby's first brief and nearly happy marriage. She had been married to a tea-planter for eight years and none of her relatives knew how she liked it, for her letters home were as dry and short as they were dutiful. Mr Digby was wondering whether or not to tell Teresa the reason for their sudden flight, and deciding to put it off until a later date – until they were under a different roof in fact, for the things he would enjoy telling his daughter about his second wife would be more enjoyable and make him feel less uneasy if Miss Digby were not close at hand. All the same it was time, high time, that Teresa was told something about her mother – what sort of a woman she was – and strictly warned against her. Even with the great distance that lay between India and England this would be a wise precaution and no more than Teresa deserved. He did then what he seldom did – looked straight at Teresa and thought directly of her, appraising her, finding little of her mother in her, and being glad for that.

II

Miss Digby drove over and fetched Teresa's things from school. Teresa loitered in the garden. Miss Digby mended the holes in Teresa's black cotton stockings; and Teresa sat on the top stair outside the attic door, her chin in her hands. Miss Digby folded the white wool and navy serge garments, and packed them in a small suitcase, with moth balls at the bottom and lavender bags under the lid; Teresa pressed her way through the laurel bushes, climbed over the wall, scraping her knees, and fell on her feet into the road. The sun was dropping, the wind was mounting. Dust blew, a little this way, a little that, and subsided, as morning mist rises, in white spirals. Teresa drifted down the road towards the sun and into the dust, with her heart beating in her throat from confusion, and the hungry sensation she usually felt in her stomach extending all over her. For she was deeply, almost painfully, impressed by her coming departure. Her father and her aunt had thought her unresponsive and had been, in different ways, disappointed by her. Painfully, deeply, she had responded, more than she herself could gauge, more than she with look or word could show. India in physical terms meant nothing to her. It was a name written in capital letters round a huge dark hole into which she was just about to step. Wrapped in her misty astonishment she wandered on and on down the road, on far enough to make her late for supper, for her feet followed her mind and led her on to nowhere: she was walking down a road to nowhere with the dust blowing in her face and the sun declining.

Miss Digby's indignation, far from growing less, had waxed as the day progressed. Her brother had taken her by storm and whipped away her strongest weapon: displeasure. Displeasure, which had won her many battles before, required the agencies of silence and slow time if it was to be really effective, and he allowed her neither. Her telling silences were bawled out of all significance by Mr Digby's loud triumphant voice, and as for time, he banged it to bits like a paper bag and nearly as noisily. He had chased her up to her bedroom and thumped on the door.

'May, let me in. I've got to talk to you.'

And into her sacred apartment he had whirled, not lowering his voice or modifying his gestures in the least, but rampaging round, saying: 'Do this, do that; fetch Teresa's things; tell Teresa's mistress', until, throwing aside all pretence at calmness, and trembling again from head to foot, she cried out in a voice strained louder than his own: 'Stop!'

He stopped, in some surprise. 'What is it?'

She could say nothing. She had been affronted, she knew, but could say nothing. '*Inconsiderate*!' was the only word that burst out of her mouth, while she panted in vain for others.

'My dear,' he said, looking towards her quite kindly, 'you can hardly expect me to be considerate to a woman who has never considered my feelings for one moment since the day we met.'

He was talking of Lilian. His sister, through sheer amazement remaining silent, he went on to say – glancing at his watch – that the train he was just about to catch was the one by which he would expect Teresa the following day. 'I'll write

to you this evening,' he added, 'from London, but I can't wait now. The boat sails on Tuesday and God knows there's a packet of things to be done before then.'

Seeming to notice her reticence for the first time, he searched about in his mind for the tactful ending. 'My dear May, I don't know what I'd do without you. I depend on you – always have done, eh? Too much I dare say.' For tact it was his custom to snatch up whatever came to hand and, after the manner of a brick hurled at the head of a yelling baby, it generally sufficed. He polished off his diplomacy and his visit with a kiss which landed haphazard on the nearest part of her face, and so left. Such kisses are interesting. For it might be thought that lips which had once, however many years before, given off those dark flames of roses must always at a touch bestow a scent, the merest whiff, a pot-pourri of passion. But no, nothing like it. The mouth of Mr Digby, like the mouths of a thousand thousand others, had become ashes without perfume. It ate, and it talked, and moved about rather too much, and had no cunning beauty left, no flowery breath, and kissed, as it now kissed Miss Digby, more as one signs a cheque than as one signs a letter.

He had kissed her, and left her, and was out of the door when she stopped him with a last faint cry: 'Randall – your career? Torrington?'

It was a kindness on her part, though an unintentional one. For he was able to stand in the frame of a doorway and toss away his career, his dull career of teaching, with both hands. How magnificent he felt doing it – a lion out of his cage, off to his desert. No bars were meant to hold him. In the end he

could escape his bars, for his heart, he wanted his sister to know, was a lion's heart. Everything sawdust and trammelled he left to her.

'Finished! Over! Done for! I was born again – born yesterday!' Then, forgetting his uplifted expression and dropping his voice to a meaner level, he added, his eyebrows twitching malevolently, 'My dear May, you should have seen their faces! It put them in a fix, I can tell you.' Perhaps it was for this reason – that his own feelings were ever stronger than those he adopted – he had never become the remarkable actor he knew he might have been, or, alternatively, the remarkable playwright, or, failing both these, the remarkable novelist – successful in any case – but instead only a capricious schoolmaster teaching the diviner words of literature to boys under the age of fourteen. Then, girding up his garments of glory again, he threw her a look of brilliant wickedness, and disappeared. She heard him shouting in the garden to Teresa, who was skulking at the top of a fir-tree. So he went. He left Miss Digby shattered, more shattered than she remembered ever having been before, and she stuck herself together painstakingly throughout the day with the glue of outrage.

All, all was directed against herself. Not only Randall's latest hideously selfish act, but all Teresa's perverse refusals, all the distant slights and snubs of Randall's second wife, Lilian; even the conception and birth of Teresa, she now perceived, were for one purpose only – the spite of herself. Injustice, she thought, as she sewed up a long stocking-ladder which could very well have been left for her good maid Eileen to do, falls

heaviest on the meek of the earth that their reward in heaven may be the greater. But oh! how very great her own reward in heaven would have to be to compensate for this! Bear witness! her stabbing needle seemed to say, bear witness I have always behaved in an upright and honourable manner, and this is how I am served, by my own relations. Since her feelings were sincerely, though obscurely offended, and since, though not for love, she was going to miss Teresa very much indeed, it would have been understandable had she wept a little at this point on to the black cotton stocking she was mending. But whereas Teresa might learn to weep as she grew older, Miss Digby's tears had all been shed in her childhood and had stopped flowing the day that she put up her hair. Upright in her chair, upright in her mind, she sewed rigorously on. Coals in this way, she felt, were being heaped on somebody's head, though how or on whose she was uncertain.

Teresa, in the space of a few hours, had turned into a mouse. How provoking this was! She slipped into the dining-room late for supper, accepted her rebuke mildly, sat on the edge of her chair, nibbled her food.

'What are you thinking about, Teresa? I've spoken twice to you. Are you deaf? Have you forgotten your old aunt already?'

Teresa stared at her.

'Oh, come, Teresa,' said Miss Digby with irritation, 'it may have been foolish of me but I really thought on your last night you'd make some attempt to show good manners. After tomorrow, of course, you'll have no need of them, for your father never notices good manners and Ruth has lost her own, I should think, after living so long in a jungle.'

But Teresa continued to stare at her with clouded eyes across the little pieces of table setting, across the purple flowers, across a distance. The words spun round in her ears needing no answer, being senseless. As water deflects the slap of a hand descending, so this distance that she had felt to be surrounding her all day, making her feet float and her voice an echo, deflected the numerous sharp arrows Aunt May loosened at her. She saw their glint but did not feel their prick. Her eyes were like antennæ, reaching, sensitive, into the future; her mouth waited agape to catch the first sound from a new world. As she forked up her greens and cut her bread in patterns, she considered knocking over the water-jug; for nothing like that mattered any more. She imagined the stream of water, the streams of anger. There she would sit, right out in the open, with anger playing directly upon her, yet untouchable and hidden. Aunt May was speaking again and Teresa, listening and not listening, kept her hand from the water-jug, for she realised there was no need to insist upon herself in a stream of bright ruinous water. The need was past. She smiled into her tumbler lazily. Everything ended today, and tomorrow everything else was beginning. A new thought darted into her head at every noise: her spoon clinked – Aunt May would never be able to harm her again; she scraped her chair back – but she, on the other hand, could still injure Aunt May. Thought by thought she piled up her strength, and crossed the hall with a swagger, pouting her lips. But then it seemed to her that, being so strong, so extremely powerful, to harm her silly old Aunt May would be only a waste of energy. Down dropped her sails. She looked

round the drawing-room, in itself so peaceful, and yawned. Becalmed, exhausted, rippled with sleep, she said to Miss Digby as sweetly as though she was four years old again:

'Goodnight, Aunt May. I'm going to bed now.'

They exchanged their kisses gravely. Both of them were tired. Tomorrow was going to be Thursday, October the first. Miss Digby listened to Teresa's feet slowly mounting the stairs, one by one. Then she put on her spectacles and wrote a letter to her brother.

III

Teresa slept deeply and without dreaming until after mid-night. She was awakened by an owl hooting. At least she thought it was the owl that had awakened her. She lay on her back in bed listening to its hollow note, she and the bird awake while the rest were sleeping. The immense excitement which had sapped her energy during the day had left her, and the immense darkness in which she now lay kept her heart-beats slow and filled her mind with a starry clearness. The owl hooted. She slipped out of bed and touched a chair, a table, searching for her dressing-gown. Then she walked down the stairs and out of the front door, leaving it standing open behind her, and ran across the chilly grass.

Never before had she been in the garden at this hour of night and it made but little impression on her now, though later, a long way away, she was to remember its smells and silence, and its peculiar subtlety. In a light-headed dream she walked all round the house. It was the gesture of the water-

jug translated: the thing she had never dared to do before she could now do with impunity. She was saying goodbye. Or, more exactly, she was allowing a life nearly finished to say goodbye to her. Gravel shifted underneath her bare feet. Wet grass trickled between her toes. A spray of leaves tapped her cheek. She stood, unthinking, unfeeling, not yet understanding, looking upward at the solid house from the square patch of lawn that lay before it. And sleep again descended heavily on her, making her head reel and her eyes sting with water, and her purpose, if she had ever had a conscious purpose, mistily recede. The owl had flown away. There was no noise but a strong sensation that midnight was past and the morning, though still far off, was washing in nearer and whiter with every minute. Almost too sleepy to close the front door without a bang, she went upstairs to her room again, and again fell asleep.

So Thursday came, and Teresa was put on the morning train with no tears but a host of injunctions and one sharp kiss. The train moved, and Teresa never saw her Aunt May again, nor that station, nor the road leading away from it, away, away to Aunt May's house.

IV

As the train drew in at Waterloo the first thing that Teresa noticed was Mr Digby's head craned above all the other heads, and her exaltation, which for twenty-four hours had buoyed her above all common occurrences, had kept her vacant-eyed and open-lipped, had caused her to remain transfixed in a corner seat on the journey up, feet together, hands together, a bashful angel in a black velour hat – this marvellous exaltation deserted her the moment she caught a glimpse of Mr Digby's harassed face, and down she plunged like a stone from the skies. Bewilderment encompassed her, doubts, suspicions, discomforts beset her. The need for hurry tangled her feet, upset her temper. London smuts blew in her eye; London noise bellowed in her ear. From the second her father said: 'Oh, there you are,' grabbed her arm, snatched her suitcase, and propelled her by a push in the back towards a taxi, Teresa heartily wished herself at the bottom of the sea, or else grown-up, or else dead, and her vision of the golden life vanished out of all remembrance.

Running away from a second wife was made as difficult for a man as possible, and the difficulties put Mr Digby in a vile humour. Temperament instructed him to step aboard a boat and sail away, his daughter tucked under his arm: Lilian called him from the cliffs; the waves dashed up in his face; he was deaf to her cries. But vivid flight like this, his heritage, was reduced by a hundred and one minor officials to a very different level, the prosaic level of passports and inoculations and vaccinations, of visits to the shipping agency and visits to the bank. And Teresa – Teresa always with him, being as tiresome as possible, pinching her fingers in taxi doors, losing her ticket, dropping her gloves, being, last and most terrible mortification, sick in a restaurant. Teresa never forgot her father's anger, the way he hissed at her:

'You might have done it in the street. Well, for God's sake clean yourself up in the cloakroom – don't just sit there.'

'I can't. I can't get up. It's mostly in my lap.'

Her sickness was over in one burst, a nervous spasm. With burning disgust he threw her his handkerchief, his napkin. She scrubbed them stubbornly up and down her tunic, and dropped them afterwards underneath the table. The smell was horrible.

'I couldn't help it.'

'Of course you could help it. It's muscles, that's all, control. It's a matter of discipline. My fault, I suppose – you've never been disciplined.' He was tearing her coat down from a peg. Teresa was wobbling to her feet, shaky with shame and with anger at unmerited anger. Waiters kept away, but were watching. Diners looked askance at their own food.

'It's London; I hate London.' It's *you*, she wanted to cry.

'Don't talk, don't talk. You'll be sick again. For God's sake –' He pushed her shoulder. Once out in the street she stopped as though for ever, and cried: 'You're cross! It's unfair! I've never been sick before!'

'My God, if I ever catch you being sick again –' He stopped as well and they faced each other. People divided round them, bumping and jostling on either side.

'Teresa, what's the matter with you?'

'I hate it all, everything, India. I don't want to go.'

'I'll leave you behind if you make another scene like this one. I promise you I will – I'll leave you behind and go on my own.'

'Oh, do, *do*,' she cried. People glanced at her as they passed. 'I never wanted to go. I won't. You can't force me to.' Wrath overmastered him; he forgot she was a child and his daughter.

'You stupid little fool,' he shouted, 'why do you think I'm bothering about you at all? For your own good, of course, for your own good.' He gripped her bony arms and shook her to and fro with all the strength of his exasperation. Teresa was limp, fighting a returning sickness. The busy passers halted, murmuring indecisively. Mr Digby caught hold of Teresa and keeping her in front of him, shoved her forward through the crowds and on to a bus. Here he leaned back and shut his eyes. The incident was over, and India no farther nor nearer than it had been.

But he thought of her more in consequence, bending his thoughts upon her like a searchlight. She was so different from Ruth. Ruth, at the same age, had been graceful. Ruth had been serene. Ruth had kept out of his way, never exasperated him, never been sick. Ruth, to be sure, had come from a different mother, but mothers were not everything. This child stuck out like pins at every angle and the fault was her own, no one else's.

'Must you wear that ghastly hat?' They were in Mr Digby's bedroom on the fourth floor of their dusty Kensington hotel.

'It's my school hat. I haven't got another.'

'It makes you look like' – he wriggled his fingers – 'like an insect.'

'It's the only one I've got,' she repeated in a low voice.

'Well, get something else. Buy another.' She stood in the middle of the carpet, watching him painfully. 'And, Teresa, you still smell of *sick*. Haven't you washed?'

'Yes, I did wash. I suppose it's my hair. Some of it went on my hair.' She picked up a pigtail and held the end of it against her nose.

'Then wash your hair. You must think of these things for yourself. You're thirteen, or fourteen – which is it? – nearly grown up. Ruth –' he began, and broke off, frowning. Ruth had been different. For one thing Ruth was beautiful, and with that quality Mr Digby admired above all others in women, whether they were four or forty, the quality of serenity. Teresa washed her hair in Mr Digby's basin and combed it over her shoulders with a helpless gesture. She longed to go away to her own room down the passage, but until he said to her 'Go away,' she stayed. Her hair smelt, not of sickness now, but of soap and of London, or so she imagined, and faintly of her body, the sweat of her fear, her helplessness. It was half-past eight in the evening. Mr Digby crunched up a handful of the dark curtain of hair and said:

'Sopping wet. I suppose you can't go to bed till it's dry. How long does it take to dry?'

'I don't know. An hour.'

He tapped his teeth and she waited, waited for him, ringed with the scent of her hair, heavy with the weight of her sorrow.

'We'd better play cards. Do you play cards?' She nodded.

'Piquet?' She shook her head.

'I'll teach you.' He dragged the wash-stand forward and they sat one at either end of it while he taught her the rules of piquet. The marble slab chilled her elbows and she listened to him greedily with sharp attention. After ten minutes or so he said:

'Well, do you think you understand?'

She answered in a clear high voice that she understood

perfectly well: it was easy. A smile crept on to his face. He looked in a moment both cruel and jubilant.

'We'll see about that,' he said. Teresa was silent. They leaned towards one another like fighters, excited, and Teresa narrowed the large eyes that Mr Digby had given her, in a defiance more perfectly understood than the rules of piquet, though they, too, were like a natural code to her. Mr Digby opened his wallet and pulled out a pound note; then, after hesitating a moment, he rapidly pulled out two more and handed them to Teresa. 'That's the money I'm going to win back from you. That's your bank. You'd better put it somewhere safe. I don't suppose I shall get the whole lot off you tonight.'

Teresa, who had never before been given anything but shillings and odd half-crowns, took the money composedly and clipped it under a bottle of her father's brilliantine. He dealt the cards and they began to play. Teresa's hair slipped forward round her shoulders and dripped puddles on to the mottled marble, and drips, which she brushed impatiently off, spattered the glum faces of knaves and queens. Presently it turned shiny and dried, and she stuffed it inside her shirt to be out of the way.

V

On Monday morning at breakfast Mr Digby remembered the mosquitoes. India was full of mosquitoes, dangerous dreadful things, foreign pests. They must buy nets to protect themselves. Thank goodness he had remembered in time.

'We can buy them when we get there,' said Teresa.

'We'll have plenty of other things to think about when we get there,' retorted Mr Digby, and a suspicion disturbed his mind that the whole undertaking was greater than he had yet foreseen. The journey to Ruth seemed suddenly a dark and too-long path and Ruth herself, twinkling at the farther end like a star, as distant as a star. A wind of tiredness blew across him and his body slackened. Distances were terrible; they daunted him. His age shrank from all great unknowns, including death. And when he was feeble, who would sustain him? No one. Ruth perhaps. He mustered his will, the will of the wounded lion, and drew his brows together like a warning. Age should not decay him; rivers – he would cross them, mountains too, and die in the middle of his stride if necessary.

But Teresa, who had watched defeat and then recovery first line and then illuminate his face, observed the breach in his armour; he was old, and therefore weak. And she was young, with her strength growing. Age shook him as fiercely as he had yesterday shaken her in the street. Thoughtfully she ate her breakfast. That she had seen his weakness and was bound to take advantage of it was a tragedy, and a tragedy that the only alternative to his conquering her seemed to be for her to conquer him. Where had it all started, and who had struck the first blow? Or is it possible to be born afraid and fighting? Teresa was afraid, and therefore she fought, with courage and sense, whoever came near her. Though nearly fifty years divided them, Mr Digby also fought and for the same reason. Teresa was too young to know that with every year of strife her heart would shrink and her fears increase.

The tender gesture she needed from her father he was unable to give, having for too long expected tender gestures from others, and for too long been disappointed. It was difficult to imagine anyone loving Mr Digby: he was not lovable. Nor was Teresa. The one might have been and the other might later be. Yet Mr Digby's first wife had loved him. Soft and quiet as she was, she had loved him perfectly for a short time and then died. Only after her death did he realise that what he had lost was love, and ever after sought diligently to discover it in another. He took some pleasure in thinking of himself as a man soured by circumstances, and in declaring himself as such to be. Was it his fault if he was a sour man? The world or Fate, or whatever it was that doled out happiness and punishment, had denied him what he needed and like a child whose milk is withheld, he grew thin and his bitter cries increased.

Teresa and Mr Digby discussed mosquito nets, Teresa proud of her aloof contempt. Mosquito nets would be far better bought in India, she *knew*, and to buy them in England was simply a waste of time. Mr Digby *knew* she was wrong.

It happened that London was just then short of mosquito nets. The day turned into a hectic scramble to run suitable ones to earth. When at last they had found a source and the search seemed to be over, Mr Digby held up the gauzy stuff and said the mesh was too large. When assured that no mosquito in existence could possibly squeeze its way through, he shook his head. In his mind they were becoming like germs, invisible and deadly. Only material of the closest and finest weave could keep them out. Vaguely he implied a lifetime spent in tropical marshlands, and the shopman lifted his shoulders. Teresa stood by, sneering. They raced out and caught another bus. London was at its dirtiest. Teresa's feet began to ache and as her father, discouraged, became increasingly snappy so she grew stubborn. In the end they found what he wanted – mosquito nets of bridal beauty, and fine enough to defeat the most dwarfish mosquito of his imagination. To make quite sure he draped himself, and Teresa burst out laughing.

'What is it? What are you laughing about?'

Absolutely terrified by the sight of his face glaring at her through the white gossamer, Teresa cried: 'Nothing – I wasn't laughing. They're lovely; let's buy those.'

The mosquito nets were bought, but, since their suitcases were already bulging, a separate brown paper parcel had to be made of them and marked largely: 'DIGBY – BOMBAY', in case of mishap. Monday was nearly over, and sometime during its course Lilian had landed in England. Success made a new man of Mr Digby. He pranced about his bedroom, rubbing his hands. Successful in little things, he would yet be successful in big. But just at the moment how he longed to celebrate himself. He was the sunniest, best-tempered man alive if people would only not cross him as they did, if only Teresa would not stand there woodenly staring. Could she not be gay with him? Was he not gay, ready to gambol? Was it not a shame there was no one who could gambol with him?

'I thought I told you not to wear that ghastly hat.'

More out of high spirits than ill-humour he snatched the round black abomination off her head with a rough jollity and sent it spinning out of an open window. It fell and floated into

the London street, and may have been run over by a bus or picked up by someone and hung on the spike of a railing, but Teresa, in any case, set out for India without a hat.

PART TWO
THE BOAT

I

Teresa was at sea. The boat moved – would she ever forget it? – away from the land. And something was severed; she felt delivered.

'I never want to come back,' she screeched.

The grey land made no effort to hold her, gave no final sign of enticement. It lay there, apathetic, allowing her to go. The loud-speaker was playing 'Indian Summer'. Down poured a huge flood of sound, drowning the salty air, paralysing thought, emotion, everything, a vast crocodile tear of farewell, loudly lugubrious, and up against it soared Teresa's voice, like a skylark beating its frail wings. 'I never never want to come back. . . .' Strands of hair whipped across her blasphemous mouth; the tears in her eyes belonged to the wind, for she was hard with triumph. 'Never, never. . . .'

'Very well, never come back,' the flat grey mud that was England seemed to answer, indifferent to her wild cry of renunciation. She gripped the rail, passionately free. A woman glanced at her, smiling; a child stared. Buried somewhere deep in the boat she felt a throb that answered her, impulse for impulse, that drew her away from the grey land, across the grey water to bluer seas smoothed over by hot winds, and on and on, farther, even farther, to where strange golden India lay waiting.

Teresa had dodged her father when they first came on board. She left him hitting out amongst a turmoil of porters and luggage, and skipped aside down a passage. To play will-o'-the-wisp with Mr Digby in a boat of that size with its

labyrinth of passages, decks and stairways, would be easy. As sure of his needing her as she was certain of herself not needing him, Teresa looked forward to a prolonged game of hide-and-seek with satisfaction. She was a traveller; travelling was her chosen occupation from the moment she set foot on the gang-plank, and her father, in consequence, seemed to her redundant. Detached and curious, she was indeed a natural traveller, and those emotional obligations that turn travelling for so many people into no more than unhappy separations were unknown to her. Her moments of greatest joy would always be when a boat left shore, or a train moved out from a station, or when the wheels of an aeroplane lifted off the ground.

There were three sittings for every meal and by some mistake Mr Digby and Teresa had been given tickets for different ones. Teresa could have planned it no better herself. She sat up very straight at dinner and pretended she was twenty-five. At the same table as herself sat a little girl of about six and her mother, a matronly woman who took an immediate interest in Teresa; the child was so plainly alone and had a motherless air. So even before the soup was done she passed the salt and asked if Teresa were going out to India all on her own. Unpleasantly jolted, Teresa answered, no: she was travelling with her father. A simple statement, she made it sound inexpressibly coarse. Mrs Evans scented unhappiness and at once felt sorry for her. Hushing her own little girl, Rita, who was clamouring for tomato juice, she turned her full attention on Teresa and attempted to make her feel more at ease by drawing her out. Had she any brothers or sisters, and was this the first time she had been in such a big boat? Question after question Teresa answered stonily, but her primness and disdain were misunderstood as the shyness of her difficult age, and Mrs Evans grew kinder as the meal went on. And though Teresa battled and tried to be rude, it was of no use: she was twenty-five no longer and Mrs Evans had destroyed her independence. So easily can one's claim on freedom be broken. So great is the pain pretension brings. Teresa suffered through dinner and longed for her father's brusqueness.

The night outside was cold, ice-flavoured. She scrambled up and down the stairways from deck to deck and in the darkness heard waves breaking round the ship's bows. Numbers of lights winked and flashed at her from land and from the sea, bobbing and blinking all out of time with one another, in and out, off and on, giving a sense of imminent danger, like people who jump up and down and wave their arms in warning, and yet are too distant to make themselves heard. Seeming not to heed their desperate messages, the ship thrust onwards.

'I wonder if that's the Cornish coast,' said Teresa aloud, and found herself standing beside two men. They were not men, they were bulky shapes, and the night drew them together. Daylight would have made them dangerous – people, and, as people, to be avoided – but now they were anonymous and she trusted them. Darkness wrapped them in a secrecy she longed to join, for Teresa's relationships were still symbolic. Overt dealings offended her confused belief that affection was a plot in which all the conspirators were masked, and possibly treacherous. Yet she longed to be possessed by a shape greater than

37

herself, to be embraced by faceless companions. Her desire writhed inside her like a snake and was anguish. She slid along the rail until her shoulder touched an arm and behold! she was accepted. This was marriage of a sort. She was no longer alone, but one of three. She thrilled with content, and the stormy night folded her in its vast blanket.

'Perhaps that's Ryde,' said a voice, mysteriously human. The ship rushed on. Huddled in a crowd together they stared towards the shore, wondering. Their faces chilled and stung, their hair stood away from their heads, straining like dark banners, and looking out at the leaping distracted lights – 'rocks, rocks, go away' – they felt together the mighty intention of the ship beat up through their bodies and pass out of their frozen mouths in shouts and laughter.

'Yes, that must be Ryde,' yelled Teresa, having no idea what place it was, and she held her arm forward, pointing, to feel her fingers catch and lose the wind. 'There's the pier. How bright it is!'

It reached out towards them a spearhead of brilliance, glittering, flaming, like wealth itself. To one side, delicately spaced, was a string of streetlamps, as clear and pure and distant as virgins might be in a young man's dream. They ran then to the other side and leaned over, fancying they saw a shape, a faint light.

They waited yearning, and faintly, almost exhausted, the light that was land trembled and paused for them and died. They were the only people left in the world, they and their fellow passengers, packed between deck and deck and racing forward, and the land for them was a thing of signs, of smoke

perhaps and lights certainly, but of people never. It was speech-less, soundless, altogether out of touch. For days to come they were consigned to this feeling: that they might be the last creatures, and the earth manless.

Her two companions turned away from Teresa without a word of goodnight and stamped off down the deck together, laughing. She was terribly hurt that they were able to leave her like this, without a word. There had been no compact after all: she was less than nothing to them. A whole had been torn in half. She must remember: a whole could always be torn in half.

They left her lonely. Wraith-like she wandered up and down the long length of the boat, touching steel and rope for com-fort. The sound of singing drew her up to the top deck and here, crouched in a circle in the lee of a life-boat, were Indians going home, singing of loneliness. Their bundled figures swayed from side to side. They sang, she knew, or thought she knew, of sorrow and parting, of death and after-death. She hovered outside the dim ring of their fellowship, listening. Here was no sleeve she could brush, no voice to say to her: 'Oh, look – that must be Ryde.' Their soft nasal song spiced the Channel wind with ghosts of heat. The boat rushed on.

And now for Teresa it was an indifferent boat, as Southampton had been indifferent. It bore her on irresistibly, whether she wished it or not, and no scream, no splash of hers could divert it. She had forgotten again what she wished, and why and where she was going, and wandered up and down the decks in perplexity with singing in her ears and the lights from shore still wickedly winking at her. No wonder she

wandered to and fro, for this was her lost time, her passage from one state to another, a time of transformation. The waves dashed away her certainties, one by one. She rocked in a void, astonished, and with a sense of despair almost too great to be borne. Life was a boat, a wind, a sound of foreign singing, a glimmer of lights. And darkness. Only India was solid, somewhere at the end of it all, and even India she began, like a mirage, to doubt. They chased towards it, and it faded, singing.

How cold it was! She halted, shivering, outside the wide lighted windows of the lounge and looked in at her father reading a book. He read impatiently, flicking over the pages, and once or twice he lifted his head and glanced about him expectantly. The lounge spread out its warm comfort all round him, dotted with armchairs and tables, with people playing bridge, with trays of drinks and stewards hurrying to and fro. His legs were crossed; he was frowning, disliking, or merely not understanding, his book. She watched him beckon a steward and look sharply about him again. She lifted her hand, then, and tapped on the window. Tense with urgency, she stared towards him, willing his attention. But his isolation was perfect; no sound of the night reached him. He lowered his head and turned a page, too far off to hear her. Her hair blew across her face, her knuckles were frozen. Someone sitting immediately inside the window screwed his head round and looked up at Teresa inquiringly. She stepped backwards, alarmed, and hid herself. Mr Digby went on reading his book, and Teresa went away to bed.

That night she heard a new noise. She lay in her bunk and knew she was at sea, really at sea, being tossed up and down on enormous waves. Above her head she heard the light delicate sound of animal feet scampering to and fro. Invisible mice pattered across the cabin, paused, and pattered back: it was the sound of the boat straining and stretching herself amongst the gulleys of open sea. Falling asleep she saw her Aunt May's large whitish face bending towards her, saying, 'Now remember, Teresa . . .' but the train moved; the boat dived; a wave rose and the sea swamped over her its green unconsciousness.

II

She was awakened at six o'clock by the little boy who occupied the berth beneath hers, drumming his heels on the side of the cabin.

'Mummy, mummy, I want to get up.'

A silence while he lay and listened to the scampering above his head.

'Mummy, what's that noise?'

All through the night the scuttling sounds had gone on; the boat moved and creaked and forged ahead whether they slept or whether they lay awake and listened. Morning dawned, and they were still at sea. The voyage continued without pause. Without pause Teresa heard the waves breaking, not as waves break against the beach with a gathering power, a hesitation, a slow ebb, but in a steady flush, unceasingly: break, break, break, break. She expected a pause.

There was no pause. The water smashed itself forever and forever as the boat rushed on.

'Mummy, what's that noise? Mummy, I want to get up.' And he drummed his heels again on the steel partition.

'Oh, hush dear, I don't know. You can't get up; it's too early.' All this in a worried whisper, his mother having no notion how to prevent him from drumming his heels. Being a disobedient child and over-lively, he drummed them again, and shouted at the top of his voice and sprang about in his bunk.

Teresa dressed herself and left the cabin. She was hungry. The wind was outrageously strong, whipping up her appetite as it whipped her hair, and she was in time to see the withdrawal of night from the cold Atlantic. In every direction, as far as her eye reached, was water. No rock, no other boat, no bird even. Water and sky of the same colour, or lack of colour, a blended emotionless grey, was everywhere, and only water and sky. Others besides Teresa were out to have their early nip of air. Roman Catholic priests were stamping round and round the wooden boards, their long full dresses dragging them forwards or clutching them back according to whether they were on the port or starboard turn, like impatient children, the pages of their open prayer-books fluttering in a perfect frenzy of fragile tissue. What did they read about at such a time? The Creation? The Flood? Some improbable and magnificent story to which the waters of God surrounding them, acre upon fathomless acre, might be an illustration? Two nuns were bravely parading themselves, and so was an Indian Prince, and sundry other solitary spirits. They marched separately round and round, with heads bent, battling their way and hungry for breakfast. And presently, had they been able to raise their heads and keep the hair from their eyes, they would have seen a pearly light of palest yellow and faintest pink touching the cold grey sky and spreading, gleaming, all ways across the grey sea; a light so tender, so indecisive, it might have been the beginning of, not another ancient day at sea, but a new cycle of creation, a new and different night.

Rita came and swung on a rail beside Teresa. 'Ooh, look – it's all soapy!' She leaned far over till her knickers blew, and looked back and upwards at Teresa. 'My Mummy's feeling giddy. She had to have an Aspro with her cup of tea this morning.'

Children were all the time appearing, bobbing out ahead of their nursemaids, prancing up and down the boards like little horses, flinging themselves into the gusty weather with the terrible abandonment of their kind. They screamed and hollered, rolled on the decks in their neat little buttoned-up velvet-collared overcoats out of sheer fun, scrambled on and off the railings, and nearly went mad with joy when seamen came along with mops and tossed bucketfuls of water to left and right. The seamen whistled, the buckets clanked. The children behaved like burly little demons and Rita ran away to join them. At that moment Mr Digby, with a trilby hat tied on to his head with a scarf, fought his way up to Teresa.

'Hullo,' he shouted, 'didn't see you last night.'

'I went to bed.'

'Bit blowy, isn't it?' The ends of his woollen scarf lashed Teresa's face. He knew he looked extraordinary. Teresa was ashamed of him. She left him, saying she was going to have her breakfast.

Rita's mother, Mrs Evans, was missing from breakfast. Rita was there, bouncing up and down.

'Mummy says, will you look after me, she's feeling giddy again.'

The dining-saloon was full of children and from them arose a continual overtone of massed wailing. Like a sea-spray it hung above the dozens of white tablecloths, the white-coated hurrying stewards. For fourteen days that chorus prevailed: children's voices protesting first against the rolling motion and later on against the heat; children's voices crying out to be put down, to be helped up, crying for more food, for less, for something different, for none at all. Or children's voices merely lifted, wordless, howling their discomfort. The sea in bulk sloped past the portholes at a mountainous angle, fell out of sight, wallowed into view again. Everyone hurried through his breakfast in order that the second feeders, including Mr Digby, might have their turn. And Mr Digby was encouraged to hurry his breakfast down in order to give his seat to someone else. Stewards hastened in every direction. Food appeared like lightning, and everybody felt obliged to gobble.

Mr Digby was annoyed that he and Teresa had been made to eat their meals at a different time. He tried to put the matter right, but his manner was so unfortunate that he only succeeded in making the situation permanent for the rest of the journey. It was worse than unjust, he said, it was incompetent. He was astounded the boat managed to go at all with people like that in charge of her. As he split open his egg with a savage jab he remarked that such inefficiency staggered

him. 'Who do they think they are?' he added. No one at the
table answered. 'We pay, don't we?' said Mr Digby, so injured
that he had to go on speaking whether anyone replied to him
or not. 'It's an absolute scandal. I'm going to report it. I'm not
going to take this sort of thing without a fuss. No fear. Why
should I? I'll speak to the Captain about it if I must – I don't
care who I speak to. My daughter and I are travelling together
– they've no right on earth to put us at separate sittings.'

Only one man at the table seemed to welcome his outburst, a small stringy man who nodded his head eagerly, and
murmured agreement: 'Disgraceful – yes – a scandal – you're
quite right.' He watched for the time when Mr Digby should
stuff his mouth too full of egg to be able to speak. As soon as
this happened he seized his opportunity.

'Mind you, it's always the same – they don't care a hang
about their passengers. We're just like a load of cattle to them.
You know, I believe they hate us.' He lowered his eager voice a
shade. 'My name's Littleton –' Mr Digby grunted. 'I've been
to and fro this way a dozen times, and I've seen the same sort
of thing happen over and over again –' So he manoeuvred
into position and said what he really wanted to say: that he
was a tea-planter; that he had been home on short leave to see
a specialist – his stomach, he said, had been giving him gyp
for years. And his wife had said – much better get the thing
seen to. And the specialist had said – much better have it out.
Pretty nearly insisted he had the thing taken out. So there it
was, an operation sprung on him out of the blue, and his wife
in India. For they had thought – much better for her to stay
behind, all that upheaval, never dreaming of an operation

of course, and the two children – much better for her to stay where she was and keep things going. He spoke of England as 'home', poor little man, because it was the habit to do so, but his face was turned towards his home now, and death would be more welcome than retirement. His wife, he said, was coming to meet him at Bombay.

Mr Digby listened to him gloomily. These sick fellows were always such a bore. What did he care about anyone's stomach? His own was a stout organ and never gave him a day's anxiety. Mr Littleton, while attempting to go on talking and drink his tea at the same time, choked, and was out of the running.

'My son-in-law's a tea-planter too,' said Mr Digby loudly, 'up in the north. Best part of the country for tea I'm told, though I dare say you know more about that than I do. Funny sort of a life for a woman to choose, stuck away up in the wilds with nothing but tea to look at all day long. It wouldn't suit most girls, but Ruth – that's my daughter – she knew what she wanted. She always did. Even when she was quite a baby, she knew what she wanted, Ruth did, and knew what was best for herself, too. I don't mean to say she's aggressive, mind,' he added hastily, laying down knife and fork and searching the face opposite his closely for signs of a false impression, 'I've probably given you quite the wrong idea now; she isn't in the least aggressive, not in the least. On the contrary, no one in the world could have a – sweeter – you know? – softer nature than Ruth has. Feminine,' said Mr Digby, going contentedly on with his meal again, 'a real woman, out and out. Not clever, mind you' – he lifted a fork warningly – 'not by any means clever, and if you want my opinion, I say "thank God for that".

The woman who thinks she's got a brain – you take my word for it, she's poison! Keep her away from me, that's all I ask. The moment a woman sets up to be clever she turns herself into a freak, like one of these what-you-may-call-it things in a side-show, and I'll tell you why,' said Mr Digby, giving the table a bang that sloshed the tea into saucers and drew him several hard glances, 'it's because she's going against Nature. A woman ought to be beautiful, and she ought to be sympathetic. That's quite enough. I've always found that quite enough in a woman. Anything more is too much.' And Mr Digby concluded this statement of his views with a triumphant flourish that decided his unpopularity once and for all with everyone but Mr Littleton. For while Mr Digby was describing Ruth and hinting at Lilian, his opposite neighbour, though politely attentive, sat thinking in secret about his scarlet-flowering garden – so extremely missed in London – his glossy stretches of tea-bushes, and his wife waiting for him at Bombay – a woman never beautiful, as required by Mr Digby, but sympathetic, whenever the heat was not too great for her.

In this way they made friends, and clung to one another after breakfast and throughout that day. Many of the passengers thought it a duty to fight the elements as their good sturdy boat was doing; the decks accordingly rang with their footsteps and the wind carried away their voices. Others were being sick in their cabins and others, influenced in no way by their environment, sat reading in the lounges. Mr Digby and Mr Littleton were amongst the promenaders. Now and again Mr Digby caught a glimpse of Teresa leading a fat little girl by

the hand or bending protectively over her. The sight vexed him; Teresa, he was sure, had no fondness for children, and, in addition, he felt it right that when he was occupied she should be disconsolate.

'My daughter,' he said, carelessly waving his hand in Teresa's direction.

It was odd that, unable though he was to be proud of Teresa in any way, he yet spoke of 'my daughter' with a thrill of pride. They sheltered for a few moments at the stern end of B deck where Mr Digby could talk to his friend without shouting.

'She's a worry, I don't mind saying so. I'm an old chap now' – May was always telling him this; complaint and defiance mingled in his voice – 'she ought to have girls of her own age to play with – she ought to be at school, I suppose.'

Teresa's lonely days at school were over. She wanted no companions of her own age, nor did her father really believe she did, but of what she did want, or what she should have, he was uncertain. It was a problem he would have preferred to shelve, conjuring up Ruth in his mind as a general solution, but it pressed on him daily, demanding more penetration than he possessed. Over and over again he attempted to calm himself with the commonsense reflection that Lilian had threatened Teresa and he, her father, had taken the necessary step to preserve her. That was all. But it was not all. That for Lilian to gain control over Teresa would have been disastrous, he was in no doubt. But the child had been wrenched from her setting and this action, he saw, was a beginning, not a conclusion. The matter was in no way ended, and his was the responsibility. Caught in a backwash of fright and more and

more muddled, Mr Digby longed for sympathy. However, the story was a long one and the voyage lasted fourteen days. Plenty of time; no need to bawl it all out now. His mood changed. He was a rough old bustard, a regular old rascal.

'Perishing cold standing still. How about another turn?' He hurled himself into the wind and Mr Littleton trotted out to catch him up.

III

The following afternoon Teresa saw Portugal. Mrs Evans was still ill. Teresa was just telling Rita not to climb on the third rail. 'If you do,' she said, with spiteful relish, 'you'll fall overboard and be drowned.' With this remark she lifted her head and her heart seemed to sigh. Portugal, miles away, came out of the sea, and the name on a map was land in front of her eyes.

For hours and hours the pitching had gone on and her temper had worsened. Not sick, but with her head aching, she had longed for five minutes of quiet, five minutes of no movement. But for hours the lurching had gone on and the bitter gale continued. Then at midday the boat had seemed to steady herself and with afternoon came a pale sunshine, not bringing with it any warmth but seeming to glaze the back of the wind. In a weak yellowish glimmer was born this vision. Teresa forgot her temper, Rita, the ache inside her head. Land so unlike land, strange and brown, clouded with spray and distance, induced an ache no part of her meagre body recognised.

It was soundless land. White waves rose up in slow gestures against those far cliffs, poised and fell, without a whisper of noise, animated by a sadness and a resignation as endless as the turning of the world. It was as insubstantial as pictures in sleep, and as permanent as the first created moment. No life was there, no movement but the moving line of spray, lifting and dropping its long white fingers in neither welcome nor farewell, only unceasing sorrow. The boat tore past at top speed and Portugal receded. A drift of clouds came down between Teresa and those faint hills and she saw their brown heads creep over the top of it, half-vaporised, blue-shadowed, and this was her last sight of them.

Glamour had touched her eye-lids, glamour bewitched her. The sea was beginning to turn green, and everywhere it sparkled with a new liveliness. Whales were sporting on the starboard side. Romance was real, rising out of the ocean in rocky shapes, and fabulous monsters swam about. Teresa went in search of Rita, who had slipped away to hide herself, and bore the burden of the child's teasing with docility for the rest of the day.

That night she walked about the deck without an overcoat. The air was almost warm. Peace had taken the place of fury. A full moon shone. The mild water glittered with a million fish-scales, black and silver. She recognised her father leaning alone on a railing and held herself back out of shyness. For she imagined going up to him, touching his arm and saying: 'Hullo. Did you see Portugal this afternoon?' And him answering: 'Yes, of course I saw Portugal.' 'Did you see the whales?' 'Whales? No. Who said they were whales?' Such a conversation seemed to her so grotesque, and so likely that she stayed where she was in the shadows, watching Mr Digby, and thought she heard him heavily sighing. Presently a smaller figure joined his. Mr Digby's harsh voice was audible greeting it, and then his harsher laugh. A cigarette was lit. They moved off past Teresa, talking.

Next day they were in the Mediterranean Sea. Mrs Evans was present at the breakfast table, her inside stabilised and herself full of gratitude to Teresa.

'Oh, you have been good,' she said, 'and Rita simply adores you now.' Apparently Rita had not reported a slap or two. 'I felt so ill, I didn't care what happened, but she's too young to be running about on her own. She's such a monkey she'd have fallen overboard most likely. She can't talk of anyone else but you.' Rita, who was drinking, ambiguously lowered her eyes. 'Be a dear and take her up on deck for half an hour – I've just got to straighten out the cabin and do a spot of ironing, and then I'll be along. See if you can find a nice cosy corner and I'll bring my knitting up.' Rita silently offered Teresa her hand.

The unoriginal girls who had boarded the boat at Southampton emerged from their chrysalis of dowdy tweeds, and blew round the decks like butterflies. The sea was choppy, a darkly blazing blue, and the wind strong, a hurricane hot from the shores of Africa. It brought with it African sand, carried dry above miles of water to powder the honey-coloured boards of the boat with its pale scrapings of shell and rock and earth. There were rainbows chasing alongside, and flying-fish skimmed the spray as swallows skim a lake.

All that day Teresa played nursemaid to Rita. Mrs Evans joined them on B deck with her knitting and a tin of biscuits, and lashed Teresa to her side with a couple of Petit-Beurres. Teresa was admitted to her confidence as though she had been a grown-up, and, while holding a skein of wool, listened to the history of Mrs Evans' marriage and the minor troubles of married life. Using her life-jacket as a pillow, her legs stuck straight out in front, her ankles crossed, Mrs Evans chatted volubly on, occasionally breaking off to call, 'Rita – don't do that,' or to send Teresa in search of the missing child. Herself a person of much unimaginative kindliness, she was adept at the exploitation of any hint of kindness in another. Mr Evans, it seemed, was an engineer, and Rita their only child – a bundle of mischief if ever there was one. Rita edged up to hear, her rather puffy porridge-coloured face turned towards Teresa with an expression of sly pleasure. Her mother stroked back the little girl's hair and adjusted her bow while relating various of her amusing pranks.

Teresa, having been previously flattered by her adoption, soon found it irksome. Her feelings towards Rita were straightforward: she thought her loathsome. And Rita was able to tease Teresa with uncanny niceness, pulling her pigtails just a bit too hard, winding herself round Teresa's neck with suffocating affection, undoing her shoe buttons, and watching all the time for signs of the hate she knew existed. But Mr Digby hovered on the outskirts of Teresa's vision, and for this reason she bore all impositions stoically. Now and again he drew near like a moving shadow, and at once she

began to show off her new position, running officiously after Rita, dusting her down, picking up Mrs Evans' ball of wool. Look! she implied, I have my importance, my own friends who cannot do without me.

'Who is that distinguished looking old man?' asked Mrs Evans, who had her suspicions of who he was.

'Oh, he's my father,' answered Teresa with off-handed contempt, and she blushed with angry pride to hear him called distinguished.

'Oh yes, of course, I can see it now. You're very alike, aren't you? Do introduce us.'

Mr Digby sauntered up. 'Hullo, Teresa,' he called out in a jolly voice.

'Hullo. Mrs Evans, this is my father.'

Politeness demanded that Mr Digby should lower himself with squeaking knees to the boards beside Mrs Evans for a few minutes of civil conversation. With the same false heartiness he cried: 'Well, you've found a nice sheltered corner, eh?'

'Teresa found it.' She began lavishly to extol Teresa's virtues, finishing up archly with: 'I'm afraid we've stolen your daughter from you, Mr Digby!'

Unnerved by her father's increasing gloominess and deeply furrowed brow, Teresa longed and prayed for him to go away. After a short time he did, scrambling up with a muttered remark about his age and the hardness of the deck, and stumping off. 'So those are your friends,' his retreating back seemed to say to her, '– you can have 'em!' Nor did he show himself again. The bubble was exploded. Teresa's

absorption with the Evans family fell flat. Her boredom made her disobliging and ended in desertion.

IV

In the meantime Africa was the backcloth for a dozen buds of friendship, and the swimming-pool had been opened. A swarm of children occupied it as their natural playground. The square of water was a clear jewel, blindingly bright, broken in fragments by their kicking legs, and shrill and bright their voices rose, as bitterly pure as blown beads of spray.

Arms and legs were bared. Shirts fluttered. Naked flesh burned coppery under the scorching wind; men's faces turned the colour of oak; the town-mouse hair of girls was bleached to a brittle glory. And with burning flesh and leaping hair came a new demand: the need for warmth within, for the flame behind the eyes as well as the flame before; for the word of love that established Africa and made the Mediterranean to be remembered for ever. This was the time for the blossoming of that flower with shallow roots but luxuriant petals, the flower that exists without water in a blaze of sunshine to die tomorrow. Its stamens bear no pollen but its scent is intoxicating. Those too young to think about it splashed their small hot bodies with salty water instead, and screamed fit to beat the seagulls. Those too old wandered alone with its nostalgic perfume in their nostrils. But for those between such an age and such an age, the time was flowery indeed. Every windless cover concealed two worshippers. The young man bent his head forward and sand fell out of his dry

hair to sprinkle the legs of the girl beside him; and she, from behind dark glasses, noted the lovely turn of her wrist and wanted nothing else but this for ever. Deep in the bosom of the boat was a throb that promised them no ending. Dance-music bounced out of the loudspeaker and hurtled away across the silver-and-sapphire twinkling sea to confute the sombre frown of Africa. Children or seagulls – who could distinguish their voices? – were yelling. The wooden boards were fiery hot, the white paint was dazzling, the coiled ropes smelt of tar. Noisy with music, wriggling with movement, this box of a boat swept on across the Mediterranean in the full glare of the sun, old Africa as audience.

And Africa was like a beast. It was brown and heavy and huge. Its hills rose one behind the other. Its shore was as low as the lip of a village-pond, and intimately dangerous. It looked like land that had lain maturing for years without number, and had now reached its strength and was terrible, guarding a power no man was meant to calculate. Here and there a thin wisp of smoke coiled up from cooking fires, and paths like the scratches of a fingernail on wood led inland and uphill.

Mr Digby and Mr Littleton studied the chart pinned in the aft saloon and pored together over latitude and longitude. 'The first time I came this way,' said Mr Littleton, 'I was just a lad. I was eighteen. Didn't know what a tea-bush looked like. Never seen a tiger except in the Zoo. I've been on a tea-garden ever since, and for fifteen years on the same one. You don't know what's going to happen to you when you're young, do you?'

Mr Digby, whose tigers had all been Zoo tigers, felt at a disadvantage. It was the first time he had been this way. Until now his travelling abroad had been confined to Switzerland, sometimes, unpleasantly, as the chaperone of a group of school-boys, sometimes, moodily, alone. Otherwise his holidays had been spent in Sussex or London or the Lake District. There had also been one or two highly unsuccessful weeks at Lyme Regis with Teresa. Envy made him want to know how many tigers, if any, Mr Littleton, who was only half his size, had shot.

'I suppose you get pretty good hunting up in those parts?' he said craftily.

'Pretty good,' said Mr Littleton, 'you can't beat the shooting. Plenty of pigeons, you know – jungle-fowl and that sort of thing. Oh, there's plenty of sport when you've got the time for it. There's a fellow on the next garden to mine, first-class shot. We go out together whenever we've both got the time. But tea keeps you busy most of the year round, you'd be surprised.'

'Time!' cried Mr Digby, starting up with flashing eyes as though the word was a gad-fly and had stung him out of his seat. 'Who's got the time nowadays to do what he wants to do? Not a man-Jack of us. Time indeed!' – he snorted – 'you're talking about a luxury, let me tell you, a luxury like the Dodo – dead and gone. If I'd had a bit of time when I was a youngster, things would be very different now.'

And he proceeded to make clear to Mr Littleton exactly what the difference would have been had time, together with a certain amount of money, been allowed him in his youth. Mr Littleton was given to understand that had such been the

case he would, at this moment, see before him and have the pleasure of talking to, not a paltry prep-school teacher, but a man whose standing in the literary world could well be called – Mr Digby believed he was not going too far in using the word – unique. For the talent, the gift of writing – come, why not be frank and call it genius – he had it *here*. And a thump on the chest marked the spot. That is to say, he *had* had it here. When he was young, it had burned him. That was the truth. Very likely he seemed to Mr Littleton nothing but an old fool talking nonsense, but he could assure Mr Littleton, earnestly, sincerely, that when he was young it had burned him. He had carried that fire inside him – why deny it? – and had his dreams of scorching the whole world with it. Well, what had happened? Look at him! Did he have to say? Everything had been against him. The mere struggle for existence had quenched at long last that ardent flame. He wondered how many more young fellows there were like him, or like he once had been, their genius being slowly stifled to death by the pressure of miserable day-to-day necessities.

In his own particular case the blame for such stifling lay heavy, it seemed, on a good many different heads. There was Lilian, of course, but she came pretty late on in his life, and, iconoclastic though she certainly was, could hardly be held originally responsible for the destruction of Mr Digby's genius. It might be deduced that Fate had had a considerable respect for the ability of Mr Digby's Art to survive her displeasure, since she had been at such great pains to defeat it, quite overdoing herself in the abundance of obstacles she had thrown in his way. First there had been his parents, who gave

him nothing but the obligation to earn his own living. Then schools in general – institutions, he swore to Mr Littleton, that ground the very soul out of you. Then his first wife: he hurried rather guiltily over that gentle faithful creature, declaring that if she had been a drag on him it was not her fault, but just the way things were. Reproach belonged far more to that ghostly army of ill-wishers who had made ceaseless war on Mr Digby for the most discreditable of all reasons: envy. Them he might thank for being what he was today: not a great artist with a name familiar as a household word, but instead – he said it frankly – a failure. A failure, trading for his livelihood in the words of other people, amongst the most ignorant of all God's creations, schoolboys.

Mr Littleton had listened, with his mouth most flatteringly open, to every syllable. Now and again he interjected a – 'Well, I never,' or a – ''Pon my soul, you don't say.' When his friend had finally blown himself out of breath and come to a stop, he hastened to express his admiration:

'Well, who'd have thought it! Fancy having a turn for writing and keeping dark about it all this time! Though I tell you what, if I'd been a bit sharper I might have spotted it myself. You've got a sort of – you know – a sort of literary air about you. Know what I mean? Stands out a mile, only I'm such an ass. By heavens, you're a lucky chap. If you only knew! You can say what you like – all that stuff about being a failure – you're a lucky chap. I envy you. I'd give a lot – I don't know what I wouldn't give – to be able to string just a couple of words together on paper. Can't do it! What d'you make of that? Can't even write a letter. And sometimes, you know, when things hit

me, hit me hard – you know, like things do sometimes – views or – or – things that happen, you know? – I'd give my soul to be able to jot it down, like some fellows dash off a sketch of a place to be able to keep it in mind. But it's no good – I can't put pen to paper. There it is. Make what you like of it. I suppose it's a gift – some chaps have got it, like you; some haven't, like me.'

With his ready self-depreciation, his willing – nay, eager – admiration for the other, he more than repaired the damage all unwittingly done by his tigers. A soothing glow stole over Mr Digby. He felt indulgent, and indulgent first of all to himself.

'Look here,' he said, with a laugh of whimsical concern, 'I can't have you running off with the wrong idea. I'm not a writer, you know. What I've been telling you is that I might have been. There's a world of difference between the two, worse luck. But I'll say one thing for myself,' he added, with another burst of warmth, 'I'm not a mediocrity. I don't believe in dabbling about with Art, like some chaps I know. All or nothing. Art,' cried Mr Digby, entirely carried away by that glance of trusting attention fixed upon him, 'Art isn't a game you can play about with. No, by God, you've got to live for it body and soul – what?' Mr Littleton jumped. 'Aren't I right? Well, then – I left it alone. Had to. Couldn't do anything else. Of course, I've had a few articles published. Ran the school magazine – that sort of thing. But I'm not a writer. No, no, no – get that out of your head straight off. Just a poor old failure, that's me.'

He flung himself down again in a chair, with a strongly renewed hankering after the stage. The idea of an auditorium

filled with Mr Littletons quite went to his head. The applause would be stunning. All the same, something made him drink off his whisky at a single gulp, and, beckoning the steward, order two more with almost furtive haste. Mr Digby was at heart an honest man, but his moments of lucid honesty were few and far between, and as he grew older he had contrived to space them more and more widely. They were, when they came, so devastating, they showed him such terrifying sights, such abysmal depths, such snows and glaciers ahead, such scorched earth behind, that he lost the courage to face another day, and, but for his fear of dying, would have liked to cease upon that very midnight with as little pain as possible. Those were the times when he would have turned towards the warm comforting arms that were never there, and those were the times when he deserved them.

V

That evening a part of C deck was roped off. The boards were chalked. Lights were arranged to flood it like a boxing-ring, and there was dancing. The dancers circled inside the bright enclosure, too dazzled by themselves to see the dark company who stood without, silently watching. Lips were scarlet, long full dresses fluttered out. Teresa, whose summer-time wardrobe consisted of three faded gingham frocks, too far above her knees and too tight across her expanding chest to be counted as evening finery, sat perched high against a lifeboat, and swung her legs to the beat of a fox-trot. Mr Littleton found her here and begged her to try the floor with him.

'No, I can't. I've never danced.'

'Well, have a go now. Come on. You'd love it once you got started.'

She stared down into the carnival, half-mesmerised with excitement, half of her determined to flee away from it. Playfully he tweaked her leg, trying to dislodge her. 'Come on Teresa,' he said, as if they were old friends, 'Give me a bit of fun! I don't know anyone else to ask, and it looks so jolly.'

'No, really, I can't. I'd feel so stupid. I'd rather watch, really I would.' He looked up at her, his little gingery face smiling and persuasive, and she refused and refused, shaking her head from side to side and laughing with the pleasure of being able to withstand him, and yet so nearly succumbing. It was at this moment that Mr Digby saw them, and a shock of jealousy went through him.

His daughter and his friend, chatting away together on the easiest terms, without him! Never could he tweak Teresa's leg like that. Never could he make Mr Littleton look as he was looking now, ten years younger and kittenish. Never had either of them laughed like that with him, and that they were laughing together now from cheerful spirits was cruelty more bitter than an insult. He wanted to be their good companion, and they rejected him, and were gay with one another. Then astonishment took the place of his jealousy: Teresa appeared to him as a new creature, unlike Teresa, not a girl, not a woman, not human, not his. She leaned between the large light of the sky and the blaze on deck like a spirit of no permanence. Her hair, which for the party she had untwisted from its usual pigtails and combed long and straight round her shoulders, blew out sideways in a dark sheet against the moon. She bent forward away from it towards Mr Littleton, her sharp face strange with laughter and shadows. Mr Digby, much perturbed, threaded his way round the edge of the spinning couples, with whom he collided at every step.

'Hullo, hullo,' he called, and saw at once that he had given himself unnecessary trouble in coming across. They were not, after all, having the particular fun they seemed from a distance to be having. Teresa was not animated: she was just sitting still in a rather awkward position. Nor was Mr Littleton sparkling with wit: he was simply standing beside her ankles, uncomfortably squeezed up by the press of people.

'What a crowd, eh?' said Mr Digby. 'Let's get out of this, shall we? I can hardly breathe here. Let's go up on the top deck for a bit, away from this bedlam, eh?'

Teresa obediently slid down on to her feet. Mr Digby, who had included Mr Littleton in his proposal, turned protectively to help him force a way out of the throng, but the tea-planter had somehow been jostled away from them and was tangled up in a waltz, gyrating blindly towards an opposite corner.

'Oh, well, never mind him,' said Mr Digby, impatient at once at the man's smaller build that made him so helpless in a crowd. He and Teresa went up on to the top deck where, except for here and there a silent shape, or two silent shapes, they were alone. Dance music from lower down and the other side of the boat, sounded less insistently. They took up the usual position, leaning on a rail.

'Having a nice time, Teresa?'

'Yes – thank you very much.'

'Haven't you got a better dress than that to wear – something pretty?'

'No.'

'We must buy you something, fit you up a bit. We might have a look at the shops in Bombay – would you like that?'

'Yes, thank you, I would.' She wanted above all things to be polite to him, but the threat was there, she felt it as she always did, and more than polite she could not be. She was expectant, waiting for his next words, and afraid, so that the springs of original thought dried in her. Tonight she would have liked a meeting, what would have amounted almost to a reconciliation, but instinct warned her this was impossible. They had no conversation of feelings between them, only words. When he asked if she was having a nice time it was his mouth, not his heart, that inquired, and his eyes gave her no passages for penetration. Like windows shone upon by the sun they were blinding, and whatever rooms might lie beyond were concealed by their glare. It was his misfortune that no one had ever been able to tell him this, nor, if they had, would he have understood, for he believed himself the most tender and sensitive of men, and perhaps, in his own way, he was both tender and sensitive.

'I wonder where your mother is now. I wonder if she knows where we are. May must have let it out by this time.' He glanced towards Teresa for encouragement. She was silent. 'I don't suppose you remember your mother, do you?'

'No, I don't.'

'Just as well. Just as well. I wish I could say the same. It's

funny to think you wouldn't even know her if you saw her, and she wouldn't know you. You might pass each other by in the street, like strangers. Well, you are strangers, after all. I hope for your sake you always will be.' Here he waited for Teresa to say something, but she was silent again. He settled his arms more comfortably on the rail, and went on:

'Extraordinary woman! It's lucky you take after me; if you took after her you'd be unbearable.' Even this brazen flattery elicited no reply. 'You wouldn't be standing here beside me now with a view of the Mediterranean, I can tell you,' he said with a chuckle. 'No such luck! And yet, she was handsome – I'll give her that. Or she could have been if she'd had a little modesty. She had all the makings of a very handsome woman, your mother. Oh Lord, I wouldn't have married her otherwise. I wonder what she looks like now.' He wondered for some moments. 'A snare,' he said, 'that's what she was – a delusion. And I was old enough – my goodness, I was! – to have known better. But a woman like that, you see, she takes you in! She took me in. I married her,' said he, shaking his head with mournful amazement at this piece of long ago folly, 'actually went and married her, like a young fool of a boy who didn't know any better. Imagine that! Imagine finding yourself married – "till death us do part", you know what you say when you marry someone – married to a mule of a woman who disagreed – flatly, mind you – with everything you did or said from the word go. On principle – I firmly believe on principle, though what the principle was, God help me if I ever knew. There was no sense in it, not an atom. Disagreement on principle, that was it. And she was a big woman,' said Mr

Digby earnestly, 'it makes a difference, you know. Those big strong strapping women – well, they aren't like women at all to my mind. You can't treat 'em like women. There's no suppleness there, none of that feminine give-and-take that makes a woman what she ought to be. At least, there was plenty of *take* about her – there wasn't a thing she wouldn't have taken, as soon as look at it. But *give*? – not on your life, not on your life. Not she. Not Lilian. Know what I mean when I say the Nordic type? That was her. Plaits round her head, neck like a bull, and those damn supercilious eyes looking out over the top of her stuck-up nose without a wink of shame. Till death us do part! Lucky for me – lucky for me,' repeated Mr Digby impressively, 'she decided not to wait for death to do the parting. *She* decided, mind you. If I'd said it first I swear she would never have left me. That's the sort of woman she was. You couldn't budge her, not an inch. And she got her own way too, that's the scandal of it. Always! She always got her own way. I'm ashamed to say it, but so it was. Took what she liked and got what she wanted,' said Mr Digby, wiping his brow, on which the excitement of the discourse had caused drops of sweat to start forth. 'Except one thing, Teresa. There's one thing she ain't got and she ain't going to get – and that's you!'

He waited rather anxiously for Teresa's agreement, for recently he had begun to feel that the decision in this matter was not altogether his, and to need reassurance. But Teresa failed to remark the questioning note in his voice, and kept her silence. She had no curiosity about her mother. Her interests lay all ahead, and chiefly not with people. She listened because he wanted her to listen, but she watched the moon.

Mr Digby, as he talked, had a vivid picture of the woman who had been a grievance to him for nearly sixteen years, but for Teresa she was the merest sketchy outline, and she had no more desire for her to be made real than she had fear of it. Her father's voice rasped on, and though it sounded in her ear she heard it at a distance.

'You're better off with me and Ruth. . . .'

The night was enormous. The boat flew forward on a dead straight line with nothing apparently to guide her but her swallow's instinct. There was no noise of engine, only the sound of the dance-band and the low voices of strollers passing behind them, the tread of feet on boards and the solid flush of waves. The flat sea was pitted with diamonds, more and larger than the stars, and more white than the moon was the wake of broken water left behind, darker than whales the islands that every now and then drew near on port or starboard side and were for a few moments close enough to be hailed, though to a voice they could have answered nothing, being only empty rocks where the birds rested on their long flights from land to land. As sure and faster than a swallow, on flew the boat. On and on went Mr Digby's voice and Teresa put down her guards, for tonight, she saw, the potential dangers were in abeyance. In good faith he had come half way to meet her and, certain that she too had come half way, believed they must necessarily have met, and that the union was established for ever. Teresa knew differently. She saw the gap between them more clearly than ever before, realised how wide it was, and for the first time was saddened by it rather than despairing. However much they might feel about

in the dark, their hands would always miss. For the first time she knew it as a loss, and wished it otherwise. He was stone to her, and she would always bruise herself against him. Mr Digby had worked himself into a state of enthusiasm with his memories of Lilian, and now he thought how nice it would be to have a drink with a man friend, Mr Littleton.

'About your bed-time, isn't it, Teresa?'

He was in a very softened mood towards her, and thought what a thoroughly dear little girl she really was. As they walked across to the stairway, he was humming. He took her elbow to help her with the steps, and the kindliness she felt in him at this gesture evoked the most extraordinary desire to weep. For a moment she nearly loved him. Two tears did in fact rise up in her eyes and even escaped on to her cheeks, but with this her weeping fit was over. That he should believe the long monologue under the moon had brought them together as close in sympathy as they were in blood, seemed to her so inexpressibly simple-minded that weariness and melancholy overcame her, and tears alone would have been no relief. When she left him, ostensibly to go to bed, she made a swift detour and came out on the other side of the boat. Here, for over an hour, she stayed, meandering in her thoughts, watching and listening to the sea.

VI

Friendships on board ship have a way of fluctuating with almost the same speed as the temperature can change, in a matter of hours, from cold to very hot. They are tasted rather

than proved, and a constant reshuffling goes on. Teresa, after the rapid growth and decline of her intimacy with Mrs Evans, found herself annexed by a girl called Ann. Ann was eighteen and so unattractive that most people took care to avoid her. She was, in consequence, a lonely girl, destined to spend most of her life searching for a best friend. Her good qualities were so well concealed by her large and clumsy body, by myopia, and by an apparently incurable skin disease, that so far no one had wanted to be her best friend, or to make her theirs. The constant betrayals and disappointments suffered during her long crusade to win one passionate attachment had never made her lose her incipient loyalty, or her confidence that some day she would find her heart's desire and be welcomed.

She rescued herself from the loneliness of her first few days on board by approaching Teresa and offering to lend her a bathing-dress. Teresa, who had no bathing-dress, had been obliged till then to content herself with watching the enjoyment of others luckier than she. The heat was tremendous, and as the most desirable place in the world at that moment appeared to be the swimming-pool, she eagerly accepted this offer and allowed herself to be tied up in a thick woollen garment several sizes too large by a beaming Ann. The result, with straps knotted high about her neck and pantaloons descending half way down her narrow thighs, could hardly be called chic, and another girl, catching such a glimpse of herself in the mirror as Teresa caught, might well have preferred to swelter fully-clothed than cut so comic a figure. But vanity in Teresa was a disadvantage still undeveloped, and she rushed helter-skelter off to the pool, Ann blundering after, with no other thought in her head than to get herself wet as soon as possible.

Poor Ann: for her this loan of a bathing-dress implied a compact. She had imagined they would dally together delightfully on the brink of the swimming-pool, daring each other in with the little pushes and little screams that make girl-friends so dear to one another. Alas, she was deceived again! Teresa felt herself under no such obligation; bounding on ahead, she flung herself immediately into the water – or, rather, into the midst of a squirming mass of children – and proceeded to splash her way across to the other side as best she could without a single backward glance. Here she clung to a rope and, coughing, dashed the salt away from her eyes. Ann was left stranded on the steps with the miserable sensation of having been deserted. She cried out desperately:

'Oh, Teresa, you do swim well! I can't swim – will you teach me? Teresa, come and teach me how to swim.'

Now Teresa did not swim well. On the contrary, she swam feebly with no skill and was fully aware of it. She guessed that Ann was only sucking-up and, instead of being flattered, despised her very much for these slavish remarks. Regarding her contemptuously across the pool, she thought how ugly and what a fool Ann looked amongst the swarm of agile eight-year-olds. So she ignored her cries and letting go of the rope, struck out again amongst the squealing urchins. They swam about her like tadpoles and sprang in from the side without fear, holding their noses. They fought and splashed one another, sank and came up bubbling, used their arms like flails, and ran round and round the pool outside, yelling with joy. As Teresa

drew breath at the shallow end a little girl leaned over above her and whispered:

'Take me for a ride. Please take me for a ride.'

Teresa, who could just touch the bottom, reached up her cold arms and lifted down the frail sun-warmed body. 'Hold me,' whispered the child, winding her thin fingers together. Her hair was pinned on top of her head and smelt of sweet hay; she smelt like a field in August.

'Climb on my back,' said Teresa authoritatively, and tried in this way to swim forward. But the rough little boys overcame her and they sank. The little girl screamed and clutched her neck. The confusion was brilliant, daggers of green and silver, and sturdy limbs flashing. Teresa caught hold of a rope and loosened the two hands throttling round her throat.

Happiness tingled over her. Never before had she felt the desire to protect another. Now she felt it. She longed to possess something alive, like this child, that she might shield it with her own person. 'Don't be afraid, it isn't deep. I won't drop you.'

The little girl, gasping, clinging, urged her forward again; again they struggled and again, choked and blinded with water, they sank, and came up into the sunlight holding a rope. Exhilarated, laughing between splutters, they played at drowning until they were exhausted, when they climbed out on to the side and the little girl ran away.

'Hi – Teresa!'

In a daze, panting, salt on her tongue, her skin glittering wet, Teresa turned her head and saw Mr Digby hanging over the rail of the deck above.

'What a guy you look, Teresa! Where did you get that awful thing you're wearing?'

He had to shout to make his voice heard above the yells and the splashes. His voice was like a fog-horn. Previously unaware of an audience, Teresa now saw that a number of people were standing along the same rail watching the children's antics, and, at this moment, attending amusedly to Mr Digby and herself. Their smiles scalded her. The stupid bathing-dress had stretched as far as her knees and she did look a guy. She felt a guy. In dreadful shame she hid herself inside the pool, wishing the water could cover her head as well as the woollen horror.

'Why don't you dive, Teresa? Can't you dive?'

Mr Digby stayed where he was, enjoying himself without any thoughts of malice, though a little irritated, it is true, by his daughter's unathletic behaviour and unsightly appearance. Again she gave him no cause for pride. However, he was not too ashamed of her to find pleasure in showing everyone that he was her father. And so he continued shouting, half-jovial, half-chivvying, and between his loud advice to Teresa he spoke in confidential parenthesis to those standing round about him.

'Try an over-arm stroke, Teresa. It's no good paddling about like that. Lift your arms out of the water – it's a funny thing, they don't seem to give 'em any swimming instruction at girls' schools. Teach them deportment instead, I suppose. Teresa, look at that little chap over there – he knows how to dive. Ask him to give you a lesson. He'll show you how to do it.'

Teresa's swimming-pool had become a hell. She could not leave it, for to leave it she must walk in full view several hundred yards, and this was now impossible. She heard her father's voice terribly echoing inside the caves of her ears. This was the man who could humiliate her with a glance at any moment, who could petrify her, strike her dumb; who could torture her, moreover, with impunity, for he did not know he tortured her and this ignorance of his made him invulnerable. His stupidity – for so she termed it to herself – was his armour-plating, and every blow she struck fell glancing back on her. She might scream or burst – he would never understand that he was to blame.

Now she defended herself in the only way that occurred to her, by ridiculing Ann who was still planted squarely on the steps.

'Fancy going bathing in your glasses! Why don't you take them off? Why don't you come in properly instead of standing there like a silly lump?' And rather hysterically she flung up a handful of water which, catching Ann across her spectacles, made the poor girl more helpless than ever.

'Oh, Teresa, don't.' She lost her footing and fell heavily on to a small boy who was practising the breast-stroke. Teresa mixed herself up in the scrimmage, roughly trying to pull Ann deeper in. But however hard she tried to divert herself with cruelty the pool remained a hateful place, and nothing she did or said could kill her enemy, Mr Digby.

She looked up and found he was gone.

The world was calmer, the cries softer. The water had a chill and muddy look. She climbed quickly out and wrapped a towel round her waist, shivering with tiredness.

'Oh, Teresa, don't go! Come on – it's lovely.' Not knowing what to do with herself amongst the clamouring brats who surrounded her, Ann gazed up with beseeching eyes through her smudged spectacles. Teresa walked scornfully away without replying.

'Oh, Teresa!' The wail followed her. She ran up the hot steel stairway on her bare feet and from the railing of the deck above, where her father had stood, turned to shout back an answer.

'I'm sick of bathing. It's beastly and crowded. If you only knew how silly you look with all those babies down there.' Then she rushed along the passage to her cabin and was literally and thoroughly sick in the lavatory.

For the rest of that day she had a headache, and lay on her bunk too hot to sleep. The fourth occupant of the cabin, a Miss Spooner, found her in this condition and touched her forehead lightly, whereupon Teresa buried her head ungraciously, saying: 'I'm not feeling very well.' By evening she was hotter, and tossing petulantly over to mutter: 'No, I don't *want* any dinner,' she was sick again. Miss Spooner took her temperature and sent for the stewardess. The stewardess sent for the ship's doctor, who diagnosed sunstroke. Her temperature rose during the night, and all next day she was in a fever.

VII

Teresa was ill and Miss Spooner nursed her. That is to say, she sat in the cabin sewing, and now and then she fetched Teresa a glass of water, and sometimes she rang for the stewardess to

bring a cup of tea. She made no fuss and she spoke so little that Teresa hardly noticed her at all. She was small and dry, with sharply active eyes behind her pince-nez spectacles. The sick-bay was dealing with an outbreak of measles, and so Teresa had been ordered to stay in her bunk. It was Miss Spooner who had arranged for the speedy removal of mother and noisy son to another cabin, herself volunteering to stay behind and act as unofficial nurse. Or, rather, she did not volunteer, she merely stayed, behaving as though there was no question of her doing otherwise.

Teresa lay on the evening of the second day, out of her fever but in a light-headed dreamy state, and watched the competent fingers embroidering flowers on a piece of white material. It was a camisole, as Teresa saw when Miss Spooner held it up and gave it a shake. She asked drowsily who it was for. Miss Spooner replied that she was making it for herself, an answer that very slightly shocked Teresa, who felt it wrong that such an old lady should care about her clothes, especially her underclothes. For herself, she had always considered clothes ugly but necessary, and thought little more about them. Beautiful clothes, such as she occasionally imagined, belonged to the fantastic, not the real world. If you were four-teen you wore black gym stockings and white shirts. If you were old, like Aunt May or Miss Spooner, you wore black or grey dresses with white spots. If you were Eileen, Aunt May's maid, you put on a blue sateen blouse for your afternoon off. Miss Spooner was saying:

'I like to feel I'm looking nice underneath, whatever I look like on top.'

Teresa was puzzled. Miss Spooner threaded her needle with lavender coloured silk and started on a Michaelmas daisy. The camisole was edged with lace. Teresa looked from the lace to Miss Spooner's face, and found it uninteresting, an elderly face with a small mouth.

'Why are you going to India?' she asked nosily. Miss Spooner made no reply. It was certainly none of Teresa's business and this silence should have snubbed her. But with the fretful licence invalids are all too inclined to allow themselves, she repeated her question. Miss Spooner then answered calmly, with no hint of reproof in her voice, that her sister, who lived in Calcutta, was ill, and she was going out to look after her until she was better. While Teresa was turning this over in her mind, together with various other inquiries which, in view of Miss Spooner's plain disinclination to be communicative, would have been extremely impolite, Mr Digby's head was pushed through the cabin window.

'Hullo, Teresa. How are you? Better?'

'Yes, thank you. My temperature's normal. The doctor says I can get up tomorrow.'

He looked at Miss Spooner too, and also found her uninteresting. She seemed, strangely enough, to feel the same about Mr Digby, for her smile was a restrained one and she said only 'Good evening' – not another word.

Teresa lay slackly. Her illness had soothed her. She said to her father: 'How's Mr Littleton?'

'Oh, he's very well; he's fine. He's a good chap, I like him.'

'I like him too.'

'He's been telling me a lot about tea. There's more in it,

you know, than you'd think. Funny thing too, he lives quite close to Ruth, only about a hundred miles away.'

'That sounds an awful long way away,' drawled Teresa from the depths of her indolence. She was lying on her back, her hands loosely joined across her stomach, and the sheet covering her lay as lightly as her own thoughts. It seemed easy enough to float all the way to Ruth in this faint state of disembodiment, but a hundred miles farther was too far.

'Why, that's no distance in India,' said Mr Digby, laughing, 'is it, eh?' he added, appealing to Miss Spooner, but she was sewing and thought him to be addressing Teresa, not her. 'He's invited us over to stay if we want. I said we might. So we might if we feel inclined, but time enough to think of that sort of thing later.' All his efforts tended towards Ruth and there his life broke off. It was for her to decide what must happen afterwards, what he must do with himself and what must be done about Teresa. He must get to Ruth. His mind used up its energy in the thought of reaching her, and could go no farther.

'Oh, well, I must be off for my dinner.' Teresa wished he was not so jocular. She was sure it tired them both, but in a good mood he was always jocular. When he had gone away she waited for Miss Spooner to say something – something about how nice or nasty he was, or how alike they were, or to ask what was his occupation. Miss Spooner snipped off a thread with her scissors and seemed content to say nothing. Such reticence surprised Teresa, but she found it so agreeable that she presently went to sleep.

When she awoke the cabin was empty. Miss Spooner had

gone to her dinner and the camisole lay neatly folded in a piece of tissue paper on the foot of her bunk. Teresa missed her, which was odd since they had spoken so little to one another and since Miss Spooner had shown Teresa no friendliness, only consideration. All the same she missed her, and the half hour before she returned seemed a long one and was boring.

'What did you have for dinner?'

Miss Spooner described the food she had just eaten and asked if Teresa was hungry. Teresa said she was. Miss Spooner sent for a plateful of bread and butter and while Teresa was eating her slender supper she undressed in the bathroom and arranged herself more comfortably in a kimono. All her movements were brisk but unostentatious, as though she did them to please herself and no one else.

'Would you like a biscuit?' She never called Teresa by her name, giving, by this fastidious avoidance, the impression that even so slight a familiarity would have offended her independence. I believe she's hard, thought Teresa, munching a biscuit with her knees under her chin; I wonder if she likes me? She watched Miss Spooner's decisive preparations for bed. The silences between them were in this way busy, not awkward ones.

'I'm glad that little boy's gone, aren't you?' said Teresa cautiously.

'Yes, I am glad. He was a very tiresome little boy, but I found his mother much more tiresome. Perhaps your sunstroke's done us a good turn. I'm going to leave those biscuits beside you in case you feel hungry during the night.'

'Do you like children?'

'It depends on the children,' said Miss Spooner, 'I have known some horrid ones.' Before turning out the light she read to herself for half an hour, sitting primly up in her corner with her hair tidied away under a pink silk net.

Lying awake in the darkness Teresa listened to the noises of the sea. She felt vaguely troubled, and vaguely comforted. Just as she was dropping off to sleep, she thought: I don't believe she likes me.

'Miss Spooner?'

'Yes?'

'Nothing. I thought you might be asleep. Good night.'

'Good night,' said Miss Spooner, kindly and softly.

VIII

'She's a funny sort of woman, that Miss what's-her-name,' said Mr Digby. They were cruising down the Suez Canal. Teresa sat in the shade with a straw hat, belonging to Miss Spooner, shielding her head and face. For Miss Spooner had said: 'You must wear a hat if you sit outside today.' And Teresa had answered: 'I haven't got a hat.'

'Then you'd better wear mine. It isn't very pretty, but if you tie it under your chin with a ribbon, I daresay it won't look so elderly.' And it was she who produced the ribbon and she who sliced holes in the straw to thread the ribbon through, apparently unconcerned whether or not she ruined her only summer hat for ever. It was a flat straw hat, rather the shape of a boater. Miss Spooner was accustomed to skewer it on to her own head with pins. Strangely enough, with the bow under her chin, it suited Teresa. It gave a gentler air to her usual gravity. Miss Spooner smiled with pleasure. 'Why,' she said, nodding at Teresa with a sudden perkiness, 'you suit it very well. You make it look younger. It's really quite a pretty hat now.' Teresa was pleased.

She said to her father, 'I wouldn't call her funny, exactly. She's ordinary. This is her hat.'

'Oh, well, I suppose you know. She's certainly been very kind to you. But I don't think I care for her. I don't like her manner. I met her this morning and I said How d'you do, that sort of thing, to show I knew who she was, and I thought she was very stiff. Not rude, but very stiff. I hope you haven't offended her, Teresa. Perhaps you haven't thanked her enough.'

'I haven't thanked her at all,' said Teresa, flushing. 'You can't thank people *like that*.'

'Like what?' Teresa was silent. 'Well, all I can say is, I didn't take to her a bit.' Mr Digby was more than ever decided about his feelings for Miss Spooner.

'Now that other friend of yours, Mrs Evans –'

'She isn't a friend of mine.'

'I thought she was.'

'She was. She isn't now. I think she's awful.'

'Ah, well there I disagree with you. I've happened to bump into her once or twice while you were ill, and I found her very pleasant. Very sympathetic. She's common of course, but she can't help her voice.'

'Sympathetic about what?' said Teresa crossly, knowing

exactly in what fashion Mrs Evans had pleased Mr Digby. He waved his hands.

'Understanding in a general way – you know what I mean, Teresa, don't pretend. Now that other one, Miss Spencer –'

'Spooner.'

'She hasn't got that nice generous womanly approach. The trouble with her is, she's suspicious of men. I can tell it a mile off – it's written all over her. 'Tain't her fault, I suppose– she's a spinster. Spinsters always get like that – suspicious of men. It turns 'em acid.' And he champed his jaws as though the mere thought of Miss Spooner left a sour taste in his mouth.

'I don't think she's acid,' said Teresa thoughtfully, 'I think she just likes to be private. Mrs Evans talks too much.'

'Oh, rubbish,' said Mr Digby, who had the gift of always talking the most, whoever he was with. 'You're too young to read characters, Teresa. Don't give yourself airs.' And with this he silenced her.

The previous night the boat had lain at Port Said. Teresa had been awakened by the noise of the anchor rattling down, and by voices shouting. In the morning she wondered what it was that made her feel so strange. It was the stillness and there being, after six continuous days and nights, no sound of waves breaking. She had dressed and gone outside without waking Miss Spooner. Houses greeted her eye, amazing sight, square dung-coloured and yellow houses close at hand in the bright sunlight, with painted signs in an unknown language fixed to their façades. People not English strolled about and the water was dotted with little rowing-boats, and with dhows. She could not digest her astonishment: it all seemed so natural. Within an hour the anchor was hauled up and the boat moved forward into the Canal.

Her father said: 'You missed a lot of fun last night – I nearly came and pulled you out of bed.' And he proceeded to give her an account of their arrival.

Port Said, for Mr Digby, had been a great experience. He had missed seeing Portugal altogether; the cliffs of Spain he had seen, and thought that they were sunny clouds; Africa had not surprised him. But the moment he heard a voice cry out a string of words in a high-pitched foreign tongue, he knew he was abroad. And in that moment he became, most sincerely, what he had always wanted to be: an adventurer. He clutched Mr Littleton by the arm. He swelled. His eyes flashed. He turned his great and handsomely modelled head from side to side, he snuffed the hot night airs, and so faithfully exploited his own private inner theatre, that indispensable and echoing cavern round which he was built, that soon he knew himself as a giant figure striding across the globe, dropping in on this barbaric port for a few rough hours, then off again – who knew where? – into the wilds. That exotic dust which had so miraculously rinsed Teresa in its bright glitter some five days before when Portugal discovered itself to her out of the sea, now showered down on Mr Digby – less pure, perhaps, more backstage tinsel than dust of the universe, but dust of his own kind and, for him, exotic. Mr Littleton was good-natured enough to stoke up his friend's enthusiasm, and even found himself excited by it. The boat swam up the long alleyway between the floating red and white lights. The pilot's launch came curving out to meet

it, a-twinkle with lights, the water before it splashed with rose. The pilot sprang aboard. Tall masts of dhows crossed the moon. The anchor went down with a rattle. The water immediately beneath was burning green, and everywhere else a shining black. All was lights, and darkness, and dark heat, and from the land, from those sensed but unseen houses, from the myriad shrouded passages between them, came shrill whistles, expressions of the humming vibrant half-naked altogether foreign life swarming at hand.

The water was clouded with mud; the mud settled; the water turned again a wild green. And out came the droves of rowing-boats, with oars working like active legs of insects, to tangle themselves with motor-launches, to drift and crash irresolutely like wreckage on a tide. And the sea that had for so long spoken only its profound and mystic language became suddenly domestic with smaller splashes, with horns honking and with voices beautifully and obscenely swearing. A number of lamps as powerful as searchlights shone down at the side of the boat, and beneath them showed in colours as vivid as enamel every detail of seam and rowlock, each tooth and toe-nail, every bare brown limb and fold of dirty cotton. Above this microscopic exhibition, voiceless, in shadowy rows, the passengers leaned. Officials scrambled up the stairway; illicit vendors were hustled off it. Battle went on amongst a dozen or more minorities. The moon, most large and constant, flew up the sky unnoticed. On the deserted port side of the boat a dhow, with languid dipping movements of her mast and furled sail, unloaded vegetables into a hatch. Gentle occupation: in busy peace the task went on, without haste or disorder of any kind, and the bales being swung aloft appeared like the movements of ballet-dancers, as musical and strong.

On the crowded starboard rail, Mr Digby was trading with a child of about fourteen. Carried away by the flood of his new sensations he had caught and fastened the line flung up by the boy, and was now leaning over hauling up in a basket first one article and then another. Mr Littleton beside him was indulgent but cautionary. 'You don't want that,' he said, rubbing his fingers over a travelling-bag; at once Mr Digby shouted out, 'No, no,' and sent it scudding down again so fast it nearly fell into the sea.

'Very high-life bag,' cried the disappointed urchin, rescuing and holding it up, trying its buckles in full view, pulling out its straps. 'You like this. Very good high-life carrier bag. Very cheap.'

'Well, I don't want it,' yelled Mr Digby victoriously.

'All this leather stuff's camel, you know,' said Mr Littleton in his ear, 'leather's all right but they make it up so rotten bad, no craftsmanship. All their goods are shoddy – don't last for two minutes. You'd much better keep off 'em altogether.' Mr Digby continued to shake his head and wave his arms in high good spirits at the little boy bobbing up and down beneath him on the bright green ripples.

'Looky here – you like dates? Very smart sandals? How 'bout this – cigarette case for lady?'

He wore a fez. He tilted back his smiling face to gaze up and up at the mountain above him and at the small greyish head and shoulders of Mr Digby, the foolish god who could,

if he would, shower down shillings and English pound notes. Friends and enemies all about him were doing the same, holding up leather cases, leather handbags, thumping this, shaking out that, cajoling, beseeching, refusing, agreeing, wagging their fingers, tossing up lines with an accuracy which would have been deadly had the lines been knives.

'I might as well buy a box of dates,' said Mr Digby, 'I can give 'em to Teresa – I dare say she likes dates. Hi, you – dates! Send up a box of dates.'

Up like lightning came the flat straw basket with the dates inside. 'Five shillings, sar, very good dates.' Mr Digby agreed to pay three shillings for his purchase.

'They're not worth it, of course,' said Mr Littleton, 'they're not worth more than one-and-six at the very most – probably not as much as that. They put any sort of muck in these boxes.'

'Eh? Is that right? Are you sure?' said Mr Digby, taking his hand out of his trousers pocket with an anxious expression. 'Oh, well, in that case I'll give him one-and-six.'

'You'd better give the beggar three bob now you've said you will. He'll kick up an awful row if you don't. I was only warning you what to expect.'

'Oh no! Oh no! I'll give him what they're worth and not a penny more. I know what they're like, these fellows. He can't make a fool out of me.'

Putting one-and-six into the straw basket, he lowered the string. The boy seized the basket eagerly and plunged his hand inside. Finding only two small coins, he felt again. His happy expression changed to one of concern. He shook the basket and turned it upside down. Mr Digby saw in one moment a world of confidence topple over and crash. The brown child lifted a face wrinkled with anguish.

'But sar, here is one-and-six – you promised three shillings; sar, you promised, you promised three shillings –'

Mr Digby answered nothing. Not anger or indignation, such as he had expected, raised that cry, but more terribly a primeval recognition of betrayal. The despair, so out of proportion to its cause, dumbfounded him, and his own confidence collapsed. He was right, he knew he was right, and said hurriedly to Mr Littleton:

'It's ridiculous – such a fuss about one-and-six.'

The wretched wail sought him out: 'But sar, you promised –' To free himself, Mr Digby flung away the box of dates he still held in his hand. By the merest chance it fell at the feet of the now almost hysterical boy and not into the sea.

'I don't want them at all,' shouted Mr Digby, 'they're horrible, not good dates. Bad, bad.' His voice sounded nearly choked with rage. Turning towards Mr Littleton he breathlessly cried: 'I dare say they were full of worms. What villains they are! I'm off to bed.'

For despair is a boomerang, and he who five minutes before could have lifted continents on his shoulders was now filled with miseries as vague and terrible as the torment of a nightmare during sleep. He rushed away, disturbed and disturbing, and only some time later remembered the one-and-six that Egypt had acquired for nothing. This oversight restored him enormously, for injustice he could well endure, and even enjoy. So he was able to sleep deeply after all, and

to tell Teresa about it the following day with quite a show of cheerfulness.

Teresa, since her bout of sunstroke, had been ruled by an abnormal lethargy. She listened now to all he said, but every word was transmuted as it left his mouth, and the excitable scenes he described appeared to her in slow motion, moving across her mind with voluptuous heaviness. They were vivid to her, as vivid as though she herself had been there and heard and seen it all; as though, in fact, she had seen and heard it time and time before, not only from the rail of B deck, but from the shores of Port Said and from the little bartering dinghys; as though her blood was partly Eastern, not controlled by birth and death, a very ancient understanding that pulsed inside her. She nodded her head attentively. Her father's face fogged out of focus. It was very hot.

On either side of the boat stretched miles and miles of sun-coloured land, drier than raisins, not steaming, as green and earthy places steam, but nervously shimmering, as though the whole wide territory was on the move and might at any moment take off into space as easily as its sand, having no weight, shifts and sorts and piles itself when the desert winds blow. Now and then, growing close to the water, were date-palms and tamarisk trees. Now and then Teresa, turning her face outwards, saw a village go by, the thin black line that was a road skirting the low parched blocks that were houses, and stretching away beyond them either side, mile after flat mile, out of sight. Telegraph poles, the link with distant but somewhere existing towns, strung out singly across the vast emptiness, seemed, paradoxically, the very attar of desolation.

Landscape was geometrical, a matter of lines and squares, occasional curves and perspective that lost itself in space. The mind observing it was lulled to an appreciation of the very large or the speck on the sky-line, the immediate moment or the remotely historic past: there were no middle distances.

Here was Ann, ambling up, casting her shadow, smelling of unhealthy sweat, and even so limned in shade and dazzle, unattractive. 'Teresa, where have you *been*? I've looked for you everywhere, yesterday too, and the day before.'

Teresa, fumbling for words to say whatever would send her away soonest, squinted up at her, dimly revolted. 'I've been ill,' she said, 'I've been – I've had sunstroke.'

But it is the desert, she wanted to say, that makes anything between us, even five minutes' conversation, impossible for ever afterwards. She turned her eyes towards it. I am content to be parched, to be burned, to be left forgotten in the desert. I am bones to be bleached; I am sand to be blown. None of this she said. None of this, in actual words, she thought. But she looked out helplessly into the glare, and she turned the same glance towards her father to summon him and his strength and his marvellous tongue to her aid.

Ann said: 'Oh, you poor thing, I'd no idea. Are you all right now? Come and play deck-tennis. I'm not much good at it but I'm sure you are. The court's empty, I've bagged it specially.' She even touched her, making a clumsy grab at Teresa's hand and muffing both her speech and her action through excessive nerves, for she understood, though not very clearly, that Teresa did not want her, either then or at any time. Mr Digby spoke up sharply.

'Of course she can't play games, she isn't well. Didn't you hear what she said – she's been ill. You'd much better go away.'

Ann's legs, as unpleasing and solid as reinforced concrete, were planted close beside Teresa. Sitting very still and quiet, Teresa watched these legs and, watching them, missed the rather humiliating sight of Ann's eyes filling with water behind her spectacles while the rest of her face became an extraordinary crimson. Mr Digby saw, and found her in every way disgusting. Many people were destined to be rude to Ann in the years approaching, but she never grew accustomed to the dreadful surprise of it, nor ceased, from time to time, to weep in consequence. Thick-skinned as she was physically, and fairly thick-skinned mentally, the small amount of sensibility she had been granted was just enough and no more to ensure her being a most unhappy person. Teresa saw the legs withdraw themselves. There was silence. There was a long silence. Mr Digby said: 'How about a game of piquet?' He must have had such an idea in his head when he dressed himself that morning, for he pulled a pack out of his pocket there and then and began to deal the cards on to the deck between them.

So that in future Teresa could never think of the Suez Canal without the vivid addition of playing-cards, as though scarlet hearts flowered permanently in the dry sand, and spades and diamonds danced all day long in the heat-haze; as though her bland-faced Jacks in their gaudy trappings themselves inhabited those mud-baked houses.

Mr Digby defeated Teresa. The cards were shuffled and re-dealt and Teresa defeated Mr Digby. An hour, or more than

an hour, went by. Then Teresa lifted her head and received a small but definite and lasting shock. Mr Digby, noticing her inattention, thought it was the camels.

'Look at them – what a bunch!' he said, allowing himself a pause in the game as well, for the camels were indeed a comic sight.

A ferry full of these animals was drawn up beside a small quay, waiting till the great boat should have passed. The camels were crowded together. Their long necks waved complainingly over the sides. More camels waited on shore, some lying down, some standing in patiently disdainful poses. It was impossible to guess from where they had come, for there was no house, no sign of human dwelling in sight, only acres of unspotted sand. Yet here they were, camels by the score, gathered together out of nowhere, waiting to cross the Canal. And standing guarding them, equally out of nowhere, were a number of men, chatting and laughing together in the liveliest of humours. Their business, whatever it was, seemed without connection to time or place. There they were, these men and their camels, very much and healthily alive in a land as barren as the sun itself, and nearly as hot. It was strange to see them so close – close enough almost to share in their feelings for one minute; and strange to reflect that after the minute had passed they would be lost again to Mr Digby and Teresa, buried again in silence and obscurity, as though they had no existence except for those sixty seconds. Somewhere they must have been born and raised; somewhere they would grow old and die: their span was the same. Yet save for the time between one blink of an eyelid and the next, they and

the passengers watching them aboard the boat had no more bearing on each other than they would have had were they dead.

It was not, however, this thought that startled Teresa, nor the sight of a man stark naked, brown all over, that caused her to drop her cards and forget completely about piquet. One of the camel-drivers was wearing a long loose pink cotton robe. The rest were in white. What astonished Teresa was that dab of colour.

It was a very pure pink, the pink of campions in English country hedges. In all those aching stretches of dun, where occasional touches of sorry green and blinding white were the only relief, it came like the quenching of a thirst. It jolted Teresa out of a fourteen-years-old indifference. For the first time she noticed colour as being beautiful in itself, and realised that it could and should be more than merely the means of identifying one object from another. She thought it was lovely, this garment covering an Arab whom she would never see again, and asked herself: why was it lovely? Undoubtedly because it happened to be of a certain pink. This was such a simple discovery, and such a tremendous one. She made no mistake about its importance. .A world of colour opened out before her, exquisitely pleasurable, promising revelation after revelation. Some aesthetic sense, long sleeping inside her, had been tapped and responded joyfully.

'Come on, Teresa, stop goggling. I've got a cinquième.'

'I've got a carte,' said Teresa automatically.

'Well, it doesn't count. I've got a cinquième and a carte.' Mr Digby threw down his aces and kings with a flourish.

Teresa, carefully picking out her low cards, laid them one by
one on top.

IX

Teresa's dream-state was broken only by India. From the Canal
to Bombay she remained inside her cocoon of unreality. And
Mr Digby, as they drew nearer what, for him, meant action and
responsibility more than he could gauge, grew increasingly
apprehensive. With apprehension he became quieter. He fell
back into the old habit of tapping his teeth. In such frames of
mind he and Teresa were drawn to one another, preferring
their own erratic and side-stepping methods of companion-
ship to more rough-and-tumble friendships.

Sometimes they were joined by Mr Littleton, but recently
he had formed an attachment with a young woman missionary,
and it was with her he was more often to be seen, walking
together and deep in earnest conversation. He was outwardly
a little ashamed of his predilection, and found it necessary
with his friends, Teresa and Mr Digby, to laugh off that mawk-
ish word 'missionary' by a pretence that his interest was only
in order to get what he called 'the young idea'.

'Doesn't seem right,' he said to them, 'for a girl like that to
go and bury herself in some God-forsaken place, all bugs and
malaria and swamps. She's just throwing her life away. She
ought to be having a good time at her age. I'm trying to make
her see sense.'

In fact, he was trying to make her see nothing of the
kind. Secretly he was awed by her, and she increased his

humbleness. He had been born a disciple, as some people are, glimpsing glory through the eyes of more splendidly esoteric spirits, and happy in the reflection of it. The instinct for hero-worship had survived his long since discarded adolescence and was ever-present at his elbow, prompting new allegiances. This young woman of thirty with her pale bright face, its delicate bone-construction and peculiar sweetness of expression more disguised than disfigured by the over-large horn-rimmed spectacles, fired his always inflammable gift for admiration. In mind they were much the same age, both eager, unselfconscious, ignorant, and bursting with any amount of undirected enthusiasm. Mr Littleton was able to unburden himself of the many questions he had shovelled to the back of his mind as a boy and left there ever since through diffidence. Though she could answer none of them conclusively, she yet said a number of things that seemed more wise than they were and which he remembered till the end of his days. Indeed, Mr Littleton, his timidity quite conquered by her zeal, came dangerously near to falling in love with his missionary, and was only saved from this catastrophe by knowing her so short a time, and losing her altogether at Bombay. Perhaps he even, to some extent, did fall in love. At any rate, for fifteen years he kept her leaning over a rail in that blazing sunshine, talking ardently to him and making him believe what she said. The flesh is insubstantial, but the memory a most formidable preserver of life. For she died a year later from a surfeit of impossible living conditions, and, while he still confidently thought of her, lay buried in one of the thousands of isolated and

starving Indian villages. From then on her unhesitating voice and intrepid spirit belonged to Mr Littleton, and to anyone else who remembered her, so that for many years he did indeed possess her, though without knowing it, and in a more ghostly fashion than he once or twice contemplated on board ship.

Ann was vanquished and left Teresa alone. Mrs Evans each day after breakfast made for one particular *spot*, and since she had no variety it was easy enough to avoid her. Of Miss Spooner, Teresa saw little. This she regretted, though numbly, as all her reactions now were numb: she no longer felt excitement or fell into fits of uncontrollable trembling, as she used to do. But dully she regretted the loss of Miss Spooner, who, Teresa having no further need of her, had withdrawn, as it were, one step. They saw each other now and again, as sharing a cabin they were bound to do, in the mornings and going to bed at night, but contact between them, other than mere politeness, seemed to have been broken. Miss Spooner was not by any means cold: she was detached. Nor was she impersonal. She would not, however, extend her personality. She was like a flourishing little island set aside from the main trade routes and perfectly satisfied that no ships should call. Why should she wish them to call? They could only be a nuisance. On her island was all she wanted. Mr Digby, bucketing by at a great distance, had mistaken this small kingdom for nothing more fertile than rock and gravel. Teresa, canoeing closer through delirium, had seen the vegetation there and suspected hidden orchids. She would very much have liked to pay a visit, but lately the energy necessary for such an invasion had been mislaid, and so she drifted away, back into the wash of greater ships, and could do no more than cast a glance over her shoulder at the dwindling green dot and feel that she was leaving unexplored some possible happiness.

After Port Suez, Teresa slept or read or played piquet with Mr Digby, their substitute for conversation. The swimming-pool continued to sparkle with children. Love matches were made and re-made with energetic inconstancy. The loud-speaker broadcast news of missing children: 'a little girl in a blue dress has been found wandering near the Purser's cabin.' Corridor rails were strewn with drying nappies. The dining-saloons were noisy with the voices of passengers under ten. Mothers knitted. Fathers, of whom there were not very many, drank. Games of deck-tennis and deck-quoits, like the liveliest of exclamations, went on from sun-up till sun-down. There was another dance on B deck. And the Red Sea was whipped all over into sharp white crests by the hot wind that blew all day long without a lull.

The world was rippled; the air was like a continuation of sea, like the very spirit of sea relieved of weight and colour, ripples of it blowing across and across in evaporated counter-part of the waves, heavy and green, beneath. And the flying fish that all the time broke surface, streaked above the water, and disappeared, seemed scarcely to know the difference between the one element and the other. Arabia on the port side appeared at first like a cloud formation, a grey and bluish shape low down against the horizon, and later, when it drew nearer, as a legendary land, spiked with rocky pinnacles and turrets, its distant hillsides pocketed with sunlight. Teresa looked towards it apathetically, with wide eyes, as though too many drugs had killed her vision. The word 'Arabia' murmured inside her head fainter and fainter. The boat raced on, and no more land was seen until Bombay.

Two nights before they arrived, Teresa, undressing, said: 'It's so awfully hot. I wish I could sleep outside.' 'Why not?' said Miss Spooner, 'I think it's a very good idea. I'll sleep outside as well.'

It was easily done. They pushed their mattresses and sheets through the cabin window and, with some slight feeling of indecorum, tripped down the passage in their night-clothes. Most people had already gone to bed. Except for a few late walkers the decks were empty. Teresa leaned over the deserted rail, her night-gown blowing round her bare ankles, and watched the huge and deeply orange moon lumber over the rim of the sea, begin to climb, begin almost at once to fade and turn pale as though defeated by too many stars. Then she lay beneath her sheet, drew it up to her chin and tried not to go to sleep. But the sound of a couple a few feet away quietly talking together made her drowsy; the ceaseless splash of waves, the round and solitary ring of last footsteps passing close beside her, all these increased her drowsiness and so she slept.

Before six o'clock she was awakened by a hand on her shoulder and a voice in her ear: 'Scrubbing decks in five minutes.' She awoke to freshness, not to cold, to the sea still running and day half-born. The light was grey. The sheet was cool. Buckets were clanking and she heard the seamen whistling

tunes merry enough in themselves, but transformed by the strange lingering quality of shipboard to dirges, flute-like and sorrowful. Hollow and floating sounded their voices, their whistling, the rattle of their buckets against the heavy wash of the sea-waves. Forever and forever, as long as she remembered anything, the dying echoes of that early morning waking at sea never ceased to haunt Teresa, reverberating to and fro, dying but never final, an echo descriptive of her whole passage through a void from one state to another, when nothing was solid, least of all herself.

X

Early on Wednesday morning Miss Spooner awakened Teresa. It was six o'clock. 'Do you want to see India?' she said.

Teresa dressed and ran on deck. The water-front of Bombay was approaching through layers of greyness. Lights winked from shore. The great boat altered course and headed directly towards it. The water was dotted with numbers of little triangular sails, all leaning over in one direction and blowing past as soundless and frail as a host of withered leaves. High up in the sky the moon was still brightly shining, but the sun was close at hand and so, with every moment, she grew paler. The tide of night had ebbed away and left her stranded like a fish on the sands, gasping for breath and dying. Passengers who had risen early leaned over the rail, grey-faced, and spoke in hushed voices.

Then the sun appeared. The land turned into buildings, the sea and sky to flame and colour. Faces were flushed with radiance; hands reached out, pointing. There was the Gate of India, as small as a key-hole – there! As she followed the direction of their fingers and saw what her companions saw, a feeling of sickness surprised Teresa. Her flight was over. Though a boat could move away from a quayside and make short work of human ties and demands, though the world was round and the seas immense, somewhere waiting was the other quayside, the other land on which, however freely the glorious boat sped, she must eventually stub her bows. There was no departure without arrival.

Teresa shuddered. The very word 'Bombay' was like a threat. Oh, *boat*, she thought, actually striking the rail in her fit of despair, you are stupid not to be able to save me! With what indifference the boat had borne her over hundreds of watery miles, and how she had exulted in that indifference. Now she saw that her pride had been false. The boat was no more nor finer than a machine, and, as a machine, could carry and deliver her, and turn and go back the way it came, without her. How often she had loitered along these decks, imagining herself a familiar spirit. What a conceit, how pitiful! What spirit could be familiar with a machine, except perhaps the cold corroding spirit of the sea? Not a vow had been exchanged, not a response given, not a print of herself remained. All, all had been a delusion. Oh no! why must it end?

She rushed in search of her father, for the living mind to reassure her where matter had betrayed. But her father had disappeared. His cabin was empty, and Miss Spooner, she presently discovered, had already quitted theirs. Her belongings had been packed the night before; she was gone. She had vanished as seasons and shadows vanish, soundlessly, imperceptibly, while the attention is turned another way. Teresa was alone.

I am alone, she thought; I must be calm. And her heart at once began to thump inside her with the anguish of her situation. She knelt down on the floor, and scooping up her few garments crammed them unfolded into her suitcase. Then, casting wildly about her for toothbrush and sponge, she came upon Miss Spooner's hat. Up she sprang, squashing the straw with both hands against her bumping chest. Miss Spooner had gone without her hat. Was it an oversight? Had she really forgotten it? Or had she meant to leave it behind? Was it her dry way of saying goodbye? Teresa tied the ribbons beneath her chin with trembling fingers and picking up her suitcase, hurried out into a corridor that had become, during the last hour, a stream of human activity, a stream blocked every few feet by the piles of ever-increasing luggage.

The boat had docked and was at a standstill. With every minute the windless morning grew hotter. With every minute disorder aboard increased. It was as though the end of the voyage was unexpected and not a soul prepared. Hither and thither scurried the passengers, obeying as best they might the overwhelming voice of the loud-speaker: Do this. . . . Do something else. . . . Your passports must be stamped. . . . Money can be changed. . . . The Purser's Office will be open . . . . Poor things, as scatter-brained as sheep, they tried their best to do all they were told and queued and shuffled for

hours on end, with unaccustomed clothes clogging their limbs and the sweat pouring down their faces. The boat now had become untenable, and their only desire was to leave it as soon as possible.

At the very moment when Mr Digby had most need of him, Mr Littleton was missing. Mr Digby believed he had slipped away on purpose to be vexing. One second he was there, at his elbow, looking worried, the next he had disappeared, dodged off, ducked under someone's arm and gone. Mr Digby craned his head above the sea of craning heads, and searched in vain for Mr Littleton's sandy top. Teresa, too, had deserted. Not a sign of her all morning. Oh, curse them, why was he left alone? The queue moved on a couple of feet. With a savage gesture he wrenched off his tie and stuffed it in a pocket. Why should he dress himself up, as these silly clowns about him had done, to disembark? Why mince about on land, which was twice as hot as it was at sea, in twice as many clothes? And where were Teresa and Littleton? Sneaks! they were keeping out of it all, hiding while he struggled.

He was unjust to Mr Littleton, who, not a malicious man at any time, was just then bidding goodbye to his young lady missionary, and finding the task a grievous one. For he was discovering that at the last of all possible moments, when words are inadequate and looks unsuitable, only silence can sufficiently well express the inexpressible, and even silence ticks away. So, leaning over a rail at the deserted stern end of G deck, they indulged in a final silence together and, although to anyone seeing them they appeared to be merely

absorbed in watching the busy wharf-side below, each of them was thinking that a friendship so inchoate was a sort of failure. They only cheered up when the sad parting was over.

As for Teresa, she had been searching up and down the length of the boat for her father. She was not tall enough, as her father was, to see over heads. Her hat was knocked over one ear, her neck was very sharply poked by elbows, her nose ran irresistibly into bosoms and linen waistcoats; all this she endured without discovering Mr Digby. Her dread was mounting. More and more the thought of going ashore dismayed her, and her dismay grew to be terror. She paused to lean over a rail, absolutely aghast at her image of an India that would tear her presently limb from limb. She remembered those days of empty ocean left behind her, days she had suffered to pass in a dream-like lethargy, when the sea had stretched out its horizon in a complete circle round her, and only the sky was otherwise visible, empty as well except for the sun. She had been living in a dream and now the dream was breaking up like an orange-box split for firewood. Here she was, on the verge of this flat and burning land whose terrible cries already reached her ears, whose people she already saw swarming about beneath. Every dozing nerve in her body sprang awake. Reason had gone. Sense had gone. Go ashore she could not, no! she would not; nothing would induce her! It was at this moment that she saw Miss Spooner picking her way carefully down the gangplank.

Instead of a hat – for Teresa had her hat – she carried a white cotton umbrella above her head. She made the whole scene commonplace. Turbans, topees – she stepped in amongst them as naturally as though she was on a shopping expedition in an Oxford street. And, thought Teresa, leaning so far over that she nearly lost her balance and tumbled headlong at Miss Spooner's feet, it was not yet too late to say goodbye.

'Miss Spooner!' she yelled. 'Miss Spooner!'

The white umbrella ambled on, unheeding. All right, she would fall at her feet, she would do anything, anything to make that white umbrella stop and Miss Spooner look up.

'Miss Spooner!' she shrieked again, piercing the distance between them with all the power of her lungs, and the white umbrella halted. It was shifted to one side and there was Miss Spooner's face looking up at the towering boat and still not seeing her. Someone had called. It was me, waved Teresa, look here, I am here. Miss Spooner saw her. She was smiling and nodding, waving her umbrella in reply. Teresa snatched off her hat and held it out.

'Do you want it?' Her words, like seeds, scattered abroad on the air, too light to fall. But Miss Spooner seemed to understand. She lifted up her umbrella significantly, as though to say: 'I've got this instead. I don't like hats. I'd rather have an umbrella.' Afterwards she stayed where she was for several moments, looking up at Teresa with an air of indecision. She seemed to be regretting the distance and the limited compass of her voice. Whatever it was she was thinking had to be left unsaid. Finally, she raised the white umbrella again and shook it, not discreetly, but with a jolly energy from side to side. Then it was clamped down over her head and Teresa watched it move resolutely away through the loud dock-side fuss towards the Customs shed. Reflecting that where Miss Spooner had gone it was possible to follow, Teresa left the rail and began again to search for Mr Digby.

PART THREE
INDIA

I

Somewhere between the boat and the shore Mr Digby's mosquito nets had disappeared. He remembered distinctly putting the brown paper parcel on top of his suitcase. Now it was gone. Someone had stolen it – someone *must* have stolen it, there was no other explanation. The heat inside the Customs shed was stunning; the noise was incessant. Hordes of passengers, stupid with worry and the noonday blaze, clustered and fought to get their luggage cleared, their forms of declaration stamped, and themselves dismissed.

Her father's frenzy, on top of everything else, was too much for Teresa. Her face was the colour of tallow; her lips were glued together.

'Wait here,' he commanded, and dashed away, imagining he had caught a glimpse of his property being whisked off at the farther end of the shed. She put up her hands and gripped her pigtails, holding them tightly as though they were two hand-rails for support. A man, an Indian wearing uniform, called out to her in a peremptory voice:

'Come over here, please.'

Her father had told her to wait, not to move. She stared at him. What did they want her to do? A creature with brown naked legs and huge flat bare feet picked up her suitcase and said something to her – what was it? – jerking his head. 'No,' she cried, 'no, no.' He dropped the bag, but instead of going away stayed there beside her, menacingly close. He wore only a navy-blue smock. How hideous the navy-blue seemed to her against that dark brown skin. She was afraid to lift her eyes to his face. The Indian official was calling out to her again, impatiently, but she must be going deaf: she could hear nothing clearly. She was going blind: everything swam. Before she could scream her father was there, grabbing her arm, pushing her forward, picking up the cases, bellowing:

'Quick, you've lost your place. It wasn't those confounded nets after all. I saw Mrs Evans, she's in a pretty stew – little girl blubbering, half her stuff gone. Talk about inefficiency. Go on, push yourself in. Have you got the forms? No, wait, I have. Hang on to this a moment.' He rummaged in an inside pocket. 'I wonder who's got those nets. Some damn Indian I suppose. And, Teresa, don't let these coolie-chaps get hold of your stuff. Hold on to your bags whatever you do.'

She obeyed him dumbly. Whatever he told her to do, she did. She was thirsty. Her head roared with the heat and the babel of voices; her body ached with the heat and the shoving. When her father abandoned her again, plunging off to lodge a complaint or chase another parcel, she nearly fainted. She took two steps to go after him, and turning back found a coolie piling her suitcases on to the head of another coolie. Her intense distress was seen by a Customs official, an Indian with a handsome well-bred face, who leaned towards her and said civilly: 'There is no need to worry. He is only taking your luggage outside. Here it is in the way. He will take it outside for you. Don't be alarmed.'

She followed the coolie, believing that all was lost. The glare that greeted her outside was like a savage salute. She closed her eyes for a moment's relief. She would have stuffed up her ears as well had she been sure of arousing neither anger nor derision. The squeeze-hooters belonging to a number of taxis were furiously braying, all at her, and the taxi-men who, disguised in turbans and beards, looked more than anything else like a band of marauders, hung out over the sides of their rickety old touring-cars, and beckoned and shouted wickedly. Her baggage was dropped. Coolies hemmed her in, their faces, with yellow-balled distended eyes, grinning or glaring, she hardly knew which, surrounded her. With brown arms like sticks extended towards her, they gabbled of money, claiming, each one, to have carried her baggage. It was worse than a nightmare. Teresa screamed for her father – and there he was, hustling her into the nearest taxi, tossing the cases after her, climbing in himself and all the time waving his arms round and round at the coolies and shouting as though he was mad:

'Go away! Go away!'

Then to the driver he shouted, still at the top of his voice: 'The best hotel – I don't know what it's called. Wherever it is, the best hotel.'

He had meant to ask Mr Littleton where to stay, but the fellow had let him down, tricked him, disappeared. His mosquito nets had gone, not a trace of them anywhere. One of those unspeakable natives had probably pinched them. And what could he do? Absolutely nothing. When he complained they shrugged their shoulders – practically said that he was to blame. Of course it was one huge conspiracy, one skin against another, black against white. He swabbed his streaming face with a handkerchief, mastered by furious thoughts. Teresa sat screwed up in a corner, silent. The ancient touring Buick whirled them along at a mad speed and for both Teresa and

Mr Digby, each absorbed by their personal fears and furies, the streets of Bombay passed by them as a buzz, a miasma, a pillar of white dust, and nothing more. The driver, obeying his instructions, drove them directly – or, more exactly, in a series of wild swerves – to the Taj Mahal Hotel, that enormous building that stands on the water-front of Bombay alongside the Gate of India, its back to the sea. In a few minutes Teresa found herself alone in the biggest bedroom she had ever seen. The ceiling was high and the windows were twice as tall as herself. The floor was marbled in large black and white squares. Teresa locked the door, and crossing the room like a small and solitary pawn travelling across a chess-board, subsided face down on the bed and gave herself over to panic.

It was simple; and it was not simple. She was afraid; but unable to define her fears, she was unable to overcome them. Since earliest childhood every person she met had been considered in the light of a potential enemy. In this way, by being always on her guard, she had scraped clear of a good many dangers, and walling herself tightly up within her own sufficiency imagined herself a match for any comers. Thus, barricading herself against enemies, she had become her worst and most insinuating enemy, her own incipient destroyer. Her fortress was her prison, stunting her growth. Behind its bars she must slowly and inevitably shrivel. Of this she had no suspicion, and thought herself well adapted to fight the ladylike savageries of the civilisation in which she had been born and reared. Then there had been a respite from fighting, the briefest heaven, when she had floated across the world in a boat. During this holiday she had forgotten herself and become childish with enjoyment. India had caught her unprepared, and India was a force whose antagonism was immeasurable. India was very old, very hot, festering with life; not tame, not lenient, but the natural land of the tiger. Of what good were her little arts of defence against an enmity so mystical and so immense? She clung to her bed, which was stable and cool in this giddy afternoon, and waited for the blow to fall.

All that day and all the next she refused to put a foot outside their hotel, displeasing Mr Digby very much. For having, in spite of Mr Littleton's desertion, broken single-handed through a web of opposition and established a base, he now wanted to stroll out, as conquerors do, and glance about him at the local colour. Teresa seemed to have no idea of what she owed to his resourcefulness. She sat at table with her eyes cast down, munching bananas and ice-cream as though they were dry bread. He needed a companion – he had never made good company for himself – and a fine sort of companion Teresa was. Mightily proud of himself, and in his present cheerful humour, they could, he thought, have been having such a splendid time together. He felt misused, injured by his own daughter. It was her part to encourage his cheer-fulness, instead of which she chose to be sullen and dull. What was the matter? He asked her: 'Teresa, what on earth's the matter? Why can't you speak? What is it? Tell me.'

How could she say to her father: 'I'm afraid'? These words were as difficult for her to pronounce as it might be difficult for some young man to say to some young woman, 'I love you.' She sat there stiffly erect, mailing herself in a pathetic armour of non-observation, armour as unavailing as the shell of a snail in a garden full of thrushes. She would notice nothing, so that nothing could notice her. She would close her ears; she would say as little as possible. Mr Digby continued to rally her.

'I can't understand you, Teresa. At your age I'd have been half off my head with excitement. Most normal children would give their right hands to be you. Haven't you got any sense of adventure? Upon my word, Teresa, you don't deserve to be shown the world. I suppose you'd rather be stuffed up in school learning Latin verbs. That's where you ought to be, of course,' he added gloomily, *sotto voce*. 'Well, what's the matter – can't you answer? Are you feeling sick?'

His growing irritation flustered her. And so at last, goaded, confused, she lifted her black pupils directly into line with his own and said, 'I'm – I'm afraid.'

Mr Digby reacted to this with impatient incredulity. 'What an extraordinary thing to say! What on earth are you afraid of?'

So they came to another full stop, for Teresa could give no reason. She took refuge again in one of her infuriating silences. Mr Digby, half laughing, half in anger, drove his inquiry persistently forward.

'Teresa, what do you mean? You can't just leave it like that. Why can't you tell me? You must be afraid of something. Has someone frightened you? What is it? What are you afraid of?' On and on, until at last, all her control deserting her, with stiff lips quaking, she cried out:

'I don't *know*.'

Now her trembling was apparent; even her nostrils quivered. She shook from a dread beyond explaining, and she shook

110

from shame at having revealed it to the one man in the world who could have no possible understanding or sympathy for such a dread. But oh! please, her silence begged, don't ask me more, don't say another word.

Mr Digby was frankly nonplussed. Fear was a perfectly normal emotion, one he easily recognised, but it was bound to be experienced for a reason. One was afraid because the house was on fire or the ship was sinking; or one might conceivably be afraid at those times when Ruth seemed too far away, or because one's heart was dicky and woke one up in the middle of the night with a rattle like falling masonry. For a good plain reason fear was justifiable – he was the first to agree with that. Fear made heroes. Fear made history. But not to understand *why* one was afraid – that was the ignorance of a fool, and he said so without mincing his words. Teresa, thought Mr Digby, must be neurotic. A neurotic grown-up was unbearable enough, but a neurotic child was far worse – disgraceful, unhealthy. And why he of all men – bluff old Randall Digby with a will of iron – should have such a daughter, was really more than he could fathom. Perhaps she was only doing it to draw attention to herself. The best cure, in any case, was to deal with her curtly. So, laying down his knife and fork, he spoke emphatically across the table:

'Teresa, this rubbish of yours has got to stop, d'you hear? You're acting like a baby and I won't have it. Pull yourself together; think of your age.'

Her age had nothing to do with it, nothing at all. What did he mean? It was he who was talking like a fool, with a stupidity that hurt her more than rough hands. Teresa was so much agitated she lost her head. Hectically blushing, she sprang to her feet. She tried to steady herself; things on the table fell over.

'I hate you,' she cried out, stammering, choking, and then before he could answer she had bolted away, running with her head down between the little white tables, and leaving her vanilla ice half-eaten and her spoon under the chair.

Mr Digby was not dismayed. Teresa, he knew already, was an excitable child and such an outburst was not to be taken seriously. Her momentous words, therefore, sailed over his head and were soon forgotten. He picked up her napkin, sighing. She was a handicap. Some little girls were good and quiet. Teresa was highlystrung – highlystrung, that was the phrase, that was the explanation of her tantrums. It was really a sort of compliment to himself, like royal blood inherited without the royal strength that makes a monarch. As he sipped his coffee the vague worry he had been feeling about Teresa persisted, only the context was lost: what was the matter? What was the matter with what? He felt most confoundedly sleepy. What he needed was a short nap with his shoes off. That long journey, England so far away, and with such a distance still to go; and this weather, this heat – no wonder he felt a bit tired. Ten years ago, he thought, a cold shower would have done the trick, but he found cold showers disagreeable nowadays, and preferred a snooze. But what was the matter? Something, he knew, was depressing him. Then he thought he remembered: Teresa was highly strung, that was the matter. Still not altogether satisfied, he trundled off to have his afternoon nap.

He was awakened half an hour later by a knocking on his door. The knocking had gone on for some time, for Mr Digby was a heavy sleeper and the knock not so much a knuckle-rap as a light persistent tapping. Mr Digby heard it at last. He lay still and listened. The tapping recurred.

'Who is it?' he roared. 'What d'you want?' And then, 'Go away.'

There was silence. Whoever it was had either withdrawn without the sound of footsteps, or else he was still there. Mr Digby rolled off his bed and flung the door wide open. Outside stood a small and disreputable-looking Indian. His face was bright with welcome.

'Who the devil are you?' said Mr Digby.

The Indian made a gesture almost as if he was going to salute. That is to stay, he stiffened his body from toes to chin, and pushed forward as much chest as he had. 'Sir, I am your bearer.'

Mr Digby was taken aback. 'Oh,' he said, with some alteration of his former tone, 'are you? Well, you'd better come back in half an hour, I'm having a sleep now.' And he slammed the door in order to think about it.

He was a little perplexed about the actual meaning of the word 'bearer', but after walking once or twice round the room and staring out of the window, he came to the conclusion that it meant, anyway in this case, a personal servant. Mr Digby had never had a personal servant. He looked at himself in the mirror as he passed it, and rather liked the idea. Apparently the hotel supplied its guests with bearers as a matter of course, and had sent him this one. It did not occur to him that the statement, 'Sir, I am your bearer,' was an alternative way of saying, 'Sir, would you like to have me for your bearer?' for in some ways he was a credulous man, suspecting only what appeared to be ambiguous on the surface. After twenty minutes he opened the door again. The Indian, who had been squatting immediately outside, shot to his feet. His appearance was certainly far from trim, nor did he seem very clean, but he had a willing air.

'What's your name?' said Mr Digby.

'My name is Sam, sir.' And he stiffened himself again, like an urchin making the best of himself in front of a magistrate.

'That's a funny sort of name for an Indian.'

'Sir, I have worked many times for Americans.' He inclined his head gaily to one side. Mr Digby, at this, felt some distaste. 'You'd better come in,' he said, frowning, 'and make yourself useful.'

His acquisition troubled him more than it gave him pleasure; he was not quite certain of how he ought to behave. He guessed that a certain lordliness was expected, but the situation was tricky. He was not dealing, he reminded himself, with an English servant. There could be no subtle understanding between them. This grubby little creature had the advantage: he knew the rules and Mr Digby felt his own ignorance keenly. So, with his back turned, he said loudly and quickly: 'I think I'll take a bath.'

Sam disappeared into the bathroom. Taps were turned on. His dressing-gown was brought to him. The water, he found, was the perfect temperature, half-way between cold and hot. I am a sahib, he thought, happily splashing himself with a

sponge. And he realised that whatever he said was bound
to be right.

II

Someone tapped at Teresa's door, a tap so light it was more
like a scratch, and a voice cried out: 'Oh, Missie, Master says,
tea is in his room, come quickly. Missie, here is Sam.'

It was on account of these last four words that Teresa
opened her door and looked out at the shoddy little figure who
said his name was Sam. The moment she saw that confidently
grinning face, the wide mouth, the flap-ears, the bulging eyes,
Teresa's panic over India was at an end. For Sam was not an
enemy, though an Indian. His brown skin added nothing but
further comedy to his face. He demanded nothing from Teresa
except that she should be affable. This was enough for him
to spring inside her room and switch on the fans that she
had overlooked. To fetch his friend, the dhobie: 'Missie, here
is dhobie-man.' To bring photographs of himself out from
a greasy inner pocket: 'I have worked many times for Americans.' To writhe his body about in boneless contortions for her
amusement – 'I dance for ladies' – and break off his exhibition
in a fit of giggles. He became immediately her attendant,
admirer, entertainer, bodyguard, and, because he was all these
things and friendly as well, her friend. Teresa emerged from
behind her barricades and proceeded to look about her.

The Taj Mahal Hotel was huge, and as cool as it was
possible for any building to be in that great heat. Innumerable stone corridors led away from the centre well, and up and

down these corridors at any time of the day moved a silent army of coolies, washing clean the floors by skating dreamily to and fro on large wet rags. Bearers squatted drowsing outside bedroom doors, while their masters drowsed within. Fans hummed ceaselessly and blew upon, but never dried, the sweat that every movement, even the least, induced. Footsteps were soundless, or had the slipshod patter of sandals. Teresa's window was dominated by a bubbling mosque-like building, painted more blindingly white than snow. Kites wheeled and screamed in a colourless sky. From her father's window she looked out on the sea she had left, dotted with little sailing-boats. On the different landings, displayed behind glass, were magnificent gold and silver saris, with the names and addresses propped beside them of shops where such saris could be bought. What wealth was here! What indolence! What a vast pause in the heat of living, a parenthesis of languor.

Teresa and Sam became inseparables. He said that his real name was Dil Mohammed. 'It's a very pretty name,' said Teresa politely. He said he had many dependants. Many, many dependants, he said, sketching in the air with his fingers, his supple fingers that seemed to have no joints but wriggled about like worms at every word, the scores of relations who depended on him.

'I am poor man,' he said, trying to make his smiling face look downcast for a moment. Teresa said how sorry she was to hear this.

'Missie lives in London?' He was proud of his good English. He made a point of calling Mr Digby 'sir', not 'sahib'.

'Not exactly. No, I don't. I don't know where I live. I don't think I live anywhere at the moment,' said Teresa, wondering where in the world she did live.

Mr Digby sent them out to get fruit for the journey the following day. 'Get a Thermos,' he said to Teresa, giving her money, 'and oranges. You know where to take Missie?' he barked at Sam, as though he was speaking to a not very responsible schoolboy. 'Thermos – you know what Thermos is? You know where to buy a Thermos?'

Sam jerked his head to one side, a gesture that was to become all too familiar to Mr Digby, who knew where he was with an honest yes or no, but found his temper sorely tried by this maddening Eastern compromise. An Indian, he discovered, would always prefer to indicate – though never exactly – a yes rather than a no, to please by assent rather than disappoint by denial, and this with cheerful indifference to the end in view, implying, with a sideways shake of the head, a promise of possible success while at the same time disowning the responsibility of a possible failure. It irritated Mr Digby, who liked all things to be definite, very much indeed. He waved away his daughter and his bearer with an impatient hand. He wanted to write letters. In particular he wanted to write to Lilian, a letter not too triumphant but proving, just in case she still had any doubts of his ability to score off her, the indisputable *fait accompli*.

Teresa found that the compass-needle of her feelings for this strange continent had veered in a few hours hard round, and pointed now in an exactly opposite direction to the one it had at first. She was no longer afraid. On the contrary, she welcomed the strangeness; the teeming life, the palpitating noise and colour, heated her blood with excitement. She skipped along behind Sam in a transport of pleasure while he, with manly strides, attempted to keep ahead and importantly clear a path for her through the crowds.

Never had she seen so many people. Never had she dreamed so many people existed. They were everywhere, lying asleep on walls, stretched on the pavements, crouching, walking, dawdling; in topees, in fez, in turbans; wearing white European suits, or dhotis, or shorts, or practically nothing; Indians in sandals, barefoot, in shoes; well-fed Indians with stomachs and spectacles; emaciated Indians, their dry flesh wrapped against their bones; the nimble children, the beggared, the sick, the idle, the busy; Indians carrying brief-cases or babies, with baskets of fruit on their heads, or shapeless bundles; or Indians empty-handed, empty-headed, with empty blistered eyes, opening their bloody-red mouths to spit out, like consumptives, gouts of betel-nut juice; policemen, dressed like schoolboys in navy-blue shorts, wandered hand-in-hand; women, their cheek-bones standing out from their faces like the hips of cows, silver bracelets winking in the shadows of their rags, squatted over piles of green unripened oranges; crisply-laundered students tripped along with lesson-books tucked under their arms. The pavements were loaded with an intricately interwoven mob on foot, as the road was interwoven as intricately with a mob on wheels.

In the road were horses, as thin as latch-keys, trotting hectically on with whips cracking above their heads and stinking gharris rocking behind; taxis, old-fashioned yellow-painted tourers, hurled themselves forward with all the gusto of buglers charging into battle; rickshaws bounded; bicycles swerved; and the imperative warnings that issued incessantly from every whip and hooter, every bell and every hoarse throat, rose like vapour sucked up from the fuming earth by the high sun to be dispersed as though it had never existed in the measureless wastes of that silent arid sky.

This hot white over-exposed light drained away the colours as it drained the virtue out of shade. Glare lay in flat horizontal planes. The chalky buildings were baked to such a dryness that it seemed at any moment they might change to powder and crumble. And bullocks, dusty fly-tormented creatures, drifted through the hubbub to establish their incommodious bulks with familiar ease on pavements, or on the doorsteps of banks, or in the very middle of the road like boulders wedged in the spate of a mountain torrent.

With wide eyes and open mouth Teresa drank in the confusion as though she tasted a new wine and could never have enough of it. Her fears were gone, her caution; her former instinct, as old as herself, to repulse externals, gave way to a reckless rush of confidence. She flung down her defences; she threw open her doors. She longed to be occupied by this anonymous turmoil which she felt to be so safe, for in all these crowds not a single face looked at her threateningly, not a hand touched her except by accident, not a soul knew who she was or cared. And Sam guided her swiftly and surely. She followed him with elation and no alarm.

They bought their Thermos flask. They bought, in fact, two of them. How this happened Teresa was never quite sure.

But Sam and the shopman were both so certain that two were better than one – that one was of practically no use at all – their heads wagged, their hands flew with such a happy persuasion, that before she knew where she was she had paid with Mr Digby's money for two Thermoses – two very large Thermoses, moreover – and Sam, a Thermos in either hand, had darted out of the shop and was leading her triumphantly towards the market.

And the market was cool and dark, roofed over, floored with stone, piled with dreaming fruit, and flowers cut to hold their fragile petals stiff for one day only. An odour of moisture sweetened the air, hinting that somewhere deep down the earth guarded still the dampness of germination. Here and there a shaft of light, seeming to be more than light, to possess as well the power to originate colour, stole an entrance overhead and piercing the twilight buried its tip in a pool of vivid fruit – fruit that seemed to enrich the beam that discovered it more than it was enriched. Oranges, melons, pineapples, lemons, bananas, pomelos, astonished the gloom with splashes of brilliant health in a world jaded with heat. Every shape of ripe achievement plumped tight the yellow rinds, the polished skins of red and purple lying one against the other in the impermanent abundance of the moment.

'Missie should have a flower,' said Sam, 'she is a lady.' And there was the flower, a rose, being held out for her from the shadow by a brown hand with a brown face smiling behind it.

'Two rupees, memsahib.'

'Two rupees!' said Teresa aghast, 'Why, that's three shillings.' The market was full of roses. 'Two rupees for a rose – Sam!' she said. 'That's *much* too expensive.'

No, no, that was the good price for a rose – see, everyone said so, everyone nodded his head, everyone was smiling, assuring her two rupees was not too much for such a rose, the most beautiful rose in the market, the flower for a lady. See, the shopkeeper nodded, full of good humour, pressing the rose upon her for only two rupees.

She chose her oranges one by one, and the dusty-footed spectators who had gathered round helped her choose, stretching their arms past her to pick out and offer the roundest, largest, most sunburnt specimens anyone could desire. They waved them in front of her nose; they muddled her considerably. But it was all a game, played expressly for her. They were so gay, vying with one another to catch her attention: 'Looky, memsahib – this one good orange.' She felt like a grown-up at a children's party.

And it happened all over again with the lemons – orange-juice for one Thermos, lemon-juice for the other, said Sam – for when she moved away towards a pile of lemons nearby, her crowd moved with her, treading close on her heels, delighted to make her business theirs. Why, how kind and cheerful everybody was, she thought, and how pleased they were to try and please her, though she was a stranger to them and would never see them again; though every lemon looked the same, neither better nor worse than the next one; though really she had only wanted oranges, not lemons at all. How could one disappoint this friendly interest, this playful goodwill that asked for no reward beyond smiles and equal goodwill from her? At last she freed herself, flushed, confused, pulsing with pride and affection, and out into the sun again they went, Sam darting ahead to make the way, a small boy trotting behind with the fruit they had bought in a basket on his head.

III

'But I don't like lemonade,' said Mr Digby, peevishly. 'I told you to buy oranges.' His letter to Lilian had been very difficult.

'I got oranges too.'

'Good lord,' said he, frowning round at the large-eyed urchin who stood in the doorway. 'There's enough there to keep an army going – what on earth were you thinking about, Teresa? And why couldn't Sam carry the stuff? I'm not made of money, you know.' Then he saw the two flasks. 'Teresa!' he said, giving an angry laugh as though he could hardly believe his eyes, and noisily scraping his chair back from the table as he got up. He wore bedroom slippers; his shirt was unbuttoned down to his trousers. 'I simply don't know what to make of you. *Two* Thermoses – *two*? In the name of God, why? Did I say two? Aren't you fit to be sent out shopping alone? I should have thought it was simple enough – "get a few oranges, buy a Thermos." But apparently not, for you have to come back with a mountain of fruit and two enormous Thermoses.'

But Teresa was high in the clouds, her successes still too recent for her to be abashed by her father's frown. She was certain, too, that for some reason he had been angry before she came in, and his present wrath was therefore so much air escaping through a safety-valve. So she stood her ground, courageously scowling, and mute.

'It isn't just the money,' he went on, 'though I hardly dare to ask how much it's all cost – that side of it wouldn't interest you, of course; it isn't just the money, Teresa, it's the thought that you simply can't be trusted to use your head. You don't seem to have any natural common sense. I've got to be your nurse as well as your father.'

His tone had altered: he sounded now like one whose sense of humour is strong enough for him to think amusing what would have driven any other man into a justifiable rage. For Teresa's uncommonly bold attitude was disconcerting, to say the least of it. He had expected one of those pleasant little victories of strength over weakness – victories that for all their littleness and all his strength were not to be despised – which would have enabled him to forgive generously, dismiss grandly, set him up on good terms with the world and himself, and helped him to write that distressingly difficult letter to Lilian. In his school career nothing, he had long ago discovered, was so good for an out-of-sorts temper as the frown of intimidation, the responsive cringe, and the following royal pardon. For this medicinal routine he could usually depend on Teresa, but not, it seemed, today. However tight she clenched her hands behind her back, her mouth was scornful. This would not do. This was going to throw him out of his equilibrium worse than before. He wavered. He changed his tactics. He banged her on the head

with the palm of his hand to show they were pals again. He laughed. He peeped at her anxiously.

'Well, *I* like lemonade better than orangeade,' said Teresa, on whom none of this changing mood was lost, and with a coolness she herself found surprising, 'and it wasn't very expensive, if you want to know. And anyway Thermoses aren't a waste of money, they're always useful. And as for him,' she said, nodding towards the little boy who still stood with his burden of fruit in the doorway, 'you only have to give him twopence or so.' Having delivered herself of this final dart, she wandered across the room and stood looking out of the window at the sea as though the entire argument bored her excessively.

But this was unfair. She distorted his whole intention, his character even. Money was not his first consideration, he had never said so; never meant to say so, anyway. It was the principle he stressed, the principle of carrying out one's duties, of Teresa – but in any case the whole thing was a joke now, he had turned it into a joke, laughed, patted her head. It was unfair, it was really spiteful of her to go on taking him seriously. And now, in order that he himself might be free from harassment he was put under the ludicrous necessity of wooing her into a more amiable temper. First he cleared the room of servants.

'I say, Teresa. How about a little stroll? Stretch our legs a bit, eh? I can finish my letters later on.'

But the sea, the memory of lemons being plucked out of the shadow by brown hands, the rose – she had lost it, dropped it somewhere – the minarets, the shutters, the feet swarming, the noise: all this had already done his wooing for him and he could have saved himself the nuisance. She skipped round, full of life.

'Oh, yes. Do let's.' So he had to go.

They walked by the huge cool Gate. Beggars lay asleep in the shade. Old men, sitting with their knees above their ears, roasted nuts. Soldiers lounged along the wall, spitting over it into the sea. And the sea spread out its waveless greyish matter, away and farther away, spotted with still sails and the larger shapes of anchored steamers, water opaque as metal and glinting with metallic lights. Crowds and noise were absent here. The large open place behind the Gate was almost deserted. A languor, an air of approaching siesta, prevailed. Then a snake-charmer, his basket slung across his shoulder, ran up to them.

'Sahib, you see snaky dance? Snaky dance for sahib? Sahib, sahib!'

'Oh,' said Teresa, stopping, 'I've never seen a snake dance. I've never seen a snake.'

The Indian immediately squatted down, put his pipe to his lips and whipped the lid off his basket. In sluggish coils the cobra lay, unmoving. It might have been dead. Still piping, the Indian dug his naked toe into the turgid mass and stirred as though it was so much dung.

'How *can* he?' murmured Teresa. She stood two or three feet away, not daring to come any closer, but leaning forward, her hands pressed together.

'There's no danger,' said Mr Digby. 'It's all a put-up job – they take the poison out, you know.'

The thin wail went squirming on, coaxing, beseeching: 'Dance, little snake.' The creature was asleep, or sulky, or tired of heeding this monotonous chant. It took no notice. Mr Digby snorted. The Indian again applied his urgent toe. Six inches of cobra reared itself up, stiffly erect. Teresa saw its eyes, blankly open. Still piping, the Indian bent and sharply slapped the snake's head, once, twice. The wail increased: 'Dance, dance, little snake.' With unwilling slowness the monster heaved itself up another foot and swayed in a circle from left to right, and swayed again from left to right. Then it flopped down on to its belly, unwound itself over the side of the basket with a gesture as indolent as a yawn, and began to crawl away. The Indian moved himself only to plant one foot on its vanishing tail, pinning it firmly down. The reedy complaint continued, wavering onwards without a break. Mr Digby was disgusted. Well, what a dud show, he thought. He threw down a coin and pulled Teresa's arm. She resisted him. He wrenched her away. At once the snake-charmer sprang to his feet and came running after them, crying for more money. It was not enough for seeing a snake dance. Dance indeed! Mr Digby bristled with indignation. Teresa, turning her head, saw the abandoned snake racing off across the hot bare place. 'Teresa, come *on*,' said Mr Digby, walking faster.

Now they were fair game. The supplicants pursued them. 'Tell your fortune, sahib, you have lucky face.' And Mr Digby was trying with futile gestures and long and longer strides to be rid of them, worried about the journey tomorrow, the letters not written, the impossibility of saying without vulgarity what he wanted to say to Lilian. He was disappointed by that snake, wretched mangy brute with the poison taken out of it, a hoax like so many things in this world, too many things. Here was a chap with a monkey on his shoulder, dashing across their path so that he had to dodge, dragging Teresa with him. 'Memsahib, monkey dance?'

Everyone wanted to dance for Teresa, everyone wanted to amuse her. This was India, made for her amusement. Even the sun invited her to pour out her gladness, to soak up its immense generous heat and sweat out her salty thanks. Even the beggars pranced with hope. The burning sea spread wide, hard enough for her to run across it and pluck the little still grey sails like daisies dotting a lawn. The soldiers spat. They were in no haste. They sat there unmoving as the water they faced, while the hours swelled out fuller and hotter and the shadow of the Gate moved slowly over them. Only Mr Digby was in a hurry, cumbered by thoughts, by worries that clung on to him like the claws of a beast not to be shaken off. He fled from the pestering riff-raff – could one not even take a stroll without annoyance like this? – lugging Teresa, who showed a contrary eagerness to be pestered, after him into the Taj Mahal Hotel's expensive coolness where he could tap his teeth in leisure and fret himself silly with anticipation of the morrow's bill.

IV

Sam had contracted to travel with them up to Assam. 'What about your dependants?' Teresa asked him. He looked too

much of a scallywag to be a breadwinner, but still he had said that many depended on him, and Teresa believed it.

'Is all right,' said Sam airily, 'I leave money behind.' He dealt an imaginary fortune into the air. 'They wait, two weeks, three weeks, maybe four, five weeks. All right, I bring money back. Very glad to see me.' More money was scattered abroad in pantomime. 'Master ask me to go with him. All right, I go. He very good to me, very good man, so I very good to him. I look after him. You see. I very honest man,' added Sam as an afterthought, pronouncing the aitch firmly. Teresa wondered how old he was. He seemed ageless, a Puck without hair on his chin, holding his responsibilities about him like tattered garments. He carried himself erect, taking steps too big for his miniature figure, his undersized chest puffed out with the pride of being such a good bearer, a man who spoke English, who had worked many times for Americans, who carried photographs in an inner pocket, who could dance for ladies, who maintained like any Rajah or man of the world a host of submissive relatives to whom his word was law and his coming and going unquestioned.

They took the evening train to Calcutta the following night. Sam was drunk on the platform, having taken, no doubt, an emotional farewell of his many dependants. Bruised flowers hung round his neck. Officiously snatching the Thermos flasks, for which he had a personal regard, from a coolie, he dropped one of them and they heard the broken glass inside it tinkle.

'Sir, I am lucky man,' cried Sam hilariously. 'This one is lemon Thermos. Master like oranges.'

Mr Digby cursed him till the tears ran down his dirty face. His necessary pride collapsed. He looked a shabby little oddment of humanity in his suit of shrunken European clothes with the frayed cuffs, and his draggled garland of festive flowers, snivelling onto the back of his fist. The night was hot. The lights burned thickly, a dim orange that made the darkness more bewildering.

They fought their way down the platform. The station was jammed with a seething mob. The hubbub was deafening. Cries and whistles resounded on every side. The air was heavy with the sweet sickish stench of sweating bodies. Eyes rolled with wild-horse fright in the gleam of lanterns. Coppery skins shone for a moment. The ground was strewn at every step with recumbent forms, wrapped in their white cotton wings, asleep on mats, as though the struggle to keep even a weak hold on life had exhausted their strength and caused them to lie down at the feet of their stronger fellows, careless of whether they were trodden on or shovelled aside as rubbish, so long as they might remain insensible. Only the vendors seemed to have an object, thrusting their way forcibly alongside the train, with trays of bananas and sweetmeats, magazines and chocolate, trays on which candlesticks an inch high burned with a cosy feebleness of flame, and their voices harshly intoning scraped above the general babble of the lost hundreds.

For it seemed like a station of the lost. It seemed impossible that any so definite a move could be made as for the train to pull clear of this shadowy chaos and steam away, leaving it all behind. No one appeared to know why they were

there or where they were going. Not urgency, for the crowds smothered any spark as vital as haste – even Mr Digby, head and shoulders above the rest and armed with a keen determination, could do no more than struggle forward by sweating inches – not urgency, but an indeterminate flux prevailed, an air of seeking without the hope of finding, of seeking more than lost baggage or lost relations: reason, identity itself, like sleepers who mistake a nightmare for the real hell and cannot break down the walls of sleep to escape.

Mr Digby, his daughter and his bearer close behind him, achieved at last – and it was a real achievement – the box reserved for his occupation, a box in which he and Teresa were to travel for two nights and nearly two days from Bombay to Calcutta. It was the size and rather the same shape as a horse-box, and smelt as strongly though considerably less agreeably. It had four sometime upholstered bunks, now in an advanced state of blackish decay, two fans and a lavatory, and at that moment represented, both for Mr Digby and Teresa, the most satisfactory of strongholds. Their cases and rugs were tossed inside. They clambered up. Mr Digby flung off his hat and wiped his face. Teresa leaned out of the window. Then she gave a cry. She leaned farther out, stretching the backs of her knees to their utmost limit.

'I saw Miss Spooner, I'm sure I did. She must be catching the same train – I'm sure it was her.'

'Well, I hope you're wrong,' said Mr Digby, 'I'd much rather she found herself another train.'

Teresa was still straining her neck out of the window, repeating with vexatious eagerness: 'I'm sure it was her.'

'I can't think why you like her,' said Mr Digby, hunting
about inside a case for his sponge-bag, and turning everything higgledly-piggledy as he did so. 'Dull little dried-up
creature,' he burst out with surprising viciousness; certainly
effort, and even emotion, was too expensive in this climate:
the sweat began to roll down inside his shirt again. 'Where the
hell did I put that sponge-bag? Sam must have – why doesn't
the train start? What are we waiting for?'

His heart gave a couple of louder bangs than usual and
he sat down on the side of his bunk with a weakening of
fear. 'I don't like her,' he said more calmly, but as though it
was important to make this clear once and for all. 'She's disapproving. And how a woman like that dares to be disapproving
– good lord,' he went on, warming once more to this theme,
for the root of the matter was that he felt Miss Spooner
disapproved of him personally, and this rankled, as any hint of
disapproval, which was always unmerited, always did: 'Good
lord, Teresa, what's *she* got to be proud of I should like to
know? She's a lot of use in the world, I must say.' By this he
meant that Miss Spooner had never justified her womanly
organs by being the comforter and support of a man, or the
maker and preserver of children (little boys whom he
hated, little girls who bored him – but it was the principle
that counted). 'She could do with a bit of proper shame,
your Miss Spooner, instead of all this nose-in-the-air stuff,'
said Mr Digby, putting his hand inside his shirt to ease his
heart-beats. 'She's going to be taken down a peg one of these
days, you mark my words.' At which prophecy his head ceased
to swim and he felt some satisfaction. Serve her right – serve

'em all right – anyone who didn't realise what a good chap he was.

Teresa left her window – for it was useless to search that uneasy sea, amongst whose midnight waves white cotton garments appeared to be tossed up like a yellowish scum, for one particular face – and came and sat herself down on the bunk opposite him. Her long pigtails hung down in front of her shoulders. Her eyes were bright and huge. She appeared to be stimulated rather than fatigued by their recent trials. But then the onus of packing and leaving the Taj Mahal Hotel – bearing with him, however, the wound of that cruelly large bill to suppurate and give him pain for days to come – the responsibility of finding a taxi, dealing with porters and baggage and Sam and crowds, all this had belonged to Mr Digby: Teresa had only had to follow him.

'I like her,' said Teresa, thinking it equally important for her to make this statement, and more, to understand why she made it.

'Well, I know that. You keep saying it. Though I can't think why in the world you should. I'm simply telling you I don't. That's all. That's all. You needn't say another word. I'm tired of hearing about that woman. I don't even want to think about her.' He waved his arm.

'I like her,' said Teresa carefully, 'because I don't think she'd ever be cross with me unless I'd done something that *I* knew was bad. Unless I expected her to be cross with me.'

'That's enough, that's enough,' shouted Mr Digby, 'I told you that's enough of her.'

Teresa stared at the floor, considering, trying to get it

clearer in her head. What was it about Miss Spooner? she wondered. Not only the thing about her not being cross, though that was a part of it. She carried no unpleasant surprises up her sleeve, you could be sure of that. She was scrupulously fair, yes, just – but more than that. What else? It was difficult to know for certain. Was it because you felt she enjoyed herself, very quietly, all the time, whereas with other people, though they said they did and seemed to try so much harder, you never really believed they enjoyed themselves, you suspected they were pretending? Was it because . . .? And she pondered, with her head bent, sitting on her hands, the mystery of Miss Spooner.

'Teresa,' said Mr Digby miserably. 'Would you lend me your sponge a minute? I can't find my bloody bag.' Usually he tried not to swear in front of her. She gave him her sponge and as he went into the lavatory with it the train began to move. He stuck his head out and said: 'I hope to God that little fool Sam got on. Do you think he did?'

'Oh, I expect so.'

'He was drunk,' said Mr Digby. 'I should never have taken him, of course. I ought to have got someone else.' And worry, more worry, another worry, made him shove Teresa out of the way and lean through the window, the sponge dripping from one hand, searching for Sam who was more likely than not lying dead drunk on the platform. The train was packed. Indians rode on the steps, clinging to rails. Heads could be seen all the way down appearing not, like Mr Digby's, from a desire to see out, but because the open air offered more room for a head than the inside of a third-class carriage. Though

the train was gathering speed many doors were still not shut from the near impossibility of shutting them. Mr Digby saw a man climb into the aperture of such a window hanging open, and be shut into the carriage with the shutting of the door as the easiest, or perhaps the only possible way of being included. The sight angered him: why on earth could this wretched country not organise more trains or less people, and be a bit cleaner about it too, and have some method? And for all that the train was overflowing and drawing away faster and faster with its load of compressed humans, it left behind it a platform as packed as when they had first arrived, the boundaries of which stretched out of sight, lost in a blackish-orange obscurity. Swarms of winged insects batted senselessly round the dusky lights in a parody of the larger confusion below. The sleepers slept; the seekers sought; the harsh cries made a criss-cross of discordant noise through which the whistles sounded like knives attempting to make order of a tangled skein by cutting apart the knots.

And where was Sam?

Why was the worrying, he wondered, that should be done by other people, always left to him? He was a magnet for the weak, the frivolous, the merely silly who came and dropped their burdens of responsibility at his feet for him to shoulder. But why did he? he asked himself, why was he such a fool? He needed all his strength to save himself, for the current was strong, the farther bank was never reached. Yet he spent himself – he had always spent himself – in attempting to carry the cares of others when his own were already too numerous and weighed him down: worrying in case they

missed their trains, or forgot their tickets, or failed their exams. Incompetents exploited his sense of duty, fed like the parasites they were on his capability, and would find themselves soon, he savagely told himself, feeding off his corpse, for even a giant has limits. And his was the fault to allow such abuse, for the weak deserved to fend for themselves or perish. Every man for himself. Only he was too much of a fool to follow this eminently sensible precept and suffered terribly in consequence, suffered for others because it was his nature. And now it was Sam, left behind for certain, and too late to do anything about it except worry. Mr Digby squeezed Teresa's sponge over his face, sucked a corner of it to moisten his dry mouth, remembered the water was probably foul with diseases, and hastily spat the poison out.

Sam, however, appeared, much sobered, at the first stop and said that dinner was now being served in the dining-car further up the train. While they ate he would stay behind and mount guard. There was no corridor. Mr Digby and Teresa raced up the platform and flung themselves into the dining-car, where, as though by natural law, they found Miss Spooner and Mr Littleton sitting easily opposite one another and already half-way through their soup.

When the mutual exclamations of astonishment were finished they all sat down together. Mr Littleton's wife, it appeared, had not met him at Bombay. One of the kiddies was ill, he said; nothing serious, some kind of kiddies' illness, like the measles. Miss Spooner was at her liveliest. Teresa was proud of her and kept glancing towards her father as though to say: There, you see! she isn't dull, I told you so. Mr Digby

wondered whether the old girl was a bit tiddly. She drew a vivid and ludicrous picture of herself as a sightseer in Bombay, describing, in such a way that Mr Littleton had to lay down his knife and fork to laugh and even Mr Digby let out a guffaw, her first, and she swore her last, ride in a rickshaw. She had to do it once, she said, to know what it felt like, but once, thank you, was quite enough. She had felt a perfect figure of fun, she said, with her heels as high as her head, and bobbing about for all the world like a baby in its perambulator. She began to laugh herself there and then, her eyes blinking behind her pince-nez, her prim little mouth puckering as she tried to restrain her merriment at the thought of how absurd she must have looked, holding her old white brolly aloft with one hand and her skirts down with the other, determined for the sake of experience to stick it out for ten minutes though she had fervently wished to be set down immediately and allowed to walk along on her two feet like a decent Christian woman.

'You ought to take care where you go on your own,' said Mr Littleton warningly. 'I never let my wife walk about by herself, it isn't safe. The country's in a very peculiar state at the moment. Riots going on all the time in one place or another. They were throwing acid about in the markets yesterday. Nasty stuff, acid.'

'They weren't throwing it about in my market,' said Teresa. 'Everyone was awfully nice.'

She remembered the rose, the smiling faces, the deep shadow, the breath of ripened fruit, the lemons. That was Bombay. Acid and riots were out of place; it was not like that. Her esteem for Mr Littleton lessened. She felt herself draw away from him, remembering the sleepy snake, the burning water beyond the great Gate of India, the soldiers idly spitting, the monkey – *this* was Bombay.

Mr Littleton glanced at her with a slight frown, wondering for the first time if there was not, after all, a touch of disagreeable pertness about Teresa, something which, should he ever remark it in his own children, he would describe as precocity and put an end to quick enough. He had thought she was such a nice child, and felt a disappointment. An inclination to punish her by not saying another word held him silent for some minutes. Mr Digby, between and through large mouthfuls of underdone fish, was describing Sam's drunkenness on the platform, at which Mr Littleton cheered up and resumed his rôle as mentor.

'Never trust an Indian,' he said sententiously, looking from one to the other of these three neophytes. 'And I'll tell you something more, something worth remembering: never be kind to an Indian. Be fair, but never be kind. It doesn't pay. I've been in India twenty-six years, so I know what I'm saying.' And yet he did not look an unkind man; indeed, though he would never have admitted it, he very often made the mistake – much too often, his wife said – that he was now warning them against. Mr Digby thought it seemed like a piece of sound good sense and nodded approval. Miss Spooner pursed up her lips and gave a quiet sniff that might have meant almost anything, though it was hardly encouraging. And as for Teresa, her face assumed such an expression of mutinous refusal that Mr Littleton was more certain than ever she was not the little girl he had taken her for at first.

Back in their own compartment they found that Sam had unrolled their bedding for the night. Mr Digby wondered if he had stolen anything as well, and reinforced his resolution never to leave valuables lying about. Though it was bad enough if he stole their fruit or chocolate. He looked at the pile of oranges they had laid in at Bombay and it seemed to him to be smaller. He ought to have counted them, he thought; next time he would. Sam, still subdued but without any obvious sign of guiltiness, had disappeared again into the night, retiring to his own particular hole-in-a-corner, wherever that might be. The train clattered on across the dark miles of India.

'She is nice, isn't she?' said Teresa, wanting to hear her father say that she was – and how could he deny it now? She had made him laugh.

'She's not as bad as I thought,' said Mr Digby grudgingly, 'once she gets going. Though I still don't like her face. She needs to be taken out of herself. I dare say she hasn't mixed enough in the world, and I must say she's left it a bit late now. I say, Teresa, how about a game of piquet before we turn in, eh?'

So out came the cards and Mr Digby gave her a thorough beating, for Teresa's attention was too often distracted. Every time the train stopped – and it seemed to spend more time in stopping than it spent on the way – Teresa had to throw down her hand and rush to the window to lift the blind and look out. Every time the train stopped the noise started, as suddenly as the buzz of a party in full swing bursts into the silent hall outside when a door is jerked open. The flat belly-

rasp of cries as the vendors passed down the platform with trays on their heads rent the air. Bells tinkled. Goats bleated. Lanterns swung in all directions. There were the same groups huddled armless in their cotton wrappings, waiting for something to happen to them, only their eyes catching afire as the lights went by, their feet patiently rooted. Out tumbled the passengers to stretch their arms and legs, and Teresa felt a wistfulness that not a single word in all the chatter that filled her ears was intelligible.

They took it in turns to undress in the lavatory, dabbing their faces gingerly with a sponge and brushing their teeth with dry toothbrushes. Mr Digby also decreed that the floor was not to be trodden on barefoot. Before lying down he made sure that his sheet protected him from any possible contact with the mouldering leather of his bunk, for such a touch, he was convinced, would cause his skin to wither or break out in immediate spots. He would have preferred to hang himself up in a hammock, but reminded himself that when one travelled abroad – when one was a tough old adventurer – risks of all sorts had to be taken, sometimes worse than this. So he laid his cheek down with a sigh and only then found himself wondering what it was they had been given to eat for dinner. This occasioned him five minutes of unquiet speculation which then relaxed in slumber and a few uneasy snores.

V

Teresa was wakened off and on during the night by the jolting of the train as it stopped or started, and heard, half in sleep, the harsh cries sounding outside. Once she was wakened by her father, who leapt from his bunk crying that one of the fans was blowing a hurricane on to him, and his neck was frozen. Once again, hours later, he started up, the same fan having ceased to function altogether, with the loud shout that he was stifling. He was still fiddling with it and mumbling curses when she fell asleep. Because of these many interruptions and the dreams they brought her, the night seemed to go on for a long long time, and was as tiring as though she had had to walk the distance the train carried her on foot, mile after plodding mile.

Sam's face was the first she saw in the morning. The train was at a standstill. He was pushing a tray of tea and biscuits through the door, happily smiling, for yesterday with its sins was now in the past, and buried. He poured out their tea, handed them biscuits and bananas, and then vanished. It was a quarter to eight.

The day that followed was a day of extreme heat when time seemed to be dragged out to twice its usual length, for there was nothing to do except play piquet, lounge beside the window looking out, eat oranges, sleep, and every so often race along to the dining-car for a tepid meal. They passed acres of liquid green paddy-fields where small white cranes stood on one leg or floated up like feathers into the empty sky. They passed acres of dry land where the ground was the colour of dust and the men with oxen and wooden ploughs who drove slow furrows through it were the same colour as the ground they strove to cultivate, and almost indistinguishable from it. They passed villages leaning their thatched roofs against the stems of palm-trees. They passed through miles of desolation without the sign of a human face or hand, and flat as far as the eye could see. Sometimes, rarely, they crossed a river, gracious and rich in that roasted land, its wide bed occupied now by the merest trickle of water, and on its banks a sudden profusion of greedy palms and green bushes. India went on and on, on and on, as though it had no end, as though it had no beginning, as though seas and shores and other continents were only part of a feverish dream, as though this was the whole world and nothing existed beyond it, a world flat and baked and dry on whose immense surface, far apart from one another, dwelt men and their beasts, living and dying together, generation after generation. Every so often the train drew in and stopped at a little station. The hoarse clamour began at once. Children came crowding round outside.

'Baksheesh, memsahib, baksheesh, sahib, baksheesh, memsahib.'

Taught to beg, they joined their hands together, rolled up their huge brown black-fringed eyes beseechingly, their tender beautiful mouths ready to grin like children instead of beggars. Nothing drove them away. Their husky maddening prayers went on like India, on and on. Mr Digby, to begin with, threw out pice, the equivalent of farthings, to be rid of their plaguing, but presently discovered that the children who came round the door station after station were the same

children, travelling on the same train as himself, and at this he was not amused but ordered Teresa to pull down the blinds and keep herself away from the window. Even so they could still hear the soft voices droning on outside, and the heat was so overpowering that soon he abandoned his precautions and stood in the doorway, haughtily staring over the supplicants' heads or sometimes flapping his arms and crying out, 'Jao, jao' – a word he had picked up as being a useful one, but which appeared to have no effect.

Some of the children were lovely and complete, light-limbed, top-heavy with a tangle of black hair; but others were terrible, sightless or handless or pitted with the holes of smallpox. At one halt a boy of about nine or ten was led along the platform by his sister, a year or two younger. His legs were as thin as rusty knitting-needles; no hair grew on his head; he was blind. The little girl who led him was like a flower or a moth, something so naturally beautiful that it seemed like an accident. She stopped at the feet of Mr Digby, held up her small curving hand and whispered for baksheesh. Instead of the angry dismissal Teresa expected, her father pulled two rupees – a small fortune – out of his wallet and with clumsy haste thrust them on to the little girl. His generosities were ever like this, welling capriciously up within and disturbing him with their urgency, their force.

'Poor little devil,' he muttered, slamming the door and jerking down the blind to hide such misery from his sight; 'poor little devil,' he muttered, over and over again. His pity swamped him, gave him almost unbearable pain, so that his face twitched and wore an expression of gloomy foreboding

for some time to come: and this in spite of having seen other beggars in the streets of Bombay far more terribly mutilated – things scarcely human, all stumps and knobs of flesh – and been unmoved.

The water-sellers passed to and fro selling, as well as the water, red earthen bowls out of which to drink it, and these bowls after drinking were thrown away to smash on the line. Or a man would crouch down and cup his hands before his face, the water-seller pouring the precious liquid into the spouted hands, some of it escaping between the fingers and going to waste on the dusty platform. And afterwards the drinker would wipe his wet hands over his face and rub them together with pleasure at the feeling of dampness that was not his own sweat. All this Teresa observed with curious interest, and saw much besides: a goat with three legs, at which she called her father, but he was feeling dejected at that moment and would not stir; a woman, who appeared to be dying, carried along stiff on the back of her husband, her cotton cloth trailing behind on the ground, unwinding at every step to expose her nude and shrunken buttocks; shirts, she noticed, were always worn loosely like smocks, whether over shorts or dhotis, with their tails flapping outside; and the passengers who were not either beggars or invalids seemed to be a robust and cheerful crowd, tumbling out in hordes at every station to gabble and spit, and, if there was a fountain, as sometimes happened, to wash their arms and faces and pour the water over their heads.

The stations were links in an endless chain. The day went bumping on interminably. Inside their compartment the

muddy air was churned round and round by the two fans. They read. They played piquet with fretful inattention. They stared out at the achingly monotonous landscape. They dozed, and their dreams loomed large, half-real, half-fantasy, studded with incongruous cries from the outside platforms that roused their languid lids a moment and were softened again as they sank back into a sweaty sleep. The chocolate they had bought at Bombay had been attacked by ants and was uneatable, ants like the ghosts of ants, miniature spindly pale-brown insects that swarmed over the food in their thousands, and over the bedding, and over their heavily hanging hands. At every station Sam appeared, to stand grinning and useless till the second the train began to move, when he disappeared. Each meal taken with Miss Spooner and Mr Littleton became increasingly silent. They felt one another to be a burden and ate the unappetising food in hurried gulps to have it finished as soon as possible.

The night passed in the same way as the night before. Morning came and they were still travelling. Early that afternoon they reached Calcutta. Mr Littleton shook hands with them at the station. He was not staying in Calcutta, not even a night. He wanted to press forward, he said, wanted to get home and be done with it; what with the kiddie ill, and his wife – he hoped to see them again some time, they must come and stay. Yes, he had their address, he would write. Yes, he would write. Hoped they'd manage the rest of the journey, the worst was over. He shook hands all round again, and began to deal with coolies.

Rather to Mr Digby's dismay, Miss Spooner said she was

staying in the same hotel as they were, anyway for one day. She thought it might be inconvenient to go straight to her sister's house as she had not told her sister the time, or even exact date, of her arrival. Teresa, who had her own ideas of Miss Spooner's independence, interpreted this as meaning that Miss Spooner was not sure if she wanted to stay in her sister's house. In any case they shared a taxi and were driven to the Grand Hotel.

VI

Mr Digby dined that evening alone in his room. He had a headache. He was also suffering from a form of persecution mania. The journey from the train to his hotel bedroom had been beset with wretched unworthy creatures demanding tips, demanding, even when he tipped them, larger tips, and, moreover, confusing Miss Spooner's tipping obligations with his own. As an additional effrontery the booking-clerk had mistaken her for his wife and tried to put them in the same room. Miss Spooner's imperturbability – once he even thought he heard her, in the worst possible taste, give a snigger, but her face when he rounded on her was unsmiling – only added fuel to his frenzy. And still, past the desk, down the corridors, into his bedroom the bare-legged coolies trotted carrying his luggage on their heads and insisting on their due of baksheesh. They clustered round him.

'Baksheesh, always baksheesh!' shouted Mr Digby wildly. 'Sam,' he cried to his nerveless bearer, who was being of no use at all. 'Can't you get rid of these fellows?' Then, rashly,

pressing money into Sam's hand, he added: 'All right – give them baksheesh. Get rid of them. Take them outside. Don't let me see them again.'

They were drawing nearer to Ruth. There was only one more lap to go. But one more lap, he felt, was one lap too many. He was not defeated, no, certainly not defeated, but reduced, very much reduced; he wanted to rest, he had to rest, and he wanted to be alone. He was extremely tired of having Teresa with him every moment of the night and day. So he lay on his bed that afternoon with his shoes off and in the evening had his dinner sent up to him. Teresa dined downstairs with Miss Spooner.

There were few people eating, but those who were ate stolidly, with an air of trying to appear unabashed by the white-turbaned white-coated bearers who dotted the large room so plenteously that they outnumbered the diners by at least six to one, and who watched so vigilantly that not a second's breathing-space was allowed between one dish and another, and who performed their insufficient duties so zealously that they snatched the plates from one another's hands and thrust forward second and sometimes third helpings without being asked. Teresa in this way consumed three ices and felt she would never be able to eat another mouthful. Miss Spooner, who had visited her sister during the afternoon, said:

'I don't know if you know, but today is the first day of the Festival of Lights. It's a Hindu Festival. The Kali Puja I think they call it. My brother-in-law is calling for me here at nine o'clock to show me some of the sights. It ought to be quite an experience. I don't know if your father would let you come as well. Would you like to?'

'Oh, yes. Yes, I should,' said Teresa. 'I'll ask him. I'm sure he will. He must.' She hurried away to ask Mr Digby's permission.

'Well, I suppose if there's a man – I suppose it's all right. He lives here, doesn't he? He must know what he's doing,' said Mr Digby. Inwardly he was not so sure. He suspected that Mr Littleton, who was a careful chap, would have counselled him against allowing Teresa to go. But he did so want to be alone this evening; he did want to be left in peace. And if there was a man, who must know the ropes if he lived here . . . . So he persuaded himself there was no real danger and said she might go.

Teresa's surprise was very considerable when she found that Miss Spooner's brother-in-law was an Indian. A quiet scholarly elderly Indian with white hair, a little dried-up man in spectacles with an air of having suffered much in patience, an Indian who spoke a perfect English when he spoke at all, but who was more generally silent. Teresa thought it just as well her father was ignorant on the point of Miss Spooner's brother-in-law. His permission, she felt, might not have been so readily given had he known that the colour of her protector's skin was brown. And there was more to the expedition than either Miss Spooner or Teresa had envisaged: Mr Mulik had a car and suggested the ladies might care to be driven across the Ganges to a monastery on the other side where worship would be going on all through the night to the goddess Kali. Only as a curfew was now imposed at ten o'clock

– times, said Mr Mulik, with a deprecating gesture of his head, being troubled – this would necessitate them staying there till four o'clock the next morning when he would drive them back. He had brought blankets and ground-sheets with him; it was just a case of what they would like to do. He waited courteously. Miss Spooner was all agog to go. So was Teresa, but she thought of her father and her heart failed her: this he would never allow.

But having permitted a little, Mr Digby permitted much. Above all else he wanted to be left alone; he had been asleep, happily so, when Teresa burst in this second time. At that particular moment he hardly cared if she ever came back to him or not, just so long as she went away and left him now.

'Yes, yes. Do as you like. It sounds a horrible way to spend the night, but that's up to you. Go if you like. This chap, what's his name, Miss Spooner's brother, he's going with you, eh? He'll be there?'

'Oh, yes, of *course*,' said Teresa, in hearty accents, discreetly revealing nothing further about Miss Spooner's brother-in-law.

Mr Mulik took them first to the fair. They parked the car and walked through streets where no vehicles passed or would have had room to pass. The roadways were thronged with people, all Indians; they saw no other Europeans. Brown faces and white garments pressed round them.

'Perhaps you'd better take my arm,' said Miss Spooner; she held her arm, with Teresa's inside it, loosely, implying that they were thus linked together not in intimacy but only as a safeguard. The trees were lined on either side with stalls, and the stalls were decorated with hanging tinsel and coloured

paper cut in patterns. Sweetmeats, golden and sticky, were everywhere for sale, and images in brass and plaster of the goddess Kali, whose festival it was, trampling the breast of her beloved Siva. Everywhere there were brass bells, and plaster animals, tigers and elephants and horses, gaudily painted, and figures, half-doll, half-god, hewn roughly out of sticks of wood and wholly terrifying. And everywhere, everywhere there were lights, for this was the Festival of Lights.

Lights, no bigger than the candles on a Christmas cake, fringed every balcony, every wall, every stall, every hovel, a multitude of tiny red flames flickering alive in the huge dark night. They were still being lit: glistening haunches bent forward, hands poured a trickle of oil into saucers, careful fingers set up the little wicks. The crowd moved excitedly, mystically, in no direction, impelled by currents of emotion that broke above the surface of restless heads in shouts and cries. Drums were beating. Squibs peppered the ground underfoot and rockets soared aloft, ever and anon to blot out the starry skies with flakes of falling fire. Mr Mulik led them away from the yelling explosive mob, along a paved path, down to the bank of the River Ganges. And here the noise was distant. Shadows were rounded by a yellowish glow. Voices were lowered. The warm air was soft with sorrow. They trod among the muddy unseen ashes of the dead. Widows lay along the slushy steps, prostrate in grief, or crouched forward silently setting afloat their candles in little boats of tin the size and shape of withered leaves. A murmur of pain arose. The tiny steady flames drifted away. The sky was crossed with the dying stars of rockets.

They returned to the car and drove away from the fair, away from the squibs, the sweetmeats and tinsel, the prayers of the widows, the dark weedy steps. They passed over a bridge. Teresa sat alone in the back of the car. No one spoke. Mr Mulik drove for a long time. Buildings ceased. They seemed to be in the country. Teresa had the feeling of driving across land unmapped, extinct, discarded like the moon after her last eclipse. The car bucked and jolted from one rut to another and the bumps she gave her head against the roof were real enough. The car stopped and they climbed out at the gates of a monastery. Mr Mulik left them standing there and went away. It was very quiet. The air smelt of grass. Crickets were chirping. Presently he came back and said: 'It is quite all right. Come with me.'

They followed him through the gates, across a deserted quadrangle to the open door of a temple. Light and the sound of singing flooded out into the night. Here, doing as he told them, Teresa and Miss Spooner took off their shoes, and Miss Spooner, without being told, rolled off her stockings as well, as they ranged their shoes neatly along the bottom step. Then, barefoot, they tiptoed inside the temple, and felt the cold stone caress their strangely naked soles, and closed their eyes against the blaze of illumination. Mr Mulik whispered, and pointed to where the women had to sit apart, and then he left them. Miss Spooner and Teresa sat down with their backs against a pillar, and their legs in front of them.

The goddess Kali faced them in her brilliant shrine of lights and flowers and greenery. Teresa's eyes were riveted by this terrible creature, larger than life-size, coal-black except

for the long white fangs, and treading victoriously upon the fallen body of Siva, her beloved, who smiled with content- ment. She was clad in a glittering raiment, and round her neck was hung a garland of heads. Her four arms were held out: with one hand she grasped a sword, with the second a head; one hand was raised to heaven, the other was extended in love and kindness to the suffering world.

The singing had stopped. The priest who sat in front of the shrine was murmuring in a rapid undertone, at the same time touching or indicating different parts of his body, smoothing his eyes, running his fingers lightly backwards over his head. Every few seconds he was handed a lighted joss-stick by a man who sat behind him with a lantern.

In the meantime the congregation, far from preserving a reverent silence, set up a buzz of conversation, leaned sociably towards one another, laughed, nodded, wiped their heated faces. Newcomers arriving knelt down, placed their hands before them on the marble floor, bowed their heads on their hands in prayer, and then settled themselves back on their heels and looked cheerfully round. To the right of the shrine with shaven heads sat an encampment of devotees, or perhaps they were priests, dressed in apricot coloured robes. These were the singers. Their leader sat in the first row; his head was unshaved, matted with thick black hair that fell to his shoulders and with his wiry beard parted down the middle. He wore horn-rimmed spectacles and cradled an instrument with four strings. At a sign from him the whole pack broke into song, swaying their torsos ecstatically as the weird tuneless chant rose and fell. The leader had a friend,

sitting some yards away, a man with a lean cynical face, and as they sang they leant forward locking their glances together, rousing one another to greater and greater heights of enthusiasm and nodding and smiling at the same time under the pressure of their satisfaction.

In addition to the stringed instrument there came from somewhere at the back a sound like the clashing of knives and forks, and besides the strings and the knives and forks the time was kept and enforced by the clapping of hands, a clapping that swelled and died away and swelled again. Their songs or hymns or dirges, whatever they were, went on and on, monotonous, wavering, repetitious, and then just at the moment when Teresa was sure they were never going to stop – they stopped! – quite suddenly in mid-air, as a thread that has been unwinding and unwinding inexplicably snaps; and Teresa came awake with a jerk to hear the priest intoning again, and see the slender tapers being lit, and platters of food being carried in from the farther end of the temple by another priest, this one very portly with a heavy resolved face like the face of a pugilist, who, for all his portliness, walked lightly, swaying his hips at every step like a dancer or like a woman. The food was laid in front of Kali, the goddess of destruction. People were constantly moving about and new arrivals were coming into the temple, walking, not like Teresa and Miss Spooner on tiptoe, but unashamedly, searching for a place where they might sit – for the floor was crowded – and settling themselves down with a business-like thoroughness.

Then the black-bearded long-haired song-leader waved his hand to his followers and they were off again, their voices

rising like a weird and marvellous incense, their yellow figures rocking to and fro like a bed of daffodils stirred by a wind in Spring. Teresa noticed one man in particular amongst the crowd, a thin devout man who sang with closed eyes and lifted chin, turning all the mystery of his existence into praise for this strange savage goddess, and so creating a reason for himself: the shred of dust becomes a vessel of praise, and as such is necessary.

Teresa cautiously moved her head to look at Miss Spooner and found her asleep. She herself had toppled more than once on the dizzy border-line between waking and sleeping, not knowing, when she came to her senses, whether she had slept for five minutes or only five seconds, for the air was close and the lights were stupefying. The song and murmuring acted on her as irresistible narcotics. Her legs felt stiff and chilled by stone. She touched Miss Spooner's arm gently. The old lady awoke, all her wits about her on the instant. She gave one sharp nod, as though she had shut her eyes merely for a moment to consider whether or not it was time to go, and had decided that it was. They scrambled on to their feet and crept stealthily out.

They walked across the soaking wet grass holding their shoes in their hands, their heads reeling from all they had left behind inside the temple, their ears stung by the present chirp of a myriad frogs and crickets, sounding fresh and busy everywhere about them. They wandered over and stood on the high bank of the Ganges. Rockets were still shooting up from the farther side of the river, nervous twitches animating what was otherwise a motionless jumble of dim lights and

dimmer buildings. They could hear faintly the thud of distant drums, but near at hand the conversation of insects sounded more loudly and with a greater insistence. A police search-light raked the dark bosom of the river, hesitated, and swept back again. At their backs, now detached from their senses and belittled by the largeness of the night, they heard the intermittent chanting surge out of the open mouth of the temple like gusts of hot air from an oven door.

Mr Mulik noiselessly joined them. They had nothing to say to one another. They stood together, wide awake and silent, looking across the Ganges and up at the millions of clear stars above them. Their breathing was calm and even. Everyday questions had slipped from their minds, leaving behind a state of vacant contemplation. They felt both satisfied and emptied.

Teresa, walking back across the wet grass, was reminded of some other time, some other place, very remote yet bearing a resemblance to this moment. The memory escaped, but continued to tease her. She stopped still, crinkling her bare toes in the dew, voyaging back into the cloudy recesses of her mind. Then she remembered: Aunt May's garden; flitting round the house in her nightgown between one dream and another; everyone asleep; the midnight lull that came before departure. Exactly as though she had just experienced it, she heard the scratch of gravel, felt the stray branches of climbing roses touch her face with thorny fingers. The night was the same. She expected to hear the owl hoot at any moment. Only the place had changed. Seas, oceans, continents, lay between her and that night, but the time was with her still. Time, she

thought, her mind a-swim with the effort to capture her vague meaning, made no progress. Like the air it surrounded her and she breathed it in, like air, wherever she went. Time is like air, she said to herself, finding only this small hard pebble resting on the sieve of her consciousness when the rush of intuition was over. Confusion came upon her, dulling her reason and bringing with it a yearning for sleep. Time is like air, she repeated stupidly, jogging after the others. It sounded nonsense now, but tomorrow, she promised, she would think about it again and remember what she meant.

They laid out their ground-sheets, Miss Spooner and Teresa next to one another, Mr Mulik, prompted by delicacy, on the other side of the car, and fully clothed drew their single blankets under their chins. This is how we slept on the deck, thought Teresa, side by side, with the sky above us. Time is like the sea, she thought in a muddle, like waves, like the beat of the engine, like voices going by. The frogs argued hoarsely. Crickets trilled. Distantly from the temple came the clash of hands clapping, the rise and fall of a chant, the whimper of strings. They slept.

VII

At four o'clock Mr Mulik roused his companions. The return journey for Teresa was a greyish blur with only the jolts emerging, rising out of the soupy sea of her drowsiness like rocks against which she crashed again and again, never entirely drowning in sleep before the next crash resurrected her. When they arrived at the hotel she staggered immediately off to

her bed, forgetting to thank or say goodbye to Mr Mulik, and plunged into a profound and dreamless abyss. Awakened some hours later by Sam with tea and the usual banana, she felt as though she had slept away an age and opened her eyes on a new world that clothed her in fragrance like a sheet just taken out of the linen cupboard.

'No milk this morning,' said Sam, rolling his eyes. 'Milkman dead. He stabbed,' said Sam, stabbing himself with an empty fist.

Teresa tried to understand what he meant. 'No milk?' she murmured. The tea tasted bitter. 'Stabbed?' she said, dropping back on her pillow. And she saw the rockets soaring, the fire falling. But that was long ago, long ago. Today was just beginning. She was just beginning with today. The flavour of banana was sweet in her mouth. She yawned. Her hands lay limp, not ready yet to touch or pick things up. She turned her head towards the window and saw the sunshine outside waiting for her. Sam had gone.

Mr Digby showed no desire to hear about the night's adventures, and as Teresa had no desire to tell him, nothing was said. They were leaving the following day. Mr Digby felt refreshed and philosophic. The way smoothed itself out ahead of him. Ruth was nearly within his reach. He had almost won.

That evening standing by her window Teresa saw the bats come flying in away from the disappearing sun, as numerous and large as rooks. The sky was volcanic. Its glaringly unemotional daytime stare had given place to signs of wrath and destruction. The low clouds heaped themselves in angry

colours round the great red torch departing from them. The stain of fire spread and spread across the pale greenish moon-expecting wastes. Buildings turned black. Spires sharpened; mosques and domes were swollen; the ground simplified itself in outlines and darkened every moment, holding itself to petrified attention till the boisterous hurly-burly of abdication be done and the other light creep up on the other side to breathe away the black ashes of death and tender a second life, a white and bodiless awakening. Meanwhile the clouds wallowed with heavy luxuriance, now purple, now carnation, rolled and shifted, re-formed, dissolved, presenting to Teresa's eyes one lurid composition after another, and all the time the bats came flying straight towards her out of the heart of the sun, heavy-winged and silent, like a flock of smuts blown from a garden bonfire.

She was thinking, as she watched, of Miss Spooner, thinking of her, as she always did, in the form of questions, wondering what sort of education she had had in her odd fifty or sixty years to make her so courageous now. For it seemed to her an act of courage in an old English lady to sleep on the wet grass outside an Indian monastery. She could not by any stretch of imagination see her Aunt May doing the same and she thought that her Aunt May, who was a hale enough old body for all her fatness, would refuse through a fear of some kind or another – fear of rheumatism, or unseemliness, fear of behaving in an extraordinary manner, or fear of discomfort. She asked herself if it was possible for her to be equally brave at Miss Spooner's age, equally calm and decided, and what one had to do now to reach that state of

emancipation from the fear of evil. For she had thought – she had looked at her father and thought – that one weakened as one grew older, one grew more and more afraid, one's courage went as the years increased. But it might, she saw, be otherwise. Only how? Was there a secret? Was there an answer? Would Miss Spooner tell her? And how could she ask Miss Spooner? 'Tell me, Miss Spooner, aren't you ever frightened? Why aren't you frightened? Do you know what you want? How do you know?' A conversation like this was outside the realm of reality. And Miss Spooner did not instruct, did not correct, seldom talked and never about herself. So while the clouds faded before her eyes and the sun relinquished at last its dominion, Teresa played with the cord of the blind and wondered about Miss Spooner, and wondered about herself, and about tomorrow and the next day, and the year and years after that.

When dinner was over, Teresa and Mr Digby took a stroll together down Chowringee. They stepped out from the door of their hotel into the warm brawling stream of Calcutta's night-life, out of the frigidity of a mannered existence into the pavement's spawning pulsing vitality. The lights were mischievous, playing at hide-and-seek with the darkness, neither fully revealing nor altogether concealing, smoky orange, golden black, blurring the shadows with a suggestion of intimacy, and confusing, with a very Eastern casualness, the tawdry and the splendid. The pavement was crowded. All the way along against the wall were the sturdily entrenched pickets of vendors, candles and lamps a-glow, selling anything from shoe-laces to Swiss-made watches. They grew out from

the side with the same air of natural occasion as fungus sprouting out of the cracks and corners of a cellar. Beggars who might have come straight from the racks of the nether pit, their malformations appearing in that fantastic light to have a ghastly appositeness, humped themselves hurriedly along between the nonchalant feet of pedestrians, their shrill pleas unheeded. Rickshaws lined the gutter with jangling bells. Taxis sounded their squeeze-hooters continuously as though it was necessary all the time to pump out sound, as air is pumped into tyres, lest otherwise the vociferous breath of Calcutta might falter, subside and be interred in a hushed and deathly peace. Clip-clop went the horses' hooves, and their underfed haunches shone like coal as they trotted by. The rich and the poor were there, princes and paupers jumbled together, silk to cotton, shoulder to shoulder; naked perfumed flesh rubbed against the naked diseased. Fat paunches and empty bellies were neighbours with only their different hungers dividing them. One blessing, one mercy alone, was shared by every creature, wretched or fortunate, in that conglomeration of human beings: the warm air, the warm soft air of night that allowed no man, however poor, to die of cold, and no man, however rich, to shiver. Nature handed the responsibility of death back to man, seeming to say: Look to your fellow. If you do not feed him, do not instruct and nurse him, he will die. Yet though he die at midnight without a rag on his back, his death shall be balmy.

Sellers of trinkets, of balloons, of toys, of American fashion magazines with shiny covers, of cigarette-lighters, of roses – dark red roses wired into button-holes, lashed about with

silver-paper – sprang in front of Mr Digby as he strode along, thrust their trays under his nose, bobbed their balloons at his elbow, grinning, beseeching, holding out their flowers in unclean skinny fingers. Behind them marched a little boy playing 'Deep in the Heart of Texas' on a pipe; playing it fast, playing it flat, playing it over and over again, sticking to their heels with a bundle of pipes for sale slung over his shoulder, his rambling hair on end, his eyes smiling. Ponies trotted, bells tinkled, hawkers yelled, the horns hooted, and 'Deep in the Heart of Texas' dogged them with its frolicsome out-of-tune persistence.

'Here,' said Mr Digby, turning sharp round, determined to end his wincing at whatever cost, 'give me one of those things, one of those pipes. How much, how much?'

But at once half a dozen or more children came running to them, dodging up with pipes or flowers or nothing but prayers, children unchildishly wide awake, unchildishly thriving amidst the feverish mill-race of Chowringee's night-time activities. 'Baksheesh' hovered huskily on all the lips that were not piping. The hands reached up, the eyes shone. Mr Digby, holding his pipe like a baton, spun round and began to make for home. The pipes followed, madly playing. India, thought Teresa, this is India! This upside-down inside-out lunatic night is India! Anything may happen, at any moment. I want it, I'm ready: let anything happen.

The pipes followed, the bells jingled. A little girl ran beside them, whispering, '*Give* me something, sahib, *give* me something, sahib, *give* me something –' Her face was smeared with scabs, her eyes were black and huge with age.

'Oh, confound you,' cried Mr Digby, stopping short. He glared at the little girl who was like an imp and not afraid of him. '*Give* me something, sahib.' He gave her four annas and dived into the hotel.

VIII

They left the next day, but before they went there was trouble. Sam refused to go with them. He had changed his mind. His dependants, he said, his many dependants needed him. He must go back to Bombay. Mr Digby was very angry. His voice became loud. He was determined not to touch the little beggar, not to shake him, not to threaten, but all the same his voice became louder and louder. It boomed. It thundered.

'Look here, you can't go back on your word just like that. You said you'd come with us, up to Assam. You undertook it. You can't back out at the last minute.'

However, Sam could and would, and he did. He crunched himself tightly up, he wriggled and jerked and looked a picture of woe, but his will was firm. His dependants called. He was fixed. Nothing would budge his decision. He would not go with Mr Digby up to Assam. Mr Digby recognised defeat.

'The trouble is,' he said to Teresa, 'I can't force the fellow. I've nothing in writing. Nothing in writing,' he kept repeating under his breath, as though this was the missing key to the whole misfortune. The words of Mr Littleton flashed on his mind: Never trust an Indian. 'Never trust an Indian!' he

exclaimed aloud, slamming shut his suitcase and kneeling on it. 'And by God, I never will again!' He sounded triumphant. The point had been proved: he would never trust an Indian.

Sam offered two friends in place of himself, but Mr Digby turned them down. He would do without a bearer altogether. He could do just as well without. Sam, when he came to think of it, had been pretty nearly useless on the way up. And one was sure to be as bad as another: they were all the same. Nevertheless, he felt let down, grievously so. He felt he was fighting the last few miles on his own, deserted – Mr Littleton had left him – his back to the wall. But that was how he had always fought all his life, his back to the wall, deserted. One more fight then, one more fight and the battle won in Ruth.

Sam came to the station with them. At the last minute he was weeping. 'Is never forgetting,' he said to Teresa. 'Never forget missie, never forget,' he wept, snuffling, grimacing, stretching his tentacles of faithfulness round her, although tomorrow he would have forgotten, in two hours' time, or less. She felt a pang of profound loss, though no tears fell to match his own. For they had talked together confidentially. He had been India close at her side, friendly, dependable. There was a bond. The bond broke. It was painful. Friendliness departed.

'Goodbye,' she said, leaning out. 'Goodbye. Goodbye, Sam.'

What a scallywag the fellow was, thought Mr Digby. It turned out to be good riddance. He wondered how many things he was going to miss from his effects during the next few days.

And so they were off again, jolting again, father and daughter shut up in another smelly box, clattering northward none too rapidly with only their own company eked out by a pack of cards. Teresa's head was full of sound and colour. Her head was a receptacle for tumbled rags of impression, rags torn from exotic garments that could never be pieced entirely together again; but the rags were better. They were her own, suggesting, reminding, forming a crazy patchwork pattern of excitement and mystery within which walked the diminutive figures of Mr Littleton, Sam, Miss Spooner. Lemons and snakes for Bombay; a three-legged goat, a rasping cry, for the journey; rockets and pipes for Calcutta, and singing. England seemed as small as the head of a pin; as cold as the moon; as far away as death.

But this final stage of their long pilgrimage, which for Teresa continued to unfold with the inevitability of the seasons changing, had begun for Mr Digby with the hitch of Sam's renegation. The hitch multiplied with snowball rapidity, becoming soon an obstacle of such enormous proportions that it well-nigh blocked his path and defeated his indomitable will. Since Sam was not there to guard their compartment they took it in turns to eat their meals: for Indians, said Mr Digby, might easily creep along the roof while the train was moving and thieve their belongings. This necessary division caused him much anxiety. Teresa was too young and too foolish to sit and eat alone in these conditions, too young to be left alone while he was eating. But so it had to be. As every mealtime approached he grew haggard, deciding that she must eat first, bidding her speak to no one and to answer nothing if anyone spoke to her.

'Keep mum,' he told her. 'Understand? It's the safest thing.'

Then he suddenly changed his mind and said he thought it better if he ate first. While he was gone she must keep the door bolted and the blinds drawn down. Then he bethought himself that if this was so he might miss the compartment, find himself locked out while the train began to move, with Teresa perhaps asleep inside, not hearing him rattle the handle as he clung to the step. So after all she must not lock the door, but keep the blind up when the train stopped and her head sticking out for him to see. When *she* was lunching or dining he sat for half an hour thinking how certain it was that she was going to get left behind on the platform at the next station when she changed back; cursing her for being such a fool and Sam for being absent; cursing the train for having no corridor. When *he* was lunching or dining he shovelled the food down with uncritical haste, concerned only with getting back to the compartment in double-quick time, finding Teresa with a knife in her back or her throat cut, and knowing the worst at once.

Teresa, however, remained unaffected. Her ears were deafened by echoes. Her eyes turned inwards, dazzled by hoarded treasure. The past week lay like a buffer between her and the twirling swords in her father's chariot wheels. She was not mown down. She was not even scratched. She obeyed him with docility. She played him at piquet with a dreamy concentration and beat him twice, increasing his gloomy humour. She opened her mouth in the dining-car only to fill it with food or lemonade.

The train plugged on across miles and miles of paddy-fields, more water than land, the green shoots intersected by little paths and policed by the long-stemmed delicate white birds that had grown so familiar. The sun dropped hastily out of sight. The little paths drew together. The bushes thickened. And thin as a crook of silver wire, brighter than metal, whiter than silver, up drifted the new moon, nursing the old exhausted full-blown moon in her young embrace. A single star was guardian of her immaturity, rising above her as she rose. Moon and stars dabbled the dark wayside water, where paddy and little paths alike had disappeared, with serpents of icy flame. Fireflies blew past the windows in a shower of sparks no engine ever fabricated. And when the train whistled and stopped Teresa saw a man come slowly down the steps out of the night with a leopard-skin flung about his shoulders, to stand beneath a light with his head thrown back in a cloud, a pillar of dancing mosquitoes. Where had he come from? Out of the hills? Was there blood on his hands? He walked like a king. And the train went on.

IX

Teresa slept, but Mr Digby stayed awake eyeing his watch, for at twelve o'clock they were supposed to reach a river. Here they would have to get out, board a ferry, and catch another train the other side. Contemplation of the unknown hazards of this undertaking was enough to ensure that Mr Digby remained awake and alert, playing tunes on his teeth while Teresa slumbered. However, long before they reached the river, the train stopped. They were not in a station. Land dark and secret, uninhabited, unlighted, lay all about them. Mr Digby put his head out of the window. Lanterns, farther up the line, were agitating themselves. Whistles blew. He could hear shouting.

'Wake up, wake up!' he cried, shaking Teresa by the shoulder.

'What's the matter? What is it?'

'I don't know,' said Mr Digby. 'Better be ready.' Privately he believed the train was being attacked by robbers; either that or the crew had mutinied and was running amok amongst the passengers. But having no wish to alarm Teresa before it was time, he kept his thoughts to himself and looked round for a weapon of defence. There was nothing, not even a stick. He would have to use his fists and his feet. Well, he would use them to some effect. He wished he had another Englishman with him, even Mr Littleton, small though he was. Two Englishmen, he thought, could repel an undisciplined rabble. One Englishman could, but not so easily. Lights were approaching. He made himself ready. He leaned fearlessly out.

'Well?'

An Indian in some sort of uniform, carrying a lantern, halted under Mr Digby's window. His mild face when he lifted it, shone like oiled wood, with yellow highlights. 'Sir, there is delay,' he said.

'Delay? What sort of delay?' said Mr Digby, still ferocious though he felt his muscles, one by one, relaxing.

It seemed that a length of the line ahead had been torn

up. By whom? The Indian shrugged his shoulders. Who could say? But before the train could go on the lines would have to be laid again, and this would take one hour, perhaps two hours, perhaps more. The delay was indefinite. The reason for it uncertain. The river would never be crossed. Ruth would never be reached. India had interfered with delay . . . delay . . . delay on the way. . . . And sitting on the edge of his bunk, lulled by these despairing thoughts, Mr Digby dozed off to sleep.

He was awakened by the train beginning to move, more whistling and renewed cries. It was one o'clock in the morning. He had been asleep for two hours, though it seemed to him like five minutes. His clothes were twisted round him, his limbs were cramped. The train crawled forward, doubting every foot of the line. Would the rails hold, he wondered, would they topple over now, the next moment, now? But the whistle screamed, they gathered speed; delay was over. They rushed through the darkness of early morning towards the river.

It was the river he dreaded, signifying more than a river, the final impediment. Once across the river, he said to himself; once across the river, he repeated like an invocation, once across the river. And in his mind he crossed the river, this unknown river, not once but many times, put himself on the other side and his troubles behind him, and each time just as he was beginning to feel relief he knew that the crossing had only been imaginary, it still lay ahead, and so he began to cross again.

But when at last the train reached the end of its track and stopped, it was like arriving at nothing. There was no sign of a

river. There was no platform. A few lights, spots in the darkness giving no illumination, burned outside a miscellany of ram-shackle sheds. Derelict carriages stood about – so much he could see – but no path, no road, no sort of order, only a chaotic exodus of passengers spilling out of the train, and a band of hungry coolies storming up from nowhere. He had a moment's inclination to bolt the door and sit tight where he was till the world blew up. Then a head crowned by a dirty turban appeared below on the step, with two or three others crowding in behind, each fighting to be the first, and Mr Digby's faculties returned to him. He singled out the nearest coolie and motioned the rest away with firm gestures.

'Teresa,' he said – she was standing sleepily behind him – 'look alive! Are you sure you've got everything? Got your overcoat? Got your case? Here, give it to the fellow. Where's the Thermos? All right. Are you ready? Come on then.' He marshalled her down the step. 'Jao, jao,' he cried to the coolies who still hung round, scuffling for left-over pieces of baggage.

So: they were out of the train and on the ground. Now where? He had no idea. He saw the fringes of the crowd melt-ing away over a rise or a hill, disappearing into the limbo. They were being left behind. They were nearly the last. The ferry would leave without them, he thought with a surge of panic. The porter was walking unconcernedly forward under his mountain of baggage as though he could pick his way out of the darkness from habit. The only thing Mr Digby could do was follow blindly and hope for the best. The ground was pitted with craters. His feet were caught in snares of twisted metal. Teresa was lagging behind. He paused to catch her wrist.

'Come on, come on,' he urged. He shook her arm. 'Wake up! We've got to hurry.' For the porter was getting ahead; they would lose him: all would be lost.

'I can't see,' complained Teresa, stumbling into a run.

'Never mind,' cried her father impatiently, 'I can't either. Take care, take care,' as she tripped. He held her arm tightly, bearing her up and dragging her on at the same time. The ground dipped. They were blundering down a wide track of dry and crumbling mud. Lights wavered ahead. They could see a vague congregation of people. Voices reached them. Goats were bleating. It was the river.

They thumped across a gangplank and at once the heavy stench of humanity surrounded them. They fought their way through a crush of bodies. The black thick air like dirty water blocked their nostrils, bleared their eyes. Mr Digby had lost sight of his coolie, but thought he caught a glimpse of his bedding-roll disappearing up a stairway. He thrust himself after it, digging arms and legs aside as though they were so much warm stinking dung, and Teresa followed closely behind in the trench he cleared. They reached the stairway, drew a victorious breath and mounted. The upper deck was deserted. The boards gleamed emptily. There was their coolie. There was their luggage, dumped about his legs. There were the stars above, the water below, white-painted life-belts, brass railings, a long wooden table set round with chairs, the whole scene pervaded by a weirdly out-of-place

air of royal privilege. The table was large enough to bear a banquet. The chairs were numerous enough to seat the long-dead Empress of India and all her entourage, and looked as though they awaited visitors as ghostly and fantastic as these. The stage was bare save for Mr Digby, Teresa, and a very fat heavily-turbaned Indian who sat himself down apart by the rails and at once began to snore.

Nothing happened. The ferry showed no signs of moving. Mr Digby strode first to one side and then the other, peered down the stairway at the inferno still raging below, suffered himself to be torn by the battle between his impatience and his impotence. Ten minutes passed and they were still chained to the wrong side of the river. Fifteen minutes passed, twenty minutes, and it dawned on him slowly that this was Delay again, Delay that would have no reason, no logical explanation, and no immediate cure; Delay that was Indian and inevitable.

Teresa had slumped on to one of the knobbly little wooden chairs; her arms lay on the table, her head on her arms; she seemed to be asleep. Since there was nothing to do, nothing he could do, Mr Digby tried to compose himself as satisfactorily. He sat down. The calm stars derided him. The water flickered. He looked at his watch. He strove to achieve a commonsense philosophy. He put a maximum limit on Delay. No delay, he argued, even in India, could last for more than two hours. Two hours was as good as ever. Very well, he was prepared to sit here for two hours. And if, at the end of that time, nothing had happened, then he would do something; he would – he would speak to someone; he would

give them to understand that if – he would say – he would insist – But at this point the mercy of sleep overtook Mr Digby and he was liberated. Nor the stars mocked nor the opposite bank tormented him. His own tiredness cradled him as gently as a mother, and childlike he slept.

The sound and throb of an engine brought him back to his anxious senses. Chains rattled. There was the thud of planks falling. Voices, sounding afraid and angry, shouted against each other. A cloud of smoke bellied out across the unsoiled and starry sky, and the ferry moved. He sprang to his feet. An intense excitement gripped him. He wanted to shout: hurray, hurray! Happy light-hearted anticipation, dead since boyhood, awoke and tingled through his whole body. This was an ending and a resurrection, the penultimate arrival, the beginning of an end that was an end and a beginning. He leaned over the brass rail and ruffled his grey hair with both hands, filled with innocent and heady rejoicing. His care took wings. He was crossing the river. The river was crossed.

He pounced on Teresa and shook her alive. Stupid with sleep, she found herself being whirled ashore on the strength of his energy, up a steep path, into the smells and indecisions of another shadowy station. The night, she felt, had already gone on for years of her life, like a rambling sentence, incoherent, interrupted only and for ever by the commas that were stations, coming to no full stop. Sleep, so cruelly chivvied, departed from her, and an appalling tiredness took its place.

'I'm hungry,' she said.

But Mr Digby was not attending to her. He was talking to the station-master, who wore a bandage wrapped round his forehead – or was it a sort of turban? – and his peaked cap on top of the cloth. He was saying that the train had gone. There was no train, not for another hour, or perhaps two hours. They had missed their connection because of the rails being torn up on the other side of the river. He swung his lantern. Teresa stared at the bandage, wondering if it was a bandage and whether, if so, it concealed a wound, or was it a sort of night-cap; for her brain nagged her with trivial questions, too exhausted to dwell on larger.

'I'm hungry,' she said again in a low voice.

Mr Digby groaned. His fervour had left him. So had his impatience. His eager spirit had died. Not even disappointment, much less wrath, sustained him.

'We'd better play piquet,' he said.

They sat in the waiting-room and by the light of a borrowed lantern played their gravely absurd little game of kings and queens and aces, building a papery stability, an illusion of strictness, into the gap in this irregular journey where no rules held good and Delay in the shape of rivers and broken rails and departed trains continually bewildered their intention.

'I've got a tierce.'

'I've got a cinquième.'

Moths beat their frantic wings against the sides of the lantern. The night paled. The moths lay dead, or disappeared. Whites turned bluish. Faces looked sick and were lined again with daytime furrows. Teresa yawned. Mr Digby was adding up figures. And a vendor went down the platform selling hard-boiled eggs.

'Oh, I'm hungry,' cried Teresa, remembering how hungry she was.

Quite suddenly, as she saw her father standing a little distance away, buying eggs, she experienced a sense of deep surprise that verged on awe. If there were difficulties, he would surmount them. If there was danger, he would protect her. He was her security, her rock of strength, without whom she was helpless, on whom she could rely, who would never desert her, come what might, because of some marvellous binding connection stronger than affection or understanding, the original promise of blood to blood. When she was tired, he would find her beds. When she was hungry, he would give her eggs. It was a revelation. And in the same flash she understood all that the journey had cost him: the hardness of the struggle for him and the greatness of his victory. He had it within his scope to be heroic. She had sought always, deliberately and often with pain, to minimise him, to lessen and lessen him until she could enclose him within her fist and so crush him. Now she saw that he enclosed her, and in a manner different to any she had imagined. A feeling of admiration and gratitude, totally foreign to all her previous emotions for him, overcame her, bringing with it an impression of release that was like a great sigh. She had had her revelation. The poignancy of it faded immediately and, but for the merest flavour lingering on, too faint to name, was soon forgotten.

At long last their train materialised, a most inferior train, a really disgraceful train with neither dining-car nor lavatories. They ate their meals at stations where the fly-blown rooms were termed 'European Style' and the food was cooked in a hurry, and the train waited with a personal regard upon their eating. The day pressed down on their brows like a headache without relief. All joy had departed. Dirty and dull-witted, they sat in a state of passive endurance while the hours bumped slowly by. The landscape out of the windows affected them like the sight of sickness: they kept their bored eyes away from it. And the day passed. Another night laid its weight of darkness over another day, extinguishing light. Again Teresa slept, not lying down but limply bundled into one of the dingy corners. It was ten o'clock when Mr Digby climbed out of a train for the last time and Teresa fell wearily down the steps after him.

There was nothing to show that this station was different from any of the other scores of stations they had seen and rejected. Nothing to distinguish this as the fervently-sought and long-desired goal. There were the bunched figures sleeping, the huddled figures standing. Lanterns waved. Goats were bleating. The train whistled and left them. And there was Edwin.

X

He came forward stooping, as though accustomed to hitting his head if he straightened himself, and it was his voice, his living touch, that made arrival real and the endless journey ended.

He spoke in ordinary words: 'I've got the car outside. You must be terribly tired. Here, let me carry that.'

Teresa could hardly see him. Her lids were heavy, water-logged with sleep. But she could feel him, a fact, a solid, the weight that gave equilibrium, the down-to-earth positive. They were in a car; in front of her was Edwin's head, shining in the moonlight, a fair head. She remembered a photograph of him, and was confusedly surprised to find that that static lifeless print had been made from an actual man who talked and drove a car, and was even at this minute driving them towards a house hidden somewhere – in a jungle, Aunt May had said – a house familiar to him, where he lived, and where they too were going to live. The photograph, which had been propped for weeks and weeks, for months, until one forgot to notice it, on Aunt May's mantelpiece, had been all she had known of Edwin, all that there was of him except his name. There he had stood, as breathless and stiff as a paper doll, with an equally meaningless Ruth standing next to him and looking forever sideways down at the ground. Now the photograph was out of date, a silly piece of rubbish, and here was the man, Edwin himself.

This was Assam. The Assamese moon shone brightly over-head. The air was littered with fireflies, and tasted pure and sweet, of open country. She thought they crossed another river. She thought she heard boards creaking and water splash. The voices of Mr Digby and Edwin talking in front came back to her, wordless, in waves of sound.

Edwin was saying: 'I'm afraid Ruth's away. She's staying with some friends of ours on a neighbouring Garden. I'm sorry. It's not much of a welcome for you. But I'm driving over tomorrow to fetch her back, so you'll see her then.'

Mr Digby's high hopes were dashed. Ruth away? How could that be? She was the natural terminus, the star of welcome at the end of the long tunnel. It was necessary to make a readjustment. Tomorrow, Edwin had said. Oh well, tomorrow was nearly today. Perhaps it was better. He was tired now. He could rest. But Ruth away? And again he was shocked. Edwin seemed to sense his disappointment.

'Difficult to put these things off sometimes,' he said. 'She sent you her love, of course. But anyway you'll see her tomorrow.' He stared ahead at the road as he spoke, driving with care. His voice was unemotional, a slow deep-pitched voice giving no more than its sound. 'I met the mail train,' he said, swerving aside to avoid a hole in the road, 'and when you weren't on it I guessed something had happened down the line. Something's always happening down the line. Not that anyone here knew what it was.'

'Hopeless, they're hopeless!' burst out Mr Digby, bounding up and down to the rhythm of the car-springs. 'Never trust an Indian! I've only been in this part of the world for, let me see, what? – less than two weeks, but I've learnt that already.'

'Yes, they're a hopeless lot,' said Edwin, but he was smiling. His hands on the wheel looked confident. And Mr Digby's focus shifted very slightly. He felt very slightly out of his element, bouncing about in the car like an old maid. Edwin did not bounce, he jogged, as though he was on terms of intimacy with even the bumps in the road. There was a breadth about him, a certain large air of acceptance. They were climbing a hill. The road divided. They turned to the left and

drove in between two gateposts. The road had ended; there was no path. They slid smoothly across grass and stopped in front of a bungalow with lights burning under the roof of its wooden verandah.

'Here we are,' said Edwin. He turned round in his seat and spoke to Teresa. 'It's time to wake up,' he said, 'we've arrived.'

Teresa opened her eyes. She saw the lights and the wooden steps that led up to them. And in the moment after the engine had finished throbbing, in the silence, she heard a chorus of far and ghastly screams, noises of terror that swept nearer like a rush of wind in the still night. She turned to Edwin, horrified, not knowing what to expect.

'It's all right,' he said to her, 'it's only jackals. They're a long way off and they don't hurt anyone. They're not dangerous. You'll hear them making that racket every night, but you needn't be frightened.' He held out his hand to help her and she took it, and stepped stiffly down on to the grass.

PART FOUR
RUTH

I

It seemed impossible, right up to the last minute, that they should have come. Even running up the steps of her verandah she refused to believe it. But there were lights in her living-room. Firmly she pushed open the mesh door and stepped inside. The worst had happened: there they were, faces turned expectantly towards her. The shock was so great that she stayed where she was in the doorway, slowly unwinding the scarf from her head. Insects of the night followed her in and buzzed round her as though her head was a candle-flame. She brushed them away and shut the door behind her.

'Father!' she said aloud in her pleased and pleasant voice, and came across the floor towards him, trailing her yellow scarf. But had he always been so wild and loose, she wondered, such a large man? And must I kiss him? He was on his feet, swaying with emotion. He blundered to meet her. Still smiling, she held out both hands, repeating, more faintly:

'Why, Father!'

Mr Digby grabbed her hands, dithered a moment, then grabbed her altogether in a huge hug of relief and triumph.

'Ruth!' said Mr Digby. This was his miracle, wrought by himself, the bringing together of name and creature. He embraced her, his own creation, made, lost, recovered. 'Ruth – it's really Ruth!' he said.

She found her cheek pressed against his cheek. She was smiling into his ear. Over his shoulder she saw again the little girl standing in the corner beside the lamp, watching them. No, worse: watching her. She pressed her hands affectionately down on his shoulders and drew away.

'You must be Teresa,' she said, turning gracefully towards the child. The scarf had fallen round her feet and she stepped across it, holding out her hand with a friendly gesture towards the little girl of whom she was afraid. I am afraid, she thought, as Teresa took her hand, of any child who stares so unwinkingly, who is so white and thin, who stands so still. 'You've grown,' she murmured vaguely, hesitating. Then she stooped down, kissed the little girl on the top of her head and quickly dropped her hand. She began talking, lightly and hurriedly:

'Edwin's just putting the car away. I'm so sorry I wasn't here when you came. Did you have an awful journey up?'

Mr Digby had thrown himself down in a chair. He was delighted with everything; all his fears had vanished. This bungalow: so comfortable, so luxurious even, in place of the jungle shack he had more than half imagined. Ruth: so beautiful, so reassuring.

'What did you think when you got my telegram? Bit surprised, eh? Didn't think you'd see your old father again this side of the grave I dare say.' He was excitedly complacent.

She nodded. She went on smiling. As he was talking she looked round with veiled astonishment at this room from which she had fled ten days before with tears rolling down her cheeks. How much stronger, she thought, are events than one's futile efforts at shaping them. They form silently behind one's back, round about, beneath one's feet. They are like weeds covering a derelict garden, like mosses creeping over the stones of a fallen house. The sun shines, the rain pours down, the seasons change. Everywhere the vegetation flourishes. Who can stop the sun or the rain or prevent one season from changing into another? Who can interrupt the vegetation? With a trowel I dig in one little patch of ground trying to make a path for myself, and while I bend, while the blood rushes into my head, bushes spring up on every side, even the grass disobeys me, and the stealthy woodbine puts out long tendrils to tangle my feet. Why do I not acquiesce? Events are more powerful than I am. Why do I not let them master me softly, for master me they must? I should not be unnatural. Then, as Edwin came into the room, she thought with a meek despair: I make no scars that are not forgiven even before I hack with my little knife or dig with my little trowel.

Edwin looked first towards his wife when he came into the room. She was smiling; she smiled at him. His father-in-law was talking. Then he looked across the room at the little girl, Teresa, who was standing in a corner beside the lamp, hemmed in by a low table and one end of the couch, like a prisoner. He looked at her, and looked away. She reminded him too much of Ruth, or of the soul of Ruth as, in his sorrow, he sometimes imagined it, strained of her smiles and gracious gestures.

'I must go and have my bath,' said Ruth, 'and then we can eat. I've kept you all waiting, you must be hungry.'

The meeting was over. Relations, she realised, were as easy to deceive as anyone else: they came no nearer, they saw no deeper. It would be no more difficult, she thought, than presiding at one unending tea-party – tiring perhaps, but not perilous. Her father was an old man; she knew already what he wanted. Teresa was a child to be occupied. She could manage. She was still a hostess, not a daughter, not a sister. So she murmured, 'I must go and have a bath,' and then dallied to pour out whiskies for the men, painstakingly careful not to appear as though she escaped.

'Where did all these insects come from?' said Edwin.

'Aren't they a nuisance? I brought them in with me. I should have come in by the other door.' She turned towards him a face of dazzling good humour. 'Look after them both, Edwin. Give Teresa a lime-juice. I won't be long.' She went away with a light step.

II

All through dinner Teresa watched her sister. So this was Ruth! And what did she see? She saw what Ruth intended everyone who looked at her to see: a very beautiful woman. The disguise was flawless and only two people knew that besides being a beautiful woman she was also a most unhappy one. These two people were Ruth herself, and Edwin.

Mr Digby once said to his friend, Mr Littleton, that Ruth had always known what she wanted. He would have been more correct in saying that she had always known what she wanted to be. Long ago, at an age when most little girls are more concerned about the appearance of their favourite dolls than their own, Ruth had discovered her beauty and marvelled at it. There and then she had decided on the sort of character that would display this beauty best, and not only did she choose her part but she devoted herself to it through all the stages of her growing up. Every person she came across unwittingly strengthened the lie. 'Ruth never loses her temper' – and she was at pains never to lose her temper. 'Ruth is so obedient, never argues, never makes a noise, never leaves her toys lying about as you do' – and Ruth, in consequence, washed her hands without being told, hushed her voice, ran on countless errands and suffered her cheek to be pinched in gratitude as many times without her pretty smile diminishing or any naughty attempt to draw away.

It might be thought that application to so model a pattern could have nothing but good results. But there is a difference, and a profound one, between trying to be good because goodness is a virtue, and trying to be good so that people may think you good. Ruth revolved in a world of mirrors, for every person she met was her looking-glass in front of which she arranged herself, blind to everything but her own image reflected in faces that were, on their own account, of no interest to her whatsoever.

At seventeen she was finished with school and at liberty to enter on the great adventure of conquest. Success was all too easy. It exceeded even her anticipation. No matter what she did or where she went, every eye was turned towards her. When she came into a crowded room she heard the conversation die down to the farthest corners. And this was only the very beginning. She was seventeen and radiant, as radiant as the future promised to be.

She would marry. She would entertain. She saw herself in diamonds at the Opera. Eminent men would leave their cards upon her, kiss her hand. She would be praised in London and envied in Paris. And in her imagination Ruth was already reigning hostess on both sides of the Channel, gifted like

a goddess and courted like a queen, when she met Edwin Tracey, a young tea-planter home on leave.

Edwin's reaction to Ruth was not original. He thought her the most wonderful creature ever seen, ever invented. No one else so young had ever been so lovely. Tranquillity hung about her like a scent, some certain downiness that gave to all her movements a mysterious air of maturity beyond her years. He was overcome.

So, much more surprisingly, was Ruth. Edwin had a thoroughly upsetting effect on her. For with the first few words he spoke to her she recognised his salient quality: sincerity. It was a quality she herself, necessarily, did not have, and the lack of it, she realised, made worthless all those other virtues she so enjoyed counting off on her fingers as she lay in bed. They were sham, and so was she. Panic filled her breast. For suppose Edwin discovered it – his contempt would be greater than she could bear. She was torn with despair, one moment determining that he should never find out; the next, longing to throw herself at his feet and confess. What a load off her mind that would be! Surely he would understand – she could not imagine him being angry – surely he would be-friend her, be her teacher, and she would humbly obey him, and then they would be happy together? But confession was impossible, for how could she start? What could she say? There were no words for it.

'Edwin – I'm not like this; I'm a fraud.'

'A fraud?' he would say. 'Ruth, how can you be? You are what you are. I know what you are.'

'Oh, but you don't. I'm not like that. I'm different, different.'

'Then what are you like, Ruth?'

'I don't know. I've forgotten. But not like this – this is pretence. Help me.'

Such words were wild. How could she utter them? They would lead her nowhere and she would lose Edwin. Her plight was pitiful, for she was not stupid and she saw that her long apprenticeship had killed all true enjoyment for her. She could only watch herself simulating enjoyment, and criticise the performance. Neither could she reconcile herself to the alternative of doing without Edwin: she needed him, as a sick woman longs for health. His integrity was a magnet, irresistibly attracting her. It is true to say that she married him in the end because he was sincere and she was not, and she had in her head some confused idea that after marriage she would share, not only his worldly goods but his spiritual ones as well. She persuaded herself that if she was zealous in playing her part he would never guess. In her passion for him she could hide her coldness of heart towards everybody else. And finally she told herself that even if he did find out, if he loved her truly he must love her whatever she was. In this she was not far wrong.

But she was mistaken in believing that Edwin could be deceived. Ruth was eighteen when she married him. She had charm and uncommon beauty. These she took to India and buried in the northern hills. Within a year Edwin Tracey realised that his wife, against her will, thought of herself as wasted. Not by any means a conceited man he was ready to agree with her at once. Wasted – of course she was! Would any rose, if it had sensibilities, be content to bloom in a desert where none could see or smell it? His love was not sufficient

compensation; many men might love her and to better effect than he. With absolute justice and generosity he confronted Ruth, saying: I know how you feel. It's natural, I don't blame you. If you think this is the wrong place for you, then certainly it is the wrong place. Leave me and find whatever world it is you long for. You are young and beautiful: it's your right.

He thought that then she would leave him and that he would somehow readjust himself. His readjustment, in any case, was of secondary importance. He wanted Ruth to be happy, and even went so far as to blame himself for having brought her to this outlandish station, as though he had carried her off by force.

Ruth, however, refused to admit to the truth of what he said. No, he was wrong, she cried, wrong – was he trying to drive her away? This was the only place she wanted to be: with him. She swore it was so, her very vehemence making Edwin deeply uneasy. A new Ruth was shown to him, one whose calm assurance had gone to the winds; one who clung to him in a perfect storm of denials and tears, with the light of panic in her eyes. So he said no more for the moment, but the seed of disquiet was planted, growing in time to a tree of unhappiness so great that it overshadowed them both.

Edwin was a candid man; he was made candid as his hair was made fair and his feet big. To such a man the idea of shaping a character like a suit of clothes was fantastic, but this, he presently knew, was what his wife had done. And he continued to love her, not because her garments of charm fitted her without a crease; not for what she appeared to be, and for what he had first loved her – a woman balanced and

gracious, sympathetic, sufficient unto herself and complete within herself; he loved her because he now knew that with a childish ardent obstinacy she longed to be what by struggling she could never be: simple and loving. Neither could he tell her what no one else but he could have told her: that this forgery of herself was no achievement but a slow destruction. He could not tell her because, a candid man, he was also inarticulate. So he shared her suffering as she had once thought to share his sincerity, and the fierce pride that sustained her chosen pose racked him like his own anguish. Her secret raging unrest was his companion wherever he went and whatever he did.

This dissatisfaction showed itself first in her efforts to change the bungalow. She refashioned it as nearly as possible to the pattern of that home in which she had planned, not so long before, to receive her eminent visitors. She scrapped the leather; she flung out the bamboo. She pored over London catalogues, as a result of which yards of glazed chintzes arrived by post and carrier, beaded cushion covers, useless bibelots – even pieces of furniture, at enormous cost, were crated out from England and gradually, year by year, supplanted the serviceable local product. Instead of calendars, mirrors in curly gilded frames hung on the walls. The stripes of the long fringed curtains had been faded by nearly a century of use, and in a sunlight far less intense than the hot Indian beams that now shone through and faded them still more. Silver, not brass, caught and reflected the light. How Ruth did it no one knew, but even on the hottest day the bungalow was cool and shadowed and smelt of roses.

It was a byword in the district. The other planters' wives, whose husbands hung up spears and tiger-skins on their walls for decoration, thought Ruth wonderfully clever, and said so over and over again without a hint of jealousy. So she was clever. With no one to help her and no experience she accomplished what was little short of a miracle. Her skill and good taste were manifest, and Edwin might well have been proud of her and the home she had made him, as scented and elegant as herself. He was congratulated often enough to have made another man silly with pride. But to Edwin his wife's craving to set a stage where no players could act was the sign of a sick heart. The branched candlesticks and Dresden shepherdesses were symptomatic, and he hated them.

He came in from the Garden one day, dusty and soiled with sweat, to find Ruth on her knees unpacking a crate that had just arrived from England. His Aunt Trudie had recently died, leaving all she had to her nephew, and Ruth, who had once visited the old lady, making, even at that time, a mental list of what was desirable amongst her possessions, had benefited accordingly. For some time he watched her hands feverishly tearing away the shavings to get at her treasure, an early-Victorian bureau. At last he said heavily, and with apparent irrelevance:

'Ruth, you're deceitful.'

She stopped what she was doing at once and looked up at him. Tears came into her eyes.

'What do you mean?'

He sat down on the arm of a chair, sighing, and instead of

answering her directly, said: 'You can't make a drawing-room in a jungle.'

'Why not?'

'Why, because it's a wrong idea, don't you see? It isn't true. I hate anything out of place. And you're not doing it for fun, are you? It wouldn't matter if you were. You could paint the ceiling scarlet if it amused you – I wouldn't care. But this is different. It's deadly serious, I know. Ruth,' he said earnestly, seeing her sit back on her heels with a guarded air, 'it means a sort of strife that I can't bear. Don't you understand that you're fighting more than just the bungalow or the local fashions? You're fighting me too – or you will be soon,' he added, with a sudden sense of disgust and weariness. Whatever it was she was after was not worth the fighting for. Not worth his fighting, in any case. He would rather – rather it was all over and he alone again, as he used to be, than that he should be drawn into such a miserable friction. He saw her steeling herself, saw her eyes cloud evasively. She would argue with his words, a field where he was clumsy and she adept, pretending an ignorance of his real meanings. In this way she was wanton. She was, as he had said, deceitful.

'But I like pretty things,' she had cried. 'Must we live like clumsy apes just because we're miles from anywhere?'

'I like pretty things too,' he answered, not losing his patience because he knew that she loved him, at the moment, more than anything else, however obstinately she pitted herself against him. 'But that's not the point. If we had to live in a slum, you know I'd help you to use them as a sort of charade, to pretend. But the jungle isn't sordid. You can't ignore it

either. Why should you try?' He ran his hand along the top of the bureau. 'Of course this is pretty. I'm not denying it. I can remember seeing this years and years ago, when I was a boy and used to go and stay with Aunt Trudie in the Christmas holidays. It looked fine with all her bits and bobbles. It was part of Aunt Trudie, and before that it belonged to Grandmamma. But to see it standing here, Ruth, hundreds of miles away from the land it was made in, and made for – why, it seems to me nothing else but downright silly.'

He said too much and he said it too forcibly. Ruth knelt amongst the shavings and wept tears of chagrin. And when the tears and the moment of reconciliation were over, the wound closed, and nothing survived but the small scar of stubbornness. The bureau was put in its place and Ruth, with a sense of fierce pleasure in having salvaged yet another piece of flotsam from the general shipwreck of her dreamworld, wrote her letters at it every afternoon.

As time went on Edwin was made to realise more and more the weakness of this woman whose deliberate appearance was one of calmness and strength. Her spirit was suicidal, like a moth frantically beating its wings against the outside of windows shut on a lighted room. But with every year her dependence on Edwin increased. Every year enfeebled her; less and less was she able to tear herself away from his strength, which was her only strength; yet with every birthday her desperation grew. The idea of escape, of flight before too late she found herself old, became a mania. Appreciation was what she longed, she yearned for. Not admiration, for admiration came all too easily from everyone who met her, but appreciation on an unadoring and more intellectual plane: this she guiltily believed to be her due, and she had been deprived of it. Then turning hard about she would scald herself with reproach. Edwin not worthy of her? No, it was she, wretched she, who was not fit to live under the same roof as he, much less be his wife. She was odious, vile – and so it went on.

Edwin, frayed almost beyond endurance by her ceaseless conflict – conflict which she continually refused to acknowledge honestly, but known to him, nevertheless, as well as he knew his own handwriting – Edwin urged her again and again to go, and was never proof against the tears and fear-stricken embraces that these entreaties of his induced. When she said she would not leave him, he knew she could not. When she said she loved him he believed what she said, but not as an argument, as an inescapable and sorrowful fact. Every time she lied, he knew, and her lies increased as her remorse, year by year, grew, introducing a sense of sin where no sin had existed.

Then, one day in October, Mr Digby's telegram arrived. Ruth was horrified. Last of all people on earth she wanted to see were her father and this little almost forgotten half-sister. She felt she was being hounded, followed. They were trying to trap her, to peg her down with family ties like a tent just at the moment when she was convinced her resolution was hardening. No! she declared, it was more than she could bear. She would not have them; absolutely she refused.

Nothing, replied Edwin, with stolid practicality, could stop them now: they were on their way. At this Ruth quite lost

control of herself, wept as though the world was coming to an end, and finished by packing a bag and rushing away to seek asylum with Mr and Mrs Miller on a neighbouring Garden – much to their surprise, but equally much to their delight, for they had no idea to what they owed such a visitation; being simple people they put it down to a gesture of impulsive friendliness and were very flattered.

Edwin made no attempt to argue with Ruth. He drove her over in silence, and eight days later returned to fetch and drive her back in silence.

'I can't do without her,' he said as explanation for cutting short her visit, and felt a spasm of ironical pain at the words. Both he and Ruth avoided any mention of Mr Digby to the Millers, as though there was something scandalous about his arrival. Indeed, so much anger, so many tears attached to it that their instinct now was to hide it, like a scandal, for as long as possible. 'I can't do without her,' said Edwin instead, and observed their fatuous pleasure at the idea of a young couple so inseparable.

Ruth was docile, for she had found the Millers, though just tolerable as occasional visitors in her own bungalow, insufferably boring as host and hostess. Their kindnesses wearied her. Their admiration aroused in her only contempt. Edwin, moreover, was exercising his will, and his will was compelling. On those rare occasions when he did impose it, Ruth came nearest to being happy. Overruled she became nerveless, sinking back into a stupor of beatitude that resembled an early innocence out of which any flower and no evil might grow. Hope revived. She could still, she allowed herself to

think as the Austin bounced and crashed along the rutted road, start again, fresh, if only Edwin would help her, still make herself a different sort of person altogether: be loving, be simple, nothing else. She reproached herself for despising the Millers. She would learn not to be supercilious. She would learn, she swore, staring up at the moon that it might be a witness to her vow, she would learn to be true.

All through dinner that evening Teresa watched her sister. How enchanted and how far away she seemed, though only the table divided them. They dined by candlelight. Between the tall stems of wax she saw the long neck waver and turn, creamy-coloured and rounded like the candles themselves. Across her sister's face flickered expressions, as the little golden flowers of flame flickered before it. The whole room palpitated with waves of mellow illumination, and the glow centred round Ruth, emanated from her. She breathed it out. It attended upon her in misty infatuation.

Small green insects hopped down the table and drowned in Teresa's soup. Her plate was taken away by a brown hand. She sat, silent and mazed, her senses swimming. What a crowd of people there were! Impossible to reduce them to four. With their shadows they made a crowd. She felt on her left a fairness that was Edwin, a positive fairness that reached her like a scent. For the rest of them were dark: her father, though grey-haired, was a dark man; she and Ruth were dark; the servants in white turbans were dark – looking down and turning her head she could see their bare dark feet soundlessly flitting about the floor. Ruth leaned towards her father, plying him with animated questions; her long dress rustled.

And he responded delightedly, jerking himself about in his chair and stuffing his mouth as he spoke with loads of fish and curry. Now all the signs were falling into a pattern: Mr Digby was a voice, a harsh and obvious noise beating against the ears; his knife clattered, his chair creaked. Ruth was a movement; round her the insects hopped, the flames quivered; bare feet went and came. But embedded like a rock on Teresa's left side was Edwin, giving off no sound, no movement, like a bleached stepping-stone round which the strange glistening gurgling waters divided.

'We'll go for a picnic next Sunday,' Ruth was saying. 'Shall we? Would you like that? We'll go up the river in dug-outs. Edwin, will you arrange for dug-outs? We might ask Richard to come as well.' She turned towards Teresa almost caressingly, with a bending movement of her head and shoulders, the very spirit of kindness. 'Do you like bathing, Teresa?'

'Yes,' said Teresa, while a shiver of fearful surprise went through her. Ruth was looking at her, but the stare was sightless. It was stony. The mouth smiled, the voice was gentle, but the large and beautiful eyes, directed towards her, were blind. Then why does she bother to look at me? thought Teresa, why does she bother to ask me questions? She is not sincere. She's only pretending. And she hardened her heart against Ruth in secret.

Later that same evening Ruth said to Edwin, with a hint of anger in her tone: 'I don't understand Teresa.'

'Well, of course you don't; you try so hard. Leave her alone. She'll explain herself in time, or else she won't. It's no use trying.'

'But she isn't like a child.'

'How do you know? She's just another sort of child, that's all. She hasn't got used to things yet. She'll be all right.'

III

Teresa was lulled awake in the morning by the placid song of pigeons cooing. She heard the bang of a gun, soft in the distance. Flat as the polished floor of her room, the lawn spread out on every side, already ripe with sunlight. Scarlet flowers hung down, vivid and still from the surrounding trees. Day began with the anticipation of coming somnolence. Teresa dressed herself, combed and plaited her hair, aware of being cool and freely moving in a world that was breathless and bound with heat. On the verandah she met Edwin, a gun under his arm and two dead pigeons swinging from the other hand. He was wearing khaki-coloured cotton trousers.

'Hullo,' he said, 'I've been out to get your breakfast for you.'

She touched the warm feathers and felt underneath the hard body of the dead bird. 'Are they really for breakfast?'

'Why? Don't you like pigeon?'

'I don't know. I don't think I've ever eaten one. I heard you shooting. At least, I heard a shot, but I didn't know it was you. Do you always shoot pigeons for breakfast?'

'No, not always. That's to say, I go down to the office every day at half-past six and I usually take a gun along with me, just in case.' He stood on the steps with an air of peacefulness, looking out from the shade into the sunlight. The garden-boy was just beginning to mow the lawn, his brown skin and white dhoti glistening like wet pebbles against the greenness of the grass. He moved slowly. The machine broke into a whirr. Pigeons were cooing. A peacock screamed across the valley.

'What was that?'

'It's a peacock,' said Edwin. 'It lives in the village the other side of the river. It makes that noise all day long. You'll get used to hearing it soon. Would you like to see the village?'

'Yes, I should.'

'I'll take you over some time,' said Edwin. 'We might have a look at the peacock too.' He leaned his gun against the wooden balustrade and went inside the bungalow. Teresa heard his voice in the kitchen quarters calling the cook.

Edwin's notion of entertaining guests was not extravagant. To introduce them to his own daily habits and familiar sights and afterwards leave them to make whatever amusements they cared to from these sights and habits, seemed to him sufficient. The following day he took his father-in-law down to the coolie-lines early in the morning. Outside every door a fire was lit. White smoke dwindled upwards and the whole compound was lazily astir with a slow mist rising into the pale sky and pierced through and through with shafts of sunlight as straight as swords. There was little noise. There was no bustle. Women stood by taps without talking, wrapped in white cotton, filling their earthenware pots. Children, half-awake, sat naked, staring. Here and there men squatted loosely down to whet their working-knives on stones. Or a woman leaned against a door-post, suckling her child. Or a man with long hair combed it out as a woman might, and like a woman raised his arms above his head and twisted it into a knot. Hens ran about and small bristling pigs careered in circles as though animated by sudden fits of madness. And all the time occurred a gradual exodus, men and women drifting out from the compound on to the road that led to the tea-garden, a broad road running straight for half a mile and then bending aside into the acres of glossy bushes and airy shade-trees. Groups came together every moment and floated apart again as lightly as the fluff of a dandelion dispersing. While one bound his head in a turban and stooped to gather up his tools, another had already wandered off. Down the road they went, their single figures gliding forward as dreamily as people walk in sleep, some with pots or baskets posed on their heads, all upright as flower-stalks, and clasping their empty hands together behind their backs. As they walked their bare feet roused the surface dust, and up it bellied round them, whiter than the mist and irradiated with sunlight, so that they seemed, in their white garments, like a host of saints going serenely on the way to heaven.

Mr Digby was a collector of facts. There was no fact that might not, some day, be useful, and was therefore worth attention. He stood in the mist and sunshine, darting glances round him, or strode up and down between the mud and thatch huts, frowning with concentration. With Edwin, impressions came first, and he afterwards related them to facts. The sight of a little boy sitting cross-legged on the ground smoking a hubble-bubble pipe half his own size, gave him a feeling of amusement and some tenderness.

How solemn he is, thought Edwin. He went up to the child and said, speaking in Urdu: 'Is that a good pipe you are smoking there?'

The child rolled his eyes up at Edwin and then, taking the stem of the pipe from his mouth, turned his head away across his shoulder, grinning with pleasure and wanting his relations to come and listen to this banter. His mother stood in the doorway behind him, smiling. 'It is his father's pipe,' she said.

The father, hearing his name, looked up from his occupation and moved his head with willing agreement. 'Yes,' he said, 'the child has taken my pipe.'

Passers-by halted. Children appeared.

'Well,' said Edwin gravely, 'it is a very good pipe. If you smoke that you will soon become a fine man like your father and be able to cut down great trees.'

Mr Digby, unable to understand either the conversation or the lively amusement it aroused, moved away impatiently. Edwin followed.

'What were you saying?' asked Mr Digby, almost jealously.

'Oh, nothing. You know – a joke. They like jokes.'

'What are they? Assamese, I suppose.'

'Oh, lord, no. They're none of them local – not originally so, at any rate. They're imported labour. It's a changing population. They come in from all parts of the country. Sometimes they only stay a little while till they've made a bit of money, sometimes they settle here altogether and never go back to their own village. Oh no, we get the most peculiar assortment – some wild, like animals, and with just about the same

intelligence. You can see it in their faces, you know. I've often thought what a study one could make of it. Faces – what an extraordinary production they are! I must say, it's an idea that – that fascinates me,' said Edwin, using the word delicately as though it was not a usual one with him. Mr Digby made no remark but restively fidgeted his head. Edwin went on, still with the same uncommon eagerness that suggested this was the subject he most enjoyed discussing, and that, like all hobbyists, he was not particular in his choice of audience: 'Some of them are really ugly – ugly from a sort of meanness of countenance. You could almost call them degenerate-looking except that "degenerate" implies they've sunk from something higher, and I should imagine myself they've never got farther than one stage from the monkey. But then there are others' – his expression brightened; he even straightened his shoulders a bit – 'who are – really they are beautiful. Well, I feel like a hulking great oaf beside them. So I am, but I don't notice it most times. I look at their faces and the way they hold themselves when they're walking and I say to myself: "Now there's nobility." Interesting, isn't it? I wonder what it means? It doesn't really make sense, does it? Pushes home the lesson that beauty's got nothing to do with the intellect – I mean the intellect of the beholder. It exists for absolutely no reason and in any old place, swamps and jungles. And gets born every day, and dies every other. One ought to remember that and learn something from it.'

He was musing to himself by this time, whether he knew it or not. His father-in-law, quite at sea and always bored by monologues not his own, broke in:

'What's that? – a beautiful Indian! Sounds like a contradiction in terms to me.' He laughed at this absurdity.

Edwin stopped short and slowly turned to stare at the older man. His enthusiasm, so misdirected, fell from him with the sharp rending of flesh torn from flesh, and lay at his feet like his own shadow, leering. He had misbehaved, babbling away like any chatterbox, and shame filled him. 'Oh, God,' he said, 'how sick I am of hearing that! I ought to be used to it by now, but I'm not. Whose point of view is it, I'd like to know? The fools of this blasted earth? God knows there are plenty enough of them and they all catch each other's tricks, like cowards.' Anger struggled inside him. He hated to feel it there, weakening him. 'But you must be *blind*,' he burst out finally.

Mr Digby, though injured by such an attack, was more inclined to make light of the whole question than turn it into an issue. 'Well,' said he, with jolly inconsequence, 'taking the Greek idea of beauty for a pattern, you must agree –'

'Oh, rubbish!' said Edwin, loudly and rudely. 'There are some things you can't deny any more than you can argue about them. That girl, for instance, over there' – he pointed – 'if you think your face is prettier than hers because yours is white and hers is brown, all I can say is you must be mad.' He strode on, trampling all fools and madmen under his boots.

'But I never said –' complained Mr Digby, hastening after him and beginning to be really huffed.

'I know, I know.' Edwin halted again, at the same time making an impatiently conciliatory gesture. 'I'm talking

nonsense. We both are. I don't know what the hell I'm saying,' said he, lapsing into an old contempt for himself, 'but then, neither do you, so what's the odds? Everyone talks too much. The fact of the matter is, I like that lot back there. You know, they're just a bunch of silly kids, so responsive. Gay. Wanting their little joke. And they like me, too.'

'But that's got nothing to do with it,' said Mr Digby, feeling as though he had been on the winning side, but unfairly cheated out of it, and not in the least grateful to Edwin for checking his outburst of temper.

IV

That evening Edwin drove with Teresa down to the river. Teresa sat forward straining her neck, turning her head from side to side to look at everything they passed. Oh, she said, how ugly those water-buffalo were. Did they have to keep their heads stretched up like that? – they looked so uncomfortable. Were they fierce? What long horns. And their skin was such a nasty pinkish colour, almost hairless, was it sore? Edwin, attending to ruts and hummocks, answered that no, they were not particularly fierce, nor sore, nor, as far as he knew, uncomfortable. At that moment they met an old man walking along beside the road. He stopped and bowed as they passed, touching his forehead. Teresa turned round to look at him again, but he was lost at once, smothered out of sight in the cloud of dust that followed behind the Austin.

'Oh, Edwin, it does seem rude. We've choked him with dust. He was being so polite.'

Edwin drove on without answering. On a spur of land above the river he stopped the car and lit himself a cigarette. 'Teresa, why do you say things like that? If I was being rude why do you worry about the old man? He's all right. You ought to worry about me.'

Teresa, not understanding how she had irritated him, sat staring down at the river. It curved below them gleaming and still. Cows slopped down to the water's edge to drink. A woman was beating her washing against a board on the opposite side. The thump-thump of wet material floated across to them all out of time with her movements, for whenever she raised her arms they heard the small tardy thud.

'We behave,' said Edwin, seemingly involved in an old argument, 'as we're expected to behave. How can you behave in any other way? What harm can you ever do except to yourself?' The tone of his voice was puzzled and unconvinced. 'Teresa,' he said, less sharply, 'I can't explain anything to you; nothing can be explained. Only here you must think of everything differently. Now you see that ferry down there – that's how we're going to cross the river in a minute.' The ferry, built of two long narrow boats boarded together, was strung on to an overhead cable. 'And you see beside the ferry they're building a bridge.' Men stood idly knee-deep in water. Others pushed themselves out on rafts to where immense poles stuck out of the river's wash. The sound of a leisurely tapping drifted up, voices, and splashes like single notes of music. 'In a few weeks they'll finish that bridge and it'll last very nicely several months. Then what happens? The rainy season comes along; that river turns into a torrent – you'll

probably see it. The bridge gets swept away like so much straw, and we use the ferry again till this time next year when they build another temporary bridge. Why not build a permanent bridge? Why not use the ferry all the time? Why build a temporary bridge every single year to be swept away every single year? Isn't it a waste of time and labour and everything? But is it, *is* it?' said Edwin, throwing away his cigarette and speaking earnestly. 'Isn't it just as good a way to spend your life, building a bridge, as any other way? Why do we think achievement's better than repetition?' He took the brake off and let in the clutch. The car began to bump downhill. 'They look happy, don't they?' said Edwin, nodding towards the casually occupied gang of bridge-builders. 'I believe they are happy. Well, then – but you'll have to get it into your head, Teresa, right from the start, that everything's different here. You can't judge because judgement is logical. We're logical because we come from the West, it's a Western habit to judge. But here – what do we know of motives? We can only guess them and you can't judge by guesswork. Judge not –' he began, and broke off, adding to himself impatiently: 'But that's absurd of course. We are ignorant, you and I, Teresa. And what I'm saying is that here you really can't be certain of –' He paused and she turned her face, waiting. 'Why, of anything at all,' he finished, catching her anxious look and suddenly smiling.

He guided the Austin carefully over the planks on to the ferry. He wanted, he urgently wanted to say more, but hesitated, not wishing to antagonise her. He wanted to say: Yes, everything is different; differences are bewildering. Do not, in order to be rid of your bewilderment, attempt to reduce what is extraordinary to the limits of your ordinary appreciation. That is what most people do. They try to commonise, to reduce, because they are afraid of being bewildered. Let yourself be astonished. Be small. That is enough for you, and for me.

This he wanted to say, and much besides. But he was more a feeling than a speaking man: words offered him little in the way of communication and he feared, too, she might think him affected or priggish, so he let it go at that.

Several other people were crossing, a man with a bicycle, a boy leading a goat. One of the ferry-men pushed off from the bank, the other with a broad oar kept the clumsy craft pointing half upstream into the current, and the current working down upon the side of the ferry forced it across, the cable overhead ensuring that it was swept only sideways and not away. Edwin sat in the car, his arms crossed on the steering-wheel and his head put down on his arms. Teresa climbed out, walked all round the ferry, looked over at the muddy water and came up on Edwin's side of the car. She asked: 'How long are we going to stay with you?' wanting to say something, anything, to show her confidence in him. She had annoyed him by some remark and she wanted him to know that his annoyance had not estranged them.

He answered without raising his head. There was something almost indecorous in seeing that large skull laid so babyishly low before her. Yet the attitude was reposeful and the repose dignified it. He smiled at her upside-down, slanting round his eyes to see her face. 'Good lord, Teresa,' he said in a drowsy voice, 'I don't know. How long do you want to stay?'

'I don't mind,' she answered, pleased and confused to find that, after all, there was no estrangement. There was between them a familiarity that sharp words from him could never dissipate. He might be cross with her again, but there was no need for her to be anxious: she could bear such crossness, it was not serious. So she thought, climbing back into the car and wondering at the same time why she found such relief in Edwin's remark that one could be sure of nothing. Her father and her Aunt May were forever telling her that this was right and that wrong, this good and that bad. Such definite pronouncements, far from being convincing, made her extremely uneasy. Something deep within her refused to believe what they said, suspecting perhaps that they themselves were not absolute believers in what they said, or at any rate had not, at first hand, proved the truth of their words. 'This is right,' they said, and at once she thought it was wrong, and asked herself: 'What is right?'

But now here was Edwin saying, 'You can be sure of nothing,' and how comfortably this sounded in her ears. For in that case there was nothing with which to argue, nothing to defy. Everything was for acceptance. And if one started off by being certain of nothing, biased by no argument, why then, at any moment one might be certain of something; and if, coming upon it in this way, one was certain of something, how very certain one would be. And if, she thought, as the Austin bumped off the ferry and accelerated up the track, I am ever certain of something, then the first person I shall tell is Edwin,

to make him certain too. Teresa felt a warm flush of pleasure at the thought of sharing this imagined discovery, and the importance of it.

Edwin stopped the car beside a clump of palm trees and Teresa, as they walked down the single street of the village together, thought he was enjoying himself, and so he was. After twelve years of living in the same part of India he knew nothing, he sometimes alarmed his acquaintances by saying, about either India or the Indians. Nor did he want to. Nor did he expect to. He looked about him and liked almost everything he saw. He was curious, as a child is curious, about everything, only unlike a child he seldom asked why. He drew no conclusions and made no pronouncements. In this he was unusual, for even Mr Digby, after only a week or so on Indian soil, knew all about the Indian character and was quite ready to talk of it for hours. Edwin inclined to the view that he lived amongst people of mystery in a land of mystery.

'If I was an Indian,' he said once to a friend of his who had just beaten his servant for stealing, 'I should understand Indians and they would understand me. And I should think of Europeans as they think of Europeans. I wonder if they know what they think of Europeans – ? However, I was born in Somerset.'

The things he understood were things like the Naga hills which were always beautiful and remote, unchanging. He knew how to grow tea, how to supervise it from the first planting of a green sprig to the time it was taken away in crates by lorry or floated down the Brahmaputra by boat to Calcutta. All his troubles were personal, centred on Ruth. He disliked very few people, disliking more, and sometimes intensely, the things they did and said. And he was quite able to be happy walking down a village street with Teresa, avoiding the bony hump-necked cows that lay down in the middle of the white and dusty road to ruminate.

Teresa for the first time saw quilts being made. They stopped to watch. The finished quilts were hung up in the sunshine. Three men sat on the ground, stitching busily. From inside the open-fronted hut came the sound of a sewing-machine.

'The cotton's poor stuff,' murmured Edwin. 'It doesn't last and the dye fades if you only so much as look at it; but aren't they pretty now?'

The houses, or shacks as they seemed to Teresa, lay on either side below the level of the road with a deep ditch running between. Bridging the ditch were strips of slatted bamboo. Every dwelling was a shop or a work-shop; various wares were laid out before them with the undisturbed air of never being sold. Here were stacks of earthenware pots, as light in the hand as paper and so brittle that only a jolt was needed to smash them, but cheap, a few annas each and made in every size for carrying any quantity of water. The bigger ones were decorated with brown lines swirling in loops and commas. Oranges, bananas and coconuts lay in heaps out-side nearly all the doors, covered in roadside dust. And here the brass-and-copper smith lived. They heard his hammer ringing, but his shop was closed in more than the others and too dark for them to be able to see him at work. His brass jars and bowls thronged the doorway and shone like little

earth-bound planets of golden fire. They passed the barber's. They passed the temple, built more solidly, not of bamboo but of earth and sandstone white-washed, and with a red tin roof and carved eaves. A tinkle of bells sounded and tattered fringes of coloured paper hung down from the painted gateway through which cows and goats wandered at will, there being no gate to stop them.

'It's quite a grand sort of village, this one,' said Edwin. 'It's got a telegraph office, and it's a halt on the main Calcutta line. The station I fetched you from is just over there' – he pointed – 'you can't see it from here. The children go to school. In fact, nearly everyone's a babu and thinks a lot of himself in consequence.'

Cyclists, their shirt-tails hanging loose outside their shorts and billowing behind them, came wobbling down the road, weaving in and out between the cows. There were many children visible, but no women, and for every one man working, four stood about to watch. It seemed like neither Tuesday nor Wednesday nor any day of the week, but just the daytime, those hours between sunrise and nightfall recurring endlessly throughout a lifetime. The young men might change their positions and lounge in different attitudes, but the shadows from the palm trees lay in the same lines across the dusty road, day after day, and shrank and lengthened at the same pace. Time became like the sky, enormous, empty, hot, covering everything, lasting for ever. Who would wish to fight against the sky? As there was no attempt to alter the sky, so there was here no struggle against time, and this Teresa sensed with satisfaction. Tomorrow

would be the same as today, with the one difference: that she herself might not be here.

An ox-cart came heavily zig-zagging down the road towards them. Not a single cow got out of the way. It moved from side to side to avoid them, on occasion almost toppling over into the ditch. Its bamboo hood made it look like a huge bonnet with the shafts sticking out for starched ribbons. The driver, crouched well forward on the board behind the rumps of his animals, knees crooked as high as his ears, urged them on by alternately wringing the tail of the left-hand one and thumping with a stick the flanks of the other. Teresa and Edwin stood aside to let him pass. A smell of warm animals lingered behind in the dust that covered them, and an increase of flies.

'You see,' said Edwin, blowing his nose. 'Dust! It isn't a special privilege to rouse it. Even the chickens kick it up. Hi! Teresa' – she was looking behind her at a silversmith breathing on his coals through a hollow stick – 'we didn't bow, but we're full of dust. D'you feel better about the old man now?'

The silversmith saw her staring and jumped to his feet. He was heftily built, like a Rugby forward. 'Please come into my poor shop,' he called, smiling excitedly. Teresa glanced at Edwin and then crossed the ditch. A chair was fetched at full speed from an inner room and dusted for her. A stool was brought for Edwin. 'Is sitting please.' They both sat down.

'We must go,' said Edwin at once in a low voice. 'It's getting late.'

But the silversmith was bringing out trays and boxes and strewing in front of Teresa a litter of bracelets and earrings and heavy ornaments studded with coloured glass. She picked them up uncertainly, one by one, and the author stretched his arms above his head and cracked his finger-joints with a gauche pleasure. Little children came peeping out from an inner room.

'This is my nephew,' said the silversmith, pouncing on one, 'and this is my nephew, and this is my nephew.' The three little girls looked shyly up and shyly down. On the road above a group of neighbours gathered to watch. They paid no attention to the silversmith who every few moments waved his arms at them indignantly and shouted out, trying to make them go away.

'I suppose we ought to buy something,' said Edwin. 'What would you like? Choose something.' Doubtfully she touched the tray of silver goods. 'How much is this?' asked Edwin; he held up a silver nose-ring.

The silversmith shrugged his shoulders, put his head on one side and suggested five rupees. Edwin paid him without bargaining and then, looking suddenly tired and haughty, turned towards Teresa. 'Listen,' he said, in explanation so scrupulous that someone older than Teresa might have thought it amusing, 'I've bought you a nose-ring because you can't wear it. Understand? I don't like English women wearing Indian ornaments. They were made for Indians.'

Teresa put the nose-ring in her pocket with a feeling of disappointment. She had wanted a bracelet.

What's the matter with me? thought Edwin as they left the shop and began to walk down the road towards the car, I'm a prig after all, I'm just a fool like anyone else. The sun had dropped. There was no evening. At once, even before they reached the car, it began to get dark.

'I suppose you really can't wear it? Haven't got a hole in your nose, have you, Teresa?' said Edwin, much depressed by his own clumsiness and trying to set it right by an even clumsier attempt at being playful. But it was too late. Teresa, walking awkwardly, stumbling in the pot-holes, felt separate from him again and saw no joke. Again she felt he had reproved her, and wanted to say: I understand more than you think. There's no need to go on and on explaining. You should trust me to know what you mean without putting it all into words. You called me a woman a moment ago, and then you treat me like the youngest child.

Neither child nor woman she was lost, a nothing, and exiled by misunderstanding. His conscientious kindness hurt her, thrust her away when she wanted to come closer. As they reached the car she put her hand in her pocket and dropped the useless piece of metal into the grass. Then she regretted the waste and stooping down to find it again ran her hand quickly here and there.

'What is it?' said Edwin. 'What's the matter? What have you lost?'

'Nothing.' She climbed in, discouraged, and he started the engine.

As they sat, both listless, aboard the ferry, the moon was just rising. Looking towards it Edwin said in a flat soft voice, as though continuing some long conversation with himself: 'Certain of nothing except yourself. You must be sure of yourself or you might as well be dead.'

He was thinking of Ruth, as he was always thinking of Ruth, and she was half of himself. How, if he was honest and she dishonest, could he help but fall, he and she, the two one, falling together. She hates all this, he thought coldly and as if convinced of it for the first time, she always has hated it. Even the moon gets up in the wrong place for her. And so it's wrong, it's wrong of her to stay. She mustn't stay. She must go. For though he was non-committal, or even indulgent, with every one of his fellow-creatures, allowing them possible reasons for any piece of bad behaviour and too humble not to be forgiving, yet with himself he was austere and Ruth was himself. As they crossed the river the moon rose by inches, amazing them.

'Edwin,' said Teresa sadly, 'I dropped that nose-ring you gave me.'

'On purpose?'

'Yes.'

'Oh well, never mind. I dare say you did the best thing. It wasn't any use to you. Good. I'm glad you dropped it.'

They drove past the coolie-lines and saw children in the light of flames, their naked bellies glistening. The air was winking with fire-flies. They turned to the left and the flat fleshy leaves of tea-bushes slapped against the sides of the car.

'We never saw the peacock.'

'Nor we did,' said Edwin, 'but we'll hear it tomorrow, screeching away.'

'And the day after.'

'For ever and ever until it dies; unless we die first.' They laughed, and the gap lessened. Edwin accelerated, turned the car in between the gateposts, swept it in a wide semi-circle across the lawn and braked in front of the bungalow.

Richard, Edwin Tracey's new young assistant, was having a drink in the living-room with Ruth and Mr Digby. He lived in a bungalow a quarter of a mile away, alone except for a host of servants and lonely enough to drop in on Ruth and Edwin a good deal more often than they wanted him. A certain terrible cleanliness linked to an extreme regard for every aspect of his own appearance were the only distinguishing idiosyncrasies of this otherwise unremarkable young man. His most characteristic and most often repeated gesture was to smooth back his smooth and slightly oiled hair with a small pocket comb that he carried everywhere with him. Nothing was so impossible to imagine as a bristle showing on that always closely-shaven chin, and for Ruth he was a real trial having early developed an adoration for her that she was unable to defeat. The alacrity with which he leapt to his feet gave her a nervous headache. His insistence on taking things out of her hands with a commandingly servile 'Mrs Tracey – let me do that – you sit down' occasionally pushed her beyond her much-tried patience. Occasionally she could not forbear to stamp her foot at him, and giving a great tug at whatever she was holding and he attempting to take from her, would cry: '*No*, Richard – leave me alone, I shall scream if you don't. I *want* to do it myself.' To Edwin she said, 'For heaven's sake, why can't he stop showing us all how well brought up he is?'

But Richard thought her perfect, and admired even these rare bursts of peevishness as signs of spirit. All his ambitions were orthodox and well within his reach, except perhaps the one of marrying a girl as beautiful as Ruth. He was so punctilious that even in his dreams he called his manager's wife: Mrs Tracey. He wanted to be a manager himself one day, to be the most popular fellow round about, to marry an awfully nice girl – this quite soon – to win the tennis tournament, and later perhaps take up golf and be good at that as well.

Edwin, as usual, kept his opinion quiet and his lack of enthusiasm for the new assistant was no more marked than on other occasions. Only his wife knew how distasteful to him were the sodden stubs of cigarettes left about everywhere by young Richard, how he hated being called 'Sir' with every other word and hated even more the thought of being called 'Edwin'. To be fair, he had made a point of telling several people what an excellent worker Richard was, never sparing himself, never slacking, up at all hours, willing, quick to get the hang of things. Such a recommendation from Edwin Tracey went far with the neighbouring planters, so that, after six months, Richard had made his initial splash and registered a small success. Still, he was lonely. Being a popular boy, with only two club-nights a week and the club-house ten miles away, was not enough.

He and Mr Digby were getting along like a house on fire when Edwin and Teresa came into the living-room. Ruth, wearing a long black dress, was standing beside them, radiantly pretending to listen. She had just decided to force Teresa and Richard together, solving a dozen problems with one stroke. When she turned sweepingly towards her husband

and sister she broke off, as she might have snapped a twig, the thriving conversation between Mr Digby and his new young friend.

'My dears,' she cried, 'where have you been? We thought you were lost.'

She looked quite magnificent. Edwin's cold-hearted thoughts were swept away on a wave of admiration. Everyone in the world, he thought, should see her as she was at this moment. Of course she was wasted! Men ought to paint her, to adore and remember her, just like this. Such a glorious woman was made to be seen. The wave crashed and dissolved, and immediately a small cool ripple lapped round the edge of his mind, insisting: This is only her lovely skin – what about the poor silly thing that lives inside, unpaintable, unadorable, but more real than all of that rich hair or this wonderful outstretched hand.

Edwin took the hand, saying compassionately, 'Ruth!' as though they were alone together, and coming at last near to an understanding.

Ruth knew his thoughts: they were all old ones. She knew them as well as her own. So first she had flushed, and seemed to swell a little out of pride. And then she had paled and contracted, watching him beseechingly. Her arm remained flung out between them in the original gesture of welcome, but lifeless for as long as ten seconds. When he took her hand she made a great effort, infused herself with warmth, pressed his fingers, tucked her arm under his elbow and, holding up her noisy skirt in the other hand, drew him across the room with every appearance of gaiety.

'Pour out your own drink. I don't see why I should have to do it for people who come in so late and so secretly. No, but really, where have you been? You must be careful, you know there's supposed to be a tiger in the district? Nidar was telling me about it this morning. Teresa, what would you like to drink, my dear, and how would you like to see a tiger?'

Edwin bowed his head and put the tips of his fingers against his eyelids, thinking: 'This is confusion. This is panic.' He felt immensely tired. 'I took Teresa across the river and showed her the village,' he said flatly. He could hear the boy Richard gabbling on again to old Digby, and Teresa was saying:

'I'd like a lime-juice please. Is there really a tiger round here? What'll happen? Will it kill someone?'

V

Tomorrow was club-day. Before dinner was over Ruth had arranged for Richard to pick up Teresa the following after-noon and drive her over to the club-house, an arrangement that cast a gloom over the rest of the evening. Richard had no desire to be saddled with Teresa, a little girl who neither played tennis nor danced, was too young to drink and would have to be brought home early. Teresa had no desire to go. Ruth, however, settled the matter, and packed young Richard off to his bungalow as soon as possible afterwards.

'Half-past two then – don't forget,' she called from the verandah steps. He hung about on the grass below.

'You're coming too?'

'I don't know. I might. It depends how much I've got to do,' she answered, afraid he might wriggle out of his promise if she told him she had no intention of going.

Richard, arriving the following afternoon at exactly half-past two, dressed in white shorts and a red-and-black striped blazer, found Mrs Tracey, his dream of fair women, sitting in a deck-chair on the lawn with her hands in her lap, talking to her father. There was no sign of Teresa.

'Aren't you coming?' he said. It was plain enough to see that she was not prepared for a social occasion. She leaned her graceful head back against the canvas and looked up at him, smiling.

'No, I decided not to. I've really got too many things to do – I can't spare the time. And my father's got a touch of indigestion,' she added, making it sound like the best sort of joke in the world, 'so he's staying behind with me. And Edwin, as I dare say you know, is somewhere out on the Garden seeing to something – planting, I think he said. So it's just you and Teresa. Where is Teresa? Be nice to her, Richard, and introduce her to people. You *know*.' Teresa came out on to the verandah behind them.

'There she is,' said Richard. They all turned their heads. She looked, with the green space dividing her from them, smaller than usual, a long way off. No one called her name. And to Teresa, hesitating inside the empty verandah, the group of three at the far end of the lawn seemed so remote she felt it hardly worth her while to reach them. She came across the grass with dragging steps.

'I don't want to go,' she said.

'Why not?' said Mr Digby sharply. 'Aren't you ready? Not feeling sick, are you?'

'I feel perfectly well. I just don't want to go. I'd rather not.'

Richard stood by Ruth's chair, glumly banging his racquet against his leg. Ruth reached up and patted Teresa's hip.

'I want you to go. You'll meet all sorts of people. It's dull for you here. And Richard's waiting.'

'Oh, Ruth – please!'

'Teresa, my dear, what nonsense. You'll enjoy it when you get there,' said Ruth, with a hint of firmness creeping into her voice. 'And Richard's going to take great care of you, he's promised. Now hurry – it's a quarter to three already, you'll miss half the afternoon if you don't go. Richard, give my love to the Millers and Mrs Lawson.' How badly she wanted them to go, now, quickly. She shooed them whimsically away with her hands. Richard, looking neat and sullen, crossed the grass to his battered two-seater and climbed in, slamming the door. Teresa followed him. They drove away with Richard's discontent grinding aloud in the change of gears.

'Wait here; don't move,' cried Ruth. 'I must fetch some sewing. I can't sit idle.' She came back holding a crumpled pink garment in her hand, and using great energy with a pair of scissors began to tear the seams apart. Mr Digby settled himself, tilted his hat more over his eyes, and slanted a glance.

'What's that thing?' Tea in an hour or so; nothing to do; alone with Ruth. This was his time for a snooze, but not today; he wanted to stay awake and talk to Ruth.

'It's an old dress of mine,' she said. 'I'm going to cut it up and turn it into one for Teresa.'

She felt guilty towards Teresa who was, after all, a sort of sister, and so poverty-stricken, without clothes or grace or mother. For neither loving nor understanding the child she blamed herself extravagantly. But Teresa existed for her only as a further reproach, another finger pointing at her crippled emotions. Wishing to yearn towards Teresa, she yearned towards herself. When she would have wept over Teresa's condition, she wept over her own. For this was it: she was bankrupt. With maternal gestures she sought to make up for the maternal love she wished she could have given, and slashed away at the pink stuff with a sort of desperation.

Mr Digby had accidentally dropped asleep. The afternoon was very hot. Every few seconds a ghost of wind made the palm leaves above her head crackle like tinfoil. Pigeons were cooing in the stretch of woodland that ran downhill to Richard's bungalow. The scarlet hibiscus flowers hung still. Bees were humming. Mr Digby began to snore. Someone in the coolie-lines was trying out a drum and the deep faint thrumming sounded at intervals, sleepily disturbing. From the back of the bungalow came the light clicking noise of wood being chopped, and the murmur of voices. It was half-past three. Each sound was minimised by heat or distance to the close importance of an insect in an English hayfield on a summer afternoon. Only no drum, however softly, ever beat in an English hayfield. Beyond the river-valley rose the Naga hills, unchanging, soundless, blue. The peacock screamed. Ruth let fall her scissors. The far hills rested on her lashes, offering only silence. Then the peacock screamed again.

Oh, that scream! All the dust and ashes of imprisonment, so long that even despair has forgotten its reason, sounded in that cry. Inhumanly hopeless, as the face of a monkey shows the marks of inhuman suffering, it yet seemed to Ruth more laden with human grief than the echo of it that escaped from her own mouth, awakening Mr Digby.

'Hullo,' he mumbled, struggling up. 'I went right off. My dear, did you shout? I thought I heard you.'

'You were dreaming,' said Ruth. She picked up her work, bent her head. 'Dreaming about those little boys you wish you'd never left.'

He knew she was chaffing him. Someone else he might have taken seriously. With someone else he would have sat bolt upright, run his fingers through his hair, protested hotly that he never wanted to see another little boy again. Little boy indeed! – little pig! But no, there was no need, for Ruth, only Ruth, knew how to chaff him. He cuddled himself in his chair and chuckled. And with his enjoyment came a piquant desire for confession. To reveal himself as a fraud – what a comfort that would be. Ruth was threading a needle, delicately smiling, receptive. She had always understood him.

'I was never any good at teaching. I hated it all the time – you knew that, eh? I hated the guts of it,' said Mr Digby happily. 'Why does someone go on doing a job they hate for forty years? Why, because they can't do anything better, of course. I couldn't do anything better, Ruth, that's the truth

of it. Couldn't even do my own job – I was a rotten bad school-master, I can tell you.'

'Oh, no,' murmured Ruth, 'it isn't true.'

'Of course it's true,' he cried, fire leaping into his eye. 'Why d'you think I've been messing round in one footling little prep school after another all my life? Never got further than a prep school – boys under fourteen. Because I was a failure, Ruth, couldn't even teach – and they knew it – and I knew it.' He dropped his voice, took a new breath, and plunged mournfully on. 'I thought I could write – thought I was too good to be a schoolmaster. Of course I couldn't write.' His voice shook with contempt. 'Good God, I knew it all the time, but I never let on I knew – fooled myself I was a genius, what a farce! And acting – same thing – had to pretend. Had to think I was a great man – light under a bushel – that sort of stuff. The world's loss, damn the world, I said – kept saying it, year after year. But what's the use? – In the end you've got to admit you're just another drop going down the drain. There you are Ruth,' he spread out his hands, 'your poor old father's a failure – been a failure from the word go.'

By this time he felt a magnificent one, light-hearted and very hungry for his tea. Peace entered his heart. He leaned forward and touched Ruth on the arm to console her for the sadness of his story. She lifted her face in reply, puckered with sympathy. He was surprised by a suspicion, gone the next moment, that she was looking ill; perhaps it was seeing her face so close and with her eyes screwed up against the sun.

'You make it sound much worse than it is,' she said. 'You can be proud of yourself in so many ways. You've always worked hard, and if you worked hard at a job you didn't like, why, so much the greater credit to you.' She built up the castle again, brick by brick, with deft and gentle fingers. 'Everyone pretends he can do things he can't do, there's no need to be ashamed of that. And then there's Teresa – what would have happened to her, do you think, if it hadn't been for you?'

He pushed at that brick and made it wobble for the pleasure of having her steady it: 'Oh, well, I suppose Lilian would have had her. Who can say, it might have been for the best.'

'But Lilian hasn't wanted her for ten years,' said Ruth, correcting him with a sweet reason. 'She's only just begun to want her now. Father dear, you mustn't be morbid about yourself. And just think, if it wasn't for you I shouldn't be alive today – isn't that something?' she asked, her head bent very low, sewing blindly. He let the question go.

'Poor little Teresa,' he mused from the heights of his re-established confidence. 'She hasn't had it easy all the time. It's not all her fault she's such a – a difficult child. May did her best – she meant to be good to her I know. But I sometimes thought she was just a bit hard. Children aren't really up her street, she's said so herself. And girls aren't like boys – you can't handle 'em all the time with a stick. I'm not suggesting May beat her; but you know what I mean. Girls want spoiling. I don't mean spoiling exactly, I mean looking after, under-standing. Love,' said Mr Digby in a loud cross voice. 'That's what they want, and if they don't get it, they miss it, poor little beggars. You know, I've sometimes wondered if Teresa's got a kink. Once or twice I've really thought she wasn't quite normal.' There was a silence. 'But she'll be all right now,' said Mr Digby. He looked at his elder daughter adoringly, folded his hands, put away worry with a great sigh of satisfaction. 'Edwin's a nice fellow,' he added, to round off the whole agreeable conversation. More and more he inclined to the feeling that everything was all right now. Overdue tides of relaxation engulfed him, lifted him on a pacific swell, washed him like a cork, this way, that way, in no direction.

The house-boy carried a tea-tray across the lawn, and almost immediately afterwards Edwin drove in. He came over the grass with a tired step, clogged with sweat. He looked like a walking piece of rope, unfashionably dull-coloured amongst the greens and scarlets, the sunlit whites. Yet he is more dramatic, thought Ruth, he and his shadow approaching, than any part of his exotic surroundings. If only, she thought, he could always be coming across the grass towards me, like this, and I could always be waiting, like this, to pour him out a cup of tea, everything would be all right. And she tested herself, saying: supposing that tiger bounded out between us now, should I be afraid? I admire him too much, she thought, as he dropped down into a chair beside her, it blocks the way. If, she thought, we could only live in the moment, and, since it will neither repeat itself nor petrify, die when the moment passes without a word, then everything would be all right. If I said to him now: Go back and come across the lawn again, it would be no use – the moment is over. To remember it is madness. As she reached out for the silver tea-pot, Edwin said:

'Teresa and Richard go off all right?'

'They went – in the end – reluctantly. Teresa didn't want to go.'

'And Richard didn't want to take her?'

'I wish they'd make friends. They'd be such good company for each other, and after all there isn't really much difference in their ages.'

'It isn't a question of ages,' said Edwin equably. 'You can't feed Teresa fourteen-year-olds, even supposing there was someone else of fourteen round here, which there isn't. Teresa's age doesn't go in years. And as for poor Richard, think what sort of a girl he's dreamed of driving about in that car of his; pigtails must be an awful substitute.'

'But that's absurd, Edwin.'

'No, it's not absurd. I should think Teresa's having a terrible afternoon. Lots of good women being nice to her and not a word to say for herself; but if Richard wins a couple of sets he'll be all right in spite of Teresa. I've fixed up for two dug-outs on Sunday, by the way. Or have you forgotten – you know, your picnic.'

'But Edwin, we'll want three dug-outs at least, and anyway it's not my picnic – it's *a* picnic, *our* picnic.'

'Well,' said Edwin, stretching out his legs in front of him, 'I thought it might be nice for Richard to paddle Teresa up in the little flat-boat. Don't you think so too?'

'Oh, Edwin, you mustn't laugh at me.' She was laughing herself, and with a sudden gesture of confident friendliness, put her hand in his. He took it, enclosed it, without surprise. Mr Digby had fallen asleep, satisfied or exhausted by a plateful of cucumber sandwiches and a number of buns. They sat

there hand in hand, while the bees buzzed round them and the old man slept. And their moment of marriage lengthened itself into five, into ten minutes, began to imitate eternity, while nothing stirred and no one spoke except the husky pigeons out of sight. And Ruth was able to lift her eyes and regard the blue feathery Naga hills without pain, for in her hand she held a silence and a constancy to equal theirs.

VI

Sunday's picnic began in the classic manner, with a bickering departure. Richard arrived on foot, puffing discreetly, having scrambled up the steep short cut through the woodland. He was dressed much the same as on Thursday, in spruce white shorts and his expressive blazer. Instead of a racquet he carried a fishing-rod.

'Hullo,' said Edwin. 'Where's your car?'

'I didn't bring it, sir. It's such a little way I thought we'd all pile into yours.'

'Oh, well, I suppose we can. I suppose we'll have to. But five people, and fishing-rods and food and all the rest of the stuff – I thought you were certain to bring yours along.'

'It never occurred to me, sir,' said young Richard, quite wilting with the onus of his error. 'You never mentioned it. But it won't take me two minutes to nip back and –'

'Nonsense,' cried Ruth from the doorway. 'We've had six in the Austin before now, and Teresa hardly counts. What are you thinking of, Edwin? There's plenty of room. Richard, be a dear and help my father – he's lost something, I don't know what it is, and he can't make the servants understand. Teresa,' she called, 'are you ready? We're just going.'

But before they finally succeeded in going many things had to be lost (where was the bottle opener?), searched for, and found. House-boy, sweeper, chokidar and cook were all sent running in different directions. Richard turned the subject of his own car into a thorough nuisance by reiterating as often as a stammer how willing he was to slip down and fetch it. Mr Digby thought he'd like to try his luck with a gun and was offended when Edwin, who, for a number of very good reasons was unwilling to lend him one, offered a fishing-rod instead. Various disputes were waged over trifling matters, such as where each person was to sit in the car, and in half an hour the impending picnic had turned sour, and no one wanted to go. Nevertheless they doggedly continued to go. Teresa had the bad idea of riding on the running-board.

'Teresa, don't be ridiculous, of course you can't. Get in behind quickly and stop making a fuss.'

'You'll be scraped off,' said Edwin in an undertone. Teresa, without another word, abandoned her determination and squeezed herself between Richard and Ruth on the back seat. They started. Just outside the gateway Edwin stopped the car.

'Richard,' he said, 'have you got the beer in behind?'

They began to search beneath one another's legs for the bottled beer. No beer.

'Oh, chokidar!'

The chokidar came running after them over the grass. Edwin waited until the man had caught them up and then he said quietly: 'Beer.' He sat impassively, looking ahead. The bonnet jigged, the engine throbbed, and a hush fell on the others, like over-rowdy children rebuked by an elder.

'Teresa,' said Ruth in a low voice, 'have you taken your hat?'

'No.'

'Well, never mind, you can have mine,' she said, still speaking hurriedly and glancing at the back of Edwin's head, 'I never get sunstroke.'

The beer was brought.. They started again, and drove up and down hill along paths channelled through acres of close-packed tea-bushes until the neat cultivation ended, wilderness fronted them, and the car could go no farther.

They parked and left it. Two men were waiting for them, naked except for loin-cloths and turbans, and wearing silver earrings. These were the boatmen, wilder in appearance and taller in build than the bungalow-staff. A footpath, so insignificant that it looked as though a worm had wriggled its way through the undergrowth, led into the towering, falling, jungle face. 'Watch your step,' said Edwin, walking forward into the gold-spattered gloom, and the others followed. Last of all came the boatmen, their feet turned out like fins, laden with rugs and baskets and fishing-lines and bottles.

The path dipped and grew muddy. Mr Digby began to groan, labouring down with a slipping sideways movement. Ruth managed her descent neatly, avoiding assistance from Richard. Teresa hopped from place to place. The startling thing about the whole outing, she realised, was Edwin's shirt: it was blue. She had grown accustomed to seeing him dressed in duns. The blue shirt altered him, made him seem a different colour all over, almost a different person. Every now and then it showed up ahead, as bright as a parrot's feather, flashing across occasional shafts of sunlight that clove the overhead layers of green. She noticed the huge leaves tangled waist-high about her and so still it was hard to believe an impetus of growth had thrust them up out of the ground. Innumerable creepers hung down from a great height, unstirring. The jungle was alive, and hid incalculable life, while seeming breathless. And light was everywhere, dark light, pale light, captured, imprisoned, deflected, reflecting, light unlike light and green as the bottom of the sea.

They reached a small stream and began to file across it one by one. Then Mr Digby muffed an easy stone in the middle. Hearing cries from Ruth and some slight splashing, Edwin turned round to see his father-in-law with feet under water indignantly waving Richard's proffered hand aside.

'Are you all right?' he called.

'Quite all right, quite all right,' retorted Mr Digby, much mortified. He strode ashore and rolled up his dripping trouser-cuffs. 'Go on, go on,' he shouted testily. 'What are you waiting for? I'm all right. Feet wet, nothing to worry about.' He slopped up the incline. Ruth began to laugh. 'Oh, poor Father,' she said apologetically. 'How awful for you.'

All at once the echoes of light gave way to a full blaze and they stood in the open, immediately above the broad and scarcely moving river. There were the two dug-outs waiting, and moored beside them the little flat-boat, like a punt cut in half.

Ruth and Mr Digby were settled in one dug-out, Edwin and the gear in the other. The flat-boat was left for Richard to take upstream with Teresa for his passenger. Off they started, Richard making no attempt to keep up with the others who were soon well ahead, stringing out round the first curve. They moved forward into the still beauties like a speck of dust creeping across a giant eye. Such largeness of scenery confounded Teresa. The floor of water spreading round her, polished as though with deep green oils, seemed to have no currents but to lie quiescent in a mild and wide reflection. Not overshadowing, but spaced grandly apart, the steeps of jungle rose on either side to what appeared to be an immense height. The head of every tree, packed against its neighbour, showed as clearly as though it grew in miniature close at hand. And here and there where one had sprouted even taller than the rest, a thin sickly stem leaned out from the green precipice, as white as flesh. Teresa, discounting Richard, which she found easy enough to do, and with her back turned on the two dug-outs, fancied herself alone, and gave herself over to one of her most dangerous conceits: that of identification with inhuman powers. She, small but intensely human, crawling at the foot of these old hills, became their focal point, bringing into them her sensational and beating heart as sacrifice and receiving in return their vast dimensions like a confidence, their heat like a thinly veiled secret.

'Teresa,' said Richard. 'You might sit in the middle. The weight's all over on one side and it makes it hellish hard to move the thing, I can tell you.'

There, after all, was Richard. Her frenzy broke. She saw

the patches of sweat staining his shirt. His face was unbecomingly flushed. Looking at him critically, she wondered if all men's knees were as ugly as his.

'Shall I take a turn? Are you tired?'

'Good lord, you couldn't shift this tub on your own for five seconds. But there's another paddle somewhere – you're sitting on it. You can help a bit with that if you like. But you'll have to turn round.'

'Well, I know that,' said Teresa contemptuously.

'Careful – for God's sake – what do you think you're doing?'

'Turning round. It's got a flat bottom, hasn't it? Flat bottoms don't overturn.'

'Don't they just! If you dance about like a lunatic anything overturns.'

'I don't suppose it's deep,' said Teresa calmly. 'Anyway, I'm sitting now; you needn't be nervous.'

Richard looked at the narrow back in front of him with hate. Teresa undid him completely. He would have liked to ignore her, or, failing this, to patronise her, but somehow she made either attitude impossible and he was a schoolboy again, wanting to pull her pigtails right off her beastly little head. Useless to remind himself that he was assistant manager on an important tea-garden. When Teresa scornfully said: 'You needn't be nervous,' he wanted to shout: 'Who's nervous?' and give her a big push. And it was not the assistant manager but the dignity of the sixth form prefect that prevented him from doing so.

They struggled on, occasionally speaking.

'Shove a bit deeper, can't you?' Teresa did her best to oblige.

'You're dripping water down my back,' she said.

'I'm sorry – it runs down the handle of the paddle. I can't help it.'

'Oh, I don't really mind. In fact, it's rather nice. I was just telling you.'

Ahead of them the calm face of the water broke into widespread confusion. 'We have to get out here,' said Richard. 'Rapids. It's all right, it only comes as high as your knees.' Teresa took off her shoes and obeyed him. Her bare feet slithered over round slimy stones that hurt her instep and rolled across her toes. Water churned and bubbled round her shins and leapt, spitting, above her knees. A fuss of breaking water filled her ears.

'I don't call these rapids,' she called. 'They're more like shallows. I thought rapids were dangerous, like waterfalls or something.'

'You're meant to be pushing the boat, not hanging on to it,' said Richard.

The hubbub ceased. The buffeting was behind them. The water joined itself together, mirror-smooth, ahead. Richard held the boat steady while Teresa clambered in. Without a word exchanged they set off, dipping their paddles like a team. Puffing and splashing, they rounded a bend, and there were the two dug-outs drawn up on a spur of rocks and shingle, and Edwin swimming to meet them. He flung an arm over the side of the boat. 'Ruth says, you must wet your head. She forgot to give you her hat.'

'Wet it,' said Teresa, leaning down. He scooped handfuls of the bright river water over her bending neck until she lost her breath and laughed and shrieked: 'Enough, stop it, that's enough!'

Suddenly, without reason, like a flame springing into being without a match, the picnic turned itself into a party. Ruth was standing, tall on the shore, calling out and waving. A little way off pottered Mr Digby, draping his shoes and socks on a boulder to dry. At the farthest end of the beach, as far away as possible, the two boatmen had built a fire and were boiling water for tea. It was reunion, camp in the jungle, travellers meeting travellers: they were bound to be glad. Then Richard stretched out his hand and pressed down her dripping head to submerge it altogether. With a loud 'Oh!' of surprise, she toppled overboard, and the party turned into nonsense.

'Can you swim?' said Edwin, grasping her arm.

'Yes, a bit,' she answered, her eyes drowned, her mouth full of water.

'Hang on to my shoulder.'

Richard's petulance had vanished. He paddled alongside, apologising, offering help. 'I didn't mean to push you in, Teresa, only your head.'

They waded ashore. Everything sparkled hot and cold, like the water on her lashes. No one was angry. Ruth was laughing. 'You must change, Teresa, quickly. Did you bring your bathing-dress?'

'I haven't got one.' She stood meek, in a daze of happiness, rooted to the burning shingle.

'If you wait two seconds I'll make you one,' said Richard. Edwin put his wet arm round Ruth, and she made no objection, standing like a pillar for him to lean on. Richard pulled a cushion out of the flat-boat and taking a knife slit it open at one end.

'I don't see what you're going to do,' said Teresa.

'Wait a minute; I'm making you a bathing-dress. I did the same thing once before for my sister. You'll see. It's easy.' He rummaged out the horsehair stuffing, and then, holding up the empty bottle-green cover, beat and shook it and slapped it on the stones. Teresa, overcome with curiosity, sat down in a puddle beside him to watch.

'But it's a bag. It's a pillow-case.'

'Wait. Wait.'

Edwin and Ruth had wandered away with erratic steps, like lovers. Richard sliced two holes in the cotton. 'Those are for your legs,' he said, 'and these are for your arms. You see – there you are.' He lifted his voice and screwed his head round. 'Mrs Tracey, have you got two safety-pins?'

'Lunch is ready,' said Ruth.

'I never knew you had a sister,' said Teresa to Richard. She took the ruined cushion-cover from him, liking him and smiling, and went behind a rock to put it on. Holding it to her shoulders with both hands she then went over to Ruth, who was kneeling by a basket, and said: 'Pin me, please.'

Ruth looked up and began to laugh. 'Oh, Teresa! Richard, what have you done to her?' She called out to Mr Digby who was prowling about on his own, searching for any indigenous objects of curiosity: 'Father, you must look at Teresa.'

She was funny. She had rocketed to stardom. She was popular. They were all laughing at her. Gratitude made her tremble. She recalled another bathing-dress, another time, a time of pain; but that was long ago, a part of the old past. Ruth stood up and with unmistakable affection fastened the oddity of a garment on either shoulder. As a finishing touch she heaped Teresa's plaits on top of her head and secured them there with two of her own hairpins. Teresa saw their unguarded self-forgetful faces looking up at her and felt they were strangers. And if Teresa had died next day, it was like this she would have been remembered: torso boxed in a bottle-green cushion cover, arms and legs emerging from the corners, her neck recovered from schoolgirl disgrace and appearing for the first time as long and white as a stick of celery newly pulled out of the earth, the whole droll spectacle maturely crowned with a heap of dark and dripping hair. Then she sat down and they ate their lunch.

It was afternoon. They yawned. They lit cigarettes. Anxiety to keep awake drove them apart on different occupations. Their bay was bounded on one side by a spearhead of rock and Richard, taking his fishing-rod, scrambled out on to the farthermost tip and began casting with an air of great keenness. Edwin, leaning on an elbow, watched him for some moments, his eyelids lowered from a sort of emphatic laziness. Then he picked up his own rod and pushing the flat-boat out a few feet, waded after it. He bent and held the boat with one hand from gliding away. The water lying under the lee of the rock was calm as a pool, and of a slight pellucid greenness that seemed, even at close quarters, to be intrinsic rather than borrowed.

'Ruth,' he called back. 'Come with me, will you?'

'If you like.' She smoothed her skirt and sauntered down the shingle.

They slid forward without the touch of a paddle, turned idly in a half-circle, and began to drift towards the torrent that poured round the point of the rock where Richard stood.

'If we get too close, shove her back with the paddle a bit,' said Edwin, speaking over his shoulder.

Ruth, leaning against the remaining cushion, dipped her fingers overboard. As the boat spun slowly round each facet of their picnic-world appeared in turn before her. There were the boatmen, gravely patrolling a strip of fine white sand that fringed the far end of the shingle. They carried sticks with which they were carefully poking the soft ground. Teresa, mystified, hovered as near as she dared behind them. Their still-smoking fire swung into view, then a long stretch of neglected shingle, its virgin desolation presently interrupted and claimed by a litter of bags, baskets, sunshades and cast-off clothing. Some yards removed sat Mr Digby who, having found a large flat rose-coloured slab of stone, was engrossed in the creation of an impromptu sundial. He had taken his watch off his wrist and laid it beside him on the pebbles for frequent reference. At this moment, not knowing that Ruth observed him, he picked it up, looked at it crossly, gave it a disappointed shake and held it to his ear: sun or clock, one or the other, had disagreed with his calculations. The boat continued to revolve on the same light current and her vision

was carried on. She saw where the bulwark of rock sprang hugely out from its screen of trees and green growth, and how it sloped, bare of any covering, unfretted by waves, as solid and smooth as the muscles of an athlete, down to the point on which young Richard stood, legs apart, fishing away with persistence, zeal and hope, and striking the eye, if not the sympathy, in his bright white shorts and shirt, erect against a leaf-and-water background. And still the boat revolved, till leaf-and-water, dark in the shade, was all that lay in front of Ruth, all except Edwin's calm immutable back, which, as a constant, had revolved with the boat a complete circle. He fished. His face was turned away from her.

How could he be content, she wondered, to wait for fish that never rose, while she sat so close and subtle behind him? How was it possible for him to remove his attention entirely from her and give it to fish, or to nothing? To be lying beside him now on the hot pebbles, their two heads housed beneath a sunshade, aware, whether they spoke or were silent, whether they touched or were separate, only of one another, and of one as another: this is how she would have had their time together spent and not wasted. And then, before the sun cooled or an extraneous thought pressed upon the bubble-state to break it, she would get up and leave him, and walking half an hour or so in the right direction, would reach England, and would never come back and never see him again. Such a healing knife-thrust as this she could and would have dealt them. But there he sat, Edwin, fishing, emptying the whole afternoon of significance, his face turned from her.

She leaned back stiffly, unable to relax, and nearly groaning from the torture of being torn between two exactly opposite desires – wanting, on the one hand, to strain herself closer and ever closer to him, and on the other, to break altogether away; but such a break would have to be made by her. Almost with ecstasy she thought of the terrible pain of this severance, a severance within her powers to accomplish. If Edwin were to be the destroyer and break from her, she would die; but breaking from him she would reach through death to life. She would surely live afterwards, strengthened, intensified by that brief anguish come upon her by her own choice instead of as a punishment. To live? To die? Or neither – life-in-death? Was it really her choice, and must she choose? She moved her foot cautiously until it lay, as though by accident, against his thigh. Edwin, who had been thinking of her, said: 'Ruth, why don't you bathe?'

He startled her. 'Edwin – you know I hate bathing.'

'You swim so badly.'

'I know I do,' she said, offended, frowning.

'I love to see you swimming badly.'

'So that you can laugh at me?'

'Yes.'

'I'm bad at being laughed at, Edwin,' she said in a low voice. 'You do it too much. It's unkind.'

'You've never been laughed at enough, old girl,' he retorted roundly.

'I don't laugh at you,' she said, with reproach in her tone and a hint of rising tears.

'My darling, you don't know how. But you'll learn. In

another twenty years or so. In twenty years you'll learn every-thing, even how to swim. More's the pity,' he added cheerfully. 'Go on, Ruth, in with you. Give us a treat.'

'No, Edwin. I'm not going to bathe. Why are you so eager to see me making a fool of myself?'

'I didn't say I was,' he answered pleasantly. 'I like to see you floundering. That's different.' She was nonplussed. 'It's the only time I ever see you floundering,' he went on, 'and I love it – love you, that's to say.'

'Edwin, no! It means you're against me.'

'Never!' he cried, shaken in earnest.

'Oh, yes. And I don't understand. It's as though you're always trying to score off me. Why? It isn't fair. Do I try to be dignified?'

'How do I know what you try to be?' he drawled, baiting her again with an affectation of cruelty.

All at once her indignation subsided. He was making fun of her. Very well. It was a part of the picnic. Was it not rather nice, after all, to be teased on this hot still afternoon that offered itself as an armistice? Her fears fell asleep. They were together now, sharing a mood. The mood was his, light-hearted as his moods seldom were, and the tightly-stretched cord between them slackened. She allowed herself to sink down into the embrace of the moment, smiling – smiles that moved her face involuntarily and made her happy.

'You're so absurdly romantic, Edwin,' she said resignedly. 'You even think the jungle's romantic.'

'And you think it's just a place where weeds grow.'

'But of course it is. Bigger and more weeds than anywhere else, that's all,' she said, nodding her head sagely with an enjoyable sense of being the elder of the two.

The jungle sheathed its claws for them, put off for once its dangerous character, and basked round about them, benevolent and harmless. But what an ambiguous and omnipresent symbol it otherwise was, symbol of an unhappiness, or an even more inflexible happiness, that lay between them always except at rare times like this when, united, they joked of disunity.

There was a pause. Ruth, looking back across her shoulder at the shore, could see Mr Digby still crouched over his stone scratching away at it and every so often lifting up his face to interrogate the sky.

'Father's making a sundial,' she whispered.

Their thoughts focused upon the old man, so near yet so unconscious of them. 'Always on about his writing,' said Edwin, keeping his voice down as well, for here distance acted on sound only to delay, not to diminish it. 'Every time he gets me in a corner it's the same thing.'

'And all nonsense, of course. He doesn't write. He can't. Anyway, I've never read anything of his except his letters.'

'You don't read them,' said Edwin.

'Well, they're always so full of blots and smudges I don't see how he can expect me to.'

'Poor old boy,' said Edwin softly, remembering those devoted scrawls and Ruth's distasteful: 'Oh, another letter from Father,' as she tore one open and two minutes later tore it in half. 'Funny to think of him teaching English. If I didn't know I'd have said he was games master. Much more likely from the way he talks. You know what he calls Richard? – a decent young shaver.'

Ruth began to laugh. 'Yes, I've heard him. Poor Father, he doesn't know how absurd he is, or how boring. How he used to bore me! Stamping up and down in front of the fireplace – I must have been about ten or eleven, younger perhaps – thundering out yards and yards of *Paradise Lost*. I had to sit there and listen. No wonder Lilian left him.'

'He's tremendously proud of his memory.'

'Well, it is astounding. Or it was, at any rate, though much good it ever did him. What's the point of knowing hundreds and thousands of words in their right order if you don't know what they mean? Browning, of course, was his chief passion – *The Last Ride Together*. "Since nothing all my love avails" – I can almost remember it now, I heard it so often. I think he used to pretend to himself that he'd written it. I must say he had a great reputation for keeping discipline – the little boys were frightened of him.'

Her soft, unhurried and very feminine voice dawdled on behind his back. That gentle stream of sound, it never varied. It was as exactly controlled as the turn of her head, and as she neither snatched nor fumbled, so she never shouted, nor spoke curtly, nor tripped over words in haste or vexation. When most angry, she was silent. When most offended, she wept. When she lied, not her voice but her eyes changed. Nothing, he thought as he sat there fishing, his back towards her, sounded with greater sweetness than her voice in agreement with him, discussing with mildly ironical amusement

her father, Mr Digby. And he considered that peculiar manifestation of the Present, living within but never beyond the Present: a voice. Voice: that gave to treachery its actual poison; voice: that commanded more ably than a veteran in war every shade of disingenuousness; voice: that was at the same time her weakness and her strength, shielding her, as she intended, with every word and with every other word betraying her as cynically as her best friend might do, behind her back. This voice he distrusted and loved was Ruth, more Ruth than any physical part of her to which he could reach out his hand and touch. For he could remember her words, the way she looked, the clothes she wore, but distance or death could kill her voice for him and, her voice once out of hearing, Ruth was gone. While he listened to her she was the Present and as the Present she was his, his heart, his pleasure and his loneliness. "'Since nothing all my love avails'" he murmured absently, and laid down his rod. Ruth had fallen silent.

'We ought to be going soon,' he said, turning round at last and looking at her. He touched her skirt, rubbing the stuff between finger and thumb as though appraising its value. They sat still, both reluctant to move, full of sighs. She put her hand over his hand and held it tenderly against her knee. 'Shall we have tea before we go?'

At this he looked searchingly up at her and began to smile. 'Yes. Let's have tea before we go. Kiss me, Ruth.'

She kissed his forehead. Edwin picked the paddle up and delved it overboard. The boat darted forward, stung by his sudden energy.

No fish had been caught. Richard blamed the weather. A day of rain, he said, would make all the difference.

'Does it ever rain here?' asked Teresa, incredulous.

Richard attracted his manager's attention to this remark – 'I say, sir, did you hear that' – and laughed heavily. Teresa followed her sister.

'Ruth, do you know what those men,' indicating the boatmen, 'found in the sand, buried? Two lots of eggs.'

'Turtles' eggs,' said Ruth automatically. Her mind was distracted.

'Were they?'

'Yes. What did they do with them?'

'Wrapped them up in leaves and then in a little piece of cloth.'

'I expect they're going to sell them,' said Ruth. She turned aside, as though her purpose – to tidy up their scattered belongings and make ready for departure – had been forgotten, and instead, holding up her skirt in both hands, took a step or two forward into the river, and then stopped and stood looking down with a perplexed frown at her submerged feet.

'I didn't see any turtles. I suppose they were hiding, were they?'

'Yes. Teresa, if your dress is dry you'd better put it on. We're going in a minute.'

Steps crunched on the shingle. The child had gone. Silence. But silence was not enough. She wanted silence itself to speak. She waited for a blessing. But no blessing came. And she knew however long she waited, still her attendance would be in vain. Her deeply-rooted hostility, the hostility of civilisation for savagery, would always prevent her from being received by this green kingdom. For she was no lump of raw metal dug up out of the ground, but instead a jewel exquisitely tooled and in need of a setting equally finely-wrought. She was essentially refined; the jungle, essentially crude. No amount of wishing on her part – and she wished it at this moment very much indeed for Edwin's sake – could close the gap and persuade a sympathy between two such incompatibles. Since this was so, since she finally realised this was so, the great reserves of vegetable silence and strength surrounding her became an embarrassment, as embarrassing as her own brief and futile supplication. She dropped her skirt, not caring that its hem draggled in the water, and turned away with a smile of self-derision. Edwin, dressed, came down to meet her. She took his outstretched hand and held on to it tightly as he helped her up the shingle. Teresa had put on her crumpled dress. Richard was combing his hair.

'We thought we'd go on, sir, if that's all right. I wanted to have a shot at fishing that pool above the bottom rapids.'

'All right,' said Edwin. 'We'll give you half an hour's start and pick you up at the lower landing. But watch those rapids, Richard, they're not so easy.'

'Oh, I know, sir.'

He and Teresa set off. The stream carried them easily down. A parakeet split the stillness with its wildly excited laugh. An insect somewhere started humming on a note so shrill, so vibrant, it might have been a noise inside the listener's head. Teresa banged her ears to be sure it was no illusion. They drifted close under the impenetrable eaves of the left-hand bank.

'I don't like being so near,' whispered Teresa. 'Do you think we're being watched? Animals – oh, Richard, there might be tigers in there.' He dipped a paddle. They glided away.

The next moment they were hurtling down the same rapids they had earlier toiled up with such laborious slowness. The water in places was so shallow that the bottom of the boat bumped and scraped over stones. They proceeded down in rushes and jerks.

'The other rapids are much more fun,' said Richard when they reached the calmer level, 'deeper than these.'

They passed the creek from which they had started that morning. Then the river turned and spread out in wide lake-like proportions, bearing on its surface the green impression of hills and streaks of light. Richard laid his paddle down and picked up his rod. The boat rocked. Some distance off a fish jumped. They heard the single plop distinctly, as though it was close at hand. Teresa sat, not stirring. Another parakeet cried out. Two men appeared on the bank of the river about a quarter of a mile further down, where there was a ford. One of them began leisurely to pick his way across, the other presently following. Where had they come from? Teresa wondered, where were they going? To see them strolling forward, apparently unconcerned at being without car or gun or clothes on the edge of day and miles from anywhere, affected her strangely. How frightened she would be, yet they were undismayed: this was their familiar suburb. They were their own policemen. One of them sang: his nasal wavering chant began, broke off; he waded on a few yards, lifted his voice again; again the long pause while the grave jungle attended with heat and silence; and again he broke the silence and made the heat ripple like water disturbed by a pebble. His song was incomprehensible, having no beginning, no climax, no conclusion. The cadenced notes reached their boat with absolute clearness, and the jungle became intimate with melancholy. Then the leading man called out to his companion. There was a brisk exchange of words, laughter – how extraordinary their laughter sounded in that immense auditorium! – then, reaching the farther bank, they walked forward and at once disappeared.

'Who do you think they were?' said Teresa.

'I don't know, I wasn't really looking. Probably Nagas,' said Richard. 'In fact, sure to be. The hills are stiff with 'em.'

'Where do they live?'

'Oh, dotted about. Here and there. I'll take you up to one of their chungs some time if you like.'

'Will you, Richard?'

'If you like,' he said, regretting his offer immediately, 'though it's a hell of a stiff climb up, mind, and there's not much to see when you get there.'

'You've promised now.'

'All right.'

The light turned golden. The green heights were suffused with a honey richness. 'Oh, lord!' said Richard. 'We'd better hurry. I'd quite forgotten the time. It's going to be dark in fifteen minutes.'

They scraped over the ford. A loud rustling sounded on one side.

'Oh, look!' whispered Teresa.

The rustling came from a host of monkeys swarming in a tree. It was impossible to count their number. They leapt off the boughs like suicides. Bamboo stalks, doubling under their weight, bore them to earth. It was nearly dark, still quiet except for this and other rustling, but a nervy quiet, and the trees seemed to have thickened.

'Sit tight,' said Richard, 'rapids ahead.'

The boat began to hurry, gave a violent jolt and was torn out of control. 'Look out!' Teresa ducked. A branch swept the air where her head had been.

'It's rocks I'm afraid of,' yelled Richard.

They were whirled past a stranded tree-trunk, appearing on their right like a black monster. Richard was bending forward, plying the paddle with no more effect than if it had been a straw. The water hissed; its lather showed whitely through the gloom. They were tossed, bumped, scraped, damped with spray, and finally cast forward on to comparative calmness.

'I say, that branch nearly got us,' said Richard, sounding much exhilarated. The river had narrowed to a form of gully, closely overhung with shadow and shadowy substance. It seemed to be as dark as in the middle of the night. 'I bet you were frightened, Teresa. You mustn't fall overboard now, it's deep here. That's an island on our right.'

'I wasn't a bit frightened,' she cried.

'I bet like hell you were,' he repeated stolidly. 'I could feel the whole boat shaking.'

After a moment's thought she said: 'I was exactly as much frightened as you were, and not a bit more.'

Richard held his tongue. It's just like being a kid again, he thought, resentful no longer at being betrayed into this former state. That was jolly fun, he thought, guiding the boat dreamily down the phantom channel. It's a wonder we weren't smashed though, it was quite a tricky bit, he thought, smiling all to himself in the dark. He held the paddle rigid and the little flat-boat, obeying him, turned in to the side. 'Here we are. Hop out, and mind how you go.'

'I can't see very well,' said Teresa. 'What a creepy little path. Are you sure it's all right, Richard? What about snakes?'

'What about them?' said Richard. His sense of elation continued. 'I'll go ahead. You'd better hold on to my belt. It isn't far. Pity we haven't got a torch.'

'I don't like talking so loud,' whispered Teresa. 'Nobody else is.'

'Well, don't be an ass, there's nobody else to talk.' 'That's what I mean,' said Teresa, clutching his belt. They trampled up the steep path, slipping and grunting. Then suddenly all the danger was over. There was the Austin, its headlights shining with welcome. Voices called out. Doors slammed.

'We thought you were drowned.'

'We nearly were,' cried Richard.

Teresa's heart seemed to break apart and shower out flowers of gladness. The picnic was over. For the second time

that day they were re-united. They had grown used to one another since the morning and now, joined by the exploits of a picnic, felt themselves to be inseparables, a loyal band. Richard and Edwin had caught no fish. Mr Digby, fired with ambition to make a professional sundial, had lugged his rose-coloured stone along with him, and now sat hugging the slab to his bosom. Teresa's hair was still pegged on top of her head. Ruth sat in front, staring into the beams of the car, her hand on Edwin's knee. Crammed together as close as the most devoted comrades they drove towards home, each warmed by the fleeting and misty delusion that some pledge of faithfulness had been made to last for ever. They were all, at that moment, in love with one another, and it was this that made the picnic remarkable and caused them to remember it for some time to come with astonishment.

VII

The picnic was more than a point in history: it was a turning point. Immediately afterwards the pattern changed. The red coals cooled overnight, became as ash and clinkers and fell apart. The strong instinct of love that had drawn them together exhausted itself in the second of integration, and a monotony began to harp on their brains like a cricket chirping.

Mr Digby had a special reason for depression. Lilian had written only once to him from England, a brief and oddly laconic note instead of the vituperative pages he had been expecting. Some of the zest went out of his life. Had she

changed her mind? Had she been fooling him all the time, pretending she wanted Teresa simply to put the wind up him? Lord, it was hard to understand her. 'I'd no idea you felt that way about Teresa –' she had written. What did she mean? He had never said he felt any way about Teresa. In his carefully-phrased letter to his former wife Mr Digby had confined himself to compiling a long list of her own failings, and this answering indulgent scrawl both piqued and hurt him. He had indeed expected more from her, some show of fight at least. Had it been only a passing whim, her previous claim, or a trick or what? He felt disappointed. Disappointment haunted the bungalow.

Every morning Teresa was awakened by the noise of pigeons. Every morning she saw from her window the garden-boy begin to mow away the grey dew from the grass in long lines. Each time she looked the lawn seemed to be bigger, the labour of mowing it too immense to be contemplated. She seemed to have seen Edwin come up from the little wood-land with dead pigeons swinging from his hand a hundred times. All day the bees buzzed, the palm leaves crackled. The flowers hung down from their bushes, bright as sores, scarlet or cyclamen-coloured or mauve. Every afternoon an old woman doddered over the grass sweeping up the leaves. She might as well have been taking grains of sand from the shore to clear it: leaves fell behind her, round her, on to her head, slid down her bending back. Sometimes she gathered a handful up and crazily threw them ahead of her in the path of her brush, and they fluttered down to litter the lawn a second time.

Teresa was sad. She ached from the sun; she ached. For she had come close to people and touched them; she had thought them warm and solid, and at once they had melted and her hand felt clammy. Ruth had been fond of her only for five minutes and by accident. The dress she had started to make for Teresa had been thrown aside, half-finished. It never would be finished. Richard was rude to her again. Her father, from habit, she avoided, and Edwin she hardly ever saw; he forgot to talk to her. A sense of failure, of having made a mistake nagged at her night and day. She felt herself sur-rounded too closely by too many people, none interested in her. There had been a moment of dependence, which now appeared as a moment of lasting weakness, when she had ventured out such a little way, but so recklessly, on to open ground, what she had believed to be a meadow-land of love. But the step was false, the ground was quicksand, and when she would have shrunk back the path was closed behind her. Teresa was only fourteen. To be forgotten the very moment she thought she had been discovered and found precious was a punishment adult and terrible.

So, in varying states of dissatisfaction, these five people continued to live, isolated together. They felt they had noth-ing. They felt they had nothing because they felt they were nothing. And they felt that circumstances had withheld that certain addition, whatever it was, that could have made their lives complete. Circumstances were blamed. And this sense of having been deliberately denied each one his due by circum-stances vague but conspiratorial, gnawed like acid inside them. They deserved good fortune, they considered, as much

or more than the most fortunate, and for no just reason had been bilked of it. Their frustration turned to an anxious ennui, emphasised by the monotonous days, the sun, the sound of pigeons, the scream of the peacock, the passivity of the Indians who served them. Nothing begun seemed worth the finishing. Ruth abandoned her sewing. Mr Digby's slab of stone lay in the shadow of the verandah, untouched. The evenings began to get colder. Fireflies disappeared. Insects no longer hopped down the dinner-table and drowned in the soup.

There was no one to teach them what they had to know to be peaceful: that they were their own experience. That they were equally everything and nothing. That they could only be everything when they were content to be nothing. That they carried this balance like air and water wherever they went, whatever they saw, whoever spoke to them, whatever happened. Neither time nor geography could dispose of one element in favour of the other. Potentially completed as mortal compositions, their breath was the dividing fire and only when they died would air and water rush together and become something not to be determined by themselves. As long as they sought to make their importance physical it must escape and deride them, fleeing ahead like the most mocking *ignis fatuus*. Only Edwin remained aloof from the chase. Mr Digby had exhausted himself in it. And for Teresa there remained the possibility of giving it up.

Edwin, whose hopes, not large ones, lay within the boundaries of each day, was the most nearly happy of the five, for his disquietude was tangible and he had come to terms with it

long ago. Having made it his companion he took it stoically
with him on his Garden rounds, treated it with an almost
matter-of-fact brusqueness, and, as with any disagreeable
companion, permitted it to distract him as little as possible.

The plucking season was not yet at an end. Every morning
he drove the Austin down the bumpy paths between the solid
ranks of tea-bushes to see the brown hands, boned as small
as the hands of children, searching out with diving darting
motions the tender leaves. Such nimbleness still, after twelve
years, held his attention out of pleasure. The girls, facing all
in one direction, baskets posed on their upright heads,
advanced towards him, pressing their way slowly through the
stubborn growth, chins lifted not in pride, eyes lowered not in
modesty, arms held stiffly forward with curving wrists to
crop the bush ahead. Their bodies were hidden as high as
the waist. Saris of a limp and flimsy cotton hooded their
brown cheeks, swathed their bosoms. Against the dark flesh
their silver bracelets smoked with sunshine. High shade-
trees speckled the brilliant green acres with sombre patches,
speckled their yellow wicker-baskets, their white saris, made
their faces black and featureless. Like a small army, well
spaced out, resolute, forcing its way across a strongly-flowing
river, they advanced towards him, plucking tea. Edwin got
into his car and drove away. Every day was the same day.

Here were two men axing the base of a dead shade-tree.
He watched them swinging their bodies in and out. Their
shoulders glistened. They opened a wound in the side of the
white and pinkish wood. Then they wiped their brows and
taking a saw pressed it into the wound. The dead tree came

alive for a moment, its great bulk hesitant and shy on the verge of falling. They stood back and it fell, crashing across the air with a final terrifying concentration of power, and at once was finished. Its sky-high twigs nestled strangely against the earth and were trampled underfoot by the men who swarmed over it, lopping and slicing off the branching wood. Edwin drove away, a tree in his mind loudly falling.

He wore his khaki-coloured topee on the back of his head. He could smell his own sweat soaking his shirt, and petrol leaking somewhere out of the Austin. He stopped the car to light a cigarette. Down the path came a pani-wallah, trotting tirelessly along with his peculiar springy gait. His bare feet made no sound, but a metallic rustle of wire and tin preceded him far in advance. His burden was two great petrol drums slung from either end of a bamboo which bent with the weight across his bony shoulder, and at every step the tins bobbed up and down. Men hoeing left their work and came out from the undergrowth to squat round him. They held out large leaves and into these leaves, as though they were cups, he poured the salted tea. It dribbled down their arms and splashed on the ground. They drank and threw away the leaves. The pani-wallah shouldered his burden and padded off, the dry whisper fading after him.

Edwin travelled all round his Garden. He visited the nursery where sprigs of the bushes were being planted out and women crouched round them thumping the ground. He saw his labourers pruning. He saw them clearing scrub. The Garden was completing its yearly cycle; the plucking season was nearly over. Strings of women filed along the path with

their baskets; the baskets of leaf were weighed and carried in trucks down to the factory. The leaf was scattered to dry and while the days grew shorter the process went on. Every morning Edwin drove himself down the long straight road, white with dust, bordered with pampas-grasses, and the road-menders' tools lifted above their heads twinkled in the early sun like the shining tops of waves rising and falling. During each day he asked himself no questions he could not answer; his mind served his eyes. He was occupied and aware of nothing outside his occupation. But at the end of the day, driving away from the turbans and saris; from the brown limbs whose various and exact movements he had arranged; away from the toes and ankles ringed in silver; away from the green acres, his cultivation – then disquietude leaned on his forehead like a headache and said: Now you shall not rest.

Today was over. His topee lay where he had thrown it, on the seat behind. He drove slackly, leaning back, elbows fallen, the wheel loose in his tired grasp. Children, caked white with dried mud, were fishing with their hands in a pool. Buffalo loitered down the road. A cart drew to one side, half-toppling into the ditch to let him pass. It was nearly evening. The first fires had been lit. Smoke had begun to ascend in single pale ribbons, tingeing the air with a smell as good as the smell of cooking food. Little boys stood by regarding them, legs apart, little boys with a string tied round their waists and one small brass bell hanging from it against their sheeny naked stomachs. Coolies were wandering home to their huts, their supper of rice and fish, their vacant sleep. Coolies, Indians,

men: men not lovers, men without thought, accidentally fashioned, obedient, beautiful to look at – what was he thinking? He pressed his hand against his brow. The car swerved. I would like the moon to comfort me, he thought, I would like to wait here until it grows dark and to light a fire of my own and not go home. He passed the coolie-lines and the road climbed and turned towards the bungalow. Smooth grass ran underneath the wheels. He braked in front of the verandah and switched the engine off, uncramped himself and climbed out – he and his headache climbing out together, with his headache the master – and went up the steps wanting a bath and a whisky, wanting peace.

The Millers had driven over for a drink. At once, as whenever there were strangers or visitors between them, he saw Ruth at a distance. Dressed in a stiff black silk she appeared to him as a figure symbolic of tragedy, the world's young widow, shining mysteriously with loss. I am her husband, he thought, watching her, but she is widowed of all her other husbands, of more than husbands, widowed of much. I make a mistake in loving her: she is for watching, not for loving; a symbol, not a woman. When she moves – at this moment she crossed the room carrying a glass for Mr Miller, that dull kind man with a large stomach – I see her mind moving, I see a perfection and an end. When she puts back her arm, smiles, turns her eyes, I see an artist occupied entirely by her art. When she stands in a doorway she has already stood in the doorway one second before and been seen, by herself as well as by others. A sneeze would be involuntary, or a glass falling to smash. But this expression on her face, this slight waving

257

inclination of her body, these are cultivated as I cultivate my tea, precisely. Yet where I practise a job, she practises an art, so why do I quarrel with it? She stands in doorways, she looks in mirrors and I must remember what I know: that her instinct for doing so is more profound than a flippant vanity, more dangerous.

Swilling the whisky round and round in his glass, he thought: She consumes herself. He looked up and there she was, in her brilliant plumage of bereavement, like a magpie: one for sorrow. She stood on the opposite side of the room stretched to her full height, with white arms extended, offering gin to Mrs Miller. The rings were alive on her fingers, sparkling messages of pride. She exhaled an air of vibrant restraint. Her long neck was powdered. And the dark hair lifted away from her ears was a town, unlit and full of secret thoroughfares. Mrs Miller, whose only child, a girl always ailing at school in England, had prematurely lined her face with worry, looked up at Ruth from the armchair she occupied like a crumpled cushion – a poor enough adorer but one whose worship never faltered – and said she would take a spot, just a spot more gin, and then they really must be going.

I am wasting her gift, thought Edwin. And the two phrases beat in his head like a muffled funereal drum throughout the evening:

She consumes herself.

I am wasting her gift.

Mr Digby, boyishly askew on the small satinwood chair where Ruth every afternoon wrote her letters, was firing questions at his new acquaintance, Mr Miller. And tubby Mr

Miller, his red face aglow with the gratification of being able to answer and instruct, stood well back on his heels, advancing his stomach more and more as his gratification grew. Edwin prayed they might so remain: shop was the last thing he wanted to talk with Bob Miller or anyone else. He wanted tonight no discussion about the new-pattern firing machines. What was it he had wanted as he came up the steps? – a bath, a drink, peace. What he had really wanted was what he wanted all of the time: Ruth herself, transmogrified, become in reality what she appeared to be in pantomime, a woman warm and deep and rich with secret wisdom. If this was possible he would have his peace. Since it was not, he translated his need in terms of a drink, a bath, something to eat, a clean shirt.

Candles in a branched holder burned at one end of the room; a fire burned at the other end. Beside the fire, on a low table, stood a shaded lamp. The lighting ebbed and flowed with a wavering softness, building the shadows into intrigues, yellowing the white, modifying the corners. Every flicker hinted a dramatic conception of home, the tired man's ultimate resting-place, the cold man's welcome. Here, implied the candles, the lamp, the fire, you may be at ease, nothing shall shock you, nothing surprise. Teresa was mercifully absent; Richard, for once, had stayed away.

'Ruth,' called Edwin, 'can I have some more whisky?'

She came across and sat on the arm of his chair, the skirt of her dress spilling over his grimy trousers. 'Edwin, Father's had a letter from his friend, Littleton, that man he met on the boat, inviting him to stay. I thought perhaps you could spare the second lorry to drive him over. Can you?'

He smoothed the black silk with the back of his hand. 'When does he want to go?'

'As soon as possible. Tomorrow. For a week or ten days. I'd like him to go. I think he's getting rather bored here.'

'Yes, of course. Of course I can, by all means. Ali can drive him.'

He experienced a sense of relief. Some crisis, he dimly felt – so dimly it amounted to less than a feeling – was looming nearer, as clouds collect themselves together beyond the horizon. What he expected or what he feared he could not say; he could not put his finger on a reason for his premonition. It was part of his headache, a warning throb. Better to make ready; better to clear the decks before the cataclysm. He wished Teresa could go as well.

'Where's Teresa?'

'Gone to bed. A little fever, nothing serious.'

'Oh, good,' he said vaguely.

Mrs Miller had risen, more to show a willingness to go than to go. Mr Digby and Mr Miller came over, Bob Miller nodding, benevolent, trying to look wise, Mr Digby still talking. How the old boy likes to talk, thought Edwin, he must have people to talk to. How he jerks himself about when he talks, darts his eyes round. His state of war is a permanent state, because he enjoys it; no declaration of peace will ever end that war in life. And he was Ruth's father. What a ragged violent sort of inheritance, thought Edwin, this was to bestow on your child. A man might withstand such a mischief working inside him, being coarse enough, but not a woman, not a frail transparent creature,

not Ruth. He laid his arm protectively across her lap and embraced her knees, hidden by her long black dress like fish within a net: she shall not consume herself. She shall not be torn in pieces by inheritance nor by her own fault. I protect, I forbid, I prevent. She leaned over him, responding, seeming almost to smother him, sitting above on the arm of his chair. The Millers and old Digby stood round. He was at the bottom of a well, too exhausted to struggle up and over-top them.

'What are your plans for Christmas?' said Mr Miller, reluctant to give up his empty glass. 'We thought of slipping down to Shillong for a couple of days or so. Why don't you people come along with us, make a party?'

'I wish you would,' said his wife, in her twittering voice. 'My dear,' she said, turning to Ruth and pushing her head eagerly forward, 'do come. Do say you will. It would be so nice, wouldn't it, Bob?' She looked appealingly from one to the other. Edwin noted, as though it was important evidence, her awe of Ruth's beauty, her readiness to be grateful: admiration and awe, these were what Ruth provoked in other women, not envy.

'Oh, we haven't made any plans, have we, Edwin?' said Ruth gaily.

'No plans,' he repeated, dully.

'We're the most boring, the most unoriginal couple,' she cried. 'You mustn't try to dig us out of our rut; we really enjoy sinking into it deeper and deeper, don't we, Edwin? It'll take an earthquake, nothing less, to shake us up. We're quite middle-aged, prisoners of habit. We never go away for Christmas.'

She stood on her feet, shrugging her shoulders delicately, screwing up her eyes with merriment.

'Then you ought to make a change,' urged Mrs Miller, in eager imitation of Ruth's liveliness.

'Oh, no! We're too old for change. Really, I mean it. You and Bob are schoolchildren compared to us. You have to have your Christmas holidays, and your crackers and paper-caps and fun; and jellies for tea, and balloons, don't you, Bob? It's natural at your age. But Edwin and I, we've outgrown all that. It's sad, but it's true. We're half way to dying. A trip to Shillong would really kill us.' She slipped an arm through her father's, and leaned her head charmingly against his shoulder, wryly vivacious.

'My dear,' protested Mrs Miller, not quite sure of the joke, 'I'm nearly old enough to be your mother.' Bob Miller was rubbing a hand over his bald head, stupidly chuckling, his eyes fastened on Ruth's face.

'Ah, you don't understand. Years have nothing to do with it. We're elderly because – why are we elderly, Edwin?'

He saw she had gone too far and was frightened. Her eyes enlarged with panic. Her smiling lips closed hard together. He thought she was going to collapse and at once, like a ponderous domestic beast, he climbed up to her rescue, taking her away from her father and holding her firmly against his side.

'You're talking nonsense, Ruth,' he said, making a great effort, out of pity, to carry on her game where she had dropped it. 'Mavis and Bob are doing their very best to go – can't you see how hungry Bob looks?'

At this they began to make a shuffling departure. Edwin, still with his arm round Ruth's waist, drove them back, and they retreated, step by step, maintaining a bluff hilarity every inch of the way. Or the hilarity, more exactly, came from Mr Miller and was echoed in the cries and squeakings of his little wife. They climbed into their car. They banged their doors. But it seemed to be very difficult for Mr Miller to start his engine. It seemed to be easier for him to poke his head through the window and go on talking.

'Edwin – I've got a bone to pick with you. Knew there was something I wanted to say. Been meaning to say it all the evening. Why don't you and Ruth come over to the Club more often? Club night twice a week and you never turn up. People miss you. People are always saying, where the hell have those two got to? You haven't been over for a couple of weeks or more. There's a new lot of beer in too, good stuff.'

'Well, we're farther off than you,' said Edwin, 'it's a long drive for us. We're the forgotten out-post, right in the wilds.'

'All the more reason. You mustn't iso – mustn't iso – mustn't cut yourselves off. Go on, it's a shame for us. We miss you. You're our popular young pair, our brightest stars, aren't they, Mavis? – You've got to live up to it. We like to see you, and the women like to see your dresses, Ruth – gives 'em something to talk about. You've got to come over next Thursday, there's a film-show. Nearly forgot to tell you, there's a film-show.'

'Oh, splendid. Of course we'll come.'

'You will? That's fine. It's going to be quite a night. Everyone's coming. New lot of beer in. Hey, Edwin, how about coming over early and having a round of golf? I'll get hold of Stevens. We haven't had a round of golf since I don't know when.'

'Yes, I'd like to. I'd like to very much. Four o'clock.'

'Fine, fine. Don't let him forget, Ruth. See you then. God bless you both.' They waved, they called out, they reversed into a flower-bed, they drove – at last – away.

'I like those two,' said Edwin.

'Do you?'

'Well, they're fond of us. Bob Miller's a silly old so-and-so, but he's got a good heart; he's really fond of us.'

'Oh, Edwin! – what a shameful – yes, *shameful* reason for liking people.'

He was tired, and therefore weak, and she stung him. 'I think it's a great deal more shameful to despise people, as you do, for believing in your pretence of liking them.'

'They bore me. I find them boring, that's all. Don't exaggerate me, Edwin. I suppose you're going to enjoy your golf on Thursday, and the film-show afterwards. You know what the film-show's going to be like, of course? A torn sheet. A 1932 news reel. Pieces taken out of a Harold Lloyd film and stuck together. And of course there'll be something wrong with the sound-track, but never mind; pretty wonderful to hear any sound at all up in these parts. And there'll be a breakdown every five minutes, and the lights going on and apologies. We've had it all before, over and over again. And we'll gape and clap like a bunch of aborigines seeing the white man's miracles for the first time. Oh, Edwin, it's insulting; how can you enjoy it?'

'You know how easily pleased I am,' he answered. 'Yes, I shall enjoy it, the golf, and the new beer; and the film-show being a total failure too. I shall enjoy it; not very much, but enough to be amused. You despise me for that.'

'You always take the easier way, Edwin. You enjoy because it's easier to enjoy than go on hating. Any fool can enjoy. It's such – *such* a waste of time.'

'Of you?' he asked, sadly. She was silent. He disengaged his arm from her as slowly and sadly as though he was letting her go for the last time, and she went into the bungalow ahead of him. A strong smell of curry filled the living-room. The house-boy was standing in the far doorway, waiting to tell them dinner was ready. Mr Digby was bending over the tray of drinks, pouring himself another whisky. The fire had fallen; embers had taken the place of flames.

VIII

Mr Digby departed the following morning on his visit to Mr Littleton. Teresa had not been invited. The lorry drove him off at half-past nine, his chin sunk in a woollen scarf, a hat crammed on his head, too fussed to be jocular, for he dreaded the hundred miles of bumping and dust that lay in front of him. Also at the back of his mind was the fear that he might have forgotten to pack something of vital importance, like his razor or his strop, and this anxiety unmanned him. At the last moment he waved, nearly falling out of the lorry as it swerved, and called something across his shoulder. It sounded like a question, but the words were lost.

His absence made a lull. The bungalow was quieter. For Mr Digby had a habit of knocking over chairs and dropping spoons and forks at table, more from nervous than clumsy fingers. Now there were no more crashes, no more upset ash-trays. The vacuum spread wider, locking the bungalow and garden in a bland conspiracy of silence. Nothing happened.

Teresa stayed in bed for several days with a slight fever and a heavy lassitude. On Thursday evening she got up and dined alone, Edwin and Ruth having driven over that afternoon to the Club, Edwin to play golf with Bob Miller, Ruth to have tea at the burra-bungalow with the burra-sahib's wife and dogs.

Teresa ate prodigiously, sitting at one end of the table, hedged in by candles. Quantities of food disappeared inside her angular body without seeming in any way to swell it. Sitting extremely straight up, but with her head reaching, even so, less high than the tall surrounding candle-flames, her ankles tidily crossed beneath her chair, she munched unfalteringly through the succeeding dishes of fish, eggs, chicken, numerous vegetables, half a pomelo and four bananas. As though it was a duty to make a feast of her solitary state, she ate without pleasure and, of necessity, in silence, served by the house-boy, Nidar. She wished they could have had a conversation. She wanted to talk politely to someone. But he understood only a smattering of English, and she could think of nothing to say beyond 'Thank you' – words which he understood less, perhaps, than any other words. He hid behind the door and watched her, appearing with

noiseless promptitude the moment a last mouthful was off her fork to whip away her plate and substitute another. She saw him peeping through the crack and called loudly: 'Nidar.' He glided up to her at once, and stood attentive in his white turban, his neat close-fitting white coat which reached to his knees with buttons down the front. The candles confused her eyes. His brown face appeared beyond them, darkly foreign, expressionless, still as wood, waiting for her order. 'Lemonade, please,' she said. He brought her lemonade. She was proud of herself.

She wandered about the bungalow eating her fourth banana, trying to enjoy a feeling of possession. But Ruth was everywhere, she pervaded every room. She moved in every shiver of flame, every twist of smoke. The doorways were her empty frames, every polished table was her mirror, waiting for her to bend above it. The bungalow was obsessed by her, holding her spirit everywhere with brooding impatience. Teresa was not allowed to be owner even for an hour of another woman's enigmatic garments of furniture. She had never felt so misplaced or so unwanted. She listened for the car. She glanced continually towards the clock, wishing them to come at once, wishing they might never come, and her heart beat inside her like the clock, keeping the same time. She wished she could have been dead without having to die. She tried to read. She stirred the fire. She could not go to bed. It was impossible to leave the house: the night outside was full of menace. Suddenly in the distance a pack of jackals burst into their wild chorus, laughter that ended in screams of torment. It sounded like the cries of children drowning, mingled with the cries of the wretches who drowned them: fear, remorse, hate and a hellish mockery jumbled together in one shrill discord, and swept towards the house. Teresa leapt to her feet, quivering with horror. The jackals – monsters, devils, whatever they were – seemed to be only a few yards away, on top of her, overrunning the garden, when, abruptly as it had begun, the babel ceased without a whimper. Not a yap, not a scuffle followed, only a dead and eerie silence.

Ten minutes later she heard the Austin changing gear on the bend of the hill. Hurriedly leaving the room, she undressed and was in bed, her eyes shut, by the time Edwin and Ruth had climbed up the verandah steps. Apparently Richard was with them, for she heard his toneless laugh, a giggle as staccato as machine-gun fire, sounding at regular intervals, shooting down any remark, joke or otherwise, with the same killing aim. Teresa kicked the sheet, glad of the chance to relax into ordinary contempt. Richard – idiotic, ass of a boy! Just to listen to him made her grind her teeth with pleasurable disgust.

They saw each other nearly every day and had become involved in a fractious relationship very much like love that hovered always on the verge of a squabble. They circled one another with an amorous enmity that called for constant wariness. Each was convinced of being the superior, but superiority such as this required proving, not once, but over and over again. And while they touched to hurt and their tongues were quick with jibes, a disdain for any form of retaliation and an immunity from it had to be flaunted all the time as jauntily as a feather stuck in a cap. 'I don't care.' 'Yes, you do.' This was the implied and rather wearisome burden of their intercourse.

The next day Teresa said to Richard: 'I want to go up to the Naga hills. I want to see a Naga chung. You promised I could.'

'Did I?'

'Yes, you know you did. On the picnic. When you were fishing. You promised; you must remember.'

'If I said I would, of course I will,' said Richard haughtily, 'though I really don't know when I can spare the time. It'll take us a whole day, you know.'

'Sunday,' said Teresa promptly. She knew he was free on Sunday.

'Sorry; I'm playing tennis.'

'Oh, *tennis*! All right, the Sunday after.'

'If you like.'

'And that's a promise too.'

'Don't be silly, Teresa, of course it isn't. I'll go if I can. It's quite likely I shan't be able to. I may be working.'

'You never work on Sunday.'

'You don't know what I do. You've only been here a few weeks. Don't pretend to know about things you don't know anything about.'

However, when the Sunday came he made no more excuses. They started early, taking Richard's elderly bearer with them to carry the luncheon basket which was stocked with enough food to feed six people. They reached the river and began to drive slowly down the steep deeply-rutted path towards the ferry.

'They'll have the bridge finished in another week,' said Richard.

Just showing above the skyline of the opposite cliff was a line of ox-carts, their hoods resting backwards on the ground, their shafts pointing skywards.

'Richard, look! What's happening? What are all those carts doing up there?'

'It's market day.'

'Oh, how lovely! Do they always have a market on Sunday morning? You never told me. Can we stop?'

'If you like,' said Richard. His policy with Teresa was one of unwilling capitulation.

The market was already hummingly alive. Scores of figures moved mazily about on the broad plateau that lay back behind the river-cliff. Their white cotton garments reflected the sun like fallen snow. And in between the white and brown people, at their feet, lay piles of sudden colour, heaps of oranges redder than gold, bananas, pomelos, and shining purple aubergines. Here were men squatting in a patient row with ducks wallowing, their legs tied together, in the dust before them. The miserable birds stretched their beaks open in soundless distress and fumbled about with their wings in a vain attempt to stand. A little further on lay a similar line of very small pigs, some no bigger than a foot long, glaring with furious red eyes through a mesh of bamboo that had been woven round them to fit as tightly as an outer skin. Here was the butcher, holding up with one hand a dripping knife and with the other hauling out guts like greasy rope, while a live goat tethered beside him moaned and shivered, and the vultures above wheeled closer. Here were the ox-carts Teresa had seen from the other side of the river, the oxen lying placidly half-asleep behind them, great mountains of beasts, while in the shade of the hoods fish of every shape and size, from the smallest serpents to creatures with huge toothy jaws, wriggled and gasped together on platters or in bowls full of cloudy stinking water. A stench of indescribable pungency arose from these dying river fish.

But it was not the silversmiths this time, or the brass-and-copper smiths, not the stalls of gaudy junk or the old medicine-man weighing up his coloured powders with the skins of dead snakes laid across his knees, that captured Teresa. For at this market there were Nagas. The moment she saw them every former foreign witchery paled and grew tame. Nagas! The rest of the market became a blur. She turned her attention on them with that almost fanatical concentration of hers which seemed at such times to sap all the physical life from her, so that it would hardly have been surprising if the thin little girl had dried up or even disappeared altogether, swallowed as fuel to supply that powerfully absorbent mental force.

How bold they looked, she thought, how savage and strong, like no human beings she had ever imagined, with their nude muscular buttocks and tightly-lashed waists, their women loaded down with brilliant cheap beads and in their own ears cartridge-cases and safety-pins, bunches of red peppers, scarlet hibiscus flowers and long swinging tassels of dyed goats' hair. They kept themselves apart from the rabble of plainsmen, to trade with whom they had come down from their hills,

bringing pan-leaves, now stuffed into baskets, and mats of dried palm, uncurling on the ground like golden skins. They had made their own encampment in the shade of a group of tall trees and here had built fires and were crouching round them, cooking food. Acrid smoke with no wind to blow it away, rose up straightly and mingled with every other smell. The men were naked except for a fringed apron; their women wore a larger piece of the same stout cloth, dark red or blue, wound round beneath the armpits and falling as far as the knees.

Teresa refused to be dragged away by Richard. She lingered, staring. These people were new. They puzzled her deeply and moved her with excitement. She was more or less accustomed by now to the coolies she saw every day in and round the bungalow, and accustomed to the idea that in relation to them a certain sort of behaviour was expected from her: much depended on whether or not she behaved according to expectation. She had accepted, too, the general precept that the coolies were weaker than herself, child though she was. But here, standing beside the Naga encampment, half in sun, half in shadow, her nostrils itching with smoke, her eyes fastened upon the activities of these small sturdy bodies, she sensed with a peculiar thrill her own weakness and inconsequence. She felt they were killers, not servants, and edged greedily closer. And if she stared they stared as hard, not dropping their glances as the coolies did, but gazing back with an equal curiosity from those slanting eyes set so far into their heads that when they laughed the flesh creased up and shut them out of sight. They were different in every way from the brown men she already knew. Even their manner of walking was different, for whereas the plains-people had a way of drifting vaguely and lightly along, these Nagas strode with fast and purposeful steps. It was indeed this air of independence that drew Teresa so magnetically to them. They showed no fear and no hesitation. Nothing, she felt, could ever intimidate them, and because of this she was full of admiration, nearly worship. At the back of her mind was always the thought that to be brave one must be wise; those who were unafraid knew *something* that she did not. Again and again she had asked herself what it was, and she asked herself now.

They had come down from the hills, naked but garnished with bright frippery and flowers. Was it the hills that had made them as they were? Did you learn *something* in the hills? She turned her head. Below lay the placid river, shining white, with children twinkling in and out, and cows moving slowly down to the edge to drink. A woman was pounding her washing beside it. A dug-out passed upstream, silently poled. Behind her the confusion of the market-place continued with its piercing smells, its loud buzz of bargaining, its churning white garments. But far away, beyond banana palms and paddy-fields, beyond the plains and faint from the full glare of the sun, she saw the blue smoky bulk of the Naga hills rise up expecting her.

Richard tugged at one of her pigtails, a gesture of his she hated above every other gesture. 'Come on, Teresa; do you want to see this chung of yours or not? If you do we've got to go, and we'll have to step on it too; it's ten o'clock.'

They drove down a road that was raised to a higher level than the paddy-fields lying on either side, so that it seemed to

be a long bridge of white dust running straight for a mile
or more away from the sun. They drove against a stream of
on-coming traffic; theirs was the only vehicle going in a
contrary direction, going from instead of towards the market.
Cyclists, ox-carts, little boys driving or dragging goats, men
with earthenware pots, or ducks tied up in banana leaves,
slung from sticks across their shoulders, women with bundles
on their heads and baskets of fruit: an unending caravan,
walking, trotting, driving forward through a cloud of sunny
dust to market. Richard held a middle course, hooting, and
they parted to either side of the car like surf dividing round
the prow of a boat. The sun was getting hotter every minute.
The sky was almost colourless.

Presently the road branched. They turned to the left and
began to climb. There were no more paddy-fields. The undergrowth closed in. The track was grassed over, unaccustomed
to motor-tyres or cart-wheels or anything heavier than a
naked foot. Soon even this ceased and only a footpath continued up and onwards. This they followed, leaving the car to
take care of itself, and attacking the side of the hill with an
energy that soon made them breathless. Their speed slackened. They began to toil upwards, hands resting above their
creaking knees, backs bent. Sometimes the path reared itself
up like a stairway with steps hacked out of the earth and no
banister to hold to. Sometimes it turned into a leafy country
lane, and here they were able to ease their muscles and
wipe their streaming faces. Once, unexpectedly, it fell sharply
into a small ravine, and they ran and slithered down to the
bottom, laughing as though at some extravagant treat. But

after this lapse it ascended unrelentingly up and up, and up and up they climbed for an hour when Teresa cried, 'Stop!'

They sat on the ground and Richard's bearer poured them coffee out of a Thermos, and Richard smoked a cigarette, and lay down flat with his head on a stone, feeling as pleased with himself as once, long ago, he had felt during the five minutes half-time of his first match in the Colts.

They went on. With every step the air grew purer. Chiefly the path wound through heavy shadow, lit here and there by sparks of yellow light, but now and again the trees opened and the sunshine fell like a douche of hot ice, so keen and clear, so invigorating. Signs of passing Nagas marked the path with an implication of secret busyness, an implication twice as odd in that, except for themselves with their loud puffing breaths and clumsy steps, there was no sound, no voice of any sort, no cry, only an utter silence. Had it not been for these ashes of newly-dead fires, these little bunches of herbs swinging from boughs, these wispy uncouth mysterious shrines, with tatters of paper and dried grasses hung from poles, these bamboos split in half and arranged like troughs to catch the dew or rain for drinking-water – had it not been for these hints, practical or mystic, of a people as prolific and industrious as bees, swarming inside their hive of hills, Teresa would have imagined that she and Richard were the first human beings to try that path.

They seemed to have been climbing for an age. Their feet were like lead; their lips tasted salty with sweat. Then, with the veering flight of a bird, the path turned and they emerged on to an open space with a precipice of trees dropping down from their feet, and very far below the land they had left, flat as a tray, blue and hazy, and stretching away for miles that looked, without a horizon, like infinity. They straightened their backs. They drew in breaths of air so sharp and strong it refreshed them as though they had drunk from a mountain stream. Teresa put her hand on Richard's shoulder and pointed:

'Look – isn't that the river?'

With a sensation of magnificence and triumph they gazed down at the ordinary ground of every day, and then turned round to climb the last few feet of their journey. The jungle was below them. Here was a pastoral sward, small bushes and a low fence, a place where shepherdesses or gods might play, or, alternatively, where Nagas might live. They stepped across the fence, and so reached the crown of a Naga hill.

An old man, the chief of the village, came out to meet them. He wore a scarlet shawl, because he was the chief. Behind him came children, and young boys, smiling and as lissom as girls, with long red leaves, like feathers, thrust through their ears.

'Tell them,' said Richard to his bearer, 'that we're very hungry; eat first. Then we come and visit.'

The deputation drew away. They ate, and the old chief honoured them by standing a little distance off, his back politely turned, arms folded, staring away over the tops of trees.

Teresa was in an ecstasy. She felt she was standing on a cloud in the sky, taken up to heaven by a hill. She felt that she had finally reached her destination, that this, though she had not known it, had been her goal when she left Southampton

– the highest, the farthest, the most remote particle of the world she knew. She cast off the bungalow with its oppressive mood of disappointment and expectation, like a garment that had irked her limbs too long. She was free at last of that flexuous interplay of emotions she sensed all the time; free of slights, demands, betrayals; free of that dangerous company of relations who called for a fighting spirit night and day; free of exhaustion. To this high Naga chung she had escaped, and here she was free. She would live like a Naga, and eat berries, and wrap a cloth round her like the women and let her hair go loose, and sleep on the ground, and grow brown in the sun.

'I don't ever want to go down again,' she said to Richard.

He laughed and answered: 'Yes, it's jolly up here. I'm glad we came.'

The huts were built on either side of a short ridge, their back verandahs supported on stilts over a sheer drop. They went into the headman's hut, a crowd of his relations or friends following. The interior was dark and, unlike the coolies' huts, spacious and neat. Vegetables hung from the ceiling, which was made of large fan-shaped leaves overlapping and shining with the same rich golden-brown veneer that covered everything. Weapons and baskets hung against the walls. The floor was of broad strips of plaited bamboo and resembled parquet. Bins of grain stood in the shadows. Baskets, bins, ceiling and floor were all constructed with the same care and craftsmanship, as cosy as a farm kitchen, and all were soused in the same spicy smell of pan-leaves and smouldering wood. Wives and daughters came out of the corners, smiling at them. They were taken outside on to the little platform which shook beneath their feet like tissue, and saw the other Naga hills retreat back and back, brow beyond brow, a crowd of hills without end and forested as thickly as hair on a head. Richard gave the old man a bag of salt. Teresa stared at the three brass heads threaded round his neck on a piece of red string.

'What are those for?' she asked.

'Heads,' said Richard. 'The Nagas are head-hunters. At least, they were. They aren't allowed to chop off their enemies' heads any longer, but you bet they do if they feel like it.' He touched the brass images on the sunken chest and said, still in English: 'You did pretty well for yourself. You must have been quite a lad in your young days.' The chief put back his head with a proud gesture and glanced round at his family, who burst into childish laughter. They were full of glee.

'They like us,' said Richard rather smugly. 'Lucky they do or they'd have your head in a bag by this time, Teresa.'

'Not really?'

'Oh no, of course not. Don't be absurd, I was joking. They think all white people are nearly as brave and clever and strong as they are. They admire us like anything. Come on, do you want to see the rest of the village? We ought to be going soon.'

'I don't want to go,' said Teresa. He was still ignorant of what she meant.

But when they had walked from one end of the village to the other, and had a tattoo beaten for them on the drum that was nothing more or less than a huge fallen hollow tree, and tripped over chickens, and been the focus of attention from a dozen or more young men decked out in beads and tassels and scarlet flowers leaning in graceful attitudes against their door-posts, then at last he understood. Teresa would not go. They were standing by the fence. Their bearer had hoisted the picnic-basket on to his head and was waiting.

'I'm not going,' said Teresa. 'I want to stay here. I don't want to go down again, ever, ever.'

Richard flushed. 'Don't be such a little fool, Teresa. It's getting late. We've got to get back to the car before it's dark.'

'I'm not going.'

All his good spirits, his feeling of being on a holiday, evaporated. 'You must be mad.'

As he said the words he realised: at this moment she was mad, out of her mind, abnormal. He was in a fix. He had no idea what he ought to do – give her a clout on the head and push her over his shoulder, slap her soundly, coax her? He tried coaxing for ten minutes. She remained rooted, her eyes dilated with demented obstinacy. Her malady was incomprehensible to him and so he was helpless. For this village on a hill was her Utopia; the bungalow signified for her the harmful world to which she was afraid to return. He tried ridicule, he tried contempt. He tried talking common sense. It was no use; she was mad, and madly resolved to stay. She refused to go home.

Richard was furious, and also frightened by such a responsibility. What would Edwin have done, he wondered, or what would Edwin expect him to do? He sat down on a stone and began to smoke excitedly, blinking and frowning. The situation was fantastic and yet it existed. Something had to be done: time was short. And yet, as far as he could see the best thing was to do nothing, to sit and smoke and hope that, left alone, Teresa would recover her wits. As a last resort he decided he would hit her, if necessary hard. Fifteen or twenty minutes passed in this way, then, glancing sideways he saw that the fit had passed. She stood a few yards away, her arms hanging limply. A hopeless and timid expression had crept on to her face. Richard got up, throwing away his cigarette.

'Come on.'

She followed him meekly, without a word, and stumbling as though she was tired.

I shall never have anything to do with her again, thought Richard, so relieved that his anger came flooding back with double force; she really is impossible. She's mad. I wonder if I ought to tell Edwin. I wonder if he knows. And he wished now that he had hit her while he had the excuse: it would have been a pleasure. He rushed down the steep path full tilt, not once turning round to help Teresa or to see how she was managing. Serve her right if she fell, he thought. Serve her right if she twisted her ankle. But then he would have to carry her; he slackened his pace. He reckoned they had about half an hour of daylight left, possibly a little more. He heard her give a cry as she missed her footing.

'All right?' he called out gruffly, embarrassed at having to ask her. She was gasping too much to answer. It occurred to him she might be weeping and so he reluctantly turned his head. No; she was not weeping. She was slithering anyhow after him, terrified now that she might be left behind, flinging herself from one side of the path to the other, her outspread arms clutching at boughs and grasses to prevent herself from falling altogether headlong.

'It's going to be worse when it gets dark,' he said with grim unkindness.

It was dark before they reached the car, and beneath the trees it was very dark indeed. Teresa, her eyes wide but unavailing, followed the sound of Richard's boots and heard him cursing. They had no torch. Teresa had forgotten now how she had felt on the top of the hill, that brief and intoxicated moment when her head had swum and she had seemed to be in heaven. She only knew she had been stupid, and Richard was furious, and she wanted someone to be nice, not cross, and kind to her. She felt hungry, too. She wanted warmth. She wanted to eat a large meal and then go to sleep. She wanted forgiveness, but not from Richard, on a huge and understanding scale that asked for no apology.

They reached the car. It stood where they had left it like an old friend. Richard drove fast and carelessly, making no attempt to avoid pot-holes. The car rattled and shook, sounding as though it was going to fall to pieces at the next jolt. The beams from the headlights jumped about on the road ahead. It was just before they reached the river that Teresa saw her first tiger. One moment an empty path of dust stretched before them; the moon was rising; the dust was beginning to glimmer. Next moment the pampas grasses on one side shivered and into the yellow glare of the headlights leapt the huge beast. It stood, blocking the road, its head turned towards the car, its tail held low and twitching.

Richard trod on the brake. The car ground to a standstill. He put one hand on Teresa's knee and dug in his fingers to keep her silent. The engine had died. There was no sound. They sat petrified.

Teresa thought her breath had stopped, but her body shook from the loud strokes of her heart. She felt Richard's fingers hurting her flesh. This was a real tiger, really alive, twenty yards ahead of her and able to kill her if it chose, to take her between its wide jaws and destroy her life. Tiger, tiger, her heart banged, tiger, tiger, tiger. It burned like a powerful flame, like a furnace, in the dark night, able to consume. Its eyes narrowed. They saw it snarl. Then without another sign it sprang forward. The farther bank swallowed it with a single rustle. The fire was gone. The road was ashy, unoccupied again and shining whitely.

Such an out-of-the-way experience healed the breach between them. 'I say,' said Richard, 'if only I'd had a gun. What a target! Lucky he wasn't feeling savage. I say – what a beauty!'

The bearer was laughing and gabbling away in Urdu. Teresa believed in tigers now: she had seen one, had very nearly touched one. They were real, not imaginary creatures, and lived in jungles and roamed about wild and appeared suddenly out of the night.

The tiger had acted like a tonic on their jaded tempers. Still with this pleasant astringent feeling of a beginning – that is to say, as though the things that had happened before the tiger no longer mattered, as though like a live coal he had burned away the dross of their complicated irritations – they crossed the river and drove merrily towards the bungalow, speculating on the reactions of Edwin and Ruth to this adventure. They had both been badly frightened and the fright having passed their spirits rose proportionately high.

Richard rushed the car across the lawn with a last burst of speed, played a tiddley-ti-pom on the hooter, and jumped out, shouting: 'I say, sir! Mrs Tracey! What do you think?'

Ruth came through the window of the living-room and ran down the steps. She went straight to Teresa and folded her arms round the child. Teresa scented her warm bosom with surprise and allowed herself to be pressed closely against it. How could Ruth know about the tiger or the hill? The embrace was pleasant, though suffocating. She heard Ruth say:

'Teresa, something terrible has happened. It's Father.'

And then she heard her sister sob, or anyway catch her breath in a peculiar way.

'Father's dead,' said Ruth, not knowing how else to say it.

Teresa pushed her angrily away and stared into her face with wild suspicion. It was true: he was dead. The compassionate glance, the puckered brow, told her it was true. The extraordinary day had reached its climax.

'Where's Edwin?'

'He's down in the coolie-lines,' said Ruth. 'There's been a fire, one of the huts. He doesn't know yet.'

Teresa stood in the middle of the living-room and looked round her. This was the room in which she and her father had arrived that first night, when every piece of furniture was unfamiliar and challenging. She had been hardly more than semi-conscious with sleep. The light had hurt her eyes. The voices of her father and Edwin, she remembered, had wrapped about her head like velvet. There were now no insects. It was colder. Tonight there were logs hissing in the grate. Otherwise everything was unchanged – except that her father was missing. He was not here. The balance was wrong. The weight was thrown all on one side, draggingly. He was gone; gone as that first night of their arrival had gone, for ever, though the room remained unchanged.

He was gone; he was dead.

He was dead.

Teresa burst into tears. Ruth, in some perplexity as to what to do, again put her arms round the child, and looked over her head at Richard who hung in the doorway, very ill at ease but willing to run on any errand. Mr Digby had been driven home by Ali, a lifeless body bumping about in the back of the lorry, not more than half an hour before. Apparently the lorry had developed a flat tyre. Ali had stopped to change the wheel. Mr Digby had got out to help him. Something was wrong with the jack. They attempted to lift the lorry on their shoulders and force a stake beneath it. They had struggled. Then suddenly Mr Digby had sat down on the ground – Ali described every detail with an awful clearness, himself falling down on the floor; Mr Digby had sat on the ground and bent over and pressed his hands against his chest and made a noise – like this – grunting and whistling, not a good noise. And then he had stopped grunting, and leaned back against the wheel as though he was well again. But Ali was afraid. He touched him. He put his mouth against Mr Digby's ear and shouted, 'Sahib!' He tried to revive him. It was too late. Mr Digby's overworked and agitated heart had failed him at last.

Ruth was more shocked by her own coolness than by the tragedy itself. She felt no grief at his dying and therefore it was easy for her to accept his death as a simple fact. Even its suddenness disturbed her no more than a household catastrophe, such, for instance, as the lights in the bungalow fusing. But her thoughts circled miserably round Teresa. She remembered something her father had once said, about children – especially little girls – requiring love; a most unusual remark to hear from him, and therefore it had lingered on in her head, significantly. She felt that he had used his last strength to bring Teresa these thousands of difficult miles in order to deliver her into the security of Ruth's protection and love, necessities that he knew he himself could not adequately give her. Having achieved his purpose, he had died. Seen in this light he appeared as a sort of hero, a very valiant old campaigner whose final effort had been honourable whatever his previous record. But his mistake was fatuous. For Ruth did not love Teresa. She did not love Teresa in the very least. She could offer her no protection. She was herself a needy and unstable creature, always on the point of fleeing from her own indecision. Her father's belief had been childishly misplaced. He had made a mistake and sealed his great mistake triumphantly and irrevocably by dying. His onerous charge he left to Ruth. She felt oppressed by guilt.

He would have liked to have known that he had his funeral pyre. For Teresa his death was for ever welded with the apparition of the tiger. The beast had leapt out of the night, burningly bright and savage, and her father had died. The night of the tiger, the night of death – they were the same, and the memory was branded on her brain. For Edwin the event was marked in the same way, unforgettably lurid, by a fire. He had come back, sooted with smoke, his eyes still dazzled by crumbling red-hot thatch and spurting flames, to hear the news of death. Only for Ruth there was no dramatic connection, nothing to remember but the empty bungalow and her cold surprise when the body of Mr Digby was lifted out from the back of the lorry.

IX

Ruth had announced that she was going to take Teresa back to England, to her mother Lilian.

'I simply cannot understand *why*,' said Edwin. The conversation had been going on for several hours. 'It seems to me completely illogical, the most pointless thing to do.'

'She ought to be at school.'

'Your father didn't think so.'

'Father's dead. He always did unreasonable things. What he thought was right for Teresa when he was alive was his business. But he isn't alive any more and everything's changed; I have to do what I think's right, and I think Teresa ought to have children of her own age to play with and grow up with. Goodness knows, she's unnatural enough as it is. This sort of life isn't going to help her to be like other children.'

'Why do you want her to be like other children? This mania for trying to force a child into a pattern. I don't understand it.'

'She ought to have a mother,' said Ruth, stubbornly.

'Oh, rubbish! You don't believe that stuff any more than I do, or any more than the old boy did. And besides, Lilian's cooled off Teresa again, you know she has. You saw that letter she wrote to your father. You're just saying all this about Teresa needing a mother for excuse. But excuse for what? Why can't you tell me the truth?'

'Oh, Edwin, don't be so ridiculous. Of course I'm telling you the truth. I'm just trying to be sensible. Lilian wants Teresa whatever she wrote to Father – she wouldn't have come all the way from America to get her if she hadn't wanted her. We've no right in the world to keep a child from its mother. Father behaved like a madman, kidnapping Teresa like that. I've always thought so.'

'No, you're not being honest,' repeated Edwin, shaking his tired head. 'Everything you say sounds as if you've learnt it by heart. It isn't convincing. It isn't even intelligent. Someone as unreliable as Lilian, a woman who can't make up her mind about her own child – if you'd an ounce of feeling you'd fight to keep Teresa away from her. I would. The old boy did. He was a fighter. What sort of a life d'you think her mother's going to lead Teresa? I can make a pretty shrewd guess, even though I don't know her. Teresa needs stability, as much as anyone can give her, not indecision.' He felt he was wrestling with air, and while he battled the ground slipped from underneath his feet. Ruth put up her hands and drew the pins slowly out of her head. Her hair began to topple and fall round her like undammed water. He saw her face in the mirror, terribly set, a mask of beauty. 'Do you really consider Teresa at all, I wonder? Have you asked her what she wants to do? Isn't what she wants important, more important than what you want?'

He watched her reflection closely. A flicker crossed her face. Her mouth moved and tightened. He said quickly: 'Teresa isn't too young to know her own mind. That was what you were going to say, wasn't it?'

She turned towards him, agile as a viper, her composure crumbling. 'Edwin, don't! What are you saying? What do you mean? Why are you treating me like this, as though I'm a criminal? I'm doing what I think is the right thing to do, what seems obvious. I think Teresa ought to be with her mother, and go to school, and have parties and friends and everything I had when I was young.'

'I see. And did parties and school and friends make you happy when you were Teresa's age?'

'Yes,' she said defiantly, 'I was happy when I was a child.'

'You've only been miserable since you married me? For eight years, in fact.'

Tears came into her eyes. He felt a deep contempt, for himself as well as for her. It was so easy to break her down. He was so much the stronger. Now she would weep and his contempt would turn to pity, as it always did. He detested himself for his cruelty. She makes me a coward, he thought, like herself, for I know the reason behind this pathetic sham. I know it all the time because it lies deep down inside me, a deposit of silver, the truth. I fight to make her admit it, only that, because admission breaks her and I break with her. We fight towards destruction; not towards finding, but towards uncovering. I force her down and down. I am cruel. I will break her, but I will have her admit the truth to me with her own mouth, truly, I will.

'You intend to take her back yourself?'

'Well, there's no one else, is there? She can't go back alone.'

'And how long do you mean to stay?' His voice was hard. He clenched his hands beside him, refusing to move near her though he saw the tears in her eyes gather and gather. Still trying to speak light-heartedly, she answered: 'I don't know. A few weeks, four or five. It's so long since I was in England.'

'We were going together next year, for our leave, anyway. Can't you wait till then? Is there such a desperate hurry?'

'The sooner I can get Teresa settled the better. She does worry me so much. And Edwin, it works out so well like this. I can see dull relations and that sort of thing while I'm on my own. Then you'll come across in May, and after your leave we'll travel back together.'

'You've made up your mind, in fact?'

'Yes,' she said, nervously, avoiding his eyes.

'Then in that case it won't be a matter of four weeks or so – it'll be five months. Aren't you going to be lonely without me for five months?'

She began to weep. The tears ran down her face imploringly. 'Oh, Edwin, yes, I shall be.'

With some difficulty he sat still. He was sweating. 'You're going for good, aren't you? You don't mean to come back with

me after our leave, do you? You've no intention of coming back again, ever. Why don't you say so?' He had urged her to go so often, to leave him, but to leave him openly, honestly, not in this underhand way, sneaking out behind the skirts of a little girl. 'You just haven't the courage to tell me now. It's so much easier to write a letter, isn't it, when you've put half the world between us as a bolster. It's so much less painful for you. You won't have to see me get the letter. You won't have to watch my face when I read it. But you know, Ruth – I wouldn't read a letter like that. I wouldn't read any of your letters. I should burn them, without opening, as soon as they came. Because I should know what was inside, every regretful, poisonous word. Every excellently thought-out sentence. You needn't bother to write to me, Ruth. I'm letting you off. I know it all now. It isn't news.'

He had forgotten whether he wanted her to go or stay. He had forgotten the laborious pros and cons of the last years, the long detached arguments with himself, the rational summing-up. His only intention was to hurt her in return for her having hurt him.

Then his bitter wrath left him. She sat on her dressing-stool, bowed over her hands. Her hair dripped round her hidden face like dark tears. Suddenly she bored him. He was sick of the whole fuss, sick of her despair, and of his own finished anger. He felt a deep dejection at the thought of the time he must have wasted in wrangling with a silly woman whose final answer was always tears.

'Ruth,' he said loudly. She was quite unable to speak. Her weeping choked her. He went across, lifted her up, set her on

his lap and began to rock her like a baby. 'Ruth, listen. I do understand. I know you've been hovering on top of this precipice for ages. But what I can't bear, what drives me into such a rage, is your weakness. You haven't the courage to jump, have you? You've got to wait for a mishap to come along and push you over. Your life depends on misadventure. Don't you think that's awful?'

He felt her cower closer in against him with anguished remorse. Again his mood changed. Great affection, existing constant and apart from his torments and doubts, apart even from what he called his love, that iron circle that so often closed round him, cramping his movement, restricting his sensible sight, distorting his appreciation – great affection, born of the eight years of her company, made him speak to and hold her gently. 'Ruth, that's enough for tonight,' he said. 'It's high time we went to bed. We can say all this again tomorrow if we want to.'

He leaned his chin on the top of her head and yawned. Unlike Ruth, he could never sustain a crisis: they always made him sleepy.

PART FIVE
TERESA

I

The days that followed were difficult ones for Edwin. He knew
that he could still, if he wanted, stop Ruth from going. He had
only to assert himself. But this was not, he felt, the time for
force. She must make her own decision at last, and he must
let her do so. Everyone's salvation is ultimately his own
affair, said Edwin to himself, and no one else's. The soul may
be born to its peculiar salvation, not once, but many times,
and interference to prevent such a birth seemed to him, in its
abortiveness, not only wrong, but stupid. Spiritual gestation,
he believed, should not be suppressed, it should be honoured,
and this however feeble or mistaken its attempts at expression
might be. To turn Ruth from her purpose now would decide
nothing, create nothing. Waste could only be added to waste.
Bully her he could, and by bullying keep her, but what would
follow? Surely, if one could imagine arteries as carrying sympathy instead of blood, a hardening of them from that time
forward. If, on the other hand, he behaved in accordance with
his faith – a faith which ruled that at momentous points of
one's life one should depend only on oneself and be allowed to
depend only on oneself – then he must hold his tongue. He
must not interfere, nor lift a finger to snatch her back, even
though he saw Ruth on the verge of flinging herself to her
destruction: it was her own destruction and she had a right
to it.

What troubled his resolution was the suspicion that she
herself had, buried beneath the complex contradictions of
her real and professed intentions, a single hope of defeat. Did

she indeed depend upon Edwin preventing her, at the last minute, from going, casting responsibility on to his adamantine will, her helplessness in face of it? But why, he asked himself, should she be traitor to her own determination? Perhaps because, fearing herself to be too frail to stand on her own, she shrank from the dangerous test, believing that she might yet escape, through him, the consequences of her stubbornness, and find excuse for escape. Or was there always, perhaps, deep in her nature a desire to be decisively overpowered? He did not know. He could not be sure of what was fact and what existed only in his imagination. The whole equivocal situation sickened him, so much so that, with every nerve and fibre of his being straining to keep her, he longed vehemently for her to go and be gone.

So the few, slow days passed. The last one came and by the end of it Edwin was alone. Ruth left him, and with her went sensation. He could feel nothing. It was like convalescence after a raging fever, and though the delirium was over he had no wish to recover. Wherever his eye turned it lighted on some token of Ruth, but no response stirred in him. His only feeling was thankfulness at feeling nothing; his only thought a prayer to the future, that it might be good to him in letting him never feel anything, ever again.

II

Slowly the train rattled along. Teresa had seen this same scenery in reverse order too recently to be interested in looking at it now. Ruth lay on her back on one of the lower

bunks, an arm flung across her closed eyes. She was feeling ill. They had hardly spoken a word to one another since the train started.

Teresa sat forward on the verge of the dirty broken leather, thinking of her father. Since his death he had occupied her thoughts exclusively. The morning after he died she had cut off her hair, sawing the two pigtails away with a knife as though they were dead branches. For it seemed to her imperative that some visible outward alteration should commemorate the tremendous invisible change that had taken place in her life. Ruth had shown neither surprise nor anger, only remarking as she trimmed the ragged edges with a pair of scissors that she liked Teresa better with her hair short.

'Your face is too thin for pigtails,' she said. 'It suits you much better like this.'

Ruth, during the past few days, had grown more remote and yet more tender, moving round the bungalow as though she was half-awake and sitting idly in the garden with her hands folded, looking away at the Naga hills, when she should have been packing her things or helping Teresa pack hers. Teresa missed the weight of her two long limp plaits as she missed her father: all the time. They no longer flopped against her back or dangled in front of her shoulders, and he was gone as well.

Since her earliest memory Mr Digby had overshadowed her. She had spent years and years keyed up in anticipation of his criticism, or his indifference, his wounding insensibility, his excitable rages, his even more jarring bursts of gaiety. For years she had attempted to muscle her puniness to meet his strength. And although she seldom saw him, she was never free of his presence. At school she had been a solitary, having none of the charms that make a little girl popular with other little girls. She was neither sly – for nothing at a girls' school succeeds as well as slyness – nor open: she was stiff, afraid of her companions even while she held them in contempt. The staff thought her secretive and they thought her sullen. She was the favourite of no one. It was as though she stood alone in an empty room lit by candle-light and the huge shadow cast behind her on the wall was not her own but the towering silhouette of her father, ever there. However, this room of hers had a window, high up and out of reach, and through it she continually glimpsed a land of sunshine and freedom. She accepted mutely the issues of clean new exercise books and obediently, as she was bidden, turned them into rubbish by filling them from cover to cover with blots and dates and theorems, for when every last page was completed they were torn in half and thrown away as so much waste paper. She suffered the prison regulations – if one lost one's rubber, if one came to class without a pencil, one was punished – with a fortitude more apathetic than disdainful. And always she kept her eyes on her bright window and dreamed of golden days.

Then her father had swooped down like a great bat and carried her off to India. During first the voyage out and then the stifling journey across India, they were thrown together in a close company and Mr Digby had been transformed for his daughter from a nightmare into flesh and blood. He had shrunk to life-size. He was more, she discovered, a dragon than a phantom, more actual fire and smoke than flickering shadow. She searched out his weaknesses. She forged herself new weapons. He was still, it was true, the dominating influence in her life, more so perhaps than ever before, but mutual experience is a first-class leveller. Their relationship in those few weeks developed a binding interdependent quality that neither could have credited as possible before. There were times when she needed her father sorely, times when he needed her. She had thought of him still as an enemy, but a familiar one, an enemy as familiar as a friend and she fought him accordingly as she fought out their games of piquet, with a cunning appreciation. And she had believed that in such a war they would continue until she triumphed.

Teresa had yet to learn that the relationships of people are never established, are ever mutable, wavering like seaweed on a tide. Places and time, new smells, new sights, new sounds, act as the green and uncontrollable ocean swells, washing emotions first one way and then the other, or bearing them altogether away from the rock to which they seem to be most firmly anchored.

Life at the bungalow, that empty even tenor of days and weeks, had imposed another pattern. Without any perceptible fracture the chain that shackled Teresa to her father had disappeared, evaporated rather than broken. Having shrunk to life-size he now faded out of all importance. He was like a dream remembered drowsily after waking. She hardly noticed him. He melted into the background of scarlet and green, and the blue distances. He dissolved for her in the hot midday sun.

Then he had died. Death brought him back to her with a rush as the old original shadow, swollen to giant proportions, vaguely reproachful as though, in forgetting to be afraid of him, she had forgotten a duty. Think of him accurately she could not, though she thought of him only. And her memory behaved with an elfish malice, flashing on to the screen of her unwilling mind pictures of him in his most absurd moments: in the Bay of Biscay, his trilby hat lashed on to his head with a woollen scarf; waving his arms at coolies; swatting flies; or slipping into the stream on the day of the picnic and afterwards bending over to roll up his sopping trousers – she remembered how startled she had been to see his legs appearing, so white, so thin, like a pair of invalids.

But worse than this, worse than any fantasy, her conscience smote her with terrible rods. For she had cheated at piquet, not once, but several times. While he was alive it had seemed a small point, an illicit victory, but now he was dead her sin became cardinal. And it was too late to confess. She had deceived him at cards as he had never deceived her. She felt unclean. The dark blot of her little crime spread and spread. Her punishment was to know that he would never know: there could be no pardon. The money remaining over from her piquet bank she had privately buried at the foot of a eucalyptus tree in the garden, a sacrificial gesture that would have pained Mr Digby very much, though this Teresa did not guess.

Ruth was feeling sick. She had intended spending only one day and one night in Calcutta but they stayed day after day. She longed to be at sea. She longed for fathoms of icy water to lie all round her, sparkling with waves. She longed for the wind to be getting colder, the sea greyer, as they left the Mediterranean behind. She longed to see clouds, black with rain, hanging over the English coast. She longed for the welcome of puddles, a glistening quay, phlegmatic men with sacking round their shoulders. She lay on her bed in a stupor, sweating with sickness, longing and longing for English weather and English commonness. Only the effort to move was too much for her. She needed to be transported to Bombay by ambulance or aeroplane, or by miracle. Her limbs felt like lead. The boiling, clattering journey by rail, burdened with trunks and Teresa, demanded of her more strength than she had. From day to day she put it off, and grew no stronger.

Teresa, who had been so glum in the train, seemed to be revived by the inferno of Calcutta. The longer they stayed the more lively she grew. Ruth was thankful to know that the child had a friend. This friend was a Miss Spooner, a little elderly woman who was stepping composedly down Chowringee the morning after their arrival, a white umbrella spread above her head. Teresa had given a cry and darted forward.

'Miss Spooner!'

The white umbrella had stopped. Miss Spooner's spectacles glinted a welcome. 'Why, Teresa,' she said, in that dry voice of hers that made strangers think of her as prudish. 'How nice to see you. It's just as well you stopped me; I don't think I should have known you. You look quite different. When did you cut your hair off?'

'Last week,' said Teresa.

She introduced Miss Spooner to Ruth as though she was offering her sister a handful of gold, instead of a tidy respectable-looking spinster in pince-nez. Teresa's pleasure was evident. Her cheeks were quite flushed. She hopped about from one foot to the other. Miss Spooner, although her manner and smile were cordial enough, showed no such signs of eagerness.

'I'm going back to England,' said Teresa, her eyes becoming round with tragedy. 'Ruth's taking me back to school.' All at once she thought of her father. Miss Spooner was bound, in politeness, to ask how he was. She dreaded having to say in front of Ruth that he was dead. She rushed hurriedly on: 'Do come and see us. We're staying another day, aren't we, Ruth? Will you come and see us? Do please come, Miss Spooner, please do.' She urged her anxiously, afraid Miss Spooner would vanish again, this time for ever. Calcutta was so immense, so crowded. There was such a glare.

Miss Spooner came to tea. Ruth and Teresa did not leave the next day, nor the day after. Miss Spooner took Teresa shopping. Together they visited the New Market. They bought little but they looked at everything. Teresa found her the perfect companion. She answered all questions. She listened to Teresa's expressions of her taste with interest. She gave her own opinions clearly. She was willing to stop in front of any window. She carried a gentleman's fob watch in her purse but never referred to it, showing no impatience and no dissatisfaction. She dealt firmly with beggars and vendors. She never lost her way. Neither the temperature nor the crowds flurried her. When they were overheated with walking they sat inside a café, their feet on cool marble, drinking lemonade through straws. Or sometimes, as a different treat, Miss Spooner ordered coffee and showed as great an interest as Teresa in choosing small iced cakes to eat with it.

She told Teresa that her own sister was better. 'There was really no need for me to have come out at all. She wasn't nearly as ill as I'd thought from her letters,' said Miss Spooner, speaking rather sharply. 'I'm afraid it's mostly in her fancy, poor dear.' Teresa imagined this unknown sister as a plump and querulous woman, always complaining. 'However, now that I'm here,' said Miss Spooner, 'I think I shall stay. There's nothing to take me back to England and I like Calcutta. It suits me very well.'

'I like Calcutta too,' said Teresa.

'Plenty to see,' said Miss Spooner, energetically. 'Plenty of life. And this lovely sunshine all the time, it's such a joy.'

'I wish I wasn't going. I don't want to go a bit.' She would have liked to have asked Miss Spooner to write to her, but felt too shy.

Ruth was thankful to be relieved of the responsibility of her sister. Every morning Miss Spooner arrived at the same time, folding up her white umbrella as she came into the dim fan-blown lounge, and took Teresa off her hands.

'It's really too good of you,' said Ruth once, apologetically. 'I'm ashamed of myself for pushing Teresa on to you like this. Only I feel so odd I simply can't face the heat outside, and I don't think it's safe for Teresa to walk about alone. But I'm afraid we're putting you out a great deal.'

Teresa's face fell. She looked at Miss Spooner anxiously.

'Good gracious,' answered Miss Spooner, sounding very much displeased, 'it isn't at all a case of putting me out. My dear Mrs Tracey, what a very foolish thing to say. I enjoy having Teresa's company. It's a great pleasure. The gratitude, I assure you, is all on my side.'

She spoke with more than her usual force, seeming genuinely upset, even offended, at the suggestion that she was doing Ruth a kindness by chaperoning Teresa. It was ridiculous but Ruth, with all her poise and easy social manners, felt abashed by this little woman's downright expression of disapproval. She saw Teresa's happy face and was touched by a puff of loneliness. She watched them leave the hotel briskly together, two figures the same height, canopied under the same umbrella, and then she went back to her room and stretched herself out on her bed under the windy fans.

Teresa's other chance encounter was with Sam. Why, after all, he had not returned to Bombay and his many dependants he did not trouble himself to explain. Perhaps for some reason Calcutta suited him as it suited Miss Spooner. Teresa found him hanging about in the hall of the hotel one morning, waiting for employment. They were delighted to see one another. He attached himself to her at once, automatically becoming their bearer, and enquiring of Ruth with solicitous concern every morning: 'Madam, how is your belly?' She sent him out to buy her oranges and melons. Her thirst for coolness was insatiable. He brought her jugs of iced water.

One afternoon as she lay on her bed in a state of torpor, Teresa burst open the door. 'Look, Ruth! Look what I've got!'

Her dark straight hair was damp with sweat as though she had been running.

She undid the parcel she was carrying and shook out a length of crimson cotton, patterned with white leaves. The stuff gushed round her on to the floor like living blood. She held it under her chin. 'Do you like it, Ruth? Isn't it lovely?'

Ruth raised herself on an elbow. 'Oh, Teresa. Where did you get it? Is it yours? How did you buy it? Had you any money?'

'Miss Spooner bought it for me. She gave it to me. Don't you like it?'

'Yes, I like it. I like it very much. But Teresa, it isn't right for Miss Spooner to give you presents. She doesn't look as though she's got much money. You shouldn't let her. She's been good enough as it is. I'm in her debt already. I wish she hadn't bought you that.'

'But she wanted to, really she did. She said we *ought* to buy it, we had to. I'm sure it's quite all right, Ruth. I'm sure she really wanted to give it to me. She never does anything unless she wants to.'

'It certainly suits you remarkably well,' said Ruth, unwillingly, 'and you do need some dresses. But it's I who ought to be buying you clothes. If only I didn't feel so wretched. . . .'

'But it is pretty, isn't it? You do like it?'

'Yes; it's exactly right for you.'

'I saw it first,' said Teresa triumphantly, with a skip of excitement. Sam had slipped into the room with a tea-tray for Ruth and now stood behind Teresa, grinning, his head on one side, foolish with admiration.

'Oh, tea,' said Ruth faintly. 'Sam, put it over here. And bring another cup.' Teresa was draping herself in front of the mirror, arranging the brilliant stuff round her with loving touches. 'You ought to wear bright colours, of course,' said Ruth, sitting up and pushing her fallen hair out of her eyes. 'For some reason one always thinks of putting children into pale colours, blues and pinks. But it's all wrong for you. I wonder I never thought of it before.'

Teresa turned away from the glass, still swaddled in folds of white and crimson cotton. Above the daub her huge eyes shone out dark and intense, so eager they seemed to lean forward in front of her, to brim over her narrow face like ripened fruits piled into a basket too small to contain them. It appeared as though all the life in her body had been sucked up and concentrated in the animation of those two wide-open sockets.

Her eyes are extraordinary, thought Ruth. They're magnificent. They make her beautiful. She saw Teresa for the first time more as another woman than as a sister or as a little girl. Her surprise was warm and human. She held out her hand, saying gently: 'Come over here, Teresa, and have some tea.'

Sam came in with a second cup. Teresa sat on the bed. A sensation of home came over Ruth as she poured out the tea, a tiny flicker of restfulness. I've been wrong again, she thought, another mistake of mine. We can be company for each other. We are quite close after all – how nice that is! How crabbed and stupid I am: I nearly missed her altogether.

The days went on and became a week. Ruth was pregnant. Her sickness was lasting, and would last, she thought bitterly,

till the end of her life. It shocked her deeply to think that at this time of all times she was with child, caught, as it were, mid-way between the bungalow and England, suspended like a tight-rope walker high in the air, unable to move either backwards or forwards. Fall she must. There was no safety-net to receive her and her balance was precarious.

And still she dallied, another day, in an agony of doubt and fear. She felt that Edwin had deserted her. Why had this mad, this tragic thing happened to her? She had never liked children. The thought of having children of her own had always been abhorrent. From this there was no flight, no deliverance. Her body had become her vice, her own destroyer, tightening its screws upon her. She could not leave herself; she could not divide herself from herself. Time, that general ameliorator in which she had laid her trust, had revoked its divine property of mending, had turned its tide in the night and now bore her away from the shore she had nearly reached on a dark and ever-quickening stream in which she was helpless and must finally perish. If only *this* had not happened, she repeated over and over to herself, tossing her hot cheek from one side to the other, everything in the end would have been all right. She had planned to be happy. She would have been happy. Green English meadows lay inside her eyelids like forbidden apples and the tears rose to drown them.

I am sick. I am ill. I am alone, afraid.

Edwin has left me, forsaken me in my extremity. How could he? Alone, with sickness, with *this* –

Oh, Edwin!

In a panic she pulled on her dress, her shoes, ran down the

stairs, through the hall, as dim and vast as a cellar, and out into the flaring street. At once the voracious multitudinous Eastern cries for life engulfed her. Bells clanged in her ears. The pavements were hot and hard as metal under her feet, strewn with beggars and cows whose panting flesh shook off the flies with every breath. She began to push her way forward through the battery of human creatures and their awful clamour.

She plunged and dived between the traffic. Her hair, care-lessly pinned in her haste, slipped over one ear. She stopped and leaned against a building, breathless, putting one hand up to her head as though to staunch a wound. On the other side of the road was the General Post Office, more like a palace with its vast and snowy proportions than a Post Office. Resting her heart, looking up at the voluptuous silver-painted dome that blossomed above her like a cruel artificial flower against a sky where no clouds, no soft thing moved, not a streamer of wind stirred the vacant sun-space – looking up from her pavement below she felt as though she had all at once become a half of her usual size, of no consequence to the world that had begotten her, abandoned by the brassy sky to be crushed by the stony walls. She felt too small – but she was a tall woman – too weak almost to lift her shoulder away and cross the street unsupported. But she gathered all the strength she had, and crossed. She went into the Post Office. Inside it was cooler, darker, but humming with a semi-hidden life. She took a blank telegraph form and addressed it to Edwin. Then she wrote in capital letters: 'Please come at once.' She hesitated, pressing her hand against her forehead.

That was not what she wanted to say. She tried to think what she wanted to say. Her fingers shook. She picked up the pen again and wrote quickly underneath: 'Darling, please come at once. Ruth.'

She stood outside, spent, her decision ended. There is no solution, her mind cried out within her. It is useless to flee. Where can we fly? We are victims of our own absolute weakness. There is no solution, no solution, no solution. Despair rent her. She stepped forward blindly off the pavement with tears on her cheeks. A taxi hooted. She heard the hooting swell and burst in her ear and felt her body crashing down before it.

I have been killed.

These four words went booming through her head. She had time to know them as her own thought and expected others to follow, but immediately all thoughts ceased.

III

'Teresa,' said Edwin. 'Shut the window. It's too noisy.' He looked at his watch. 'We'd better have lunch.'

Their lives continued in the grotesque routine of everyday habit. They still had to eat at the usual times. They still looked down the menu and chose what food they would have, saying: I should like ham; or: I should like an ice-cream. And food still had the same tastes, pleasing their palates, satisfying their stomachs, however indifferently they felt towards it.

Edwin had been in Calcutta three days, coming in answer to

Ruth's last cry before the living had sent for him. There was nothing to say, no alteration that anyone could make. A door he had thought would stand open for ever had slammed: it was simply that. Ruth had taken all his emotions with her and left him nothing, not even grief. She had left him hollow, an echoing shell, and only the echoes were of her. He had built himself about her as a shelter. What was the use of a shelter when the thing it had been built to protect was gone? His sturdy walls circled a deserted space. And the irony was that although the reason for it had gone, the sturdiness remained and would remain for an age, or ages, a useless survival of strength. His brain was as cool and methodical as it always had been. His body, though he cared so little about it, would last him another fifty years or more. But his health was unhealthy. His reason was senseless. He was a hollow man, and a dry man; a man in whom the spring had been quenched, and from whom the core had been taken.

He said to Teresa: 'I can go with you down to Bombay if you like and put you on a boat. Your mother would meet you the other end. Or you can come back with me to the Garden tomorrow.'

Teresa waited while he ate his melon. She imagined he was deciding what to do with her. She waited for him to speak again, watching with apprehension the spoonfuls disappearing into his mouth. He looked up. He wiped his mouth and fingers. He caught her glance fixed expectantly on him and smiled.

'Well? What do you want to do, Teresa?'

She understood. He was telling her to choose for herself, to decide her own future. She could do as she liked. There was to be no compulsion.

'I don't want to go back to England.'

'You'd rather come back to the bungalow?'

She nodded.

'Sure?'

She nodded again.

'You're not going to find it dull?'

'Oh, no.'

He sighed, not from disappointment, and looked at her closely, trying to probe the hidden years ahead and know if she had made a right decision, and if he had been right in letting her choose. Her grave eyes looked back at him, demanding so little.

'Perhaps this is your country,' he said. 'Perhaps you're too exotic for England. Ruth was English. I blamed her for it. Do you think you can manage to run a bungalow for me, Teresa? You'll have to learn some Urdu.'

'I wish we could take Miss Spooner back with us.'

'Do you? Would you like that? Well, perhaps we can. We'll ask her if you'd really like it.'

'She might come,' said Teresa. 'She might come for a bit, anyway. Will you ask her, Edwin? I think she might come.' For the blows fell so fast. People were suddenly precious. What friends she had left she must gather safely round her, hoard them like a treasure.

Poor little Teresa, thought Edwin, what a banging she's had. It isn't fair. She hasn't had the chance to deserve such a persecution. But which of us ever gets what we deserve, any more than we get what we expect? Nothing's ever fair. Has she learned that yet, I wonder? The child had been flung from pillar to post. He saw she was numb with the repercussions. He wanted to bring her alive again, to warm her although he was cold himself. He wanted to give her whatever she wanted, to pour a flood of generosity over her. She had had too much of death; he must promise her life.

IV

Later that day he called on Miss Spooner. They had met before when he first arrived, Miss Spooner having moved into the same hotel as Teresa on the evening of Ruth's death. As soon as Edwin came she had unobtrusively relinquished her charge to him and withdrawn from their company, even taking her meals at a different time in order not to intrude on what she felt was their privacy.

They had not, therefore, exchanged more than half-a-dozen sentences before this afternoon when he knocked on her door. 'I hope I'm not disturbing you,' he said.

'Not in the least,' she answered. 'I was only darning my stockings.'

'Oh, well, do please go on darning them. I don't want to stop you. I've only come for a few minutes.'

He went across to the window and stood in it, darkening the room. Miss Spooner picked up her mending. There was a long pause. On the mantelpiece a little travelling-clock in a red leather case ticked busily on. Edwin continued to stare down into the courtyard of the hotel where people were sitting at tables drinking their after-lunch coffee. At last he said: 'I suppose you knew Ruth?'

'Very slightly.'

'She wired for me, you know, the same day she was knocked down.'

The clock ticked, filling each silence. Miss Spooner went on sewing. Edwin stood quite still, his back turned, blocking the light.

'She wasn't happy. I thought perhaps she might have talked to you about it. She didn't?'

'No. She didn't.'

He sighed, and leaving the window came and sat down in a chair opposite Miss Spooner. 'She wasn't ever happy,' he said, watching her needle. 'My fault.'

And as, scene by scene, the last years formed again in his head, he told them over to her, speaking in a flat unhurried voice without emphasis, as without apology. Clearly, while he talked, he saw the bungalow; not a detail of it had escaped the touch of their long desperation. But surely, he said to Miss Spooner, his eyes following her needle, they should, in all that time, have found some way of putting it right? Now there was no time left, no chance to solve; he could only reconstruct and blame himself over and over again.

'But you see, I can't decide exactly how I was to blame. I must know *where* I was wrong. Perhaps, I say to myself, I should have taken Ruth back to England long ago, given up the Garden, got another job over there. Why didn't I? I knew it was what she wanted. But I never suggested it, never once. If I'd really put her first, isn't that what I should have done?

It seems so simple, so obvious now. But I *did* put her first,' he cried aloud in an access of perplexity. 'I know it sounds extraordinary, and that's what muddles me. It doesn't sound consistent, but I *did*. I thought of how to make her happy all the time. I thought of nothing else. I know that's true. I remember. Yet in that case, why didn't I do what she wanted and take her back to England?'

'You are a planter, Mr Tracey,' said Miss Spooner. 'You can't plant tea in England.'

'There are plenty of other jobs,' he said, almost angrily.

'For other people, not for you,' she replied. 'To have made yourself unhappy, Mr Tracey, was no way to make your wife happy. As you knew, of course – I'm saying only what you knew. If you hadn't known it you would have taken your wife home. But a change of scenery – you would still have been the same two people, Mr Tracey, whether in England or India.' She drew the stocking off her hand, laid it across her knee and regarded it sharply. 'Happiness, I think, is not divisible. No, not divisible in marriage. If one is unhappy, then both must be, here or there, Mr Tracey, here or somewhere else.' She put the finished stocking aside with a little pat, as though of regret.

'I don't know. You may be right. I don't know. I want to get things clear. No, it's not true, I was selfish.' The dull lowering sky of his loneliness split apart for one instant on a lightning flash of pain.

'Selfish!' he cried, with anguished joy at the relief pain brought. But immediately the skies closed round him again, heavy and grey. The one vivifying moment of despair passed.

He looked across at Miss Spooner blankly. She had set to work on the heel of another stocking.

'But a solitary state is a selfish state,' she said, mildly continuing the conversation, 'and we are all solitary, whether we wish it or not. A certain form of selfishness was put into us by our Creator like a spiritual backbone, and if we are ashamed of it we are ashamed of our Creator and of ourselves as He made us. We may well be ashamed of what we do in our lives, but to be ashamed of ourselves as we were made is wickedness. Self-respect – it's the same thing, Mr Tracey, I believe – is bound to make us suffer. We pay for the privilege of existing as human beings, and very right and proper that we should. It's a selfishness, Mr Tracey, we must not excuse but cherish with pride, and with good sense, for without it – dear me! where should we be? – back in the sea with the jellyfish.'

She was comforting him. Why? he wondered, full of gratitude. Comfort the living: that would be her argument. The dead, she would say, had no need of comfort, nor could they any longer be harmed by blame. So, carefully and kindly, for his sake, she was shifting the blame to Ruth. He was not deceived, though grateful. The blame was his and nothing should part him from it; for blame, more than the memory of her face – already oddly untrue and clouded – kept her familiar, close to him, even alive in the smothered throb of its punishment. While it was his blame, she was still his Ruth. For the first time in his life he was jealous, guarding what was his. He watched Miss Spooner darning, wanting to thank and contradict her, and afterwards thank her again.

'Ruth,' he said, 'was like one of those soap-bubbles that children blow. So pretty and light. And I was the great drop of water you see underneath, dragging it down. Too heavy – I was too heavy for her. It wasn't ever fair.'

He studied the plain little shut-up face for signs of protest, but she only raised her head and nodded at him once, not in agreement but more as though to say: It's your own business. Think as you like.

We don't agree, he thought; she's sure and I'm not, but we shall never agree and I can't be comforted. It was all my fault, Ruth, he said to himself as he crossed the room. At the door he looked back, remembering why he had come.

'Miss Spooner.'

She turned in her chair. He saw the bright sensible eyes and felt at a loss, dependent on her, lonely.

'Teresa thought perhaps you might come and live with us in the bungalow, for a while at least. It's the reason I came to see you, to ask if you can. I should like it too.' He paused, searching the suitable phrases for what he really wanted to say. 'We should both be so very pleased,' he added awkwardly. 'It's rather cut off, but there's a nice view of the hills and we're close to the river –' Again he hesitated, confused by the spectacle of Miss Spooner blushing. Her dry cheeks had gone suddenly red, as though the sun had caught them.

'You're very kind,' she said.

V

That evening he and Teresa walked together down Chow-ringee. The warm night stenches of the city filled their nostrils. Teresa told Edwin how she had cheated at piquet. She stopped in the street and held him by the sleeve to make him realise the measure of her sin. She had spilt her tardy tears over it, dreamed of it, suffered. Now she confessed. The beggars came round them with their stumps and sores. Pipes were wheedling. Ponies trotted by. Rickshaw coolies tinkled their bells in the gutter. Cars hooted. The lamps glowed thick and orange, like candles in a stuffy room. Above, the stars were numerous and white in a placid sky. Edwin took her hand and held it kindly in both of his.

'It doesn't matter any longer, Teresa; it isn't important now. It's what you're going to do that's important. That's very important indeed. The past can take care of itself. Do you understand?'

She was going to say that she understood when her gaze swerved past him. Her face changed. She began to laugh.

'Oh, Edwin – look!'

He turned round. A very dirty emaciated Indian was standing behind him on the kerb, selling toys. A bunch of balloons was tied to the strap of his tray. On the pavement was a green paper crocodile, pleated like a concertina. The Indian jerked a string and the creature writhed about, lashing its tail, snapping its paper jaws open and shut with every appearance of ferocity. The man saw Teresa watching.

'Missie, missie. . . .' He tried to make her take the string.

He thrust himself on her, persuasive, voluble. 'Very nice crocodile, very pretty. You like him, eh? Five rupees; very cheap, very nice crocodile.'

'No,' cried Teresa, shaking her head, backing away. 'No, no.'

Edwin looked down at her face again, dishevelled now with laughter and her strenuous denials. Like a minnow breaking suddenly with its small lively somersault the surface of a pool in which he had believed all the fish to be blasted, the thought occurred to him that a time might arrive – a very remote but just possible time – when he could be happy with this child.

'Would you like a crocodile, Teresa?' he said.

'Oh, no,' she answered. 'Thank you, I don't want one a bit. But it is funny though, isn't it?'

'Yes,' said Edwin, bending his eyes on the thrashing paper tail with sober consideration, 'it is, very funny indeed.'

AFTERWORD

❧❧❧

I do not linger over secondhand bookstalls as I used to; some other business always presses and our shelves already overflow. But I usually dive in for five minutes and, once in a while, pull out a plum, something out of print and long sought after, never worth much money but valuable to me.

Twenty years ago, when I was about to publish my own first novel, at a tender age, I was told of a similar young woman who had written one which had been widely and loudly acclaimed and sold well. But she had produced nothing else and the book had dropped out of sight. Last month I finally tracked it down. I gave ten pence to the funds of a school in Woodstock for a good, clean copy of *The Far Cry* by Emma Smith (MacGibbon & Kee, 1949). I had no idea what it was about or would be like but I have a certain missionary zeal for resurrecting novels which deserve a new readership and even, with luck, a new edition. So many appear and disappear like shooting stars and most deserve oblivion, but a few are worthy of a permanent place in print. What, I wondered, of Emma Smith? I expected to find a work of promise which might betray its author's youthfulness, and seem dated. I did not expect to discover a small masterpiece. I began it with

interest, and read on with growing amazement, deepening admiration. There is nothing 'promising' about it, it is a completely formed, satisfying work of art, rich in human understanding and all manner of subtleties, beautifully shaped, evocative, moving and mature.

It seems to have been written out of a long lifetime of quiet, penetrating observation and experience of a wide variety of human beings, their personalities, emotions and behaviour.

Teresa Digby is her father's second child, by his second disastrous marriage, and is living with a well-meaning but narrow aunt when her mother threatens to reappear and lay claim to her. To her surprise – for she has never been close to him – Randall Digby carries her off in panic to India and his elder daughter, Ruth, married to a tea-planter. In her presence, he is sure, all will come right, for Ruth is good, true and wise beyond description, the shining light at the end of her father's tormented journey with this awkward younger child he neither knows nor likes. Teresa is not pretty, not graceful, not sensible, she 'sticks out like pins at every angle', and throughout their passage to India by boat and hot, slow train, her presence is an irritant and an embarrassment both to her father and to her own self.

This is a most telling portrait of an intelligent, sensitive girl growing up, reminiscent of the young Portia in Elizabeth Bowen's *The Death of the Heart*. Emma Smith's novel echoes those of several other writers, without being, in any sense, derivative. She writes of English people journeying to India, and its impact upon them, so vividly that not just sights, but sounds, smells, whole atmospheres, rise off the page, and it is not merely that her subject-matter and setting are rather Forsterian; she uses simile and symbol in her way, investing certain places and incidents with far more than their immediate and obvious significance.

Yet, just like E. M. Forster, she never spells her meanings out, is never pedestrian, only, with the instinct of a novelist born, lets them stand by themselves, to be given weight, and interpreted, by the reader. There are some magnificent set-pieces of description – a Hindu Festival of Light, a river picnic, Teresa's night encounter with a tiger. Above all, though, this is an intricate study of human nature. It is about growing up, and disillusionment, pride, pretence and vanity, and the suffering they cause; for Ruth turns out to be only a poor sham of an angel. It is about simple, clear-eyed love – that of Ruth's husband, a good man.

A great deal happens to the protagonists, which advances them along the road of self-knowledge and self-acceptance, and so, in turn, understanding of others. Teresa suffers shock after shock and emerges bruised, yet stronger and wiser. Her father dies, her sister dies, the one still in ignorance of most of the truth about himself, about his daughters and life in general. But Ruth has just begun to learn, and to repent. Their deaths mean freedom for Teresa and Edwin, though they barely recognise the fact. Yet it is a hopeful novel, positive and liberating, on the side of life and goodness, permeated with all the humane values.

The prose is a joy to read, accomplished and graceful, the confident writing of a natural stylist, and there are some passages of great beauty.

I was bemused by the novel whilst reading it and it has occupied my thoughts considerably since. From it, I have learned a good many things about the art of fiction. Yet I am taken aback by the sheer accident of my finding it at all. How many people ought to be reading it too; how few can do so. Its rescue from the relative oblivion of secondhand stalls is long overdue.

Susan Hill,
1978

If you have enjoyed this Persephone book why not telephone or write to us for a free copy of the Persephone Catalogue and the current Persephone Biannually? All Persephone books ordered from us cost £10 or three for £27 plus £2 postage per book.

PERSEPHONE BOOKS LTD
59 Lamb's Conduit Street
London WC1N 3NB

Telephone: 020 7242 9292
Fax: 020 7242 9272
sales@persephonebooks.co.uk
www.persephonebooks.co.uk